The Dynasty

Charles H. Knickerbocker

The Dynasty

A MEDICAL NOVEL

DOUBLEDAY & COMPANY, INC.
Garden City, New York

*To the men and women of the profession
to which I am proud to belong.*

This novel concerns the medical profession, and I am a practicing physician. However, this is not an autobiographical novel in any sense of the term.

In my professional career, I have known several thousand physicians and perhaps thirty thousand patients. None of these real men and women is portrayed here, either directly or by implication.

I can scarcely claim that the material of this book was invented without relationship to my experiences as a physician. Almost everything in this book has happened. However, things really happened in different times and places, in different ways, and to different people. As to the characters: they are real, in the sense that they could have existed, but also they are not real, meaning that they never did exist.

There is truth in this book, and there is fiction, but the two are blended in such a fashion that I can't tell them apart.

C. H. K.

The Dynasty

Part 1

On a brisk September morning in 1931, a young man was walking through the city. Particles of grit and dried manure blew into his eyes. Debris and old newspaper swirled in the gutters, stirred by the autumn wind. Harridans lounged in doorways; juvenile hoodlums roamed in gangs; fat women scrubbed brownstone steps on hands and knees; ancient men in shirt sleeves leaned out of second-story windows, smoking their pipes and dreaming of yesterday.

John Crest was not aware of his immediate surroundings. His eyes were fixed on the middle distance where he could see the tower of the medical-school buildings rising over the slums, as an oak tree towers above a swamp. Medical schools are often found in the slums. Dirt and poverty breed disease, and disease is the raw material from which the art and science of medicine is taught.

John Crest wore an obvious stamp of status. The freshly starched knee-length linen coat; the enormous tome underneath one arm, Gray's *Anatomy*, which seemed to weigh a quarter of a ton; the fifth-hand microscope in its wooden case, clutched in his other hand; the new dissecting kit of stainless steel, as yet untouched by the grease of cadaver juice; a certain eager expression of the face—these were the trademarks of a medical student, freshman, on the first day of a new school year.

Some of the passing citizens gave him a smile. This was not the smile of ridicule; he hadn't forgotten his pants. In this wretched section of the city, where the cop was regarded with hatred, the social worker with contempt, and the sailor as a prospective victim with his wallet on his belt, the young men in the clean white jackets were treated with affectionate respect. They were not doctors yet, and at this stage knew nothing of their trade, but later in the game, it was they who would come when somebody was vomiting in the alley, or dying in the gutter, or giving birth among the garbage pails. In an area noted for an alarming rate of delinquency and crime, no medical student had ever been mugged or robbed.

One particularly slatternly old shrew smiled at him and said, "Good morning, Doc!"

The title was unfamiliar to his ears, but it gave him pride. He smiled at her as he returned the greeting.

Now John Crest was confronted by a steep flight of marble stairs, as the medical school loomed overhead. He paused to catch his breath.

"Abandon hope, all ye who enter here," he thought.

Then he grinned to himself and bounded up the stairs, leaving the drab non-medical world behind him forever, or, at least, until he flunked his examinations.

The lobby was teeming with people in various uniforms. There was an information booth in the center of the lobby, but Crest had no need to ask the obvious. There were a number of other young men in white jackets, bearing Gray and a microscope. They wandered down a long marble corridor, dewy-eyed and green, like spring lambs baaing their way into a new and somewhat frightening pasture. Crest joined the flock.

The medical school was a conglomeration of architecture which had grown by accretion over the years, like a crystal, as new wings and annexes were piled on top of the old. In the middle, at the bottom, was the nucleus of the crystal, the original building nearly two centuries old, which had once been a septic city hospital and now contained the undergraduate lecture halls and laboratories. Sunshine did not penetrate down here. The air was musty with the smell of ancient pain and death.

Crest entered an auditorium with the others in his class. The room was shaped like a well: three stories tall, circular, precipitous, narrow, and deep. There seemed to be fog at the ceiling. This room dated from the day when cadavers were freshly stolen from the grave and anatomy was taught by remote control: the professor, in morning coat, pointed out the structures with a stick, while a hired flunky did the actual dissection and the students peered down from overhead. Crest took his seat in one of the higher rows. A hundred freshmen milled about, making introductions, joking off nervous tension, buzzing like a swarm of bees.

The buzz abruptly ceased, and silence fell into the room like a stone. A figure was entering the pit far below: a big man with an unruly shock of hair, a leonine head, and an imposing arrogance of manner. Crest recognized him: Thomas Fawcell Parkindale, M.D., D.Sc., F.A.C.P., emeritus professor of clinical medicine, and dean of the medical school.

"Gentlemen," said the dean in a booming voice that filled the auditorium, "good morning."

"Good morning, sir," said a hundred voices in chorus.

"Gentlemen, I wish to make a small request. Will each of you kindly look at the young man who is seated on your right?"

A hundred heads swiveled in unison.

"Thank you," said the dean. "And now will you look, with

equal care, at the young man who is seated on your left?"

Heads turned like those of spectators at a tennis match.

"Gentlemen, one of the three of you will not graduate with this class."

The dean paused for dramatic effect, and the class was duly impressed.

"This is one of the oldest and finest medical schools in the world," said the dean. "Our standards are high, and we are justly proud of them. Although this class has been carefully selected from more than a thousand applicants, we know from past experience that one third of you are not fit to hold the diploma of this school. We weed out the rotten apples as soon as we can examine the barrel. Nothing is tolerated but the best. Kindly bear this fact in mind as you begin your work."

He paused again.

"Why are you seated here this morning, gentlemen?" he continued. "Why are you trapped in this dreary auditorium when you could be outside earning an honest living or enjoying the crystal clarity of the autumn air? You are here to become physicians. Why do you wish to become physicians? Many of you could not give a valid answer to this question. Some of you are doctors' sons. Some of you fell in love with your family physician at the age of three. Some of you are infected by that dangerous contagion, the Florence Nightingale syndrome, a misguided and romantic desire to serve suffering mankind. Some of you believe that the medical degree is the passport to power and prosperity. All of you are wrong.

"You have chosen an arduous and difficult profession, and many of you will never practice it. Those who become practicing physicians will find themselves split off from contact with the normal world. Your sleep will be interrupted and your meals will be late. You will be a stranger to your wife and family. You will be at the beck and call of any idiot with a pain in the neck or a cold in the nose. Patients will abuse and revile you, patronize and threaten you, sue you and neglect to pay your bill. You will spend your life among the sick, and you will soon discover that sick people are vindictive, hostile, rude, infantile, querulous, self-centered, stubborn, and hysterical. Most men fear infectious disease, but you will be constantly exposed. Men shun the sight and smell of blood, pus, bile, urine, feces, and gangrene, but you will be up to your elbows in these sweet substances forever.

"For one part Florence Nightingale, you must be one part ghoul; for every part of savior, you must be equal parts sadist. You will hurt more people than you help and kill more people than you cure. You must earn a livelihood off the suffering of others, as a vulture feasts off carrion. And you still desire to become a physician? Might I ask you: why?"

He glared at the class and a hundred pairs of eyes glared back at him.

"There is of course a recompense," he said. "You have chosen a noble profession and a proud profession, a profession which will always challenge you and bring forth the best in you. In a world inhabited largely by useless cowards, you must be useful and brave. On a dull and boring planet, you will never be bored. As most men waste their lives, you will give your life for your fellow man. There is no comparable occupation for a man of wisdom, courage, and skill.

"I have taken enough of your time. You have work to do. You will now proceed to the laboratory and begin your dissection. The cadavers are waiting and you have much to learn from them. Class dismissed."

The dean stepped off the podium and stalked out of the pit.

"He's an old windbag," said the boy seated beside John Crest.

"How can you say that?" asked Crest, somewhat shocked.

"With every right in the world. The dean is my grand-father."

Crest studied his companion: a pleasant, apple-cheeked boy with dimples and a cheerful grin. He had the large Parkindale head, but the unruly hair was shorn into a crew cut.

"I'm Sam Parkindale."

"John Crest."

Sam, studying Crest in return, saw a tall, lean boy, intense and serious.

"Is it true?" asked Crest. "Will they flunk out a third of the class?"

"They flunk about twenty per cent," said Sam. "Another ten per cent drop out of their own accord somewhere along the line. You needn't worry, Crest. I suspect that you'll manage to get by."

"How can you be sure?"

"Aren't you a dedicated grind, my friend?"

Crest flushed. The accusation was true, at least in part.

"Got yourself a partner for anatomy?" said Sam. "We dissect in pairs."

"I don't know anybody in the class."

"Then why don't you work with me? I may need the assistance of a grind to squeeze me through."

Crest was flattered by the offer. They pushed down a corridor with the throng and entered the anatomy laboratory, a spotless white-tiled room, starkly illuminated. Skeletons grinned down sardonically from display cases along the wall. On fifty marble slabs lay fifty ominous figures, shrouded with rubberized canvas.

"I never worked on a cadaver before," said Crest.

"You'll get used to that in a hell of a hurry," said Sam.

"As a matter of fact, I've never even seen a dead man before."

"Then take off the canvas and have yourself a look," said Sam.

"Why don't you take it off?"

"Because," said Sam, "I have seen a dead body before."

Crest took a deep breath and removed the canvas shroud. The figure underneath was male, indeterminate in age, wasted, and gaunt. It possessed human form, but did not look as if it had ever been alive.

"Like an old wax doll," said Crest.

"I didn't think you'd mind," said Sam, "but some of the class is more sensitive."

At certain tables, the students seemed afraid to touch the canvas sheeting. Several members of the class walked rapidly by, green around the gills, heading for the lavatory.

"Sometimes they walk straight out and never come back," said Sam. "Look at the big boy over there!"

The big boy was two hundred and fifty pounds and a good six feet four. Crest recognized him as a prominent selection for all-American tackle last fall. The ex-tackle, his face ashen, had keeled over in a faint and was lying on the floor. Crest breathed an inward prayer of thanks that this had not happened to him.

"Get out your scalpel and let's begin to cut," said Sam.

"Hadn't we better wait?"

"What for?"

"Until somebody tells us what to do," said Crest.

"Around this school, they never tell you what to do," said Sam. "You have been thrown in, to sink or swim for yourself."

"What if we do it wrong?"

"Later on we'll kill somebody, but our first patient is already dead," said Sam. "Come on."

"Where do we begin?"

"This bird seems to have a lot of skin," said Sam. "The first step, I should think, would be to take it off."

"Sounds reasonable," said Crest.

Sam had already begun to work, and Crest followed the lead. Sam was obviously clever with his fingers; the skin was coming off cleanly for him like orange peel. Crest discovered that this was not as easy as it looked. Often he cut too shallow and buttonholed the skin, or else he cut too deeply, bringing up pads of superficial fat. They worked intently for more than an hour until Crest had a crick in his back; his eyes were stinging and his nostrils smarting from the corrosive fumes of formaldehyde.

"Time for a break. Let's have a cigarette," said Sam.

"Can we smoke in the lab?"

"Out on the balcony."

"Are we allowed to leave?"

"Hell," said Sam, "we can go to Timbuctoo. We're permitted to do anything as long as we pass the examinations."

As they left the lab, Crest was pleased to note that they were ahead of most of the other groups.

"It's not exactly true that we can do everything," said Sam. "No whistling or singing in the laboratory. We must wear a clean white jacket at all times, and the law requires us to show proper respect for the dead. Two boys were expelled last year for this reason. They took the small intestine out of their cadaver and were playing jump rope with it in the corridors."

Crest winced.

"You'll have to get used to that sort of thing," said Sam. "If you think that flesh is sacred, either alive or dead, you won't last very long in this racket."

"That's true, I suppose," said Crest. "But you must remember that I do not come from a distinguished medical family."

"That may be an asset rather than a liability," said Sam. "Have a cigarette."

"Thanks."

They were out on a balcony which overlooked a courtyard with a high stone wall beyond. Crest noticed that there was an enormous pile of old cigarette butts at the base of the wall.

"According to tradition," said Sam, "every freshman must be able to flick a cigarette butt over that wall at least once if he hopes to pass the course. As you can see, many have tried, but few are chosen."

"It looks easy enough."

"Try it."

Crest flicked his cigarette with his forefinger. It flew out high and wide in a satisfying arc, but it fell several feet short of the wall. "I can do better than that," he said.

He took another cigarette, puffed it down rapidly, and went out into the corridor. With a running start and a lunge which carried him almost over the balcony rail, he tried again. This time the butt flew higher and farther and vanished cleanly over the wall.

"I can see that you are a determined youth," said Sam.

"I have no intention whatever of flunking out of this place," said Crest.

"They won't flunk me," said Sam. "No Parkindale has ever flunked out of this school, and surely I'm smarter than my father."

"Your father went here too?"

"There's always been a Parkindale connected with the place. One of my ancestors helped to found the school, and there's been a Parkindale on the faculty ever since. You know that my grandfather is the dean. My uncle is on the staff. He's a plastic surgeon."

"What does your father teach?"

"My father isn't here," said Sam. "He's only a general practitioner, an ordinary country doc. Quite frankly, my father is a quack."

"So is mine," said Crest.

"Your old man is a doctor too?"

"No, a real quack," said Crest. "One summer he bought a steam calliope and went tootling all over the countryside, hawking patent medicines."

"Fascinating," said Sam. "Tell me more."

"I think we better get back to the lab," said Crest.

In the afternoons they had histology, the microscopic study of tissue. This was a sleepy subject, quite worthy of being ignored, but anatomy was important.

Every morning, Sam and Crest labored over the cadaver. They soon became oblivious to the pervasive sweet-smelling

grease which soon covered their instruments, the pages of
Gray, their coats, their hands, even their hair. Often they ate
a snack over the remains, and they would have slept beside a
dead body without a second thought. They named their cadaver Long Peter, for an obvious anatomical characteristic of
this particular body.

The skin of Long Peter had vanished. They dissected and
studied his muscle layers with the origins and insertions. They
traced out the blood vessels which were injected with a rubbery colored material, red for the arteries and blue for the
veins. They followed the course of the nerves and worked
their way down toward the internal viscera. There are some
five thousand named anatomical structures, and they were
required to know, by sight and by name, each of these structures and its third-dimensional relationship to every contiguous structure in every level and plane.

Crest studied long and hard. Sam was more casual, but he
had an agile mind and a third-dimensional sense of relationship, and he seemed to acquire knowledge somewhat easier
than Crest. However, as the first examinations came along, it
was obvious that Crest, though not the leading scholar in the
class, was bucking for the upper ten per cent. Sam was perfectly content with an honorable gentleman's C.

As the form of Long Peter disintegrated under their dissecting instruments, Crest had long since forgotten that this
had ever been a living human being. One day, however, the
humanity of the cadaver occurred to him forcefully. They
were dissecting the eye. A cadaver's eye is glazed and milky,
devoid of the sparkle of life, but, as Crest was levering up the
lids on his side to cut into the film of the grapelike structure,
the man inside suddenly seemed to take a look at him. Crest
stepped back and dropped his scalpel on the floor.

"What's the matter?" asked Sam.

"Nothing," said Crest. "Where do they find the cadavers?"

"The river, the gutter, the morgue. There are plenty of un-
claimed bodies during a depression."

"Just think," said Crest. "A few short weeks ago, this poor old slob was walking through the city, breathing the air, dreaming of a bottle or a woman, hoping his tomorrow would be better than his yesterday."

"Touching but inaccurate," said Sam. "Long Peter has been dead for at least two years."

"How do you know?"

"A cadaver can't be released for that period of time. Suppose a relative turned up to claim the body while we were dissecting it? They have a room in the basement where they store several years' supply. Haven't you been there?"

"No."

"I'll take you down."

He took Crest to the nether regions among the boilers and steam pipes. The door said ABSOLUTELY NO ADMITTANCE, but Sam walked in. It was a dark cavern of a room where the fumes of formaldehyde were suffocating. Fresh bodies soaked in vats of preservative like so many bloated pickled fish. Prepared specimens hung from hooks thrust cruelly through the back of the neck, several hundred of them, like sides of beef.

"*Sic transit gloria,*" said Sam.

"I am not going to will my body to the medical school," said Crest.

"Don't you wish to serve suffering humanity?"

"I shall look for another way," said Crest.

"What do you do when the sun goes down?" asked Sam.

"Study," said Crest.

"And when the eyes are grainy and the brain has fogged, what do you do?"

"A cup of coffee and a cold shower, and then I study again."

"And when you're about to go blind?"

"I sleep," said Crest. "I never get enough of that."

"That's a damn good way to burn out the battery," said Sam. "I'm taking you out for an evening of fun and games."

"I haven't the time and I haven't the money."

"You have enough of the one and I shall supply the other," said Sam. "We are going out and get drunk and we're going to tumble a couple of broads. This is therapeutic. Accept the prescription of Dr. Parkindale."

"You may be right," said Crest. "Anatomy is running out my ears. I can't tell the difference between Poupart's ligament and the left great toe. I'll go out with you, Sam, and have a few beers and a good bull session, but no women. I couldn't afford that luxury."

"All right. We'll start with bull and beer," said Sam. "Come with me. It so happens that I know this little place."

"You come with me," said Crest. "It so happens that I also know a little place."

"Indeed?" said Sam with a look of surprise.

Crest conducted Sam to the subway, and they went to the other end of town, down to the water front, among the docks. There was chill fog off the river, and they could hear the hooting of tugs and growling of ocean liners from the harbor. Crest led his friend down a dangerous-looking alley, at the end of which was a heavy locked door.

"I forgot to bring along my switch-blade knife," said Sam.

"You won't need it here," said Crest.

He rapped on the door. A panel shot back, and a suspicious eye peered out of a peephole. Then the door swung open, and Crest was warmly greeted by a dark, hairy waiter in a dirty apron. This was a small water-front speakeasy. There was sawdust on the floor, faded red checkered tablecloths, candles stuck into bottles encrusted with old wax drippings. As if entertaining a long-lost cousin, the waiter conducted them to a table in the front and then he brought a bottle of champagne, popping the cork with a flourish.

"Do you live here?" Sam asked Crest when the waiter had gone.

"No," said Crest. "Look at the piano player."

A man was seated at a small upright piano and he had a familiar face, intense and serious.

"The old man?" asked Sam.

"Yes. That's my father," said Crest.

"I thought you told me he sold patent medicines."

"Only for one summer," said Crest. "He's done a lot of things and failed at all of them. He can only play the piano, and if you listen, you will discover that he doesn't play it very well."

Crest's father played a medley of the popular tunes of the moment, glancing at his son from time to time. Crest kept his eyes fixed on the tablecloth. At the conclusion of the medley, the older man slipped off the piano stool and started down to join the boys at the table, but then he seemed to change his mind, and he disappeared out back.

"Let's get out of here," said Crest. "I hate champagne. This isn't any fun."

He got up and left, and obviously he was not expected to pay for the champagne. Sam followed him out into the alley.

"Sorry, I shouldn't have taken you there," said Crest.

"What's the trouble?" asked Sam.

"I don't get along with my father," said Crest. "He's paying my way through school, and a dollar isn't easy to find these days. I'm grateful, but I avoid the man. I can't make myself speak to him. You tell me: what is my trouble? Why am I such a God-damned snob?"

"Lots of guys can't get along with their old man. It's natural," said Sam. "I can't stand mine. I hate the old son-of-a-bitch, if you really want to know."

"Thanks, Sam."

"It's true."

"Now I'm really in the mood to get drunk. Could you afford to buy the drinks for two? I haven't any credit at any other place in town."

"Sure. Follow me. The old man that I happen to hate happens to be making fifty thousand dollars in this depression year."

They went to another and better speakeasy, and Sam bought the drinks.

After several quick rounds, Sam said, "Now is the time for a couple of broads. What do you say?"

"I don't know any."

"I know two or three."

"That ought to be enough," said Crest.

"Good lad!"

Sam armed himself with a fistful of nickels and addressed himself to a pay telephone.

"Not very good hunting tonight," he said, "but I fixed us up as well as I can. One of them is big, beautiful, and dumb, but she's for me. All I could find for you is Em."

"Is which?"

"I can't exactly date my own sister," said Sam. "Emerald. She's two years younger than me. She's a student in the nursing school, and so is this other dame."

"What's the matter with your sister?"

"Maybe you better find out for yourself," said Sam.

Sam tucked a bottle under his coat in case of emergency, and then they caught a cab. They picked up the girls outside the dormitory of the nursing school. Sam's date was, as he had claimed, big, beautiful, and dumb. Emerald, on the other hand, was diminutive: a vivid and vivacious little creature with black eyes and black hair. It seemed to Crest that she was shooting off sparks.

"You are well named," he said to Emerald. "A dark-green jewel, cut into facets, with sharp brilliant edges."

She lifted one dark eyebrow into a question mark. "Is that an insult, sir, or a compliment?"

"I'm not sure," said Crest. "I don't know you well enough."

"Did Sam make any commitments for my side of the family?" she asked. "I don't get intimate with strangers quite so easily as my brother."

At the other side of the taxi seat, Sam was wrapped up in the big dumb blonde. She was squealing and giggling, and he was laughing, and, if the light had been better, Crest thought he might have seen a display of lingerie.

"Don't mind me," said Crest, somewhat ill at ease. "I'm just along for the ride, on temporary parole from Gray's *Anatomy*."

"Yes, I can tell," said Emerald. "The freshman medical student carries a distinctive aroma."

"I might also say that my only anatomical interest is in the cadaver."

"In that case, since I am not a cadaver, perhaps you better take me back to the dormitory," she said.

"Sorry, I didn't mean that," said Crest. "You put me into a position . . . No, I meant that I didn't want to put you into a position . . . Hell, I don't know what I mean."

She laughed and touched him on the hand. The touch was cool but pleasant. "Peace," she said, and then she added tartly, "Sam, did you expect to spend the night necking in a taxi cab?"

Sam disengaged himself from the blonde long enough to say, "Not if you can find a bed for us, Em."

The blonde seemed to find this remark hilarious.

"Driver," asked Emerald, "are they still running cruise boats down the river at night?"

"I think so, lady," said the driver of the cab. "The next boat ought to leave about ten o'clock."

"Please take us to the pier," she said.

The river which wound through the city down to the estuary and the bay below was dirty and industrially polluted, but it was pretty enough at night. There was an orchestra aboard the boat and a small space for dancing. Pop and peanuts were sold in the bilges, and romance took place on the upper reaches of the hurricane deck. The passengers were mostly young, some disreputable, many drunk. Sam and his blonde and Emerald and Crest tried dancing, but the floor was impossibly congested. Then they sat at a table, drinking soda pop in paper cups, laced with the contents of Sam's bottle. Crest thought the mixture revolting. Sam was regaling his companion with medical humor.

"There was a lunatic in the state insane asylum," said Sam.

"He was making good progress, and he was brought before the board of psychiatrists to be considered for release. They asked him what he would do if they let him out. 'I'm going to make a slingshot and break every window in this place,' he said. Obviously he wasn't ready for release, so they kept him for a few more weeks, and then they brought him back before the board. This time when they asked what he would do when he got out, he said, 'First, I'm going home and take a good hot shower and put on my best suit of civilian clothes. Then I'll telephone my girl. I'll take her out for a few drinks and dinner. After dinner, we'll have a drive in my car and we'll park on Lover's Lane. I'll kiss her and she'll kiss me, and then I'll put my hand underneath her dress. I'll run my hand all the way up her leg, above the top of her stocking, until I feel her garter. Then I'll take off her garter and make a slingshot and break every window in this place!'"

"Come," said Emerald to Crest. "Let's get out of here."

She took Crest by the hand and led him from the table, out into the darkness of the deck. Crest could feel her beside him, and she seemed to be shaking. He wondered if she was shaking with anger, or perhaps she was crying for some strange reason.

"What's the matter?" he asked.

She could contain herself no longer, and she began to laugh, giggling almost as the blonde had done.

"Sorry," she said, "but the story of the garter and the slingshot strikes me as funny."

Crest was relieved. "Me too. Did you think I was shocked?"

"I wasn't sure," she said. "My first impression was that you were staid and stuffy."

"I probably should plead guilty to the charge," said Crest. "According to Sam, I'm a dedicated grind."

"Sam also says that you're a good gent and a solid guy, but too intense and serious. He suspects that you are afraid of girls."

"So?" said Crest. "I've had my moments, but Sam wasn't there."

"Would you care to describe those moments in detail?"

"I would prefer to discuss a more fascinating subject, such as you."

"Why?"

"What is your excuse for existence?"

"Must I have one?"

"Mustn't we all?"

"I have a dream," she said, "but you'd laugh at it."

"Try me."

"I'm in the nursing school, which implies that my ambition is to be a nurse, but, God almighty, don't I hate bedpans and dirty sick old men! Ugh! Give me a cigarette, please."

Crest studied her face by the flare of the match. "I suppose your father wanted you to go to medical school like the rest of the clan," he said, in a flash of perception.

"That wouldn't get me far from the bedpans and the dirty sick old men, now, would it, dear?"

"I think you should do what you want to do, and follow that dream," he said. "Tell them to go to hell. Run away, if necessary."

"You think I'm lacking in courage? Nobody ever told me that before."

"Don't put words in my mouth," said Crest.

They smoked in silence for a time, sitting side by side on the deck in the shadow of a lifeboat. They passed freighters unloading at docks under the glare of blinding arc lights, and great factories where boilers and blast furnaces glowed crimson in the darkness. Crest was bold enough to put his arm around her shoulder. She did not withdraw, but she made no motion of response. Soon he took his arm away, and she did not respond to that, either.

"I know why Sam likes you so well," she said suddenly. "You're just chock full of moral rectitude."

"Ye Gods!" said Crest. "What am I supposed to make out of that remark?"

"On you it fits good," she said.

Abruptly and before he knew what she was doing, she had leaned over and kissed him full upon the mouth. Her lips were cold, and Crest felt a shock, as if he had been plunged into ice water. Before he could collect himself, she had leaped to her feet and was running lightly down the deck.

"Hey, wait for me!" he called.

But she was gone. He looked all over the boat, but he could not find her for more than half an hour. He finally located her at the bow, leaning over the rail, studying the curl of the wave below.

"What's the matter? What did I do wrong?" he asked.

"Nothing," she said, and she wouldn't look at him.

"Well, I certainly didn't do it right," he said.

"It's true. I do lack courage. It frightened me that you should see through me so easily."

"Purely a shot in the dark," he said.

"I ought to run away. Maybe I will some day. However, it is just some dull, decent, honest, respectable, courageous little jerk like you who could ruin everything for me. I won't let anybody stand in the way of my plans."

"I'm glad you know what you're talking about," said Crest. "I certainly don't."

"This may dawn on you," she said. "I don't think cadavers have given you total immunity to all matters of the flesh."

"Good heavens, no! I didn't mean to create that impression. As a matter of fact, I could find room for you in my plans, with no difficulty."

"Yeah," she said.

"And so . . ."

"And so, nothing, my friend, and that's the gist of this conversation."

"This conversation is confusing me," he said. "Let's return to fundamentals. You kissed me, quite voluntarily. I like that. You can kiss me again, or, if you prefer, I can kiss you."

"We can't. The boat is about to dock, and we must disembark."

The boat had nestled and crunched its way back against the pier. The gangway had been lowered, and the stream of passengers was pushing off.

"Let's take another trip," said Crest.

"The next trip won't get back till two," she said.

"And so?"

"And so, you have a cadaver to dissect, and I must push bedpans in the morning. A bedpan isn't a bit more attractive when you haven't had any sleep," she said.

"You're right. We should be sensible. I wonder what happened to Sam and the blonde?"

"I suggest we ignore Sam and the blonde," she said. "They know what they want, in a basic and uncomplicated sort of way. Why should they need us?"

"You're right again. It would be better to add a few complications to our relationship."

"No. You and I can't afford that sort of thing," she said. "We're getting off this boat, and then we find a taxi, and then you run me back to the dorm, if you can afford the fare. If you can't, I can."

"Must we?"

"This subject is not open to debate."

"You have a headache, I presume."

"Of course I don't have a headache!" she said. "There's a cab."

Crest was worried about the fare, but it turned out that he did have enough, just barely enough. The cab let them off in front of the dormitory. There was a bold light burning on the portico, and undoubtedly a chaperone was lurking just inside. Crest didn't seem to mind. He grasped Emerald by the shoulders and turned her around toward him, but, before he could kiss her as he planned, she broke from his grasp, took the few brisk necessary steps onto the porch, and Crest was on the wrong side of a closing door.

The next morning in the anatomy lab, Sam said to Crest, "Well? Did you get in?"

"This is your own sister," said Crest. "How can you speak of her that way?"

"My sister taught me almost everything I know," said Sam. "Why, I could tell you stories about Em . . ."

But the expression on Crest's face stopped Sam from telling any stories.

"I think I'm in love with your sister," said Crest quietly.

"Oh, no!" said Sam.

"You have any objection to me?"

"To you? Of course not. I was thinking of your welfare, son."

"I'll handle my own welfare, thank you just the same."

"May the saints preserve you; man the lifeboats; and may the Lord have mercy on your soul!"

"Why don't you shut up from time to time?" said Crest.

Crest phoned the dormitory several nights in a row. Once, Emerald was out. Once, she couldn't come to the phone because she was in the tub. When he was able to speak to her, she was pleasant but cool and noncommittal, and she always seemed to have a date.

So Crest gave up. Gray's *Anatomy* took precedence. He did not have the time, the money, or the energy for the pursuit of romance. If Sam mentioned his sister now and then, Crest did not continue the subject.

The dissection of Long Peter progressed. Crest was doing well on his examinations; Sam was getting by; and soon it was time for the Christmas holidays.

"What are you doing for the holidays?" asked Sam.

Crest had no plans except to stay in his boardinghouse and get a little sleep and avoid his father whenever he could.

"Why don't you spend the vacation with me in Sentryville?" asked Sam.

Although Crest put up the usual polite protestations, he wanted to accept the invitation.

"Emerald will be there, of course," said Sam casually, as if this would clinch Crest's acceptance, and it did.

Sentryville was a quiet village in lower New England. It seemed to be split into two diverse parts. On one half of town, there were wide, calm streets bordered with elms and immaculate white clapboard houses. On the other side, there was a railroad depot with warehouses and cheap brick hotels. The old and the new seemed to be in contention for possession of the town. On the older side was a village common with a statue of the sentry for whom the place was named. Sam's home was a rambling old mansion out toward the city limits, half of which was apparently dedicated to Sam's father's office suite. It was early in the morning, but there were at least a dozen cars parked in front of the office.

"Office hours at this time of the day?" asked Crest.

"At any time of day," said Sam. "Morning, noon, and night."

Sam paid off the cab which had taken them from the station, and the boys got out. The top-heavy old house was surrounded by large expanses of what must have been lawn and garden, now buried under a couple of feet of New England snow. In front of the office, a tiny weather-beaten sign proclaimed, F. M. PARKINDALE, M.D., PHYSICIAN & SURGEON.

"It is said that a man who claims to be both physician and surgeon is probably neither one," said Sam.

Crest did not comment. They entered the family portion of the house and were greeted by Sam's mother, a plump and pleasant individual from whom Sam obviously inherited his sunny disposition. Emerald was not expected from the city until the following day.

Crest made the acquaintance of Sam's father at dinner that night. Parky—as Sam's father was invariably called by friend and enemy alike—had been kept late in the office suite, which was the customary thing. He came striding in during the middle of the meal, and conversation died. Parky was a big man with the family leonine head and a shock of hair like a mane; he exuded power and strength and confidence and a sort of pure animal magnetism. Crest felt the personal force of the man immediately, and the others seemed to be in awe of him.

Parky sat down without a word and began slurping up his soup. When he had finished, a timid maid served him the main course. Parky continued to eat until he had caught up with the rest before he finally lifted his head and spoke.

"Good evening, dear, did you have a pleasant day?" he said to his wife.

Mrs. Parkindale murmured that she had.

"Sam, it's good to have you home," he said to his son. "You haven't flunked anatomy yet?"

"Not yet, sir," said Sam.

Parky turned his eyes on Crest and asked, "Who are you, young man?"

"This is Johnnie Crest," said Sam. "He's in my class, and will be spending the holidays with us."

"Welcome to my home," said Parky.

"Thank you, sir," said Crest.

"You make better grades than Sam, don't you, son?"

Crest didn't know what to say to this, but Sam filled in the gap. "Sure, Dad, of course he does. John will be bucking for A.O.A."

"You have the makings of a doctor," said Parky, still addressing Crest. "You are sensitive and intelligent, and you will go far. However, I would also guess that you are nervous and unstable, and that you must acquire self-discipline and control. Perhaps you will be better suited for research than for clinical practice, my boy."

"If you don't mind, sir," said Crest, with a spark of rebellion, "I prefer to make that decision for myself."

"Of course," said Parky blandly.

He returned his attention to his food and the subject was closed. Parky quickly finished his dinner. Then he arose, barely repressed a belch, threw his napkin onto the table in a wadded ball, nodded curtly to the company, and strode back to the consulting room where the patients were waiting, as usual.

"Well?" said Sam to Crest when they were alone.

"Rather like the bull and the china shop," said Crest.

"My father is not noted for his graciousness and tact," said Sam.

"And all the members of your family seem to delight in making snap judgments and prognostications on the strangers they meet."

"You noticed that?" said Sam. "It's a family failing. My father does it most. He enjoys dominating people. Other doctors in the area despise him; his family fears him; the community is in awe of him; his patients think he is God and worship him accordingly."

"He's a powerful personality," said Crest, "but I wouldn't be afraid of him."

"The bark is worse than the bite," said Sam. "The grand manner conceals an underlying lack of ability. He does not have direct communication with the will of God. As a matter of fact, when he was a student in medical school, I hear he was considered to have been stupid. They would have flunked him out if his name did not happen to be Parkindale. It is possible that there may be a worse doctor in this state, but I couldn't tell you where to look."

"It's possible that he may be an excellent doctor," said Crest.

"What gives you that idea?"

"I don't know," said Crest. "There's an air of strength and confidence about him, and this might be a powerful influence at the bedside."

"He is justly famous for his bedside manner."

"I admire him," said Crest. "For the same reasons I admire all your family."

"What reasons are those, Johnnie?"

"You carry the heritage of your family tradition. You are members of a medical aristocracy."

"The Parkindale manner, that arrogant and pompous attitude of self-satisfaction which has dominated American medicine for the past two centuries?"

"You are born to it," said Crest. "It cannot be acquired."

"It's a false front, Johnnie. The important thing is what lies behind. In my father's case, I think you may find a good deal of ignorance and greed."

"Harsh words, Sam."

"Oh?" said Sam. "Are you unduly fond of your old man?"

"All right, let it go," said Crest.

"Well, surely every son is entitled to be prejudiced against his father!"

"I said, let it go," said Crest.

Emerald arrived from the city the following day. Sam took the station wagon—the family car, as distinguished from the doctor's Cadillac—and drove Crest down to meet her train. She stepped off the iron vestibule of the car, dressed in a coat of black velveteen material on which a few stray snowflakes glistened, and she looked so crisp and pretty that Crest almost caught his breath. She kissed her brother affectionately and offered Crest a friendly hand.

"Your face is familiar," she said to Crest. "We ought to get better acquainted. We'll see a lot of each other over the holidays."

Crest replied that he certainly hoped so.

But yet it seemed to him that he saw very little of her over the next ten days. She was at table during meals. Often they were in the living room together, but not alone. Sam took Crest to several parties and social occasions when Emerald was present, but she was always at the other end of the room, surrounded by a cluster of boys. A couple of times he encountered her at the bathroom door inadvertently when one or the other of them was in some stage of undress, a fact which disconcerted Crest and which Emerald did not appear to notice. She wasn't exactly avoiding him; rather, she seemed to take him for granted, like a second cousin.

Finally, Crest managed a few minutes alone with her. Sam had gone downtown on an errand, and Crest was reading a magazine in the living room when she came in. She sat down close beside him on the sofa.

"Hi," she said. "Got a cigarette?"

Crest supplied her with one and lit it for her.

"I smoke like a chimney but never carry any of my own," she said. "Vicious habit, isn't it?"

"Smoking?"

"Borrowing when I never have any intention of giving anything back."

"It probably has some psychological significance," said Crest. "At least, it gives me the opportunity to be alone with you just once."

"Well, there was last night, in front of the bathroom door." Crest was embarrassed.

"I hope you weren't in any kind of hurry, dear," she said.

"Emerald," he said, "why don't you like me?"

"That's a silly question; don't ever ask a silly sort of thing like that."

"Well? You must admit that it is difficult for me to see you at all, even when I'm living in your house."

"You're Sam's guest, not mine."

"Exactly what I mean," he said.

"Don't be a goose," she said. "I'm very fond of you, and even you can tell." Her eyes were twinkling at him in a disturbing fashion.

"No, seriously . . ." said Crest.

"With us, never seriously," she replied. "Thanks for the smoke. Bye-bye."

And she was off again, leaving him alone with the comfort of his magazine.

"I don't think your sister likes me very well," Crest said to Sam later that evening.

"I have a contrary opinion," said Sam.

"She acts as if she doesn't."

"The way Em acts and the way she is are two things altogether different," said Sam. "She is always trying to put on some sort of role or act."

"She's elusive. I can't pin her down."

"And my advice to you is, let her alone."

"I scarcely have another choice," said Crest.

He tried to let her alone, but late that night he found himself lying in ambush for her in front of the bathroom door. Sam was in his room, and the house was apparently asleep. She appeared, pin curlers in her hair, cold cream glistening on her face, wearing a sensible and woolly robe.

"Ooop!" she said. "You startled me."

"Don't scream. My intentions are honorable," he said. "I just want a few words with you."

"You wouldn't mind if I go to the bathroom first?"

"Of course not, but I'd like to see you later."

"*Adieu,* kind friends, *adieu,* I can no longer stay with you," she sang softly, closing the bathroom door.

Crest realized that he could hardly hang around in the corridor outside the door, within range of the noise of running water and intimate sounds. She wouldn't come into his room, and of course he could not go into hers. Besides, he wasn't quite sure what he wanted to say to her, anyway. He decided to go downstairs. He did not for a moment think that she would join him there, but he was hungry; Mrs. Parkindale had graciously invited him to raid the icebox at any time of day or night that he was overcome by hunger pains.

He was just opening the refrigerator door when Emerald said, right behind him, "A glass of milk and a cold chicken leg for me, if you please."

Crest looked at her in some surprise. "So you did come after all?" he said.

"Sure. This is me. Why not? Am I supposed to be afraid of you or something? The chicken is over there, stupid. Here, let me in."

Crest had been overcome with a fit of mechanical ineptitude. Emerald took charge, found a drumstick for each of them, poured two glasses of milk, and closed the refrigerator door. He followed her into the living room. She turned on only a dim shaded light, and the atmosphere was intimate and almost domestic. She curled up on the sofa and patted a place for him beside her, and Crest sat down. She handed him his milk and chicken leg. After they had finished, she licked her fingers, and then she wiggled the index and the middle finger of her right hand in a scissors motion. He was fully dressed, and his cigarettes were in his pocket. He stuck one into her mouth.

"I apologize for looking like the wrath of God," she said, "but what can you expect if you bushwhack me on the way to the john?"

"You look very nice," said Crest.

"Oh, damn it, is it necessary for you to make such a proper and conventional remark?"

"All right, you look like hell," said Crest.

"That's better. You do have a sense of humor, but it's a wretched timid little thing, fearful and shy. Now, what did you wish to speak to me about?"

"I don't know," said Crest. "You take the tongue out of me, and I never know what to say."

"I'm not in love, I'm not secretly married, and I'm not engaged," she said. "I have too many other plans."

"What sort of plans?"

"What sort of business might that be of yours?"

"None," said Crest.

"Damn your honesty. Now I've got to tell you all about it," she said. "You might as well know that I've been stagestruck since I appeared in a Christmas pageant at the age of three. So, I hate the nursing profession, and I want to be an actress and run away and get on the stage, and isn't that as corny as the devil? My father insists that I become a nurse. The father of this family is a very domineering man. As you told me once, I lack courage, and now you know."

"Thank you," said Crest.

"Now that you've got me started, I might as well finish it, and embarrass both you and me. I find you very attractive, but I promised myself long ago that I wouldn't let any man except my father stand in the way of my plans. That way I can get mad at Dad, as a recompense for my own lack of courage, and can still enjoy and appreciate the company of men, without getting mad at the entire sex for causing the frustration of my plans. If you find this a little bit confusing, you can understand that I'm a little bit mixed up. But please also understand, there's not one snowball's chance in hell that I would ever fall in love with you, and if I seem to be avoiding your company, it is for the distinct and definite reason that I can't trust myself. So, little boy, go away! Don't bother me! Now that you understand, are you any happier?"

"Well," said Crest, "you left me a crack so that I can get my foot in the door."

"Beware of a fractured toe."

Suddenly she had kissed him again, and then she had leaped off the sofa and was leaving the room before he could properly react.

"Damn it," said Crest. "Just like the other time. Can't you ever kiss me when I'm expecting it?"

"And lose the fascination of my mystery?" she said.

"You're laughing at me again," he said.

"It's good for you. Thanks for the cigarette. Nighty-night."

Crest was not alone with her again for the rest of the holidays. In fact, Emerald was not mentioned until he and Sam were back in school, elbow deep again in the grease of the cadaver.

Then Sam happened to say, "Did you know that my sister never checked back into the nursing school after the holidays?"

"What happened?"

"She's taking a course in dramatic art at the university."

"Well, good for her!" said Crest.

"It won't last. The old man's mad as hell," said Sam. "She'll be back in the nursing school next term."

"Maybe she won't," said Crest.

"You think not?"

"I think that underneath her superficial brilliance, there's a very hard core of iron in your sister."

"Huh?" said Sam.

Crest did not bother to explain.

Long Peter had been dissected down to the bones, and nothing remained of him but a small mound of rubbery particles which not even a forensic pathologist could have identified. The 5,000 anatomical parts were as clearly stamped in the minds of the students as they would ever be, and more clearly than they would ever be again. Now it was time for the mid-year examinations.

Sam Parkindale prepared for the exams by ignoring his books altogether for a week and staying out, drinking and sporting, until all hours of the night. Crest, of course, was hitting Gray even harder than before. When Crest entered the examination room, filled with anxious students, pens, pencils, bluebooks, and general consternation, his mind was an utter blank. It seemed unlikely that he could remember his own name. When the examination question sheet had been passed around, Crest stared at it hopelessly.

"Name the origin, insertion, structure, blood supply, nerve supply, and function of the flexor pollicis longus muscle."

"Describe the course and relationships of the femoral artery, including all branches thereof."

"Locate, identify, and define the foramen of Winslow, including three-dimensional relationships to all contiguous structures."

Ye Gods! After sitting frozen for ten or fifteen horrible panic-stricken minutes, Crest could recall nothing. Finally, seizing his pencil in a moist and shaky hand, he compelled himself to write, no matter what sort of gibberish might come forth. Soon the pump began to flow. Facts began to come, in a slow trickle at first, and then in an increasing stream, and finally pouring forth faster than he could set them down. At the end of three hours, he was still driving away, scarcely conscious of aching eyeballs and a crick in his neck and almost total paralysis of the right forearm. The instructor virtually had to take the bluebook away from him by force. Sam was waiting for him outside the examination hall.

"I failed," groaned Crest. "I flunked. I'm out. I couldn't remember a bloody thing."

"Ridiculous," said Sam. "I think you got a 93."

"And I suppose you failed the course?"

"No," said Sam. "I imagine I got a 72, two points higher than necessary, just for safety's sake. Let's forget it and go out and get roaring drunk."

"Not for me," said Crest. "I'm going to bed and sleep for thirty-six hours. I'll see you next week, if we're both still students in this school."

Monday found them both still students of the school. The grades were posted and there was a jabbering merry mob in front of the board. Crest pushed in close enough to read the grades. Although Sam had not been exactly right, his guesses were very accurate. Crest had a 94 and Sam a 78. Crest also noted the names of those who had flunked, a dozen of them, including some names he fully expected and others that were a total surprise. Glancing around, Crest noted that none of these were in the crowd around the board. He realized that word must have been given to the unfortunates privately over the weekend and that they would never be seen again in these halls.

Without pause for delay or self-satisfaction, the second half of the year began immediately. The subjects now were physiology and physiological chemistry. This involved a great deal of lecture work, hour after hour on the hard benches, looking down into the dark and gloomy pit. There was also laboratory work. In the physiology lab, they ganged up on a poor little frog. They would pith the creature, which meant driving a trocar through its spinal cord, to render it decerebrate and deprive it of pain; and they would study the functions and reactions of the still-living froggy muscles and nerves and viscera and heart, recording reactions on the kymograph, a large revolving drum covered with smoked paper.

"Not that I have ever eaten frog's legs in a French restaurant," said Crest, "but I surely could never do it now."

In chemistry, the lab work was somewhat incendiary and exciting at times. Many of the experiments involved extraction of organic compounds with ether, following which the ether was boiled off over a water bath. Some of the students could never remember that ether fumes are heavier than air and also explosive, and therefore the wise man turns his bunsen burner off. At least twice a week somebody forgot to cut the gas, and there was an ether explosion: a concussion that rattled the windows and a momentary sheet of flame from wall to ceiling.

A good deal of the work in the chemistry lab involved the detailed examination of urine samples, and each student supplied his own. If a smell of formaldehyde was the trademark of the first semester, a student lugging around a large glass carboy filled with his own urine characterized the second semester. The work of the second semester was detailed and tedious but not particularly difficult, and even Crest realized that he was not likely to flunk the course.

"In anatomy, they flunk us out," said Sam. "But in pee chem and physiology, they whittle you down through the attrition of sheer boredom."

It was in the spring term that Crest met another member of the Parkindale family.

"My own personal favorite member of the clan," said Sam.

"Who's that?"

"My uncle—Joseph. He's the plastic surgeon."

Joseph Parkindale lived in a swanky apartment in a fashionable section of the city. The boys went past a doorman dressed like a cossack and entered a building where the word "depression" was obviously never mentioned.

"By the way," said Sam, "my uncle is a bachelor, but don't be surprised if you see a woman or two about the place. He often keeps them."

"Keeps?" said Crest.

"His hobby is collecting mistresses."

"I didn't think American men actually kept mistresses," said Crest. "That always seemed to me like a continental custom."

"Perhaps you might say that Joseph is a continental type," said Sam.

In certain ways, Joseph looked like an older and more sophisticated edition of Sam: the same apple cheeks and pleasant grin and the leonine family head. However, there was a polish and smoothness to him which Crest had not noticed in the other members of the tribe. Joseph had a trim little red mustache and silky red hair. He wore a red velvet smoking jacket and an ascot with a pearl stick pin. Crest immediately noticed his hands: tapered, sensitive, beautifully groomed, the hands of a Sybarite.

"This is Johnnie Crest," said Sam.

"I know," said Joseph. "I've heard very favorable reports from the Department of Anatomy."

"You've heard of me?" asked Crest, surprised.

"Of course," said Joseph. "I keep tabs on every class. Who can tell? I may discover a plastic surgeon in the group some day."

"One plastic surgeon in our class should be enough," said Sam. "Meaning me, of course."

Crest had not heard of Sam's interests along these lines.

"And furthermore," said Joseph, "you have made quite an impression on the members of my family, Dr. Crest. There is a certain niece of mine who is quite smitten by you."

"She has managed to conceal it very well," said Crest.

"Maybe you can become my plastic surgeon. Sam has the

manual dexterity, but I'm afraid he's a little bit too dumb. He'll have to have a dental degree, if and when he graduates from medical school, if he hopes to work with me."

"You're a dentist too?" asked Crest.

"You almost have to be if you expect to do much maxillo-facial work," said Joseph.

"What is the appeal of plastic surgery?" asked Crest. "I know nothing about it, but it always struck me as a remote and superficial sort of specialty."

"Short hours, good money, and you meet a lot of celebrities," said Joseph.

"You'll hear plenty about the art of medicine," said Sam, "but Joseph is the only artist in the crowd. If you don't believe me, look around you."

Crest noticed that the apartment was full of statuary—busts and bas-relief—and many of the faces were familiar to Crest: actresses, society women, various minor celebrities.

"Yours?" he asked.

"My patients and my models," said Joseph. "Sometimes after I have finished working on the flesh, I set down the results in stone. Flesh is subject to decay, but stone endures."

"How does a plastic surgeon work?" asked Crest. "Exactly how do you create a nose, for example?"

"Ask him about his work on the female breast," said Sam. "That fascinates me."

"Yes, it would," said Joseph.

"The stuff about the reconstruction of the nipple," said Sam. "You remember, Johnnie, that the nipple is composed of erectile tissue. It isn't enough to make a reconstructed breast look pretty, it's got to function properly too. Joseph developed a technique whereby he re-creates erectile nipple tissue from tissue in the nose. I guess you didn't know that some of the nasal mucosa is capable of engorgement and erection under erotic stimulus, just like the nipple and the clitoris?"

"When I was your age and going to school," said Joseph, "plastic surgery was utilitarian and gross. It was surgery of repair, for the restoration of function. We fixed harelips and fractured jaws, skin-grafted for burn scars, performed radical neck dissections for carcinoma of the lip, took off keloids, loosened contractures around a joint, and so forth. Any surgeon with manual dexterity and a gentle touch with tissue can learn these techniques and most of this work now falls in the province of general surgery. A few of us developed the special clever tricks of cosmetic surgery, which is the unique contribution of the plastic surgeon. The profession is apt to regard us as mere surgical beauticians, but our work is more important than is generally recognized. A patient with a physical deformity develops a corresponding psychological deformity. A would-be debutante with a crooked nose or an aging movie star with sagging breasts is fully as disabled as the working man without an arm, and develops corresponding occupational neurosis. A patient who is ashamed of the way he looks is disturbed and insecure. Our job is just the same as that of any surgeon: to restore a disabled person to gainful and enjoyable activity. I like to think of plastic surgery as a sort of surgical psychiatry."

"That's an interesting point of view," said Crest.

"It isn't enough to repair deformity and change it into beauty on the terms of classic art. You asked me about a nose. Once I made a nose of classic beauty, and the operation was a failure. The patient did not have a personality of classic beauty, and she couldn't live up to her nose. She looked in her mirror a few times, and then she committed suicide. Now I always try to leave a flaw, and I pick a flaw to fit the personality. You follow me?"

"More or less," said Crest.

"I'll demonstrate," said Joseph. "Diana, my dear, come over here, if you please, and show the young gentleman your nice new nose with the flaw which fits your personality."

Crest was aware for the first time that there was a woman in the room. She was a statuesque and regal ash blonde; she walked calmly over to the light and held up her face for inspection. Her complexion was a chalky white, and Crest observed that she wore a heavy layer of powder to conceal a network of almost imperceptible scars around her nose. The nose in question was patrician and elegant, as was the lady herself, but there was just a suggestion of a hawklike crooking at the tip. To Crest, it spoke of cruelty.

"Diana is Jewish, of course," said Joseph, "and she came to me with a nose like Shylock's, desiring to be transformed into Aryan aristocracy. I have made her aristocratic, but it would be a mistake to remove all traces of her Jewish heritage. Somehow or other, though, I am not quite satisfied with Diana's nose. I seem to have made her virginal and cold, and she isn't that way, I can assure you, boys. I operated on her first and began sleeping with her second. The next time, perhaps, I'll do it the other way around."

Crest found himself disconcerted by the discussion. The intimate discussion of the lady's nose was bad enough; the discussion of the lady's bedding habits was worse. The lady herself showed no signs of being disconcerted; in fact, she showed no reaction at all. When her nose had been sufficiently scrutinized, she promenaded over to a bar at the other side of the room and poured some raw gin into a glass. For the remainder of the evening she sat wordlessly in a corner, sipping her gin as smoke and conversation swirled around her, silent as a clam.

After they had left, Crest said, "Do you suppose your uncle cut out her tongue when he fixed her nose?"

"I never saw this one before," said Sam. "I warned you that Joseph's taste in women is special and bizarre."

"I almost felt as if he had taken the raw ingredients of a woman and molded them to suit his taste and used the final result for his own pleasure. He's a sensualist, isn't he?"

"He's an artist, John."

"It strikes me as vaguely obscene," said Crest. "As if a gynecologist took pleasure in performing pelvics or as if a urologist was homosexual."

"You may see that in the profession from time to time if you look real sharp," said Sam.

"Shouldn't a doctor keep private impulses out of his professional life?"

"A doctor is also a human being."

"The more of a human being, the less of a doctor?"

"Not necessarily," said Sam. "But it is well to develop a detached and impersonal attitude."

"Which is also vaguely cold and cruel, I suppose."

"Part of that is self-defense," said Sam. "If the doctor suffers with his patient every time, he doesn't last very long."

"That will be hard for me to learn," said Crest. "I think I'll keep remembering that I and the damned patient are two damned human beings in the same sinking boat."

"I think this is why I like Joseph the best," said Sam. "All of my family has this hard, tough, professional shell."

"Yes," said Crest, "I've even noticed it in Emerald."

"In the case of Joseph, however, the shell is thin. The man and the doctor are not so vastly separated. The private impulse and the public action have the same motivation."

"Which is dangerous," said Crest.

"Yeah, maybe so," said Sam. "But at least to Joseph the patient is a human being, not a living cadaver on an operating table or a decerebrated frog."

"But still another thought," said Crest. "If the outer shell is hard and tough, perhaps the man inside is warm and sympathetic. And this might imply that your uncle is less warm, less sympathetic, than the dean, for example, or your father."

"It isn't as easy as that," said Sam. "You can't classify people into types. Joseph is a rather complicated gent."

"In my case, I know that I will have to develop a shell in self-defense, but I hope I don't entirely lose my own humanity," said Crest.

"This is known to be an occupational hazard, son," said Sam.

The relative ease of the final examinations in physiology and chemistry, and the fact that he was not likely to flunk these subjects, made the spring term somewhat anticlimactic to Crest. He faced a long hot summer in the city. During the summer he got a job lugging heavy crates for the Railway Express, and he saw somewhat more of his father than he liked. He was ready for the beginning of the second year in the fall.

In the second year, the medical work came alive for him. The subjects of the freshman year are necessary background material, but it is difficult for most students to get excited about the structure of a cadaver, the contents of urine, or the reflexes of the frog. The first half of the second year consisted of a single subject, pathology, the science of disease, which is truly basic to all of modern medicine.

Crest had previously thought of disease as a long list of individual conditions, each different, each with a name, a cause, a discrete set of symptoms and signs. Now he learned that disease has no sharp boundary lines.

No man, he was taught, is entirely healthy at any time of his life. Health is a relative state, characterized by relative minimum of disease. The body is under constant attack from a vast variety of internal and external hostile forces, against which it puts up a continuing dynamic battle. When the battle line is stable and the enemy contained, a state of relative health exists; any retreat or withdrawal at any point of the battle line represents disease.

The list of hostile forces is almost incredibly long: environmental factors such as heat, cold, radiation, electricity, and mechanical trauma; organic and inorganic poisons in food, water, and the atmosphere; living enemies from the plant world (bacteria and fungi), from the animal world (the protozoa, the spirochete, and multi-celled parasites), and from the twilight world of viruses; internal forces such as infection, metabolic disturbance, imbalance of vitamins, hormones, and enzymes; structural derangement of internal

viscera; arteriosclerosis and the aging process; abnormal reaction to stress; and finally the process when the cells turn
against the body, the frightening malignant crab of cancer.

"Holy smokes," said Sam Parkindale. "I didn't realize what
a triumph it is to be alive at all!"

Against these forces, the body puts up an extraordinarily
shrewd defense, and only when defense breaks down does
disease occur. They studied the various diseases: measles,
mumps, and whooping cough; diphtheria and smallpox; syphilis, gonorrhea, tuberculosis, leprosy; asthma, pneumonia,
rheumatic fever, coronary disease, gallstones, kidney stones,
nephritis, ulcer, appendicitis, cirrhosis, colitis, diabetes, anemia, sarcoma, and carcinoma, and several thousand more.

"One thing I'm sure about," said Crest. "I'm never going to
get out of this alive."

Crest had a tendency to discover in himself the signs and
symptoms of each disease that they studied in turn, a tendency shared by many suggestible members of the class. He
thought he was catching the lot of them, from Tsutsugamushi
fever to Carrion's disease.

"What the hell is Carrion's disease?" asked Sam.

"Another name for Oroya fever," said Crest.

"That's a big help!" said Sam.

"Carrion was a man's name. He discovered the disease and
inoculated himself with it in order to study it, and he died
of it."

"Smart guy," said Sam.

"It's an infectious disease marked by high fever, a pernicious variety of anemia, prostration, and rapid death, and is
accompanied by a warty skin condition known as verruga
peruviana. The disease is caused by a blood parasite called
Bartonella bacilliformis, which can be seen in the red blood
cells as a tiny rodlike structure. The exact nature of the in-
fecting organism is not known; it looks like a bacteria but is
probably some sort of virus. The disease is transmitted by the
Phlebotomus, which is an insect of the sand-fly family."

"Oh, sure," said Sam. "We see a dozen cases in Sentryville every week at this time of year."

"I doubt it," said Crest. "Carrion's disease is found only in Peru."

"And why do we have to fill our little minds with this sort of junk?" said Sam. "You and I aren't going to practice in Peru."

On the next test, however, one of the questions concerned Carrion's disease.

"Thanks, buddy," said Sam. "Now you see why the acquaintance of a dedicated grind is of such a help to me."

"I've got it, Sam," said Crest. "Look at this place on my skin. Doesn't it look like a verruga peruviana to you?"

"To me, it looks like a wart," said Sam. "In Sentryville, we cure 'em with toads and swamp water."

"I'm sure I'm running a fever, and I feel definite indications of prostration this morning."

"You'll be famous, Johnnie, the first case of Carrion's disease ever seen outside Peru."

"Do you think I ought to go on down to the infirmary?"

"I think you ought to realize this," said Sam. "You are bound to get a few of these diseases that we're studying, and one of them is bound to get you in the end, but you can't get more than a few of them, because you won't live that long, and nobody in history ever got 'em all. Now, isn't that a comforting thought?"

Their work contained a good deal of lecture material, and Crest found it engrossing, as if he were an observer on a mountain top, overlooking the panorama of battlefield on the plains below. In the lab, they studied slides under the microscope, sections of diseased tissue where the evidence of a skirmish lost or a breach in the battle line was stopped permanently in front of their eyes. They dissected fresh specimens which were sent down warm and smoky from the surgical operating suites or brought up cold and putrefied from the autopsy room. They wandered through the pathological museum, where instructive specimens from the decades and the centuries were permanently pickled and preserved. And they participated actively in autopsy work several times a week.

The autopsy room was in the basement, a dark, damp cave serviced by attendants who resembled albino lizards, pale, hardened little men who picked their teeth with autopsy probes and ate lunch amid the spleens and livers.

Having spent six months with Long Peter the year before, Crest thought himself immune to the presence of death. However, an autopsy never failed to produce in him a strong and mixed emotional reaction. Part of this reaction was aversion and disgust. The preserved cadaver never seemed to have been alive, but the body in the autopsy room was fresh, and sometimes not so fresh. Crest kept expecting to see the body take a breath or let out a scream as the large knife of the butcher variety cut the belly wall in a single brutal stroke. Futhermore, the prepared specimen of the anatomy lab smelled only of formaldehyde, which is an almost pleasant odor when you get used to it. In the morgue, the body smelled of putrefaction. Sometimes even the experienced pathologist must breathe through his mouth if he expects to retain his lunch. On the other hand, there was always an air of excitement and adventure connected with the autopsy. Each case presented a problem, a puzzle to be solved. Finding the telling evidence to confirm a bedside diagnosis or else to reveal an unsuspected or a rare condition was a thrill to Crest that was seldom duplicated elsewhere in the field of medicine.

"At least the patient doesn't talk back to you down here," said Sam.

"But it's hard to forget," said Crest, "that death may be just around the corner for each and every one of us."

There was a death waiting around the corner that Crest did not expect. He was sitting in the lecture room, taking notes, when the lecturer suddenly stopped in the middle of a sentence. There was a buzz among the students, and heads turned around to look to the back of the auditorium. A pair of large, businesslike policemen had walked in and come down to where Crest was seated.

"John Crest?"

"Yes. What's the matter?"

"Would you come with us, if you please?"

Crest left the room between the two cops, the center of undesirable notoriety.

"What's the matter? I haven't done anything wrong," said Crest, perplexed and a little frightened by the whole affair.

"It's your father," said one of the cops.

"Dad? What's wrong with him?"

"He's dead," said the cop. "We want you to identify the body. Just come along with us."

They hustled him out of the building to a waiting squad car, and set off downtown with the wailing of sirens and the flashing blue eye on top of the car. This was December and a wet snow was falling; the squad car, hitting a wet streetcar rail, skidded just a little bit. Over the radio came the crackling of static and occasional commands for car this-and-that to go to such-and-such a place. The whole thing had such an air of unreality to Crest that he failed to have any immediate emotional response. He had heard that his father was dead, and that he was being taken to view the remains; he accepted these facts but he could not entirely believe them. City scenes swept by like the panorama of a dream. The police were brusquely silent. The thought occurred to Crest that, if he had been under arrest, perhaps they would have passed the time of day with him, or at least would have spoken with each other. Their silence was sympathy, in a fashion. Policemen cannot react to every horror or outrage they see any more than doctors can, and their professional gruffness had something in common with the brusqueness of many surgeons.

The car was already in the water-front area before one of them finally spoke to him. "It's rough, son, you better get ready for a shock."

Crest heard himself speaking one of those foolish inane remarks that sometimes come out under stress. "I've seen a dead body before. I was doing an autopsy not more than an hour ago."

"That so?" said the younger of the cops. "I always wanted to see one of them."

"Hank! . . ." said the older policeman warningly, and the younger man shut up.

They went a few blocks further and then Crest said, not knowing how he knew, "My father committed suicide."

They did not reply. His presumption, then, was correct. They stopped in the block where his father lived. They all got out. The older policeman took Crest by the elbow, guiding him and supporting him, although Crest knew exactly where to go. His father lived in a basement one-room apartment, leading off an alley. The door was open, the room full of people, including a number of policemen in uniform, and photographers and others in civilian clothes. All of them wore hats. Most of them smoked, and crushed out cigarette butts on the floor, as if this was no longer an indoor room where anybody lived.

The object was very prominent. Crest could think of it as nothing but an object. Of course it was his father and readily identifiable, but there was an obscenity which the mind could not assimilate.

The room was high, with the ceiling perhaps ten feet from the floor, and along the ceiling ran steam pipes which supplied heat to the apartments overhead. In the summer, Crest recalled, the room was often unbearably muggy, as moisture condensed along the pipes, and in the winter, it was likely to be exceedingly hot and dry. His father had always claimed that he liked the room for that reason, since he had always been susceptible to cold, although Crest knew his father took this room because it was cheaper than the others in the building.

Crest's father had hanged himself. Standing on the small

end of an upturned orange crate, he had obviously thrown the rope over the pipes. When the noose was adjusted, he had kicked out the orange crate underneath his feet. The knot was very close to the pipes, and his head must have nearly touched the ceiling at the time. In the beginning, his father's feet had dangled off the floor the length of the orange crate, perhaps three feet.

"He's been dead, son, a matter of several days," said a man who seemed to be in charge, probably from the coroner's office.

Crest was aware of this. The odor in the room, the state of decomposition of the skin, and Crest's autopsy experience made this obvious.

"I'm a second-year medical student," he said to the man in charge, to explain his own presence of mind and unnatural curiosity over the scene.

But then there was the obscenity, which he now forced himself to observe, and he had to ask the question about that. "Why is he almost ten feet tall?"

"This happens, son, when you don't cut down a hanging man for a matter of days. The ligaments and joint spaces stretch, you know."

Crest hadn't known, although he later confirmed the fact in a textbook of forensic pathology. His father had been a man of average height, but the body now almost extended from the ceiling to the floor. Crest could only think of a dead giraffe. His belly began to churn, and he pulled the trick of concentration which he had taught himself in the autopsy room, breathing quickly and deeply through his open mouth and fixing his vision somewhere else.

"That's all, son. You don't have to look any more. We're sorry that you had to see it. He left you a note."

The man was thrusting some papers into Crest's hand. Crest glanced at them. There was a note in his father's handwriting, brief and unemotional. He had lived long enough, his father wrote, and finances were pressing him, and he had always failed, and he was worth more dead than alive. The insurance money would pay for the medical school. God bless you and forgive me and so forth.

The other papers were the insurance policies and his father's will. Crest glanced at them and gave them back to the man in charge, and then he quickly went outside and was sick in the falling snow. Leaning weakly against a wet brick wall, Crest knew that he had not been sick on account of the sight or the smell or even the act itself, but because of the ultimate manifestation of his father's failure. The insurance policies had contained a suicide exemption clause. His father had not even thought of this.

Crest was driven back to school in the squad car, but he did not return to class, nor did he go back to his boarding-house. He walked blindly around the streets and through the corridors of the hospital and medical school. Late that night he found himself on an outside porch, a sun pavilion, on top of the hospital building. He leaned over the rail, looking down into the darkness and the falling snow. The city noises were muffled. Every now and then, a car poked its way along the street below like an illuminated beetle.

Crest thought about his mother. He had never really known her, since she died of some wasting and painful disease, presumably cancer, when he was five or six years old. His only recollection was of a little white lady in a big white bed. The uselessness of her suffering and death had originally inspired him to choose the profession of medicine.

Perhaps things would have been different if his mother had lived. As nearly as he could remember, they had been respectable and happy, though poor, when she was alive. His father had been a church organist and director of the choir and had given private music lessons to young ladies during the week.

After his mother's death, his father abandoned all association with the church and took to the road, playing with small jazz combinations and with village bands. Sometimes the boy went with him and sometimes the boy was left behind with

a strict and unaffectionate maiden aunt. For the most part,
the boy had grown up lonely and alone. His father had loved
him and been kind to him, and had gone beyond the call of
duty in paying for an expensive education. The worst that
could be said against his father was that he was weak. But
the fact remained that he had failed, both in his son's eyes
and in his own, and his son was ashamed of him. It was too
late for Crest to pay back any debt of love. The thing that
bothered him most at this time was that he could not force
himself to feel any grief at what had taken place. The pain
of the moment concerned money and the useless insurance
policies, for now he could not afford to remain in medical
school. He was appalled at his own small selfishness and in
this moment had transferred the shame against his father into
shame against himself. His own potential failure now loomed
up in front of him.

"Are you thinking of jumping?"

A large figure had appeared behind Crest on the balcony;
looking around, Crest saw that it was the dean.

"You're John Crest, aren't you?"

"Yes, sir."

"Don't you think you better come out of the snow?"

"My father committed suicide," said Crest.

"Yes, we know," said the dean. "We've been looking for
you."

"The insurance wasn't any good. I'll have to quit school,"
said Crest. "I don't know where to go."

"First you'll come out of the snow and go home in a taxi
cab," said the dean. "Then you'll take a long hot bath. I have
two sleeping capsules in this envelope, and you will take them
both immediately after your bath, and then you will go to bed.
I will leave word with the landlady at your boardinghouse
that you are not to be disturbed. What's today? Tuesday?"

"Wednesday, sir, I think."

"Wednesday, of course. You are not expected to report to
classes until next week. The first thing Monday morning, you

will report to my office. There are certain financial matters which must be arranged. Now, come along."

He put his arm around Crest's shoulder and led him off the balcony, through the corridor, down the elevator, across the lobby, out the main door, and onto the street. Then he summoned a taxi with a piercing authoritative whistle.

"You'll be all right, son?" the dean asked, looking at him searchingly.

"Yes, sir."

"And you have the sleeping pills?"

"In my pocket, sir."

"I expect you at my office next Monday morning at eight o'clock," he said. "And, by the way, suicide is not a crime, a sin, or a moral weakness. In my considered opinion, it is a fatal symptom of an emotional disease. Your father could have died of a heart attack or been run over by a truck. A man is frequently the cause of his own destruction, but it is not within his power to select the time, the place, and the means of his own mortality. The seed of his destruction was planted in him long ago, as it is planted in us all, and he fights it as long as he can and as well as he can, until such time as the strength of his defense is overcome. Reason is your best friend at a time like this, my boy, and when reason fails, there is always prayer, although these medicines are not carried in the doctor's bag. Good night."

"Good night, sir."

The dean paid the taxi fare in advance. The cab started up along the slippery thoroughfare. John Crest was back in class again the following Monday. His education was now supported by a scholarship and loan.

Part 2

The waiting room for the out-patient clinics was large, dark, and poorly ventilated. Here, on rows of hard benches, sat the silent poor. Often they waited for hours to be seen in one of the various clinics. There was a clinic for medicine, for surgery, and for the various specialties: eye; ear, nose, and throat; allergy; dermatology; venereal disease; gynecology; obstetrics; pediatrics; orthopedics; neurology. The clinics were staffed by third-year students under supervision. It was here that the student had his first contact with the living, breathing, and complaining human patient.

As John Crest again approached the school for the start of another year, his stamp of status was of a higher order. Instead of a knee-length linen coat, he wore a short white jacket. In the top pocket he carried a pen, a flashlight, and wooden tongue depressors; through the lapel were thrust several straight pins; in the right-hand lower pocket was a new stethoscope whose tubing coiled like the arms of an unco-ordinated octopus; and in the left-hand pocket, a reflex hammer and combined otoscope and opthalmoscope.

At five minutes of eight he greeted Sam Parkindale and the other friends in his class. At eight he was in the clinic, and the patients were ready. As always in this school, it was sink or swim, and nobody told the students what to do.

He was assigned to the surgical clinic that morning. The room contained some twenty cubicles, each shielded with a curtain. The patient in Crest's cubicle was male, elderly and cantankerous, bearing about him an unwashed fragrancy.

"Good morning," said Crest.

"And a fine good morning to you, Doc," said the patient cheerfully.

"What can I do for you?" asked Crest.

"I don't know," said the patient.

"Well, why did you come to the clinic?"

"On account of they told me to."

"And what's the trouble?"

"You're the doc," said the patient. "Why don't you tell me?"

This was not a brilliant beginning. Although the room was cool, Crest felt himself perspiring around the collar. He decided on a bold frontal attack.

"All right, my friend," he said, "I'm a busy man. There are a lot of other patients waiting to get in. Why don't you just move along?"

The patient gave a sheepish grin. The frontal approach was going to work.

"Well, sonny," said the patient, "I got six stitches in my arm, and I figger somebody better take them out."

Crest realized that he should have looked before he spoke. The bandage on the patient's forearm was quite obvious. In a surgical clinic, it was unlikely that the patient would present a diagnostic problem. Crest took a pair of bandage scissors off the dressing cart and cut the bandage, once white, now a nice vintage shade of tobacco brown.

"Old lady sliced me with the carving knife a week ago last

Saturday night," said the patient. "One of the young docs sewed me up in the Accident Room. It wasn't you."

"No," said Crest. "It wasn't me."

He yanked on the adhesive tape, pulling it off the hairy forearm of the patient.

"Ouch," said the patient.

"That was nothing," said Crest.

"Nothing to you, Doc, but it happens to be my arm. How does she look?"

Crest inspected the scar of a jagged laceration, covered with a layer of dried blood and pus-like exudate. It looked messy to him.

"Fine," said Crest.

He washed off the exudate and inspected half a dozen silk sutures which transversed the scar.

"I figger I could cut them stitches out by myself," said the patient, "but on the other hand, you doctors got a lot more experience."

"Much more," said Crest, who had never seen a suture before in his life.

He gravely studied the situation and then he popped outside the cubicle, looking for help. No instructor was in sight, so he returned to the cubicle. He found a bottle of disinfectant and some cotton swabs, painted the wound with the pink liquid, and went searching for the instructor again.

"Any theories on how to remove silk sutures?" he asked Sam Parkindale, who also seemed to be looking for help.

"Any theories on how to lance a boil on somebody's ass?" said Sam.

"I've already put on disinfectant."

"So have I. Want to swap patients? I think I'm probably more of a suture-cutting man than a boil-lancing man myself."

"I don't think I'm very good on boils," said Crest. "I suppose you just stick the point of a scalpel into the center of the thing."

"And I suppose that you just cut the sutures with a pair of sterile scissors and pull 'em out," said Sam. "Carry on."

Crest returned to the booth and managed to extract the sutures without much difficulty. Sam had no trouble with the boil. Some of the students were not so successful. One of them burned a patient while trying to put on a gelatin boot, and another, while struggling to remove a plaster cast, lacerated the skin underneath.

The problems of the surgical clinic were for the most part mechanical and could be solved with the aid of common sense. There were dressings to be changed; casts, sutures, and skin clips to be removed; minor infections to be drained; granulation tissue to be cauterized. Two or three operations were scheduled every day. This was minor surgery, done under local anaesthesia: simple vein ligations, incision and drainage of abscesses, minor rectal work, removal of warts, moles, wens, and cysts. Sam loved surgery. Crest was apt to be tense under pressure, and he did not enjoy himself in the operating room.

For the most part, these operations in the clinic were routine and uneventful, but every student had at least one episode he was not likely to forget. There was the time a patient suffered a cardiac arrest, dying on the table. And there was the time Sam Parkindale was too vigorous with the knife. He had been trying to remove what appeared to be a simple cyst of the forehead.

"I kept cutting and cutting and cutting," said Sam. "I couldn't seem to get to the bottom of the thing. I kept wondering when I would hit bone. Finally I came upon this filmy membranous structure. I cut through it, and the patient jumped. He said, 'Hey, Doc, I think you're cutting into my brain!' I looked down and damned if the patient wasn't right."

The tumor had not been a simple cyst but a malignant growth of the lining of the brain which had eroded to the skin surface through the skull. In attempting to reach the base of the tumor, Sam had exposed the open surface of the brain itself. The patient was removed from the clinic and rushed upstairs to the neurosurgical operating suite as a full-fledged and dangerous emergency.

"You almost killed the man," said Crest.

"Yeah," said Sam, "with the best of intentions, I almost did."

"That would give me the creeps," said Crest. "I'd hate to go back to the operating room again."

"It wasn't my fault," said Sam. "I was doing the best I could."

"In surgery, I keep thinking of the vital structures that I may be about to cut."

"The surgeon can't look too far ahead," said Sam. "He handles the problem of the moment. Tomorrow takes care of itself."

Crest also had an episode in the surgical clinic that jarred him. The patient in the cubicle was complaining of a growing tumor of the chest, and he took off his shirt to display it. The mass was large, bulging, dark-colored; droplets of blood were oozing from it, and the mass seemed to pulsate. Crest didn't like the look of it at all. Before he could call for help, the mass broke before his eyes. A stream of bright red blood, as thick as a man's wrist, propelled by the force of a fireman's hose, shot forth, drenching the wall. Crest was soaked in the hot sticky stuff, and the entire cubicle seemed to be awash. Not knowing what else to do, Crest put his bare hand on the hole, trying to staunch the flow, but to no avail. The patient exsanguinated and was dead within a minute.

"I didn't touch the thing," said Crest.

"This was a spontaneous rupture of a syphilitic aneurysm of the aorta," said the instructor. "There was nothing anybody could have done. You have witnessed a rare and unusual event. You are not likely to see it again."

Crest was not likely to forget it, either. From that time on, he had a lurking horror of hemorrhage, and this did not help his surgical technique. In the effort to be careful, he was slow, and the more care he took, the more crude and clumsy seemed

to be the result. His fingers had a tendency to tremble under
stress; even the simple tying of a knot became a major enter-
prise. The scar following one of Sam's operations was thin,
taut, and pretty. One of Crest's incisions looked as if he had
been hacking away with pinking shears.

"Maybe your father was right," said Crest. "Maybe I'm not
cut out for clinical practice."

"You'll feel more at home when we get to medicine," said
Sam.

In the medical out-patient clinic, the pace was more leisurely. The patients here were chronic cases: hypertensives
and cardiacs, asthmatics, diabetics, and particularly hypo-
chondriacs with functional disease. Each patient carried his
clinic record with him, a massive tome as thick as a city telephone directory. It often took an hour to study the chart, and
another hour to ask the questions which so many other previous examiners had asked before. Some of these chronic patients were gray and gloomy, living in their own gray fog,
but most of them were cheerful and socially inclined. In fact,
they seemed to take positive delight in reciting their list of
symptoms, as if it was a mark of distinction that no doctor
had been smart enough to solve their case. For some of these
patients, their disease seemed to be the sole occupation and
preoccupation of their lives.

"There's nothing wrong with them," said Sam impatiently.
"They never get better and they never get worse. They complain and live indefinitely. My grandfather says that the best
way to live a long and fascinating life is to develop a good
chronic disease."

"They interest me," said Crest. "It's a challenge to try to
help these poor souls."

"They don't want to be cured," said Sam. "There's nothing
you can do. You listen to their long, sad, boring tale of woe
for an hour; you give them a vitamin shot and a prescription
for phenobarbital; you make another appointment for them
at the clinic next week, when they can bore some other ex-

aminer. In surgery, at least, there's something you can do."

"It would be a real accomplishment to pick up some condition that everybody else had missed," said Crest.

Once he was able to make such an accomplishment. The patient had been under treatment at the clinic for many months for cirrhosis. Thumbing through the voluminous record, Crest was astonished to discover that, somehow or other, a routine blood Wasserman had never been performed. Crest ordered this test and it came back positive.

"So what?" said Sam. "Did you ever see a nigger from this section of the city who didn't have a positive serology?"

"Perhaps the patient doesn't have cirrhosis," said Crest. "Perhaps this is syphilis of the liver instead."

Crest broached his theory to the instructor. He received little encouragement. Cirrhosis is common; tertiary syphilis of the liver is rare. Crest pressed his point. A liver biopsy was performed. The patient did have syphilis of the liver.

"Hero medal for you," said Sam. "But what have you accomplished? With our present methods, we can't cure cirrhosis and we can't cure syphilis of the liver. The patient is just as sick as ever, and eventually he dies of one diagnosis rather than the other. What difference does it make?"

"The treatment is very different."

"But neither treatment seems to do much good."

"You have no basis for scientific treatment until you have established a scientific diagnosis."

"I'll take a good hot appendix any day," said Sam.

The students spent most of their time divided equally between the clinics of medicine and surgery, but they also rotated briefly through the clinics of the specialties. Each specialty clinic had a flavor of its own.

The eye clinic meant darkness. Here, in the dark, the effort was made to bring light. Most students did not master the techniques of examination and treatment of the eye, a mysterious and frightening organ; what most of them learned was, if the eye is injured or diseased, leave it alone and holler for help.

Ear, nose, and throat meant steam: the steam which arose from instrument sterilizers, from spray guns, and from the mucous membranes of the patient; steam which fogged mirrors and the eyeglasses of the examiner. Once he managed to keep himself steam-free, Crest found it easy enough to peer into the orifices of the head and visualize the internal structures, wet, red, and bathed with viscous secretion.

"The ear, nose, and throat man spends his life in a swamp," said Sam.

The allergy clinic was full of needles with which to scratch and jab the patient.

"The porcupine specialty," said Sam.

In dermatology, it was rashes and splotches and bumps.

"The patient never dies of a rash," said Sam, "and he never recovers, no matter which one of a thousand salves and greases and lotions you apply, with equal lack of effect."

The venereal-disease clinic had a gruesome fascination for the students. It was always full in those pre-penicillin days; half the population of the city seemed to carry venereal disease. The students were very much aware of an invisible layer of spirochetes and gonococci crawling all over the room; it was not necessary to remind any student to wash his hands after leaving this particular clinic.

"Life's worst irony," said Sam. "To acquire venereal disease in a non-venereal fashion."

"I intend to become a monk," said Crest.

On one side of the room was a line of naked forearms, waiting for the injection of arsenical drug into the antecubital vein, and on the other side, an equally long line of naked buttocks, waiting for the intramuscular injection of bismuth.

"Mass production, just like Henry Ford," said Sam. "Remember this when you face temptation next Saturday night."

"I stay home next Saturday night," said Crest. "This is the

best advertisment for continence and chastity that I have ever seen."

In the gynecology clinic, the long line was feminine and genital.

"What a romantic sight," sighed Sam.

"Stop it," said Crest. "This is a sight to chill a man's romance forever."

In obstetrics, they palpated swollen abdomens to locate the position of the fetus.

"They tell a story about a student in the OB out-patient clinic one time," said Sam. "One of the girls went into rapid unexpected labor, and they didn't have time to get her upstairs. As usual, there was no instructor on the scene. The student did the best he could. He delivered a baby and sighed and started to congratulate himself when another baby started pushing through the birth canal. The student pulled it out and then along came a third. At this point the instructor finally arrived. The student looked at the instructor and said, 'Sir, how do I turn this damn thing off?'"

In the pediatric clinic, the patients were small, tough, and irascible. All of them constantly cried. The larger ones were liable to kick or bite or scratch and the smaller ones sometimes urinated on the examiner. Many students were frightened by babies. Babies were quite sensitive, Crest realized; they seemed to know when the examiner was afraid and quickly took advantage. Crest found that he could get along with kids and babies very well by acting calm and unimpressed. He decided that children are tougher than they look and not half as sick as they seem to be. He also realized that the pediatrician spends more time treating the mother than the child.

The neurology clinic was often considered dull, since most of the patients seemed to be epileptics, for whom there was nothing to be done except to renew a prescription, but Crest made an important discovery here. He was struck by the fact that the epileptic had a unique and recognizable personality type. It was nothing that Crest could describe or define, but he could feel it strongly: a certain surliness, an unusual hostility and aggressiveness. He asked the instructor about this, and was informed that modern thinking did not recognize the existence of an epileptic personality. Crest was not convinced. Once, in the surgical clinic, he recognized this personality trait in a patient who had never had a fit. He ordered a brain-wave test, which was positive for latent epilepsy. He checked the textbooks. The modern authorities did not mention the subject, although some of the older texts did describe the epileptic personality.

"I know it's real," said Crest. "I can feel it."

"A budding diagnostic genius," said Sam.

"No," said Crest. "But I do seem to notice things."

Some of the students had a facility for clinical observation, and some of them did not, just as some were clever and some clumsy in the operating room. Crest attempted to cultivate his facility for observation. He realized that there were many external personality traits which could give a clue to internal disease. The tiny, ultrafeminine woman who walked with a prissy, mincing, pitter-patter gait was prone to migraine. The fair, fat, flatulent female of forty was likely to have gallstones. The thin, tense individual with premature gray hair was apt to have pernicious anemia or premature coronary disease. The bald man with the heavily wrinkled face and the mouth turned sourly downward at the corners probably had functional indigestion.

To Sam, a patient was a patient until you cut him open, and then he became a container of diseased organs. To Crest, a patient was a collection of personality patterns and traits, each of which implied susceptibility to a given disorder or disease. Sam was good at managing disease which presented itself. Crest was good at spotting a tendency toward future disease. Sam practiced tying knots inside of matchboxes. Crest liked to make hunch diagnoses on fellow passengers in a subway train.

Crest recalled a remark Sam had once made concerning Parky, Sam's father: "A man who claims to be both physician and surgeon is probably neither one."

For the first time, Crest began to understand what Sam had in mind.

In their fourth and final year of medical school, the students moved upstairs for assignment on the wards of the hospital. Here they took a position toward the bottom of a long ladder of status. Above them ranged the intern, resident, instructor, associate, assistant, and full professor. Even the registered nurse was above the senior student. Below him were only the student nurse, the gray lady, and the orderly. It is better to flirt with a student nurse than to yell at her; the gray lady may be a socially prominent person with political connections outside the hospital; and the orderly belongs to a shrewd and sometimes dangerous species which even the full professor must handle with discretion. The senior medical student does not yell at anybody. He observes as much as he can from the safest feasible distance.

The ward work in surgery was much like that of the outpatient department: the changing of dressings, the removal of sutures and skin clips plus innumerable intravenous infusions to be started. For many of the students, work in the operating room was the pinnacle toward which they had been climbing for the past four years: the glamour, the drama, the essence of the profession. Once bitten by the bug of surgery, a man stayed infected for the rest of his life. The students scrubbed in on major surgery of all types. For the most part, the student was fourth member of the operating team, behind the surgeon, the resident, and the intern. There was little room for the student at the incision, and his job was chiefly that of holding retractors at arm's length from far out in left field. The visibility was poor, and the student had little first-hand knowledge of what was going on, although if his fingers trembled or the retractor slipped, he would hear about it in no uncertain terms. The surgically oriented student gladly accepted his menial role and the accompanying abuse as the first step in the long years of preparation necessary before he would be the surgeon in charge, with the prerogative of yelling at everybody in the room. Crest had already decided that the operating room was not for him, and he was able to view the proceedings with an unbiased eye. It seemed to him that the prima donna attitude of many surgeons was a reflection of tension and insecurity, as if the surgeon knew very well that no man has the God-given right to cut into the body of any other man. Surgery is done under the premise that it will save life, correct deformity, prolong useful existence, or cure disease. It seemed to Crest that often this original premise was lost. Surgery, of course, saved lives, but one had to admit that the surgical procedure itself carried a respectable mortality. Deformity was also corrected, but some operations themselves produced deformity, which led to more surgery and often more deformity in a vicious circle which sometimes ended in total disability of the patient. The question of prolonging life was suspect in certain instances, especially the more radical and mutilating operations for malignancy; the surgical result was sometimes worse than the disease, and it was open to question whether a prolonged life of constant suffering was a worthy end. Some disease can be cured by surgery. But even a surgeon will have to admit that the knife is always a treatment of second choice, which tacitly admits no suitable treatment with drugs or other more natural modalities.

"The surgeon begins where the medical man has failed," said Sam.

"I can't help remembering the famous axiom of Osler," said Crest. "'Above all, thou shalt do no harm.'"

"The medical man twiddles his thumbs and watches the patient die," said Sam.

"I think the wisest thing a surgeon could learn is when not to operate," said Crest.

The student's presence in the operating room had a certain

hazard. Temperamental surgeons have been known to kick their assistants, or rap them over the knuckles with a hemostat. On one occasion, a student in Crest's class was burned on the hand when a surgeon purposely touched him with a red-hot cautery tip. Crest noticed that surgical temperament is not necessarily correlated with surgical ability. The noisiest surgeon is apt to be the surgeon most frequently in trouble of his own making. Some of the best surgeons were as calm and quiet as a bishop. Crest also noted that surgical dexterity and surgical judgment are not necessarily correlated. Some of the slickest and swiftest operators seemed almost devoid of judgment; some of the more mature and wiser men were actually slow and clumsy with the knife. Quite apparent in any group of surgeons was the sadist, whose pleasure at the pain of others was thinly concealed; and the showman, who delighted in the pomp and power of the operating suite; the society surgeon, who specialized in prissy little procedures on plump, wealthy matrons; and the hungry surgeon, who was always looking for the acute remunerative appendix after office hours. Crest decided that the better surgeons did represent the best side of the profession, but it was also his opinion that the field of surgery is vastly over-rated, over-glamorized, and, particularly, over-paid.

Many of the senior students enjoyed the month on obstetrics best. During this period, the student lived on the obstetrical suite, eating and sleeping there, dressed in a scrub suit at all times. He felt more like a doctor here than in any other part of the hospital. Ninety per cent of deliveries are routine, well within the capabilities of student, policeman, or taxi driver. The student was permitted much greater latitude than in surgery, doing many deliveries himself, sometimes without supervision. The drama of obstetrics—the unpredictability, the tense waiting periods when nothing seems to happen, the precipitous chain of events when everything happens at once, the supreme satisfaction of witnessing birth when the purple, wrinkled, bloody little object gives forth the first cry of life—

these were attractive elements to a younger man. Crest noticed that OB is a young man's game, that most of the staff men tried, as the years went by, to shift from the sleepless and routine obstetrics to the better-paid and more leisurely gynecology.

Crest enjoyed delivering babies. It was easy enough manually, so that his lack of surgical dexterity was no great handicap, and the satisfaction of the end result was undeniable. Sam Parkindale got a kick out of deliveries too. But neither Sam nor Crest would become obstetricians, although for differing reasons. In Crest's case, it was the mental hazard of the unexpected. Although the vast percentage of deliveries are easy and routine, disaster can be more sudden and profound in the delivery room than anywhere else. The alarming unexpected hemorrhage; the retained placenta; the rupture of a uterus; the prolapse of an umbilical cord; the delivery of a dead child known to have been alive only moments before; the delivery of a monster; the fetus impacted in an abnormal position in the birth canal—these threats seemed especially ominous to Crest in that they involved the two most precious members of the human race: the new mother and her baby.

"One thing I could never get used to," said Crest. "Telling the mother, as she is coming out of anaesthesia, that her baby is deformed or dead."

For Sam, obstetrics was too easy. He welcomed the challenge of catastrophe, but emergencies were too rare.

"After the first five or ten, it gets boring as hell," said Sam. "And, besides, the obstetrician never gets enough sleep."

It was in the medical wards, of course, that Crest felt most at home. Here, manual dexterity was of no importance. Medical emergencies were handled by swiftness of mind, not of hand. In the medical emergency, Crest was surprised to discover that he could think surely and quickly without the sense of panic he felt in the delivery room or the operating room. Oddly, Sam Parkindale seemed to fluster in the medical emergency. It was Sam's tendency to reach for the most drastic and dramatic drug and give it in the quickest way, intravenously, and sometimes the results were unfortunate.

"Sam, you're doing last things first," said Crest.

"I can't sit by and do nothing," said Sam.

"You have to give the body a chance to set up its own defenses," said Crest.

"Bleeding I can stop," said Sam. "Infections I can drain. Fractures I can reduce. Malignancy I can remove. But how can I make a heart continue to beat?"

"You can't," said Crest. "All you can do is set up the most favorable environment so the heart will keep beating by itself."

Although Crest could meet the challenge of medical emergency and enjoyed doing so, he most enjoyed the challenge of making an obscure diagnosis. Diagnosis seemed to be the field in which the surgeon was frequently inept. This is largely a matter of time. The surgeon is impatient; the diagnostician can afford to take his time. Crest poured over charts by the hour. He sat by bedsides talking with patients, going over their stories endlessly, hoping to pick up some clue which the other examiners had missed. He practiced with his stethoscope, listening to the high-pitched whistle of the systolic murmur, the low rumble of the diastolic murmur, the rub-a-dub-dub of gallop heart rhythm, the leather-like creaking of a friction rub, the dry static of fine rales, the wheezing of asthmatic rhonchi. He practiced the techniques of palpation and percussion.

While working in the medical wards, Crest fell strongly under the influence of Sam's grandfather, the dean. The dean no longer had any official connection with the medical department, spending most of his time on administrative matters, but he had never lost his love for clinical medicine. From time to time, he made rounds on the medical wards. This was an occasion like that of a procession of royalty. Every physician in the vicinity dropped what he was doing and fell in behind the dean in order of succession by rank. Like Solomon followed by his wives and concubines, the dean passed down the line of beds, pausing here and there to examine a chart, to interview a patient, to listen with the stethoscope, or to address some caustic comment to his associates.

The first time he witnessed one of these spectacles, Crest was examining a patient, and the procession stopped before him. Crest had a momentary impulse to hop in beside the patient and hide under the sheets.

"This patient is assigned to you, Dr. Crest?" said the dean.

"Yes, sir," said Crest.

"What is the diagnosis, if you please?"

Crest gave the diagnosis as well as he could. The case was not difficult: cardiac decompensation, a very common problem and one in which Crest felt himself well prepared. At the end of his dissertation, he more or less expected a word of praise. The dean stood at the foot of the bed and studied the patient.

"What's the matter with the patient's eye?" he said.

"Eye?" said Crest. He looked at the patient's eyes; they seemed all right to him.

"Pupillary reflexes to light and accommodation?" asked the dean.

Crest wasn't sure that he had examined the reflexes of the pupils of the eye. He should have done so as part of a routine examination, but in a cardiac case, he might have overlooked this finding as not essential to the problem.

"Regular and equal, sir," said Crest, hoping that they were.

"Give me the chart," said the dean to the nurse who was pushing the chart rack along at the head of the procession.

The dean studied the chart.

"All of the examiners seem to feel that this patient has normal eyes," said the dean.

Crest felt better.

"None of the examiners shows much power of observation," said the dean.

Crest felt worse.

"How long have you worn a glass eye, my friend?" the dean asked the patient.

"They took out my eye last year," said the patient.

"And you didn't bother to tell these young gentlemen about it?" asked the dean.

"They didn't ask," said the patient. "I figured they noticed it."

"They should have noticed it," said the dean. "I noticed it. Perhaps in the future they will make it a point to notice such things." The dean turned to Crest. "This patient also has a large liver, I presume?"

"Yes, sir," said Crest. "Enlargement of the liver is often found in cardiac decompensation."

"I do not doubt that this patient has cardiac decompensation," said the dean. "I do doubt that cardiac decompensation is the primary diagnosis in this case. What do you think of first when you see a patient with a large liver and a missing eye?"

Crest didn't know. One of the bright young residents did: malignant melanoma. This is a type of cancer which sometimes involves the pigmented portion of the eye and which rapidly involves the liver when it spreads. The patient had a melanoma. Many people had examined the patient and missed the diagnosis. The dean had made it from the head of the bed.

One Saturday afternoon, Crest was in the medical ward, doing a little extra work on his own. There were no other doctors on the ward. An emergency case was brought in from the Accident Room, a man in coma. Crest was permitted to make the preliminary examination while the intern was being called. He was working over the patient when he looked up to find the dean standing at his elbow. This time the dean was alone, unaccompanied by the customary retinue.

"This patient does not have a glass eye," said Crest.

"I'm glad you profit by your mistakes," said the dean. "What does he have?"

"He's in coma, sir. I think it may be diabetic acidosis."

"You think? Don't you know?"

"I have no history," said Crest. "The patient can't talk, and nobody came with him, sir."

"I will agree, Dr. Crest, that history forms ninety per cent of diagnosis, but there are certain times we must do without it and rely on our own observations."

"I think I smell the odor of acetone on his breath."

"So do I," said the dean. "That's a good start."

"I've drawn a blood specimen for sugar, pH, and CO_2," said Crest. "We should get the report in half an hour."

"Your action is sound," said the dean. "But in half an hour this patient might be dead. Do you have a urine specimen?"

"I have put in an indwelling catheter, sir. And I've sent the specimen to the lab for acetone and ketone bodies."

"Suppose you didn't have a lab," said the dean. "Let us suppose that we are not on Ward A of the university hospital. This is five years from now, and you, Dr. Crest, are in practice in a farming community. You have been called out to a farmhouse in the middle of a blizzard. There isn't a laboratory within thirty miles."

"I hope that I have carried urine-testing equipment in my bag," said Crest.

"Yes, I hope you have," said the dean. "But your car is stuck in a snowbank ten miles down the road, and you had to leave your bag behind. You know this patient is a diabetic. You know that he is unconscious. It is likely that he has either diabetic acidosis or insulin shock. When you were forced to abandon your bag, you put a syringe in your pocket, and an ampule of fifty per cent glucose solution and an ampule of insulin. You know you'll have to give him one or the other. If you choose right, you'll save the patient's life. If you choose wrong, you'll kill him. How do you tell without a laboratory?"

Crest began to recite the differential diagnosis between diabetic acidosis and insulin shock.

"This is not the lecture hall, Dr. Crest," said the dean. "We are attempting to establish a diagnosis on a dying man. The problem may be theoretical, but the patient isn't. By the time you finish your lecture, this patient will be dead. What shall we do, sir?"

"I don't know."

"Let's taste his urine."

"Sir?"

"You have a urine specimen in the catheter-drainage bottle. Taste it."

Crest had never heard of tasting urine, and he found the idea repugnant, but he took the collection bottle off the floor and started to raise it to his lips.

"Just a minute," said the dean. "I said taste it, not drink it. Like this."

The dean moistened the tip of an index finger with urine and touched his finger to his tongue. Crest did the same. He expected the specimen to taste bitter and acrid, but to his surprise it was as sweet as honey.

"There must be sugar in the urine, sir."

"And therefore?" said the dean.

"And therefore the man must be in diabetic coma."

"In which event," said the dean, "I suggest we give him a hundred units of insulin without further delay, because otherwise he will die. We used to make some pretty shrewd diagnoses, son, before they ever invented clinical laboratories. When your blood-sugar report comes back, I suspect it will be in excess of five hundred milligrams per cent."

The blood sugar was 525 milligrams per cent. By the time the report came back, however, Crest had already given the insulin and other supportive measures. The patient recovered.

"He's the greatest doctor in the world," said Crest.

"Who?" said Sam.

"Your grandfather. Please don't tell me he's an old windbag. I happen to admire him."

"It's funny," said Sam.

"Why?"

"I was thinking about your opinions of surgeons. The sadist and the society man and the showman, the pomp and arrogance of the operating suite."

"Your grandfather is a medical man."

"Yeah," said Sam. "But tell me, Johnnie, isn't he a sadist? Think of the way he cuts his junior associates down to size. You may not know about his society activities, but surely you can see that he's a showman. Have you ever seen him parading down the wards, surrounded by his dukes and his earls and his pages and his court jesters? Isn't that pomp and arrogance?"

"Well . . ."

"And yet, on the other hand," said Sam, "do you realize that by his own standards, he has failed?"

"Failed?" said Crest. "He reached the apex of the profession."

"He reached it and he passed it too soon. He was kicked upstairs to be dean of the medical school. Do you think he enjoyed being crowded out of the professorship of medicine by a younger and more brilliant man? The ambition of a man like my grandfather is to make a major medical discovery: a rare disease, a sign or a symptom to carry his name. My grandfather never did. Ask him about pernicious anemia sometime, if you dare."

"What do you mean?"

"As you know, until very recently, pernicious anemia was a progressive and fatal disease, and today we are able to control it with crude liver extract. A decade ago, my grandfather followed a patient with pernicious anemia who refused to die according to the expected pattern. The only unusual thing that my grandfather could discover about the man was his occupation and his diet. The patient was a poultry farmer who raised geese. He overfed his geese to give them a fatty degeneration of the liver, and he marketed this goose liver as *paté de fois gras*. The patient developed a taste for his own product and practically stuffed himself with raw goose liver."

"Which contained enough of the crude-liver principle to control his pernicious anemia?"

"My grandfather published the case report in an obscure journal and let it go at that. Two other American physicians made a somewhat similar observation in a butcher who ate raw calf's liver. They went a little further and found out why."

"Their names were Minot and Murphy," said Crest.

"Minot and Murphy got the Nobel Prize in medicine last year," said Sam. "My grandfather didn't."

Every two weeks a public meeting of the medical staff was held, the so-called Medical Grand Rounds, at which puzzling and interesting cases were presented. This was apt to be a fascinating show, characterized by sharp debate, by diagnostic brilliance and therapeutic controversy. The dean used it as his own private sounding board and showcase, frequently dominating the proceedings and displaying his clinical gifts.

On one of these occasions, a problem case was presented, an asthenic, frail young female who had been lying around the wards for weeks without a satisfactory diagnosis. She had been examined by everybody except the janitor and subjected to every conceivable laboratory test, with negative results. One of the attending physicians presented the case, giving an involved dissertation on the possible causes of unexplained fever, covering two blackboards with the lists of the differential diagnosis. At the end of the presentation, the dean arose.

"May I be permitted to examine the patient?" he inquired.

"Of course."

He stepped into the pit, took a turn around the litter on which the patient was lying, bent down over her, and apparently smelled her body.

"This patient has typhoid fever," the dean announced, and he walked back to his seat.

The physician in charge protested. Signs and symptoms of

typhoid fever were lacking. The urine, blood, and feces had been cultured for the typhoid bacillus with negative results.

"At certain phases in typhoid fever, cultures may be negative," said the dean. "And this patient does show a positive sign of this disease. I shall demonstrate. Would one of you gentlemen be so kind as to run down to the laboratory and bring me back a cage of laboratory mice?"

A cage of white mice was produced.

"Gentlemen," said the dean. "I invite you to smell this cage full of mice, and then I invite you to smell the body of the patient. If your nose is keen, I think you will detect a similarity. In some of the older textbooks of medicine, you will find reference to the so-called mousy odor of typhoid fever. I suggest that the blood, urine, and feces cultures on this patient be repeated daily, and it is my opinion that one of these cultures will soon be positive."

Two days later, blood cultures on this patient were strongly positive for the bacillus of typhoid fever.

It was dangerous to fall asleep during Medical Grand Rounds. The dean had an uncanny eye for the somnolent member of the audience and was quite inclined to wake him up with an embarrassing inquiry. Crest was caught off base in this fashion once.

In the middle of a nap, Crest suddenly woke up to find the audience staring at him.

"Sir, would you please repeat the question?" said Crest.

"Of course," said the dean. "I asked you, Dr. Crest, what is the function of the spleen?"

The spleen? Ye Gods! Crest thumbed rapidly through his mental file. He recalled the structure of this organ, its anatomical location, the various diseases which could involve the spleen. But its function?

"I'm sorry, sir," said Crest. "I knew the function of the spleen, but I seem to have forgotten it."

"Indeed," said the dean. "This is most remarkable. For centuries, anatomists and physiologists have been vainly searching for the function of the normal spleen. There is only one man in the entire world who knows the function of the spleen. This man is Dr. Crest. Unfortunately, he has forgotten it."

The dean's final appearance at Medical Grand Rounds was one that nobody could forget. The discussion had involved some occult point in the metabolism of phosphorus and calcium, but the dean interrupted and began to talk of something else in a fashion that seemed strangely irrelevant.

"Ladies and gentlemen," he said, "I have had the privilege of participating in these rounds for almost fifty years, and every one of the sessions has been informative or exciting in one way or another. From this group has been born some of the most truly original and brilliant concepts of modern clinical medicine. Sometimes there have been arguments and debates; the conversation is sometimes fiery, and my presence has often contributed to this fire. Sometimes I have been right and sometimes I have been wrong, and I hope that I have learned more from my errors than from my pride. It has been said that I have a tendency to dominate these sessions. One of my own grandchildren has been heard to say that I am an old windbag. However, it is the obligation for the older clinician to pass his observations down to the young. If I have been verbose, my intention has been good. I hope that the fire of the mind will continue to dominate these sessions when I am no longer able to participate in them."

"This sounds like a valedictory," whispered Crest to Sam.

"Him retire? Never," said Sam. "He'll die in the saddle."

"Ladies and gentlemen," said the dean, "I now wish to discuss a topic that is familiar to you all: coronary artery disease. This is a very common condition and a leading cause of death. In these rounds, we usually discuss the rare, the occult, the paradoxical, the bizarre. Sometimes I think we should devote more attention to the routine problems of everyday practice.

"The art of diagnosis is partly the art of disciplined observation, but more importantly, it is the art of understanding words. Nine times out of ten, the patient is giving you the diagnosis in his own words, if you can understand him. This sometimes presents a difficulty, for words are tricky. It is often difficult for the sophisticated scientist to understand the words of the man in the street.

"In coronary artery disease, the diagnosis rests almost exclusively on the patient's description of his pain. Coronary pain is unique. It is never sharp, or quick, or lancinating, or throbbing, or colicky. Coronary pain is a heavy pain, a dull, heavy weight, a vicelike constriction, a squeezing, crushing devil of a pain. I am using words to describe this pain, and these words are the best that I can find. I am trying to describe the pain I am having at this moment. It happens that I am in the early stages of a coronary heart attack. I wish that it were possible for me to describe my symptoms to you at greater length, but this crushing devil of a pain is smothering my breath, and my own mortality is staring me in the face."

His complexion was ashen gray. He seemed to stagger. He clutched at the rostrum. Then he fell on the floor. A number of physicians rushed onto the podium, surrounding him. A litter was produced. The dean was wheeled away to one of the private rooms upstairs, and an hour later he was dead. Autopsy was performed. Coronary artery disease was found. As everybody expected, his own final diagnosis was correct.

It was a hot morning in June, and the auditorium was sweltering. The students felt uneasy in academic gowns and ludicrous mortarboard caps. One by one, the students paraded past the platform as the president of the university handed out the parchment rolls. Then the class in unison repeated the quaint and archaic words of the Oath of Hippocrates.

After the graduation exercises, the students milled outside, surrounded by friends and relatives.

"John Crest, M.D., doctor of medicine," said Sam.

"Dr. Samuel Parkindale, I presume."

For two years they had been called "doctor" by patients in ignorance and by the staff in sardonic condescension, but the title was hard to get used to, even though it was now earned.

"Look to the right and to the left; one of the three of you will not graduate with this class," quoted Crest. "I wish your grandfather was alive. I was looking forward to his remarks at our graduation."

Sam drifted away from Crest into a group of his family. Crest could see Sam's father, Parky, and his uncle, Joseph, and Mrs. Parkindale, and Emerald. He had not seen Emerald for three years. Every student except Crest was being congratulated by friends and relatives. He was alone. His only relative was his aunt, and she hadn't come. Sam broke away from his family group and returned to Crest again.

"Why don't you come with us?" said Sam. "We're having a party at Joseph's apartment."

"It's your party," said Crest.

"But you're almost one of the family."

"Maybe I'll drop by later on," said Crest.

The party was in full swing when Crest arrived at Joseph's apartment about an hour later. Liquor had been flowing freely, and the room was full of smoke and noise. The only completely sober one seemed to be Sam's father, Parky. He was sitting on a sofa near the door, and he buttonholed Crest at once.

"How does it feel to be a physician, Dr. Crest?" said Parky.

"Fine," said Crest, "although I must confess I'm not used to it yet."

"Where are you taking your internship?"

"At the university hospital, sir."

"You couldn't do better," said Parky. "Went there myself, and I was hoping Sam would follow my steps. He plans to

enter dental college in the fall, hoping to work with my
brother in plastic surgery."

"I know."

"Why any man wants to be both a doctor and a dentist
is beyond me," said Parky. "And plastic surgery is a waste of
time. The money is good, but that's all you can say. Sam has
disappointed me. I was hoping he would come and work with
me in Sentryville. It seems that every young punk wants to
specialize today. General practice isn't good enough any
more."

"I'm interested in internal medicine," said Crest.

"What's the matter with general practice?" said Parky.
"There's no life like that of a country doc."

"I'm sure it must be rewarding, sir," said Crest. "As a matter
of fact, I may go into general practice after all. I have a financial problem, and I may not be able to afford residency training."

"There's plenty of money in Sentryville," said Parky. "How
would you like to work with me?"

"Well, sir . . ."

"This is a serious offer. Think it over, my boy. I have a great
opportunity for a smart young man who isn't afraid of work.
You come with high recommendations from the members of
my family."

"Thank you, sir."

"I'll get in touch with you when you're finishing your internship," said Parky. "And now if you'll excuse me, young
man, I'm going out to get a little air. The fumes of alcohol
and nicotine in here would kill a horse."

The spot which Parky vacated on the sofa was immediately
taken by Joseph. He bore a drink for Crest.

"You look as if you need this," said Joseph.

"Thank you, sir," said Crest.

"Did my brother have you in a trap?"

"He offered me a job in Sentryville," said Crest.

"And you turned him down, I hope."

"I told him I'd think it over," said Crest.

"They lead a rough and ready life in Sentryville, and I'm not sure you'd fit into the picture, but that's for you to decide, of course," said Joseph. "I wanted to ask you about Sam."

"Sir?"

"Do you think we'll ever make a doctor out of Sam?"

"He's very gifted," said Crest. "There's nobody in our class who can touch him in the matter of surgical technique."

"Sam has always been clever with his hands," said Joseph. "But I have the impression that he didn't really want to be a physician. My brother pushed him into it, you know."

"Sam enjoyed himself in medical school."

"Sam always enjoys himself," said Joseph. "The doctor's life, however, requires a certain dedication. I wonder if he'll last."

"That's not for me to say."

"Of course it isn't," said Joseph. "My inquiry was unfair. Well, good luck with your internship, Dr. Crest. I'll be seeing you around."

Joseph wandered away, and his place on the sofa was taken by Emerald. She wore a simple red velvet dress which brought out her magnificent dark coloring and the dancing highlights in her eyes.

"Hi," she said.

She waggled her index and middle finger at him, and Crest stuck a cigarette between them and lit it for her.

"I still smoke like a chimney, and I don't believe I've bought a dozen packs of my own in the past three years," she said. "You see, I haven't changed. I still borrow without any intention of giving back."

"Obviously you have a lot of friends."

"Oodles of acquaintances but nary a friend," she said. "You've changed."

"How so?"

"You look like a doctor now," she said. "Sam is the same old collegian. He wears his new medical degree at a rakish angle on the side of his head, like a pork-pie hat, and he doesn't take it seriously, and I doubt if any patient ever will."

"You should see him in the operating room."

"In the operating room, Sam can hide behind a cap and gown and mask," she said. "You don't have to hide. You have a professional manner already."

"I'm new to the role. It's stiff and strange, and it isn't broken in."

"Oh, come," she said. "You could examine me any time."

Suddenly she leaned over and kissed him, in full view of the company.

"I had forgotten that habit of yours," said Crest. "I never am expecting it. Do you make it a habit to kiss your examiners?"

"Are you drunk?"

"Me? Of course not. I just came," said Crest. "I've only had this single drink."

"I am," she said. "Take mine."

She handed him her glass.

"Drink up. Chug-a-lug," she said.

"I would prefer to sip," said Crest.

"Chug-a-lug, I command. You'll have to catch up with me. Then you won't think of me as such a juvenile fool."

"I never—"

"Come on, Doctor, this is a celebration. You won't be getting your M.D. degree again. Your internship begins on Monday, and then you'll be on call for the rest of your life, but the next three days are your own. Your last chance to drop the professional manner and make a fool of yourself. Bottoms up."

Crest drained her glass and then he said, "Perhaps I better get a little air before it hits me."

"My apartment," she said. "Etchings. I've got to show you."

She got off the sofa and staggered a little bit as she did so, clutching at Crest for support. He looked at her searchingly.

"How drunk are you?" he said.

"More than that," she said, grabbing his hand and pulling him out of the room.

"What will they think, I wonder?" said Crest.

"Whew, this is better," said Emerald. "Do you mind if we walk to my place? It isn't very far, and the air will do me good. What will who think, you wonder?"

"Your family. Seeing us leave together."

"Oh, good heavens, they know I've been in love with you for years."

"Absence makes the heart grow fonder, I suppose," said Crest.

"Apparently not yours."

"You never gave me a chance," said Crest. "I had to recover from you."

"I've been a willful and wayward girl," she said. "I really don't have etchings. When we get to my apartment, I am going to question you in intimate detail concerning your other women. Do you enjoy gynecology?"

"Would you like a cigarette?"

"Here we are. Third-floor walk-up, and no elevator, I'm afraid. So up we huff and we puff."

They huffed and they puffed up two flights of marble stairs.

"Now, where in the hell did I put my key?"

"Probably in your pocketbook," said Crest.

"But whereabouts in my pocketbook? Women are a mess. Why must we lug around such a variety of portable junk?"

She found the key. Crest had to steady her hand as she put it into the lock. This was a one-room apartment, and the bed took up most of it. Everything was feminine and frilly, pink and full of ruffles. There was a faint aroma of powder and lilac water in the air, and there were three stuffed animals on the bed.

"Got to fumigate the joint," she said. "Stinks like an Armenian—"

"You've never been in one, and neither have I," said Crest.

She sang, slightly off key:

" 'Lillian was a thing of beauty.
She lived in a house of ill repute.
People came from miles to see
Lillian in her dishabille . . .' "

Crest finished the chorus: " 'Lillian in her dishabille.' "

"Well," she said, "I'm delighted to observe that you're not so stuffy any more."

"You're slightly tanked," said Crest.

"Come on and kiss me, kid."

"I don't know," said Crest. "I'm more accustomed to it the other way, when you jump and I'm not expecting it."

"Sam was right," she said. "You are afraid of girls."

"Here. I'll light you a cigarette."

She sang, to the tune of "Three Blind Mice":

" 'Poor Johnnie Crest, poor Johnnie Crest,
Still afraid of girls, still afraid of girls.
He cut off his tail with his carving knife
Which made him sterile for the rest of his life
And then he could never acquire a wife.
Oh, poor John Crest.' "

Crest grinned at her. "Try me," he said.

"Coming, ready or not," she said. "And don't ever say that you've never been warned."

And she threw her arms around him and kissed him enthusiastically. Her momentum carried them both onto the bed and she continued to embrace him with vigor.

"Hey," said Crest, laughing and struggling to escape. "Wait up. Hold on."

"Too late," she said. "We can't wait. You and I can't afford that sort of thing."

And then she carried him into love-making so directly and swiftly that he had passed his point of self-control before he realized that he would need it. The act was quick. They fell apart, panting and disheveled on the bed. It had not been satisfactory, Crest thought, either way around.

"Now I'll have a cigarette," she said, rehooking her brassiere, buttoning her blouse, and pulling down her skirt. "And after that, I think, we both should have a drink, quite large."

"Or else we should have skipped the drinks in the first place," said Crest.

"A drunken impulse on my part, you think?" she said. "I knew you were coming to that party, and I was prepared when I came. You're a doctor. You know what I'm talking about."

"And had to get drunk to do it?" said Crest. "That's very complimentary to me."

"I've been there before."

"So have I."

"Was it like this?"

"No," said Crest.

"Why wasn't it like this? How was it different? Huh?"

"Emerald, why do you want to know?"

"Oh hell, I don't, I'm just making conversation," she said. "You ruined a marriage for me, chum. I had to prove it wouldn't have been better with you. Chum, it was worse."

"I didn't know you were married."

"Not very many people do," she said. "It wasn't a good idea. I am now in the process of getting a divorce."

"Then you can marry me."

"Oh, come, you're kidding," she said. "Repeat this performance on another stage? This is a turkey. We'll bury it."

"Give yourself a chance," said Crest.

"Oh, get lost," she said. "Stop bothering me. Why don't you go home?"

"Perhaps I better," said Crest. He got off the bed and rearranged his clothes. "Will you thank your uncle for me?" he said. "I'm not going back to the party."

"Neither am I."

"Look, Emerald . . ."

"Let's leave it alone," she said.

"But—"

"So I'm a mess, but it doesn't bother me, and you can do better than this," she said. "Farewell. Good-by. God bless, and all that kind of junk."

"All right," he said.

He left her apartment. Just as he was closing the apartment door, she was making some sort of noise. Maybe she was laughing at him. Maybe she had burst into tears. He couldn't be sure, but he decided not to investigate. This had been a very confusing afternoon.

Rat race: this was the phrase to describe Crest's internship. The pace was a killing one, which only a young and dedicated man could endure, and even some of them broke down. There were three casualties among the group of twenty-five in Crest's intern class: a case of tuberculosis, which was a very common hazard to students and interns; a severely bleeding peptic ulcer, which is an occupational hazard of the profession as a whole; and one case of a manic psychotic episode where the intern in question turned dangerously violent and had to be committed.

The day customarily began around 5:30 A.M., and after a hurried breakfast, the intern went to his ward for the drawing of blood samples for myriad laboratory tests. In most cases, drawing blood isn't very hard, but in some cases it is almost impossibly hard. To go down a line of beds and draw some twenty or thirty samples, under pressure, when you are in a hurry, when you haven't had enough sleep, can be a trying way to begin the day. At 7:00, there were early rounds with the resident and all sorts of omissions to be corrected and commissions to be performed before the staff came in at 8:00 and the proper working day began.

Then, if you were on surgery, you were scrubbed and busy in the operating room until the middle of the afternoon. The intern usually scrubbed in on one case after another through the operating schedule without a break. Between cases, there was a fifteen- or twenty-minute delay while the patients were exchanged and the room cleaned up. Residents and surgeons could take a pause for a cigarette and a cup of coffee and a chance to get off their feet, but not the intern: he followed the patient to the room (often pushing the litter himself if no orderly was available) and helped dump the patient onto the bed and wrote the post-operative orders and started an intravenous or changed a catheter or checked the dressing. By the time he got back to the operating suite, it was time to scrub for the next operation.

You were just as busy on medicine. There it was rounds, around and around, following one dignitary or other as they appeared in succession of rank, and after each set of rounds, there were a whole slew of tests to be ordered and consultations requested and procedures to be done, many of which contradicted instructions given at previous rounds.

In obstetrics, of course, it was grind away, day and night, around the clock.

By the middle of the afternoon, after a late cold lunch, the intern was exhausted, and he customarily made his way to the intern's quarters and lay down on his bed for a nap. The amplifier system would be paging him and the phone at his bedside ringing every fifteen minutes. He learned the trick of dropping immediately to sleep for five or ten minutes and waking up immediately when called. He would stay in his sack as long as he could, until half a dozen emergencies had piled up, enough to justify his getting out of bed. Then he would return to the wards, and it seemed as if the real work of the day had just begun. New patients began to come in about three o'clock and kept coming in until six or seven, ten or fifteen of them to be interviewed and examined and written up in the charts. Then came late rounds and an even later suppertime.

After supper, the evening pause fell over the hospital. The professors and the staff went home. During the hours in which most births, deaths, and emergencies occur, the institution was in the charge of the youngest members of the team: the resident, the intern, and the student nurse. At night the intern was often alone and fully responsible for an examination or an emergency procedure which he was only permitted to watch at a great distance during the day.

Every other night and every other weekend, the intern was off call and free. During the other nights, he was being paged quite regularly three or four times an hour throughout the night. Often Crest would answer his phone, give an order, and replace the phone without waking up. In fact, on many occasions he got out of bed, dressed, went down to the ward, examined a patient, put in an intravenous or certified a patient as dead, and returned to his room and went back to sleep again without being conscious of what he had done. On the following morning, he often could not remember that he had gotten out of bed at all.

There was no continuity in his recollection of his internship. He could never recall which wards he had been on, what events had taken place on any given day or week or month. He lost the sense of time sequence altogether. His only memory was that of scattered episodes, without relationship to the time when they occurred.

There was the patient who expired of cardiac arrest during an elective hernia repair; the surgeon cut into the chest and massaged the heart with his hand, and Crest got a chance to squeeze the flabby muscle of the heart; they kept the patient going artificially for hours, but he did not recover.

There was the woman who walked into the Accident Room with a ruptured eyeball and the contents of the eye running down her cheek. She had been struck in the eye by the point of a high-heeled slipper.

There was the baby who had fallen out a three-story window and had landed on a concrete pavement on its head and showed nothing whatever as a consequence: no laceration, no abrasion, no skull fracture, and no brain injury.

And there was the wino who had fallen on a railroad track and been run over by a freight, with total amputation at the level of the belly button. They brought the top half of him in, fully conscious, in no pain, drunk and happy as ever, and the top half of him lived on for a matter of many hours.

And the man who had been shot through the head, in one side of the skull and out the other, and there was a small collection of brain matter in his hat. The patient walked in and an hour later walked out, showing no apparent effects from the hole in his head.

And the time Crest saw a surgeon cut the cystic artery during a gall-bladder operation. The surgeon thought the artery had been clamped. Crest knew it hadn't. He tried to warn the surgeon. The surgeon cussed at him, and cut the artery. The wound was the approximate size and shape of a can containing tennis balls, and the entire field filled up with blood from the base within a matter of seconds. Then the surgeon lost his head completely and started grabbing around blindly in the pool of blood with a hemostat. Crest had to push the surgeon from the table forcefully, taking charge himself, compressing the aorta against the backbone with one fist, sucking out the blood with a suction tip held in his other hand, finding the end of the spurting artery, clamping it, and tying it. The surgeon was at the other side of the operating room, in a hysterical collapse, crying like a schoolgirl. This patient survived.

And the time a student nurse, removing an infant for examination from a bassinet, dropped the baby and the baby landed on the floor in such a way as to break its neck. This patient did not survive. And, since Crest was the only physician in attendance, he was forced to bear sole responsibility for the death, to the parents, to the chief of service, and to the hospital authorities.

And the time when Crest was taking a violent patient to the closed psychiatric ward alone, and the elevator stuck between floors, and Crest literally had to battle for his life.

And the time Crest sewed up a Negro after a razor fight. The patient was sliced into ribbons from head to toe, but none of the cuts was more than barely through the superficial skin. Crest had to put in more than 200 sutures, and the job took him all night.

And the patient who was stabbed, just once, with an ice pick, and nobody could find the hole, and nobody could find the internal bleeder, not even the pathologist at the autopsy table.

The maternity patient in a continuous epileptic state; the patient struck by lightning, with a small charred hole in the top of his skull and another at the ball of his right foot; the victim of the auto accident, who had flown through the air like a bird for a hundred feet until he struck a guide wire and was decapitated, and two of the cops brought in the body and another brought in the head; the college boy who died of acute leukemia; the child with the marble bone disease who suffered a fracture every time she rolled over in bed; the patient with a temperature of 109 who survived, and another, who had lain in a snowbank and come in with a temperature of 72 and also survived; the virile masculine movie star, in for a check-up, who threatened interns with homosexual assault; the prize fighter who, although full of neurological complications, turned out to be the most gentle person Crest had ever met; the paranoid lady who carried a tear-gas gun in her pocketbook and who gave Crest a blast when he attempted to examine her; the patient who jumped off the top of the hospital, crashing through the glass skylight of the outpatient waiting room, killing both himself and a waiting patient on whom he landed; the society dame who tried to pull Crest into her bed; the time Crest, while trying to draw fluid from a patient's left chest, stuck in his needle too far and penetrated the heart, which almost killed Crest and did not disturb the patient in any way; the patient belonging to a weird religious sect who died on the medical ward and whose body was stolen by the relatives and hung in a tree outside the hospital.

These were some of the incidents which Crest remembered from his internship.

The telephone rang by the head of his bed. Crest woke up, rolled over, and grabbed for it.

"I'm off duty, go away," he said. "Call Dr. Smith."

"I don't want Dr. Smith. I want you," said a cheerful female voice on the other end of the wire.

"You must be a new girl," said Crest.

He knew the switchboard operators by voice, although he had never laid eyes on any of them. The operator was the intern's first line of defense, or his most vulnerable flank. The good ones knew when the intern deserved a break; the others could dig him out, no matter where he was trying to hide.

"I am a new woman," she said. "My divorce has gone through, and I am free and available."

At last he recognized her voice. "Emerald."

"Not one of your other women, dear," she said. "I'm waiting for you in the lobby. I have fifty dollars in my pocket. You are expected to use it to take me out to dinner, unless you have something better to do."

Crest did have something better to do, namely sleep, but he said, "I'll be down in a few minutes."

He got out of his intern's white jacket and pants, in which he often slept, took a hasty shower, and put on civilian clothes. She was waiting in the lobby, dressed in some greenish shimmering material which rustled when she walked.

"Hi," she said, her eyes twinkling.

"I've brought a present for you," said Crest.

"Can you afford it, dear?"

"Have yourself a bonfire," he said, and he handed her a fresh package of cigarettes.

"Gee, thanks."

"Now you won't have to feel guilty for borrowing from me when you have no intention of paying me back."

"There's a dirty insinuation there someplace," she said. "But I won't examine it. You look sleepy."

"Hungry too," said Crest.

"Are they trying to kill you, dear?"

"Twenty-three hours of work each day for room, board, and ten dollars a month," said Crest. "Also, they do our laundry free. But they don't let me sleep in the room, and the board isn't fit to eat, and I'm not getting rich on the salary. I am grateful for the laundry, however."

"It would be a service to suffering humanity to give you a decent meal," she said. "Here's my fifty-dollar bill. Let's find the best restaurant in town and try to eat it up."

They tried hard, but they could only eat up half of the money. Crest tried to give her back the change. She turned him down.

"Well, let's kill it in a night club, then," said Crest.

"I don't like night clubs," said Emerald.

"I shouldn't stay out late," said Crest. "I'm on call in the morning and the day begins at five o'clock."

"I want a quiet talk with you," she said. "Let's go to my apartment. This time we'll do nothing but talk."

"Then please take your money back."

"Please keep it," she said. "You need it more than I."

When they were settled in her apartment, Crest said, "What do you want to talk about?"

"There's something funny about you. I don't understand. Are you really afraid of women?"

"Of course not."

"But don't you live like a monk?"

"I'm living like an intern."

"When was the last time you had a date?"

Date? Crest had to think back. It was a long time ago. As a matter of fact, the last real date he had had was with Emerald, four years ago, when he was a freshman in medical school.

"There!" she said. "There must be something wrong with you. How old are you? Thirty?"

"I'm twenty-six," said Crest.

"Most men of your age are raising a family."

"Most men of my age are earning a living," said Crest.

"Some female must have frightened you," she said, "and I'm sure it wasn't me. I'll bet it happened a long time ago."

"I had a disturbing episode when I was twelve."

"Tell me."

"Why should I?"

"Sex puzzles me," she said. "I'm searching for my own identity, and I pick the brains of everybody I meet. Please tell me about your other women."

It had been one of his father's women, he told her. His father had not remarried after his mother's death, but sometimes there was a woman living in the house. Crest never knew the exact position of these women. He had been encouraged to call them "aunt." He had been playing football that day and had been kicked in the nose. Although his nose had not been fractured, there was plenty of blood, and he was a little weak and woozy. He had gone home to clean up. His father wasn't there. The woman was. She seemed to him very old, although perhaps she was no older than twenty. She got quite excited over the blood, and made a fuss which embarrassed him. She tried to mother him, hugging him against her breast, and he didn't like that at all. Then she ran her hand over his body in a fashion that was disturbing and then she began undoing buttons and . . .

"What's the matter?" said Crest.

"Nothing," said Emerald, but she had clamped her jaws over the end of her cigarette, crushing it.

"Look out! You'll burn your lip," said Crest.

She mashed out the cigarette in an ash tray, but her eyes did not leave his face. "Go on."

"That's enough of the subject, I believe," said Crest.

"No, please!"

"Why is this so important to you?"

"I'm mixed up, and I'm trying to find out all that I can."

"Well, I'm scarcely an expert on the matter."

"And you've never had another woman since the age of twelve?"

"You, of course."

"And nobody in between?"

"Oh, there were quite a few," said Crest.

He paused, trying to think of a way to change the subject of conversation, but she was staring at him intensely, obviously waiting for him to continue.

"Well, my next affair was platonic," he said. "I was fourteen or fifteen years old, I guess. She was a baby-blue blonde my own age, and she lived next door, and I never even held her hand. She was a princess from a fairytale. To kiss her, somehow, would have seemed dirty and obscene. Then I had to leave the neighborhood when my father moved. My heart was fractured. I couldn't eat or sleep for an eternity which must have lasted three or four days."

"That's nice."

"Why? Because I didn't touch her?"

"Romance is best," said Emerald. "What does a man want, anyway? What is he trying to take from a woman? Is physical love an act of tenderness or only a knife in the groin?"

"I've sometimes thought that sex and tenderness were incompatible."

"Yes, for a man. Men are lucky. You can turn it on or off like a switch."

"Not always easy to turn off," said Crest, recalling the other time he had been in this room. "My next sweetheart was a predatory creature and I was lucky to get out of that alive. She came down with the measles. I had already had the disease, and I was certified to be immune. I was permitted to visit her, provided we left the door ajar."

"And she was in bed at the time?"

"Yes. She was still covered with fading red blotches and her skin was hot to the touch."

"How did you know that?"

"We were holding hands underneath the covers."

"You must have been a nasty little boy."

"That was the opinion of her mother. She walked in and discovered us holding hands, and her daughter sitting up in bed, leaning over toward me so that her nightgown fell away from her chest, and I was admiring the view. I could see that she had measle blotches all the way down to her . . ."

"Down to her what?"

"All the way," said Crest. "I was requested to leave the house. I was requested not to return. Perhaps it was just as well. She no sooner recovered from the measles than she came down with pregnancy. I was not involved, by the way."

"Women always seem to be attacking you. It's never the other way around."

"I have made the customary number of attacks in such customary places as rumble seats and the sofa in the back room of the fraternity house in college."

"How was it?"

"Furtive. Clumsy. Awkward," said Crest. "Completely unsatisfactory."

"That has been my experience," she said. "And so, if sex without love or tenderness is unsatisfactory, why do we bother with it, anyway?"

"There's a natural force beyond our control," said Crest.

"It's no problem for a man," she said. "You can take up your hat and run. A man doesn't let sex interfere with the serious business of his life. In your case, for example, medicine is far more important than any woman you could ever meet. For us, it's different. Love is basic to us. It can be our profession, or our weapon in the pursuit of power and prosperity, or the rock on which we build a life, but never a sport for leisure moments. We get all mixed up in it."

"I think love may be more important for a woman," said

Crest, "but in that event, she's fortunate. If love is the most important thing in life—and I'd like to think it is—a woman gets more out of life."

"Life, yes; sex, no," said Emerald. "Sex gets in the way of everything. For example, a woman can't make friends. With other women, there is competition, jealousy, and claws. With a man, there is heat but no light. If you try to get intimate with a man, he misunderstands; instantly, he's dazzled and he loses his sense of self-control. He can't seem to remember that there is a human being inside the woman, a real person underneath the hair and curves. Do you know why I married Jack?"

"I don't even know Jack."

"I thought he was interested in me, in the real Emerald who lives underneath my particular sexpot combination of shapes and smells. He was a director in the theater. You may recall my interest in the stage. Jack could draw things out of me I didn't even know were there. With Jack's help, I could explore myself. I could find a means of self-expression and perhaps I could find my own identity. I never dazzled Jack. He knew me as a person. He never saw me as a woman."

"Jack must have been as blind as a bat."

"Bats can see in the dark, and Jack had a darker side," she said. "I'm speaking of sex, of course. We could find pleasure together only by degrading one another. There was no tenderness at all. Jack seemed to take pleasure in pain and I seemed to enjoy being hurt. He was trying to kill me, I think, and I think I wanted to be killed. Ugh! Give me a cigarette, please."

"You have the package in your lap."

"I had to get away from him. He was making me sick. And now I wonder: can I ever find tenderness and self-expression in my sex?"

"Of course you can."

"Why do you think so? Don't you remember the other time you were in this room?"

"You were a little drunk," said Crest. "So was I."

"Damn it, why wasn't I born plain? Ugly girls have all the advantages. I wish I were a mud hen with plain drab feathers. Men marry the girls with the plain ordinary face and the big buttery bosoms and the nice fat child-bearing hips. They only diddle around with a bird of paradise. I'm too brittle for pleasure, too small for sympathy. I am Emerald, full of sparks and ice; I borrow things which I can't give back; I like a man who likes to give me pain. What's the matter with me?"

"Nothing's the matter. You've never been in love, that's all," said Crest. "You're still young. I don't think it's serious."

"Not for you. You don't have to live with me," she said.

"I'd like to live with you."

"Can you see me as a doctor's wife?"

"Inevitably," said Crest. "Mine."

"You don't know me from Adam's second rib."

"I'm getting to know you," said Crest. "In medical terms, I have an excellent family history: I'm learning the past history, and I'm part of the present illness. I have even done a physical examination. It was not satisfactory: I intend to repeat it soon."

"What's your diagnosis, Doctor?"

"Simple femininity," said Crest. "Incurable, thank God."

"All men are idiots," she said. "Why don't you give me that cigarette?"

"Because you still have the package in your lap."

And then, inadvertently, Crest yawned.

"Oh, dearie me, I'm boring you," she said.

"Not at all," said Crest, "but I've only had three hours' sleep in the past twenty-four."

"I have no right to keep you out of bed."

"You have a bed in here."

"Not for you to sleep in," she said. "I do have feminine pride. You are going home."

"Can I see you again when I've had a little sleep?"

"Probably," she said. "I'm a sucker for dull, dedicated,

sleepy little types like you. Like the first woman in your life, I want to mother you."

"A promising symptom," said Crest. "I can carry on from there."

"Some other time," she said.

She pulled him from his chair and propelled him to the door.

He turned to her with a grin. "I know you so well that I can predict your actions at this time," he said. "First, you'll kiss me suddenly. And then, before I can properly react, you'll push me out and close the door in my face."

"Exactly," said Emerald.

And she did just that.

Crest was too busy with the mechanics of his trade to think of theoretical matters or the progress of medical research, but even an intern was aware that a quiet revolution was taking place in medicine. The first of the miracle drugs, sulfanilamide, was introduced during his internship.

As a student, Crest had been taught to consider pneumonia as the most frequent fatal disease, which could be treated only with the laborious and frequently ineffective use of serums. Now, suddenly, pneumonia could be cured with pills. Crest had been taught that infection could be treated only after it had localized, by surgical incision and drainage. He had heard much of "laudable pus." Now pus was no longer the surgeon's friend. No longer did the medical man stand helplessly in the face of generalized blood-stream infection, studying the fever chart for signs of lysis and of crisis. Suddenly he could prevent lysis and crisis from taking place at all. It was truly said that pneumonia could now be cured quicker than the common cold. Gonorrhea was now simple to treat. Strep throat melted away and the late serious complications of streptococcus infection could often be prevented. It was now expected that the patient with meningitis could survive.

To the men of Crest's medical generation, this was truly a

miracle. During the times when Crest was not too tired, sleepy, and hungry to think—and when he did not happen to be thinking of Emerald—he thought about the miracle. With the onset of the sulfa drugs, the medical profession made an enormous stride overnight and was able to increase average life expectancy almost a decade. The doctor was no longer the man whose chief job was to console the relatives as he watched the patient die. Now he could cure many a common disease, and not by faith alone.

Yet, on the other hand, although Crest was not in the position to appreciate this fact, the medical profession lost something at the same time. After all, a miracle drug is not really a miracle; it is only a chemical made by man and given by man. What one man can give, another man can take. The curative factor was no longer faith in the doctor's curative hands; it became a faith in a bottle of pills. At the time when the physician began to carry something more specific than pain-killing drugs in his medical bag, he started to become, in the eyes of some of his patients, less of a doctor than a plumber, more of a craftsman than an artist, very much less a high priest of magic, very much more a tired, gruff, and busy ordinary man. Physicians responded to this change in the reactions of their patients by a change in their own professional mannerisms. As cure became a matter of chemistry, study of human chemistry seemed more appropriate than study of the human personality. Labeled a peddler of pills, many doctors became mere peddlers of pills and began to conduct their profession along the lines of a business. The doctor-patient relationship became less satisfactory to both parties, for reasons neither party could determine. The public began to long for the days of the good old country doc. The physician began to long for the day when his profession automatically granted him the respect, love, and admiration of the community.

In 1936, the medical profession gained one miracle but lost another.

It was the quiet hour in the hospital, 6:00 A.M. The night shift was anxious to get off duty, and the day shift was in no hurry to begin a working day. Sometimes there was a lag of coverage at this hour.

Crest was walking to breakfast sleepily. As he was passing the Accident Room, he heard a call for help inside. He poked his head through the door to see what was going on.

The Accident Room was the nerve center of the hospital, usually crowded with bleeding victims, squalling children, anxious mothers, drunks, cops, reporters, orderlies, nurses, students, interns, residents, and curiosity seekers. At this moment, however, there were only two people in the room.

One of them was a student nurse, a thin, willowy girl who looked as if she might blow away in a good gust of wind. The other was the patient, a big, tough, muscular male. He had obviously taken a scalpel off one of the dressing carts and cut his own throat with it. He had made a gaping incision across the front of his neck, cutting the superficial jugular veins and opening the cartilage rings of the trachea. He had not cut the deeper vital structures at the side of the neck, and therefore had not done himself any serious damage. Although bleeding profusely, he was not in shock and he remained as strong as a bull. Now he was trying to spread the incision by tugging at it with his hands in order to finish the job. The nurse was hanging on to one of his arms and trying to prevent him, but she was much too small. She was being tossed about like a bulldog clamped to the shank of a bear. Crest sized up the situation at a glance and rushed in to give assistance. He grabbed the patient's other arm. The three of them rolled all over the room, Crest on one arm of the patient and the nurse on the other. The patient could not speak, as he had cut open his windpipe below the vocal cords; air whistled out through the opening. Each time he inhaled, he drew blood into his open trachea, which caused him to sputter and choke, and each coughing exhalation contained a mist of finely divided particles of blood.

The thought occurred to Crest: I'm hanging on to a wounded whale, right next to the blowhole.

The three of them thrashed and wallowed in a mist of blood for what seemed like a matter of hours, actually a matter of minutes, until reinforcements finally arrived. It took a dozen strong men at last to wrestle the patient into a strait jacket before they could give him anaesthesia and repair the wound in his neck.

Crest felt as if he had spent a long day with the gladiators in some Roman colosseum. His face, his hands, his white shoes, his uniform were covered with speckles of blood, and so was the nurse, and so was the entire room. In the struggle, Crest had wrenched his shoulder badly.

"Thanks, Dr. Crest," said the nurse. "I was in a jam."

"So were we both," said Crest. "Did you hurt yourself?"

"Yes. I think I broke an ankle," said the nurse.

Crest examined her ankle and he was inclined to agree. "You help me and I'll help you, and we'll hobble over to X-ray together," he said. "Battle casualties."

"It's all in the line of duty, I suppose."

"Perhaps we should have let him finish the job," said Crest. "They'll sew him up and confine him on the psychiatric wing. In a few weeks he'll be released, and the moment he gets out, I'll bet he tries to kill himself again. I hope he does a better job next time. What's your name, my dear?"

"Dr. Crest," she said, "are you married?"

"No. Why do you ask?"

"Some of the boys are married, but the rest of your group knows us by name," she said. "Except for a couple of jerks and for you, Dr. Crest."

"Consider me among the jerks," said Crest.

"Lots of us think you should expand your social life," she said.

"How about a date next Saturday night?"

"I'll probably be flat on my back in traction on the orthopedic ward," she said. "This thing is beginning to hurt like hell."

"I'll call on you during visiting hours," said Crest.

"How will you find me?" she said. "You don't even know my name."

They had reached the X-ray department. The nurse hobbled into one of the examination rooms and Crest went into another. The picture showed no fracture or dislocation of his shoulder; it was only sprained, as he had suspected. The nurse had a hairline fracture of the external malleolus of her right ankle, as Crest had also suspected; he made it a point to examine her X-ray plates, and from them he discovered her name: Nancy Conover. They did not need to put her into traction. They applied a walking cast, and sent her back to duty.

Crest asked some of the bachelors in his group about Nancy Conover. She had the reputation of being agreeable, quiet, and probably not to be had, short of a wedding ring.

Crest kept his date with her the following Saturday night. He took her, hobbling, to a cocktail lounge for a couple of drinks and then to a restaurant for dinner. He realized, wryly, that he was entertaining her on the money left over from his date with Emerald. He and Nancy chatted about mutual patients they had known, the personalities of various staff physicians, what intern was dating which of the nurses and why, and a few generalities about the weather. By dessert, they had run out of things to say. After dinner he took her to the movies, and after that he took her back to the dorm. She expected to be kissed good night, and Crest did his duty.

Afterwards she said rather wistfully, "If the other one ever gets tired of you, why don't you look me up?"

"What other one?" said Crest.

"I get the impression that I am dull by comparison."

"You're not dull, Nancy," Crest protested. "I think you're a very nice girl."

"Exactly," she said, with a wry and quizzical expression.

Crest returned to his quarters. He was not on call that night, and under these circumstances he usually slept like death, but tonight he found himself inflicted with insomnia, a symptom which rarely bothers an intern. After thrashing around in bed for a while, he went to the intern's lounge for a glass of milk and a doughnut. He wandered down to the Accident Room to see what was going on. He prowled the hospital corridors. He stopped off at several wards, chatting with the student nurses at the desk. He became aware, almost for the first time, that the hospital was full of attractive young women. He knew only a few of these girls by sight and none of them by name, and it was now too late to correct this deficiency. Then he was telephoning Emerald before he realized how late it was.

"Hello. Did I wake you up?"

"No," said Emerald. "I just got in from a date."

"So did I," said Crest.

"How was yours?"

"Dull," said Crest. "I was with a proper young lady whose ankle I broke last week."

"Huh?"

"It's the truth."

"I was with Jack," she said. "It wasn't the least bit dull."

"Your ex-husband? Why him?"

"God knows," she said. "Don't you think you better come over here for a little while?"

"I was thinking the same myself," said Crest.

Emerald met him at the door of her apartment. She was wearing a robe which wasn't sensible or woolly; it was a pale-pink shade, and the material looked like silk.

"I forgot to bring any cigarettes," said Crest.

"I bought a carton of my own yesterday. Glory be, I'm going to change my ways! What's the matter with your arm?"

"Why were you seeing Jack again?"

"I think cordial relations with ex-husbands ought to be maintained, don't you?"

"No," said Crest. "I wrenched my shoulder at the same time Nancy broke her ankle."

"It must have been a wild night."

"Six o'clock in the morning, as a matter of fact."

"My!" said Emerald. "'He broke from his cell with a hell of a yell and eloped with the Mother Superior!'"

"Have you any liquor in the house?"

"Only beer."

"Beer will be fine," said Crest.

She extracted two bottles of beer from a microscopic refrigerator in the tiny cubicle which served as combination breakfast nook and kitchenette. Her robe parted slightly as she walked toward him across the room, and Crest caught a glimpse of slip and stockings underneath. She paused over him for a moment as she handed him the beer. He was conscious of her perfume, of a curl of raven hair which twisted provocatively around one ear, of the long white narrow V at the neck of her robe. He thought she might kiss him or sit in his lap, but the moment passed, and she sat down in her chair on the other side of the room. Crest crossed the room and attempted to sit beside her on the edge of her chair.

"Hey, there isn't room: this isn't a sofa," she said.

"It's time you made some room for me," said Crest.

She giggled and gave a little twist of her hips which knocked him off her chair. He sat on the floor at her feet, and rested his head against her thigh. She laughed and touched him on the back of his neck with the cold wet bottom of her bottle of beer. He put his hand underneath the hem of her robe and ran his hand up along her leg. She winced.

"What the devil . . ." she said.

"Just relax," said Crest, but he wasn't following his own advice; his hand was passing upward toward her thighs, and she responded with a stinging slap to his cheek.

"What in the hell are you trying to do?" she said.

Crest moved away. His cheeks were a flaming red, and he

was breathing hard, but he attempted to joke it off. "In this room which stinks like an Armenian—"

"You haven't been in one," she reminded him, "and neither have I."

"Only with Jack."

"You can keep Jack out of this," she said.

"Sorry."

"Well, that's better. You customarily apologize for everything you do."

"Damn it, maybe I'm not sorry," said Crest. "I've had enough proper little girl for this particular night, and I need a woman for a change. I thought you'd understand. You're the only woman I know."

"Chum," she said, with sudden gravity, "I don't understand myself, so how am I expected to understand you?"

"Give me a break. You know what I'm talking about," he said.

"Look, sweetie, I'm not on call tonight."

"Only for Jack."

"Will you kindly stop throwing Jack in my face? Be rational, damn it. Have some more beer or a cold shower or something. We get along just fine together as friends."

"I think that I need more than a friend tonight," he said.

"And spoil everything between us. As usual. That figures. You're only a man."

"So I'm a man, and I'm not afraid of women, and I'm not a prude, and I'm not a queer, and I'm aged twenty-six, and I haven't had a woman for entirely too damn long, and what do you propose to make of that?"

"I propose to make nothing of it," she said, "whatsoever."

"Oh hell, what's the use?" he said. "Sorry to have bothered you."

He started for the door. She grabbed at his arm and spun him around.

"Now, wait . . ." she said.

"Ouch!" he said. She had grabbed his sore shoulder, but she paid no attention to that.

"Maybe we can work out something together, John Crest," she said gravely.

"This is not a diagnostic problem," he said. "There is nothing to be worked out."

She was staring intensely into his eyes. "What do you want?" she said. "Really me?"

"You know what I want."

"The real Emerald? Not just the shape and the smell and all the sexual things?"

"I can't dissect you into parts," said Crest. "I want all of you together."

She studied him a moment longer. "You mean it," she decided. "You mean it as much as a man ever can under such circumstances. Okay, I'm willing. Why not? Let's do it right for a change. Let's really have ourselves a ball."

Rapidly and almost ruthlessly, she stripped and spread herself on the bed.

"Well? Come on," she said. "What are you waiting for?"

"Let me turn off the light," he said.

She continued to pursue a ruthless approach while he was holding back. This was partly a conscious effort for each to give the other pleasure, to compensate for the differing rhythm of the sexes. But she was trying to force herself, not against him, Crest realized, but against some deep inhibition. He also recognized a source of inhibition in himself. Some underlying Puritan strain in him, shared by many American men, could not reconcile love and lust. There was a mother figure on the one hand and a whore image on the other, and it was difficult for him to fuse the two into a total woman bearing facets of both. He recognized in her some need to be forced, an underlying confusion of pleasure with pain. This was as near as he could come to the source of difficulty which lay between them and the ultimate pleasure that they both pretended to enjoy.

"That was pretty good," she said later. "Wasn't it?"

"Sure," said Crest. "Wonderful."

But he knew that something would always be lacking if they both had to wonder what the trouble was. The last stray thought that occurred to him before he drifted off to sleep was a physiological one. He remembered having been taught that during the act of intercourse neurological perception of noxious stimuli is temporarily lost. What he had been doing did not help a sore shoulder at all. He had not noticed it then. Now it was beginning to throb like hell.

He awoke to discover a pearly light coming through the window. It was dawn. Emerald was sitting up beside him on the bed, smoking a cigarette, and the texture of her skin was pearl. It occurred to Crest that the shape of a breast from clavicle to nipple is nature's most beautiful curve. The orange spark at the end of her cigarette waxed and waned like a firefly.

"Let's not set the bed on fire," he said.

The light was too vague for him to distinguish her features clearly, but he could tell that she was lifting one dark eyebrow into that provocative question mark.

"We did that last night, didn't we?" she said.

Crest grinned. "We did our best," he said. He put his arm around her slender waist and rested his cheek against the skin of her breast.

"Brrr, you need a shave," she said.

He removed his cheek and touched her on the same place with his lips. "Penny for your thoughts," he said.

"I don't understand the how and the why of a man," she said.

"I don't think Mother Nature ever intended us to understand," he said.

"Poor Jack."

"Must we discuss poor Jack?"

"I understand him somewhat better now," she said, "because he's not exactly a man."

"Emerald," he said suddenly, "why don't we get married?"

"All right," she said.

She twisted her shoulder and shook him free, and then she got out of bed. She picked up her robe from where it was lying in a tangle on the floor and put it on. It occurred to Crest then that the interplay of gluteal muscles compared very favorably with the curve of the breast. She wandered over to the other side of the room aimlessly, looking for something which she didn't find, and then she wandered back and sat on the edge of the bed. She drew a new cigarette from the package that was resting on the blanket and lit it from the stub of the old one.

"Did you hear what you just said to me?" Crest asked.

"Surely. I agreed to marry you."

"Says she, very calm and casual."

"Did you expect a display of my theatric temperament? I made the decision last night before we went to bed. I thought that was obvious. You can't afford to support a wife, by the way. I presume that you're marrying me for my father's money."

"I've given up plans for a residency," he said. "I expect to go into general practice when I finish my internship. We can get married then. I can find a location, assisting some older man. Things may be sticky for a time, but we'll make out. I don't need your father's money."

"My father is looking for an assistant in Sentryville."

"I know," said Crest. "He offered me the job. I'm giving it serious consideration."

"Is this what you really want to do, John Crest?"

"I always wanted to be a Parkindale," said Crest. "Married to your father's daughter. Working for the father of my wife. Why not?"

"Well, if it doesn't work, please remember that this was your own idea," she said. "Nobody twisted your arm. Don't blame me."

"It was all your fault. You made me fall in love with you," he said. "After that, everything was inevitable."

"Bulls' tails!"

"I don't like that pink thing you have on," he said. "Why don't you take it off?"

"It's cold."

"I know a way to raise the temperature."

"Didn't you have enough of that last night?"

"I'll never have enough of you," he said.

"Men—honestly! It's like some sort of a disease."

"Are you going to take it off?" said Crest. "Or shall I grab hold and give a rip?"

"In a minute," she said. "Just wait until I finish my cigarette, please."

She sat on the edge of the bed, smoking, abstracted, looking across the room. Her legs were crossed. Her upper leg stuck through the gap in the robe, but she seemed unconscious of it. She appeared to be weighing some pros and cons. An invisible network of doubt, faint reservation, and ill-defined hostility covered her more completely than any robe and kept them apart as firmly as a thick brick wall.

Since she was being so rational, Crest permitted himself a moment of rational analysis.

Love, he decided, is different for a woman. For her, it contains a curious blend: a vague and nebulous romance on the one hand, an earthy practicality on the other. She wants to endow her mate with a cloak of nobility and chivalry, which no modern man could wear in comfort. At the same time, she is assessing the man on the most cold-blooded economic terms of status, income, insurance, security, mink coats, and community property. Sensuality does not seem to enter in. A woman is sensual enough once you get the motor started, and in fact she is more sensual than a man when the overdrive cuts in, but somebody has to turn the ignition key. Spontaneous sensuality does not seem to occur. Entirely egocentric in her love, she takes the man's desire for granted and does

not question her own irresistible appeal. She presumes that
he will desire total possession of her total personality for life,
just as he desires her body at the moment.

Man, on the other hand, always has a store of sensuality. A
sexual impulse will occur to him many times a day; it will be
aroused, not only by his wife, but by the wife of the man
next door, the nurse or the secretary in the office, or any passing stranger in the street. Often he will not even like a woman
who gives him the sudden impulse of desire. Sometimes, he
dislikes most strongly the woman who can arouse him most.
To the impulse of lust, the man can add deep feelings of
genuine affection and regard to only one woman at a time,
the woman he loves. Sometimes his impulse of desire and
feeling of affection are in conflict with each other. He wonders
whether a woman has a genuine affection and regard for him
when she cold-bloodedly considers his bank account, or attempts to cloak him with romantic chivalry, or coldly with-
draws from his pressing physical instincts, of which he is
faintly ashamed.

Men and women seek, but seldom find, full satisfaction in
each other. Curiosity, dissatisfaction, and the search for something better draw man and woman to each other. Without
dissatisfaction, men and women could quite easily resist each
other, and the race would perish.

"Well, son," said Emerald, snapping her fingers in front of
his somewhat muddled eyes, "it's me. I'm here. What do you
propose to do about it, sir?"

He was jolted awake, and saw that she had snubbed out her
cigarette and slipped out of her robe. The light from the window was less pearly now, and the texture of her skin was
cream.

"I thought you were going to be cold," he said.

"No," she said, "not very." She took his hands in hers and
placed them both between her thighs, where it was not cold.
"What were you thinking about?" she said.

"Huh?" said Crest. He had just stopped thinking and was beginning to react.

"Tell me. Please."

He took his hands away. "I was trying to decide why I am in love with you," he said.

"Why?"

"Contrast, I think. Your black hair and eyes in contrast to the whiteness of your skin. Your vivacity, which alternates with strange moods of withdrawal. You change in the twinklng of an eye. You are very much alive."

"Now you wonder why I love you?"

"It puzzles me," said Crest.

"I can't declare it or define it," she said. "I can only show you thusly, so . . ."

She licked her lips with the pink tip of a cat tongue, and opened her mouth and kissed him. Then, as he was reacting again, she backed off to talk some more.

"Did you hear about Sam?"

"I wish you'd stop that," said Crest.

"Well, if you're not interested in Sam . . ." she said and pouted. "You're going to be a member of the family. Sam will be your brother-in-law."

"Of course. Sam is my best friend."

Although Crest thought of Sam as his best friend, he had not seen him since the day of their graduation from medical school. Sam had drifted out of his life, now that they no longer worked together.

"He flunked out of dental school," she said.

Crest was astonished. Medical students tended to think of dental students as a highly inferior breed.

"I guess cavities and tartar didn't fascinate him very much," said Emerald. "He's been drinking quite a lot. In dental school, he lacked the assistance of a dedicated grind to pull him through."

"What will he do now?"

"He's working in my uncle's office. Sam is still a doctor, of

course, even though he flunked out of dentistry, and he
conned Joseph into letting him begin plastic surgery at once,
without an internship or a residency. My brother is a skillful
con man when he puts his heart into the job."

"I think he'll make a great plastic surgeon."

"I think he won't," said Emerald. "I think Sam will be a
brilliant failure, just like me."

"I beg your pardon?" said Crest.

"A hell of an actress I turned out to be," she said. "At
least, thank God, I never was a nurse. Only right next door
to that: a doctor's wife."

"Just a minute. Let me have that again," said Crest. "By
marrying me, you have made a failure of your life?"

"I didn't mean that just the way it sounds."

"I hope not," said Crest. "What did you mean?"

"I want to be your wife, John Crest, really I do," she said.
"I think you'll be good for me."

"But you wish I wasn't a doctor?"

"You couldn't be anything else."

"Then what do you mean? Where do I stand?"

"Why stand?" she said. "This is a bed. Why don't we lie
down?"

She flung herself on him, almost like the first time he had
been in her apartment, carrying him into love-making with
a directness that was close to violence. This time, Crest managed to hang onto a shred of his self-control.

"Now, wait . . ."

"Silly," she said. "We can never wait."

"Emerald, damn it . . ."

"Don't you swear at me, John Crest."

"We can't leave it this way. Don't distract me now. This is
important to us both, now and for the rest of our lives. Where
do we stand?"

"We'll make it work," she said, with a certain grimness. "I'm
going to make it work. I'm pretty strong. I'll show you how,
John Crest. Come on."

She fell on him again, and he fought her away, and the fighting turned to passion, and this time there was physical satisfaction for them both, because of a trace of violence.

"All right?" she whispered afterward.

"All right," he whispered back.

There was full daylight in the room by now, but Crest permitted himself to fall asleep before any small doubt could come creeping back. The issue was decided. He would try to make the best of it, and so would she, he hoped.

Part 3

Sentryville, a pleasant town of 7,000 population, lies in a fertile river valley. The river was at one time navigable by ocean-going vessels, but it has silted up over the generations, and only small pleasure craft navigate there now. The river overflows its banks each spring, and manages to produce a raging flood once or twice a decade, but it is a lazy old river most of the time. The river valley supports orchards, dairy farms, truck farms, and a few tobacco fields. Tobacco is not a usual New England crop, but the clay of the valley is favorable for a tobacco used in the outer wrapping of fine cigars.

In the center of town is a village square, which might be more properly called a rectangle, since it is half a mile long and only a hundred yards wide. The square is bordered by elms, stately gracious trees but past their prime, quietly succumbing to the erosion of Dutch-elm disease. The grass in the square comes up lushly green in the spring, but by summer it is parched and beaten dry. Except when it is covered with snow, there are always little boys on it, playing ball.

In the center of the square is a statue of the sentry for whom the town was named. Children clamber over him disrespectfully; an icicle hangs from his nose in the winter; his greenish-bronze complexion has been whitened by constant bird droppings. It is said that the sentry was looking for the British at the same time as Paul Revere, but he was looking the other way.

On the north side of the square are rambling old houses, all white, some painted recently, where dwell the aristocracy of the town to the fourth, fifth, and sixth generation. The south side of the square is the business block, with two- and three-story commercial buildings of brick. Just south of Main Street are the courthouse, the jail, and other county buildings. Railroad tracks cut the square and street at the southwestern corner, running along the river, up past the textile factory, which was once very busy and which, by 1937, was in business only now and then. Still farther up the river, a small tributary stream had been dammed to form a crystal artificial lake, surrounded by a cluster of summer cottages and camps.

All of the 7,000 souls in and around the town of Sentryville are born, and all of them die, and all of them are sick at times between the initial and the terminal event. This is the substance of the doctor's trade. There were six physicians in early 1937, and a new one came to town that summer.

Dr. Jones did eye-ear-nose-and-throat and made about $18,000 a year. Dr. Hamilton and Dr. Rhodes were general men, once partners, who sent each other Christmas cards and spoke only when they passed each other in the street. Neither of them spoke to Dr. Parkindale. In a good year, Dr. Hamilton and Dr. Rhodes might each make as much as $14,000, and in a bad year no more than $8,000, and they fought for every penny that they made. Dr. Klamp was too old, and Dr. Mordikay frequently too drunk to see patients, but neither man had any need for money. Dr. Klamp had made a killing a generation before, and it was said that Dr. Mordikay had inherited means. It is doubtful if either Dr. Klamp or Dr. Mordikay made more than $4,000 from his practice in any year between 1929 and 1937. It is doubtful that Dr. Parkindale grossed less than $50,000 in any of these years.

Dr. Parkindale was always available, twenty-four hours a day and seven days a week. It was his boast that he had never taken a vacation since he had hung out his shingle in Sentryville. He was at the hospital from six in the morning until noon. He averaged 300 deliveries a year and the same number of major operations. His office load ran thirty or forty patients a day and he made a dozen daily house calls. Dr. Parkindale seldom slept more than two or three hours in a row. He was the school physician, the police physician, the municipal health officer, and the county medical examiner. He was company doctor for the textile factory and for the railroad. He had been, for uncountable consecutive terms, president of the county medical society and, for the same length of time, chief of the medical and surgical staff of the community hospital.

The trouble with Dr. Parkindale was that he was too busy, and often patients had to wait for him. No man can do everything, although it sometimes seemed as if Dr. Parkindale was trying. In the summer of 1937, Dr. Parkindale got the assistant he so badly needed. The new man was named Crest, John Crest, and he also happened to be Parky's son-in-law.

Most of the citizens in Sentryville saw a doctor two or three times each year; some of them saw a doctor two or three times every month; some of them only two or three times in their entire lives, and a few only once. It was possible, though rare, to be born in Sentryville without the attendance of a doctor. It was impossible to avoid being seen by a physician after death; a doctor must sign the death certificate according to state law.

In any given year in Sentryville, sixty people would have tuberculosis, 800 would have hypertension, and twenty-five would have syphilis. Almost every child would have measles, mumps, and chicken pox during the first ten years of life. A few of them would have whooping cough, and one or two of these might die. There was an occasional case of diphtheria, which would alarm only the state public health authorities, and an equally occasional case of polio, which would alarm the entire valley.

Each winter, every citizen would have a cold. Influenza came and went throughout the valley in waves in the winter; so did gastroenteritis in the summer. There was one case of amoebic dysentery in Sentryville in 1937. There were never any cases of Carrion's Disease.

There was a lot of asthma and eczema, emphysema and bronchitis. Pneumonia, still very common, was fatal only to the very young and very old. Thyroid disease was not unusual; rheumatic fever and nephritis occurred far more often than was recognized; diabetes and arteriosclerosis were very common; most of the married women became pregnant two or three times, and some of the unmarried ones. Beri-beri was seen only among the alcoholics, who comprised 2 per cent of the population. The leading cause of death was coronary disease; then strokes; then accidents; then cancer; then kidney conditions; and then suicide. Manslaughter was common, especially on the highways, and homicide was rare.

Half of the people who entered a doctor's office in Sentryville had functional or emotional disease. Seventy-five per cent of the time, the symptom that brought the patient to the doctor was, at least in part, emotional. Ten per cent of the population would spend a portion of their lives in public institutions for the insane, and there were no more lunatics in Sentryville than anywhere else.

A young doctor coming to Sentryville in 1937 would face many problems for which he was well prepared by his medical education and his internship. In problems of a technical nature, whether diagnostic or therapeutic, whether medical, surgical, or obstetrical, he was better equipped than the older men in town. He would diagnose problem cases that had baffled everybody else, and he would use new therapy to effect a few dramatic cures. However, it would be his tendency to over-diagnose and over-treat; looking for a rare condition, he would sometimes miss a common one; reaching for the latest drug, he would sometimes produce more disease than he had cured. In the art of handling people, he would have much to learn.

The young man in Sentryville would face certain problems that had never been mentioned in the lecture hall or the ward of the teaching hospital. In economics, he would be hopelessly at sea. In the battlefield of professional competition, there would be many a sword for which he had no shield. In the complicated nuances of community prestige, status, gossip, politics, rumor, and counter-rumor, he would be naked and naïve.

With the passage of the years, unless he was defeated, if he kept an open eye and sympathy and interest, he would gradually become aware of certain motivating forces in human behavior which have never been defined or described in a book. A knowledge of these forces would often help him, would give him some gift for prophecy, and would sometimes permit him to solve a problem before the problem arose. At such times, he would consider his experience to be a gift of God. Sometimes, however, he would consider it a gift from Satan. At times he would be dismayed and exasperated, frustrated and put to rout by the inevitable progression of age, disability, and death; by the basic selfishness of human nature; by the stubborn stupidity of man; and by the sardonic irony of circumstance.

These were the problems facing John Crest, M.D., as he began his professional work in Sentryville. He had certain other problems as well, but these were not professional in nature.

Crest wakened early. The sun was just coming up on a brilliant morning in July; later in the day, it would be hot.

His waking dream had been an anxious one. He thought himself tied to a railroad track, the victim in a Victorian melodrama, and he heard the hooting of an on-coming train. The hooting persisted in his ears after he was awake. It could have been a train, since the railroad ran not far away, but in actuality it was an automobile horn honking underneath the window.

Crest got out of bed, a large double bed in the guest room of Dr. Parkindale's Sentryville home, and went to the window. A car had drawn up in front of the doctor's office. This car had obviously been involved in an argument with another car or the concrete stanchion of a bridge. The windshield was shattered, the left front fender smashed, and the entire frame warped out of alignment. There were two men in the front seat, and Crest suspected they were drunk. He could see that the driver's head was streaming with blood, probably lacerated from windshield glass. Instead of ringing the doctor's bell, they were honking for the doctor to come out to them. Practicing tolerance, Crest supposed that their injuries prevented them from leaving the car.

Soon the doctor appeared. Crest could see Parky striding over to the shattered car. Even at this hour, Parky was fully dressed, the picture of assurance and confident strength. He stuck his large head through the right side window of the automobile and apparently conducted a cursory examination of the occupants. Then he withdrew his head. The car started up and limped away in the general direction of the hospital. Parky went into the garage. There was the roar of a powerful engine. Then Parky zoomed out in his big black Cadillac.

Crest was wondering whether he should help. His own small Ford coupe, second-hand though new to him, was resting in that garage. Should he follow the doctor to the hospital? This was the first official day of his employment as the assistant of Dr. Parkindale. Crest considered the problem and arrived at a negative decision. The volume of practice was sufficient, he knew, for him to have plenty of work, that day or any other day. The newly installed telephone in the guest room was silent. If Crest were needed, it would ring. Probably there was time for him to snatch another hour or two of sleep. Or, he thought as he glanced at his wife's trim body coiled into a luxurious knot on the other side of the bed, he might do something other than sleep.

Crest padded to the bathroom. On his return, he took a cigarette from the package Emerald kept within arm's reach on the bedside table, lit it, and sat in a chair beside the window, watching the early mists which were rising from the valley.

During the several nights that Crest had spent in Emerald's apartment before they were married, it was always she who woke first and lit a cigarette and sat abstracted by the window in the light of dawn, mulling over pros and cons. Now Emerald was sleeping lazy and late, and it was Crest who was sometimes awake too early in the day. Often he saw a smile on her sleeping face like that of a sleek fat cat who has discovered where the cream is hid. During their honeymoon, Crest had discovered that he was smoking two and sometimes three packs of cigarettes a day, and Emerald less than one. This discovery had disconcerted him.

Her sleeping face looked innocent. Crest had never associated Emerald with innocence. Although two years younger than he, she had always seemed more experienced. Watching her now, Crest felt a sudden impulse to waken her and violate her innocence.

Rape, he found himself thinking, can and does occur in the marriage bed. In fact, in many times and cultures, this was the normal marital relationship, one certainly satisfactory to the male and perhaps even to the female too. However, in the time and culture of John and Emerald Crest, husband and wife had assigned themselves the project of being companions, friends, and lovers to each other simultaneously. Is such a relationship a normal one on psychological and physiological terms, Crest was wondering? Certainly it is not an easy one. The contemporary civilized man and woman of the educated bracket are expected to work out a complex and difficult inter-relationship. It is no wonder, Crest decided, that modern marriage so often fails, and that successful marriage so often contains broad areas of frustrated discontent.

Was it thoughts like these that were waking him so early in the day and making him smoke too many cigarettes? He lit a new cigarette from the stub of the old. Emerald stirred as he approached the bedside table; she rolled over but did not awake. The evening had been warm, and they had been sleeping under a single sheet. She had kicked away the sheet, and her thin nightgown had ridden upward toward her waist. She lay on her side, her face turned the other way, and naked buttocks peeped out provocatively in Crest's direction.

Poor Jack, Emerald's first husband, had liked to give her pain, and she had taken pleasure in that pain. Crest was suddenly tempted to give that delectable presenting bottom a sharp slap with the palm of his hand. He was at once ashamed of the thought. Analyzing his emotions, he decided that there was no reason for shame. This woman was his wife of only two weeks; it is natural for a man to feel desire for his wife, at least in the beginning; natural desire contains sadistic and masochistic elements. In slapping her, it was not his intention to hurt her in any way but to excite her toward pleasure. He had never wakened a woman in this way. He had never taken a bath with a woman, or combed her hair, or rubbed cold cream on the skin of her breast. Shouldn't one try erotic experiments with a newly wedded wife?

Yes, perhaps in Paris, France, but not in Sentryville!

He walked quietly to the bed, but, instead of slapping her, he pulled down her nightgown to restore her innocence, and he drew up the sheet, and he kissed her tenderly on the forehead. She smiled in her sleep, the fat cat smile, drifting slowly upward toward consciousness but not breaking the surface yet. All impulses of guilt had gone from Crest, but also had the impulse of desire. Now he knew that he would not return to bed with his wife. He would get dressed and go about the business of the day, which now seemed a far more important and interesting thing to do.

Crest heard the roar of the Caddy as Dr. Parkindale returned from the hospital. The engine died; garage doors slammed; even through three insulated floors of a big old house, Crest could hear Parky's heavy feet trampling around in the kitchen as he fixed breakfast for himself.

Crest knew that he was tense. It was the same feeling he had known as an intern when he was assigned to surgery and the first operation of the day would be long and hard with a surgeon of the arrogant and irascible variety. This day, and each succeeding day, would have surgery for Crest, and various of the specialties in which he also did not feel at home, as well as the problems of internal medicine, for which he knew himself best equipped. He wasn't afraid of this. Fresh out of a great medical school and a rotating internship in a teaching hospital, he knew as much as any general man. There was nothing Parky could teach him about the methods and techniques of modern medicine; in fact, more than likely, Crest could teach the old man a thing or two. Perhaps Parky could be arrogant, and perhaps he could be irascible, but no country doctor could match the authorities of a university hospital. He had no fear of the man himself. Crest always admired Parkindales. He had wanted to be a Parkindale himself. And now he would join the dynasty, in fact if not in name. This was the trouble. You can't learn to be an aristocrat. You must be to the manner born.

"I'm a poor black sheep in a flock of lusty goats," thought Crest.

He left the bedroom. As he was closing the door, he became aware that his wife was now awake. He knew he should have returned to kiss her good morning and tell her he loved her

again, but he pretended that he didn't notice, and made his
way downstairs.

"I'm sorry, dear, but I'm not totally available," he thought.
"No man ever is. We must be about our father's business. In
this case, it happens to be your father, not mine."

Crest descended to the kitchen and found his wife's father
seated at the table, attacking his breakfast. The aroma of
steaming coffee filled the room.

"Good morning, sir," said Crest.

Parky looked at him, his mouth full of egg, and grunted. It
was sort of an animal noise, and Crest felt a shudder of dis-
taste. There was something of the animal in Parky: a crudity
of manner and a healthy animal vitality. Crest went to the
stove, poured himself a cup of coffee, and put two slices of
bread into the toaster.

"There's bacon, ham, sausage, and eggs in the refrigerator,
son, but you'll have to cook them for yourself," said Parky. "In
this house, men work and the women sleep late. My wife gets
up at ten o'clock."

"Thanks, but toast and coffee will be fine," said Crest. "I
never eat much breakfast."

"I need a hearty meal to begin the day," said Parky. "Did
you sleep well?"

"Yes, sir."

This might have been a loaded question. Crest had been
sleeping well in a room upstairs with this man's only daughter.
But, if there were nuances in the older man's remark, he gave
no sign, continuing to attack his bacon and eggs as though
they were a mortal enemy.

"I heard that car drive up and honk this morning, sir,"
said Crest. "I was wondering if I should come down and give
you a hand."

"Drunks," snorted Parky. "They nudged an oak tree down at
Galen's Corners, but they didn't nudge it very hard. The
driver sliced his face on windshield glass, and the other one

bumped his knee. I patched them up before I took them down to jail."

"Jail?"

"They hadn't bothered to report the accident. Ninety days' reflection won't do either one of them a bit of harm. The driver may lose his license, I suppose, but it might help the welfare of the community."

Crest did not think that many doctors took their patients to jail. Of course, Parky was police physician and medical examiner as well as practitioner and might, therefore, have mixed loyalties. Most doctors would lose the patronage of the patient and all his friends and relatives this way. In Parky's case, however, Crest supposed it was likely that this pair would consult him again the next time they nudged an old oak tree, even though they ended up in jail.

Parky washed down a final mouthful of breakfast with the last of his coffee, threw his wadded napkin onto the table, sighed, belched, and loosened his belt.

"The schedule is fairly light this morning," he said, "and I thought we might take a few minutes and talk things over, you and me."

"All right," said Crest.

"The first few weeks may be hard on us both. You are accustomed to the routines of the teaching hospital, and everything is different in the sticks. I am used to working alone, and I may find you underfoot."

"I'll try to stay out of your way," said Crest.

"There's plenty of work for both of us," said Parky. "First of all, how are you on obstetrics?"

"I've had good training in OB," said Crest. "I've done fifty-three unassisted deliveries."

"I sometimes do that many in a month."

"I might as well be frank," said Crest. "I'm perfectly capable at doing a routine delivery—"

"Who isn't?" said Parky.

"And I can handle most of the usual minor complications, but if anything goes sour, I need help in a hurry."

"In other words, you don't feel at home in the delivery suite?"

"No, sir, frankly I don't."

"Then I'll continue to handle the OB work myself. An obstetrician is no good unless he can handle any emergency that may arise. There is no time to call for help. You won't be expected to do deliveries, if that's okay with you."

"That's fine with me," said Crest.

"How are you with kids?"

"I enjoy pediatrics," said Crest. "I seem to get along with children well."

"While I hate the screaming little snot-nosed brats," said Parky. "All right, sir, pediatrics is your department. What about surgery?"

"Surgery has always been my weakest department, I'm afraid. I am equipped to assist you in the operating room, but I want no surgical responsibility myself."

"I admire your frankness, Dr. Crest. As a matter of fact, I am glad that you have no surgical ambitions. In my opinion, there's nothing more dangerous to a community than a hungry young surgeon trying to get experience at the expense of his patients."

"You have had surgical training?"

"Nope. I taught myself."

Crest was about to inquire, "At the expense of your patients?" but he managed to catch his tongue in time.

"You are strong in medicine?" asked Parky.

"That has always been my greatest interest," said Crest.

"You don't mind the psychos and the loonies, the drunks, the crocks, the creeps, and the cranks? You don't mind dealing with the whining woman?"

"I've always been challenged by functional and by chronic disease," said Crest.

"Well, there's plenty of that junk in Sentryville," said Parky.

"I like your attitude, Dr. Crest. I think we can work well to-gether. We complement each other's strength and weak-nesses, and we won't be fighting for the cream of the crop. You weren't expecting much free time, I trust."

"Sir?"

"I can do everything you can do," said Parky. "I've been doing it alone for years. However, you can't do major surgery, and you feel uncomfortable in the delivery suite, so how in the hell would you expect to cover for me?"

"Sir, I—"

"You pass for a general practitioner, Crest. You can't call yourself a specialist, since you've had no special training or experience, and you must call yourself a general practitioner by default. However, you are unbalanced. The true general man can handle everything that comes along, and you can't. You're another of these half-baked specialists without port-folio. That's all the medical schools can seem to turn out these days."

"But, sir—" said Crest, about to lodge a protest.

"I know the philosophy under which you've been raised," said Parky. "I've heard it often enough from my own family, God knows. I'm not going to debate philosophy with you. I hired you for a practical reason. I don't need your coverage. I haven't taken a vacation since I hung out my shingle. I don't believe in every other night and every other weekend off. I believe that medicine is a full-time job. Get the picture?"

Although Crest didn't entirely like the picture, he got it.

"Cheer up, my boy," said Parky. "I didn't expect you to be a tough old ox like me. You do the things you know how to do, and do them as well as you can. If you get into trouble, just holler for me. Choose your own working hours. I'll handle the overload."

"I'm not afraid of work, sir. I can do the job."

"I know you can. That's why I hired you," said Parky. "Now, let's talk about money. My boy, I think it quite extraordinary that a young man should accept a job today without discussing financial terms in advance."

"I'm in the family," said Crest. "I presume you'll pay me well enough to maintain your daughter's standard of living."

"You're not interested in money?"

"Not primarily," said Crest. "I hope to make a living. I expect to be paid for my skill and my experience. I'd like to get out of debt some day, but I don't expect to get rich."

"Well spoken," said Dr. Parkindale. "Too many doctors are looking for the easy buck, and they give the entire profession a dirty name. There are two fine examples in this town: Dr. Hamilton and Dr. Rhodes. There's always enough money in medicine for a man who likes to work, but these sons-of-bitches want to spend banker's hours and get rich at the same time. With me, you'll get paid for what you earn, and you'll earn every penny that you get. We'll go over the books once or twice a month. After the overhead is paid, we'll split the pot according to who did the work. Is this satisfactory?"

"Yes, sir."

"I make more money than all the other men in town," said Parky, "but I do more work than any other man in town. I never charge a patient more than he can afford, or less than he wants to pay. I've sent many a stiff bill in my time, but there are thousands of people who never get a bill from me. This is the point, my boy: *dedication!*"

He slammed his big fist on the table for emphasis. A coffee cup leaped out of its saucer and onto the floor and smashed. Parky ignored it.

"You are in business to serve the sick," he went on. "The moment that you lose your dedication to service, you are dead. You'll become a drunk, like Dr. Mordikay, or a businessman, like Dr. Klamp. Maybe you'd like to run a shop, selling spectacles, like Dr. Jones. Perhaps you'd prefer to cut your brother's throat, like Hamilton and Rhodes. These men have forgotten how to serve, and they wonder why all the patients come to me! They don't teach dedication at the university.

What are they teaching? Science! Medicine has never been a science. Look at my brother: he plays around with society dames like a gigolo. My own son was so interested in money that he wouldn't even come to Sentryville: he flunked out of dental school instead. My father spent his life sucking for a Nobel Prize, and he never really treated a patient in his life. I come from a family of doctors, but I'm the only doctor in the crowd. If you want to be a real doctor, dedicated to serving the sick, you'll go a long way in Sentryville, or in any other town. If you lose your dedication, you'll be of no use to me, and you might as well move along. There are plenty of derelicts in this profession, my boy. Now that we understand each other, let's go to work. We've wasted half the morning already."

Parky gave a snort. Crest was reminded of a standing locomotive getting up a head of steam. Parky was chuffing rapidly out of the room, and Crest had to run to catch up with him. Parky went into the garage and got into the Cadillac. Crest was getting into his Ford coupe, but Parky motioned with his head, inviting Crest into the front seat of the Caddy.

"I thought you might just follow me around today," said Parky. "Look over my shoulder and get the feel of things. Tomorrow we'll cut you loose on your own."

"All right."

"I didn't mean to bury you under an avalanche of words, my boy," said Parky. "I'm not much of a talker. Most of the time I listen, but when I get going, I'm hard to stop."

"I imagine you're hard to stop at anything," said Crest.

Parky smiled, acknowledging a compliment. He drove swiftly down Main Street, past the square, onto the highway which led to the hills at the outer rim of the valley. He drove fast, constantly exceeding the speed limits, crowding the curves, accelerating on the straightaways. He was a skillful driver, and the powerful car was fully under his control. Halfway to the hills, a black sedan appeared on the road ahead of them. It bore the obvious markings and blue dome light of the state police. Parky grandly swept by the police car at eighty miles an hour, waving as he passed. Crest expected to hear the snarl of the siren. The cop at the wheel, however, merely grinned and waved back. Parky's distinctive automobile with the doctor's green cross on the license plate would be recognized by all law-enforcement officers in the area, and Parky would never be stopped for speeding. Rank has its privileges.

They had reached the grade of the hills. Parky suddenly sliced the big car off to the right, bounding along a rutted clay road, plunging through a grove of trees, and he suddenly applied the brakes. Crest rocked forward in his seat. He couldn't even see the house at first, but there was one, hidden at the edge of the woods: a filthy shack, falling apart of its own weight. The yard was full of mangy hounds who skulked and yapped. Ignoring the menagerie, Parky walked to the door, which was hanging on one hinge, and went in without knocking. There seemed to be fifteen people in the room. Crest saw a mother, blowzy and distraught; a father, anxious and belligerent; and at least a dozen skinny dirty kids. The patient was the youngest of the clan, a two-year-old girl, emaciated, pinched, and grayish. Her frail body was nearly torn in two with spasms of coughing. Crest thought she might be dying of chronic lung disease.

"Good morning, Mother," said Parky in his booming, confident voice.

"Thank God, Parky, you've come," said the mother.

"It isn't thanks to God," said Parky. "And no thanks to your lazy good-for-nothing husband, who hasn't paid a penny on his bill for the last fourteen months."

The father gave a subdued look with daggers in it and slunk out of the house to join the hounds, looking rather like a hound himself. Parky sat on the edge of the bed, ignoring the strong possibility that there might be bugs in it.

"How's the little girl?" he asked.

The little girl summoned a wan smile for him, as if the

nearness of this big dynamic man had restored a little of her own lost vitality.

"Parky," said the mother fretfully, "I think she's going to die."

"Fiddlesticks," said Parky.

The patient was seized again with a paroxysm of brassy retching cough. Parky took a long, keen look at her.

"This young lady has the croup," he announced. "Don't you agree, Dr. Crest?"

"I'd like to listen with the stethoscope," said Crest.

"Nonsense. Not necessary," said Parky. "Any damn fool can see that this is croup. This young lady needs steam, Mother, plenty of steam. Put on the tea kettle and fill the room."

"Yes, Parky," said the mother.

"Have you any ipecac in the house?"

The mother gave a negative shake of the head.

"I'm ashamed of you," said Parky. "How can you raise a flock of kids without ipecac? There ought to be a bottle in every house, right alongside the bottle of paregoric."

Although Crest would have agreed about the paregoric, ipecac was an old-fashioned remedy, and Crest had never seen it prescribed. The one-hinged door creaked open as the father stuck in his head to see what was going on.

"Have you any money, you lazy bum?" said Parky to the father.

"I got about fifty cents," said the father sullenly.

"That's enough," said Parky. "You get your ass into town as fast as you can go, and you walk into the drugstore and plunk down your fifty cents, and tell the man you want as much of Parky's croup medicine as your money will buy. He'll know what you mean. And don't you be stopping at the liquor store first and trying to get your medicine on credit. You haven't got any credit, my friend, and this child can't wait for her medicine until next Saturday night. Now move!"

The father moved.

"Steam, Mother," said Parky blandly. "And when that no-good man of yours gets back with the medicine, I want you to give her five drops every five minutes. You get that? Five and five. You keep on giving her the medicine until she vomits. I want her heaving her belly all over the floor. Ipecac isn't any good until the stuff going down meets the stuff coming back up. Get the picture?"

"Yes, Parky, five and five."

"When she gets vomiting good and proper, that croup is going to go away, and this young lady will sound as bright as a new penny."

"Yes, Parky. I can't pay you very much today, what with the cost of the medicine and all. As a matter of fact, I only have a dime. Will that be enough?"

"Certainly," said Parky.

The mother excavated into a drawer of a tumbledown bureau and came up with a dime, which she handed to Parky. He accepted it graciously.

"There's nothing like ipecac for croup, my boy," said Parky to Crest as they were returning to the car.

"Croup?" said Crest. "On a hot summer day?"

"You have a better idea?"

"It seems to me the child might have tuberculosis," said Crest.

"Of course," said Parky. "The whole damn family has t.b."

"She might die of it, sir."

"Nonsense," said Parky. "My patients don't die of the croup."

He started the car and turned it around.

"I know what you're thinking, my boy," Parky went on. "I agree that croup in the summer is pretty dog-gone rare. I agree that she may have far advanced tuberculosis of the lungs, in which case she will probably die of it."

"She should be hospitalized," said Crest.

"On whose money, may I inquire?"

"As a charity case, of course. She certainly deserves an X-ray of the chest."

"Suppose I X-ray her chest," said Parky, "at the expense of the hospital, which also means at the expense of the community. Suppose we discover she has tuberculosis. What next? We can't admit the child to our local hospital. No community hospital will accept a case of open t.b."

"The sanitarium," said Crest.

"Unfortunately, they have a six months' waiting list at the san. Do you think this girl will need sanitarium treatment by Christmas? I think she will have either stabilized her disease or be dead of it by then."

"It doesn't seem right to me," said Crest.

"Nor to me, my boy. I ought to be able to cure tuberculosis, but I can't."

"Some day soon we'll have a drug," said Crest. "In the meantime, although we cannot cure t.b., we can do plenty to control it: rest, isolation, nutrition, pneumothorax, and so forth. You can't just abandon a child with syrup of ipecac and let her die."

"The idealism and enthusiasm of a young man is a wonderful thing," said Parky, "but at my age, a man knows that he cannot reform the world. I can't get her into a public san, and there is no money for a private sanitarium. I can't hospitalize her. She does have a croupy cough and, even though it may be due to tuberculosis, it will be checked by ipecac, at least temporarily. I have eased the symptom of the child and relieved the mind of the mother. That's all I can do under the circumstances. Instead of batting out my brains about things I cannot change, I will turn my attention to the next problem of the moment."

"I should think, sir, that—"

But Parky didn't get a chance to hear what Crest was thinking. The next problem of the moment had already arrived and Parky was getting out of the car. They had stopped before a neat dairy farm in the middle of the valley. Crest followed Parky into the house.

The patient was the farmer's wife. She had a robust and

healthy body but the face of the chronic hypochondriac: a
forehead lined with wrinkles, sullen eyes, a mouth drooping
sourly at the corners. As soon as Parky walked into the room,
she launched into a lengthy dissertation.

"I've got an all-gone feeling, Doctor, and I'm wore out all
the time. It feels like ants was crawling under my skin. There's
this numbness and this tingling in my arms and legs, and
this horrid pain underneath the shoulder blade. My liver is
poorly. I got a lot of gas. The bowels ain't right. I'm sluggish
and there's this tight band around my head, and I ain't sleeping a mite, and I don't eat hardly enough for a bird, but I'm
gaining weight all the time, and I got this stinging burning
in my private parts . . ."

And so forth, with a symptom involving every bodily part.
Parky said nothing. He listened to the dissertation with a
bland expression until she ran down of her own accord. He
made no comment, no reassurance, and he offered no prognos-
tic possibilities. He wrote a prescription and promised to return next week. And yet, although he had said and done
almost nothing, the patient was smiling broadly when he left.
Crest was sure she would feel much better, at least for the
remainder of the day.

"Shall I put that one into the hospital?" said Parky to Crest
when they were out of the room. "Should I be searching for
some hidden diagnosis? Shall I X-ray her from head to toe?
Shall I do every laboratory study in the book?"

"Of course not," said Crest.

"If this patient was on Ward B of the university hospital,
they'd study her for weeks."

"They have a teaching responsibility at the university."

"They'd do better if they taught the students a little common sense," said Parky.

As they were getting into the car, the farmer stopped them
and asked if Parky would mind taking a look at one of the
cows. Crest was astonished by this request, but Parky obviously wasn't. They went into the barn, which was twice as

neat and twice as pretty as the bedroom of the farmer's wife. The cow in question was lying on her side. Parky thumped her on the belly, which produced a cavernous sound.

"Colic," Parky decided.

He opened his medical bag and, to Crest's surprise, pulled out of it a veterinary capsule, an enormous thing, several inches long. The farmer held open the mouth of the beast, and Parky stuffed the capsule down her gullet, elbow deep. The farmer thanked him and paid the fee: eighteen dollars.

"Six dollars for the wife," said Parky to Crest when they were back in the car, "and twelve dollars for the cow."

"Do you do much veterinary work?" asked Crest.

"I do what I'm asked," said Parky. "I have a pair of dental forceps in my bag, and I yank a molar now and then. I've even been known to fix a carburetor. Have you any diagnostic impressions about the cow?"

"Good heavens, no!" said Crest. "What did you give her?"

"The same thing I gave the wife: phenobarbital."

"I hope I'm not expected to treat any cows," said Crest.

"Why, hell, I even did brain surgery on a kitchen table once," said Parky. "It was in one of these farms, during a blizzard. My car was stuck in a drift way down the road. I started off on foot, but I took a nasty spill and lost my medical bag in the process. I never did find my bag till spring. They rescued me from the farm with a horse. The patient had been kicked in the head by one of the animals and he was in deep coma, a dying man. I never could have gotten him out alive. He obviously had increased pressure in his head, probably a subdural hematoma, and my only hope of saving him was to relieve that pressure. I had nothing to lose. I asked the wife for a hammer and a nail."

"You drove a nail into the patient's skull?" asked Crest, horrified by the picture.

"Certainly," said Parky. "When I pulled out the nail, there was a rush of old dark blood through the hole, and the pressure was relieved. The man was conscious by morning, and he's been alive and kicking ever since. He paid me five hundred dollars for the job. This was a patient who never paid a doctor's bill, before or since."

Crest mentally resolved that, among the things he would not do in Sentryville was abandoning a dying child, and treating a cow, and driving nails into anybody's head.

The next house call was at the edge of town. The patient here had been discharged from the hospital two months before. Parky had done radical surgery for cancer of the rectum, and the patient was left with a colostomy, an artificial opening of the large bowel through the abdominal wall. At a glance Crest could see that the colostomy opening was too small and located in an awkward place. Life with a colostomy is difficult, even a good colostomy in a well-adjusted patient. This patient was obviously nervous and depressed. However, he brightened when Parky entered the room and his depression lifted. Instead of loud complaints about the horror of having liquid feces running from the belly wall, the patient was displaying pride in his ability to live with the impossible.

"I wish he'd act like that with me," said the patient's wife when they were out of the room. "Whenever you're not around, he's whining and complaining all the time."

"Cheer him up, my dear," said Parky.

"You're the only person who can cheer him up. He thinks you're the greatest doctor in the world."

When they were back in the car, Parky said to Crest, "What do you think of that colostomy, son?"

Crest was not anxious to express an opinion.

"Go ahead," said Parky. "Tell me the damn thing is too small and too high."

"They might not approve of that colostomy at the university," said Crest.

"They are free with criticism at the university, no doubt," said Parky. "Perhaps they could have made a better colostomy. But perhaps they would have had a depressed and suicidal patient on their hands. Do you suppose your professors could have cheered him up? Which is better in your book, my boy: a patient with a poor colostomy who thinks his doctor is the greatest in the world, or one with a perfect colostomy who thinks all doctors should be hanged?"

It was Crest's opinion that a cheerful patient with a good colostomy might be the best of all.

Now they stopped at one of the old white houses on the village square. A mousy little man met them at the door, took them through an ornate Victorian foyer, up a wide carpeted flight of stairs, and into a spacious bedroom, where a portly, anxious mother took charge.

"Thank God, Parky, you have come at last."

"I came immediately, as soon as I received your call, dear lady," said Parky.

After having first seen three other patients and a cow! thought Crest.

"May I present my associate and son-in-law, John Crest, a bright young man, fresh out of the university?" said Parky.

The mother acknowledged Crest with a brief cursory nod and returned her attention to Dr. Parkindale. "Our little baby is very very sick, don't you agree?"

The "baby" was ten years old, a fat and sassy girl, propped up in a bed made up with pink silk sheets. At first glance, Crest was sure that she was an only child and spoiled. She did not appear to be sick.

"The appendix again?" asked Parky.

"Yes," said the mother. "Don't you think it should come out?"

The child was watching the scene with alert curiosity until Parky happened to glance at her, and then an expression of magnificent suffering passed across her face. She's faking! thought Crest. A spoiled brat, looking for attention. Parky sat on the edge of the bed. Gracefully, he drew down the pale-pink sheet. Gently, he pulled up the nightgown of the child.

Then, abruptly and rather roughly, he prodded her in the belly. She winced and gave a cry.

"I agree," said Parky. "This appendix must come out at once. We will take her to the hospital."

Now an expression of fear crossed the child's face, and this was perfectly genuine, thought Crest. She began to wail in protest but was ignored by Parky and the mother. The mother conducted Parky to the telephone so that he could make the necessary arrangements, while Crest waited in the hall. Somebody touched Crest on the elbow. It was the father in the case, the mousy little man.

"Doctor?"

"Yes?" said Crest.

"Does she have appendicitis?"

"Dr. Parkindale has made that diagnosis," said Crest.

"Do you agree with the diagnosis?"

"I haven't examined the child," said Crest.

"Will you examine her now?"

Crest hesitated.

"What's the matter?" asked the father. "Aren't you licensed in this state? Or do you have to ask his permission first?"

Crest thought Parky might resent an examination done behind his back. However, if he was going to work for the old man, an atmosphere of mutual trust must exist between them. This was as good a time as any to test their relationship. Crest went into the sickroom and sat on the edge of the bed. He could tell that the child was debating whether to put on her show of suffering for him or not. Lightly he touched her abdomen. She decided to cry. The belly wall was hard, but Crest thought it likely that she had voluntarily contracted the abdominal muscles.

"Look, what's that?" said Crest, suddenly pointing out the window.

"I don't see nothing," said the child, following his finger.

In the moment of distraction, Crest had pressed his other hand deep into the child's abdomen, and she had not been aware of it. Now her belly was soft, and she had forgotten to wince.

"What did she have for breakfast?" Crest asked the father.

"Juice, toast, oat meal, eggs, and milk," said the father.

"Did she eat it well?"

"Of course. She always cleans her plate."

Crest walked out of the room, with the father following.

"Well, Doctor, what do you think?"

"I'll discuss the case with Dr. Parkindale," said Crest.

"And do whatever he says, I'm sure," said the father. "You damn doctors always stick together!"

Crest was taken aback by this remark. "You don't trust the Doctor's judgment, sir?"

"Nope. Never did," said the father. "I think my child is spoiled, and I think she's faking. I think her appendix is as normal as yours and mine. But, God damn Parky, I'll bet he takes it out just the same!"

"If you don't trust him, why did you call him into the case?" asked Crest.

"I didn't," said the father. "Momma did. Momma calls the turn in my house, just as Parky's going to call the turn in yours."

Parky was returning from the telephone now, and he motioned for Crest to join him in the car.

"I see you examined the patient behind my back."

"At the father's request," said Crest. "Should I have refused?"

"You should have consulted with me first."

"I'm ready to consult with you now."

"Hum," said Parky. "And I can tell by your voice that you differ with me, as usual."

"The father thinks the kid is spoiled and faking. He thinks her appendix is as normal as mine."

"And the father is licensed to practice medicine and surgery in this state?"

"No, sir," said Crest. "But I am."

"And you agree with him, I suppose?"

"The child ate an enormous breakfast, sir."

"Obviously," said Parky. "She eats like a horse, just like her mother does."

"I was taught that acute appendix is accompanied by total loss of appetite. I never saw a case without this symptom."

"Chronic appendix, maybe," said Parky.

"I was also taught that chronic appendicitis does not exist."

"I don't give a damn what you were taught," said Parky. "Will you concede that the child has an appendix in her fat little belly?"

"Surely."

"Will you also agree that within an hour, there will no longer be an appendix in that belly?"

"I understand you plan to take it out," said Crest. "May I ask you: why?"

"To relieve the mind of a mother and to cure a child," said Parky. "I have been called to see the patient five times in the last six weeks, and the complaint is always the same: belly pain. The mother is convinced that her child has appendicitis."

"And the mother has a license, I suppose?"

"If I don't take the appendix out today, I'll have to take it out tomorrow," said Parky. "If I refuse to take it out, the mother will change surgeons, and somebody else will take it out. I might as well do the job, here and now."

"This is the justification for removing a normal organ?"

"I need no justification unless my treatment should fail," said Parky. "I'll grant you the brat is spoiled. Maybe she is faking. I intend to call her bluff."

"That's a little radical," said Crest. "Wouldn't a good spanking do the trick?"

"I'm afraid that we can't spank our patients, Crest, although it might be helpful if we could."

"What will you do the next time she complains of belly pain?" asked Crest. "Take out a normal spleen?"

"There won't be a next time, my young and learned friend," said Parky. "This brat won't be complaining of pain in her belly again."

"I'll bet you a Coca Cola you find a normal appendix, sir."

"I'll bet you two Cokes we cure this child, my boy."

They arrived at the hospital. Parky conducted Crest to the locker room, found a vacant locker for him and a scrub suit. Crest changed his clothes, and he assisted Dr. Parkindale at appendectomy. Parky was easy to work with in the operating room: not irascible, not arrogant, always relaxed and confident. Parky was quick and clever with his fingers; in fact, Crest had never worked with a more skillful surgeon, even at the university. The operation was over in less than half an hour, even though it was technically difficult. The appendix did not appear inflamed; there was no evidence of acute appendicitis; however, the appendix was buried underneath the caecum, difficult to reach, in the so-called retroperitoneal position.

"Well, son?" said Parky as the patient was being wheeled out of the operating room.

"I owe you three bottles of Coca Cola, sir," said Crest.

"You see, my boy?" said Parky. "They don't know everything at the university!"

This was the damnedest thing, thought Crest. Parky had proceeded to operate without justification, but operation had revealed an excellent justification which would not have been questioned at the university. Parky did not know the position of the appendix prior to surgery; you can't determine the position of the organ pre-operatively, even by X-ray in most cases. But a retroperitoneal appendix should be removed, even if it is not inflamed; any future infection of the organ in such a position produces a very serious situation.

How did he know? Blind luck? How did he guess? Unearthly clinical intuition?

"But suppose the child had suffered a reaction to anaesthe-

sia and died on the table," said Crest. "How could you justify
that, sir?"

"Ah!" said Parky, "but here's the point, my boy: she didn't!
Get the picture?"

The picture of medical life in Sentryville was not entirely
delightful, as far as Crest was concerned.

"Next we are booked for a hysterectomy," said Parky. "Are
you willing to assist me?"

"Of course," said Crest.

"Shall we review the history? Do you wish to point out
the reasons why I should not remove this lady's uterus?"

"Sir, I do not intend to spend my time criticizing your
judgment in every case," said Crest.

"The patient has bleeding fibroids of the uterus. Is this accepted as a surgical indication at the university?"

"I am not a surgeon," said Crest, "and I do not represent
the viewpoint of the university. I am entitled to my own
opinions, I trust. I do expect to voice my opinions and to de-
fend them upon occasion."

"You are entitled to your opinions, and I to mine," said
Parky, "but we will not criticize each other. There is too much
criticism in the profession, my boy. The walls have ears, and
these things manage to get back to the patient. If the patient
loses faith in her own doctor, she begins to lose faith in all
doctors and in the profession as a whole. There is only one
court of judgment for any physician: the jury of his patients.
If the patients like him, believe in him, trust him, and return
to him, this is a good doctor. The physician without a practice,
my boy, is the physician who has failed, no matter what his
training, his credentials, or his reputation at the university."

This was a position which Crest could not honestly oppose.
If it were true that the merit of a physician lay in the volume
of his practice, Parky certainly could not be criticized, since
his practice was enormous. And yet, Crest thought, the good
physician may not necessarily be fashionable, and the fashionable physician may not necessarily be good. A devious and

knotty problem existed here. Crest was not in a position to answer it. The matter would require thought.

Crest scrubbed and helped Parky with the hysterectomy. The uterus of the patient was as big as that in a three-month pregnancy, studded with fibroid tumors; the patient was past the child-bearing age; certainly this organ deserved to be removed. And certainly Parky removed it in the minimum time and with the maximum manual dexterity.

Then came a series of minor operations in which Crest's assistance was not required: tonsils, circumcisions, and the removal of several warts and wens. Parky did the work fast and slick, as expected. There is a school of thought, found even at the university, that all tonsils, all foreskins, and all skin tumors should be removed. No criticism here!

Then there were three deliveries. Although Crest was not to be responsible for the obstetrical work, he donned mask and gown and observed from the corner of the delivery room. The first delivery was spontaneous and normal; Parky handled it with ease, and even Crest could have handled it with ease. The next two deliveries were also normal, but Parky did not permit them to be spontaneous; he applied low forceps. Crest had been taught that forceps should never be used in the routine delivery. However, even the professors who preached against the practice in the lecture halls used forceps in their own practices for convenience, in order to save time and to facilitate the work load. If you can use the forceps skillfully, there is no reason why they shouldn't be used, and Parky was skillful, of course.

Then came rounds. The hospital seemed to have about sixty beds, all full. By Crest's estimate, Parky's patients occupied some fifty-three of the beds, leaving two for Hamilton, two for Rhodes, and one each for Jones, Mordikay, and Klamp.

There were post-partum mothers and their newborn babies; there were post-operative and pre-operative surgical cases; several fractures; a number of cardiacs and diabetics;

three terminal cancer patients; a number of children with acute gastroenteritis and summer colds; and a lot of chronic medical problems.

Crest would not have criticized Parky's management of the hospital load. There were a few matters here and there with which Crest might have made argument, but nothing in the line of major error. Crest stopped looking for error. He began to study and then to admire Parky's bedside technique.

The man was quick and clever in the operating room, but surgical dexterity exists behind closed doors. The patient cannot know the skill of the surgeon's technique. Surgical dexterity has never built a practice yet, any more than surgical clumsiness has ever ruined one. Parky obviously monopolized the medical practice of Sentryville, and the obvious reason was his bedside manner.

Parky was not always gracious and not always charming, although he could be both when the occasion seemed to demand. He was sometimes brutal, sometimes brusque, sometimes profane or sardonic or pointedly silent. At times he reminded Crest of Joseph, the plastic surgeon, dealing with a temperamental movie star. At other times he reminded Crest of the dean, parading down the ward with his dukes and his earls and his jesters of the court. Most of the time, Parky seemed to assume the role most natural to him: that of the rough-cut country sage, with a homespun crackerbarrel common sense, salted with an earthy humor.

Parky saw some fifty patients in three hours. On doing mental arithmetic, Crest realized to his surprise that the average time with each patient was three and a half minutes. It seemed much longer than that. There was no sense of urgency or pressure. Parky seemed to have plenty of time for all.

This was a trick, Crest realized. In three and a half minutes, Parky could not explore any problem in depth. A diagnostician or a master therapist would require at least fifteen minutes and often an hour or two with any of his patients. Parky was only skimming the surface, but he certainly was getting away with it.

The patients loved him, this was obvious. They brightened up the moment he stepped into the room, and he left them in a glow: even the depressed ones, even those in pain, even the hostile, the hysterical, the paranoid, the psychotic, and the scatterbrained.

Crest found himself wondering, "How does he do it? How does he get away with it? Why do they love him so? How does Parky give these people more in three minutes than most of us could give them in three consecutive days?"

Parky had personal magnetism. This was part of the answer. In common with certain politicians, actors, evangelists, and confidence men, there was something in the personal presence of the man that was strongly attractive to others. There had to be some special quality, too. These men and women were sick, and sick patients are unable to respond to superficial charm. Was it faith in Parky's curative powers?

"No, not faith," Crest decided. "Many patients do not wish to be cured. They wish to be confirmed in their own feeling of sickness. They wish the doctor to reinforce the crutch of a useful disability. Most of all, they want the doctor to agree with them."

Yes, surely this was part of it. Parky told the patients what they wanted to hear. He never upset them with unpleasant truth.

"But is this honest?" Crest wondered. "Isn't the doctor obligated to cure the patient even if it hurts? Doesn't he have to tell them unpleasant truth in order to make them well, from time to time? When Parky agrees with the patient, doesn't he encourage sickness and perpetuate disability?"

Here was another devious and knotty problem for Crest to think about in Sentryville.

Crest and Parky sat down to a late cold lunch in the early afternoon at the hospital dining room.

"Did you have an instructive morning, Dr. Crest?" Parky asked.

"I certainly did," said Crest.

"It goes on like this all the time in Sentryville," said Parky, his mouth full of cold Spam. "Perhaps you'll have an even more instructive afternoon."

It went on like that in the office all afternoon. Parky saw some thirty-five or forty people, averaging three minutes per.

"What does the patient want of his physician?" Crest was asking himself.

Well, the man in pain wants pain relief, but this is comparatively simple. Morphine, codeine, and aspirin have worked just fine for generations. A sugar pill can often work as well, if given with sufficient confidence. Parky was passing out plenty of morphine, codeine, and aspirin, Crest noticed; also, plenty of sugar pills.

"But most patients aren't in pain," thought Crest. "Most of them are bothered by anxiety and fear."

For the first time, Crest was realizing that anxiety and fear are not identical. Fear is a normal reaction against a recognized dangerous enemy. Fear protects the life and health of the individual, and the good doctor encourages it. Parky did so frequently. Anxiety, on the other hand, is a low-grade tension state of apprehension against an unidentified enemy. Anxiety serves no useful purpose, and, in fact, it makes the patient sick. The good physician fights anxiety. It seemed to Crest that Parky encouraged it.

"The anxious patient will always return," thought Crest.

But, he realized, this was not entirely fair. Parky could not have built a practice on anxiety. After a certain length of time, the anxious patient begins to identify his physician with the source of his anxiety. About that time the patient will turn to another physician, or perhaps to an osteopath, a chiropractor, a Christian Scientist, or a quack.

"A sick patient regresses," Crest was thinking. "A sick man becomes something of a child. What do children crave?

Warmth, a bed, and Mother and Daddy. Parky gives them warmth from his magnetic personality. Beds are in the hospital. Nurses are substitute mothers. And Parky is the greatest Daddy of them all."

This was part of the answer, but there were other angles in the case.

"If Parky is a father figure, I may have trouble with the man," thought Crest. "I never get along with fathers very well!"

It was after five o'clock, and the waiting room was finally clear. Parky was closing the office for the day. Crest was exhausted, as if he had been wrestling with fifty or sixty problems himself.

"House calls now," said Parky, "and then evening rounds at the hospital."

"And then, dinner?" asked Crest hopefully.

"We go out to dinner tonight," said Parky. "A meeting of the medical society, you know."

It seemed to Crest that the days were rather long in Sentryville.

Ye Olde Sentryville Tavern was the largest building on the aristocratic side of the village square with the exception of the Congregational Church, and it was authentically old. Relics of the hitching post and watering trough were carefully preserved outside. The lobby was quaint, the lounge antique, and the upstairs bedrooms picturesquely uncomfortable. The only travelers accommodated here were the occasional unwary tourist and the wary couple with dubious intent. Commercial travelers preferred the brick hotel across from the railway station. The tavern now specialized in food and drink; it was the best and most expensive eating and drinking establishment in town. The main dining room had once been the kitchen, a big low room with the original timber beams; a charcoal grille flamed merrily in the old brick fireplace; grilled steak and lobster were the specialties of the house. The cellar

underneath, once used for cold storage, had been converted
into a damp and dismal room, reserved for meetings of private
groups, such as the Elks, the Rotary, the Junior Chamber of
Commerce, and the Medical Society. What had once been the
dining room was now the cocktail lounge and bar, quite large,
quite dark. The whisky was apt to be watered, the Martinis
warm and tame, the prices a little stiff.

Crest was seated at a large table in the cocktail lounge with
the other members of the medical group. After a social hour,
they would adjourn to the dampness of the cellar for dinner,
followed by the meeting. There were some eighteen men and
half a dozen wives in the crowd. Parky had introduced Crest
on their arrival. Names had been flung at him quickly and
many of them he didn't catch. He concentrated on identifying
the other men in Sentryville, ignoring the group from out of
town. Now Parky was seated at one end of the table and Crest
at the other between two of the men whose names he had not
caught. His neighbors addressed a few banalities to Crest, and
he replied in kind, and then they ignored him, talking to each
other around him and over his head. Crest didn't mind. He
was exhausted from his long first day with Dr. Parkindale, and
he preferred to listen rather than participate.

Crest ordered a Martini, downed it quickly, and then ordered a second to be sipped. As alcohol began buzzing into
his head, he was able to relax and study the scene with more
interest.

He concentrated first on the wives who were chattering in
an animated fashion, chiefly to each other. The subjects concerned children, the weather, clothes, local politics, and gossip. He decided that these six women probably attended
meetings with their husbands regularly, but that most of the
local physicians were rarely seen in public with their wives.
A doctor's wife has either a close association with her husband's professional activities or else none at all. The associated group, those in attendance here, probably had been
nurses; they probably helped in their husbands' offices; per-

haps one or two of them had a medical degree. They were smart women, chic and sophisticated, well fed and well dressed, but none of them was beautiful. None of them was really pretty, and some might be considered plain. Few doctors marry a beautiful, vibrant, or fascinating woman, Crest decided. They choose a smart, ambitious wife or else the quiet, homebody type. There's a sound psychological reason for this. Doctors see too much of the female undraped, nervous, and uninhibited in the office suite every day to be fascinated by the superficial glitter of femininity. Instead they need a woman who will help and push them in their professional work or a wife who will run a quiet, steady home. Since Crest himself had selected a beautiful, vibrant woman, in his own opinion at least, there must have been some other reason for him to have chosen her. Probably because she was a Parkindale. He decided not to pursue this thought any further. He stopped looking at the wives and began to study the doctors instead.

The members of the society came not only from Sentryville but from other towns and villages along the valley. In Sentryville, aside from Parky and himself, there were five other men in town, and four of them were present here tonight. Dr. Jones, eye-ear-nose-and-throat: that was he, several seats down on the other side of the table, small, fat, and almost completely bald. Jones was telling vaguely bawdy stories to one of the wives, who was pretending to be more amused than she really was. Dr. Jones was laughing heartily at his own stories. Crest thought that Jones would entertain some of his patients and offend others. No doubt the man could snatch tonsils and fit spectacles with the best of them, but Crest would not have felt inclined to trust him with anything more complex, such as glaucoma or a radical mastoid.

Then there were Hamilton and Rhodes, the two general men who had gone to medical school together, who had come to town as partners, who had parted in some heat, and who now never spoke if they could avoid it. That was Hamilton, alongside Parky at the other end of the table. Rhodes was just across the way from Crest. Two very different personality types, Crest thought. They must have been contemporary in age, but they certainly didn't look it. Hamilton looked old: hair graying rapidly toward white, deeply wrinkled face, poor teeth; a nervous chain smoker; a gulper of Scotch and soda, who really did not care for alcohol. Hamilton was a chronic worrier, Crest decided: a perfectionist without a skill, who worried and badgered his patients, just as he permitted his patients to worry and badger him. Rhodes, on the other hand, looked young, so young as to give the impression of insecurity and inexperience. He was a neatly dressed man, with delicate and almost feminine manners, who did not smoke, who was bothered by the smoke and noise in the room, and who had a glass of sherry in front of him only because he was sitting in a cocktail lounge. He would be kind to his patients, Crest thought: gentle and almost tender, afraid to hurt them. Certain of the old ladies would love him; children would take outrageous advantage of him; most adults would like him, but find it difficult to take him seriously.

He could work with either Hamilton or Rhodes, Crest decided; he would trust Dr. Hamilton and like Dr. Rhodes, but he would not choose either man as companion on any desert island.

Dr. Klamp, the semi-retired gentleman, looked strangely out of place in this gathering, an anachronism from a previous generation. He was a silver-headed dandy who wore spats and a carnation in his buttonhole and carried a cane. Dr. Klamp owned majority stock in one of the local banks and also in the textile factory. Crest was sure that Klamp read the *Wall Street Journal* far more faithfully than the *Journal of the American Medical Association*. Medicine was no longer his profession, but his hobby, with which he dallied now and then when he had nothing better to do.

This was the local group, plus Crest and Parky and the town drunk, Mordikay. Crest was sure that Dr. Mordikay was not among those present. Crest had not caught the name during the introductions, and he felt sure he would have recognized the man at sight.

After an hour of social drinking, when most of the group was mellow and one or two of them rather high, they trooped down to the cellar for their dinner. There was a limp shrimp cocktail, a rather dull and heavy slab of beef, cold potatoes, stringy beans, and a tough old apple pie for dessert. The tavern was noted for the excellence of its grille upstairs, but the quality of the food was not extended to the group meetings in the cellar. At dinner, Crest was wedged between a general man from up the river and a surgeon from the other corner of the valley. The generalist was talking about modern art and the surgeon about duck shooting. Crest listened to both and nodded politely now and then.

After dinner came a short business meeting and then an outside speaker, a specialist who discussed in great detail a rare neurological disease which had been seen in the county only once within the memory of those present. He illustrated his remarks extensively with slides. Crest was two-thirds asleep after the lights had gone out. The effects of a long hard day, some devious problems which had arisen in connection with Parky, three Martinis on an empty stomach, too much heavy beef and apple pie plus duck shooting and modern art were more than Crest could comfortably digest.

There was only one incident during the lecture that interested Crest. Midway during the slides, when the lights were lowered, somebody bumbled into the room and chose the wrong door. The screen for the slides was in front of it, and the newcomer knocked it down. He muttered apologies and tried to pick it up and somebody had to help him. The speaker paused in irritation during the interruption, and a small titter spread around the room. Crest could not see the newcomer clearly in the subdued light, but he felt sure that this was Dr. Mordikay.

When the slides were over and the lights turned on again,

Crest searched for Dr. Mordikay. The man was seated way
down at the end of the room, all by himself, at an angle where
it would have been impossible for him to see the screen. There
was a highball on the table in front of him. When the light
came on, he was looking downward at his hands. He brought
his face upward toward the group and there was sardonic defiance on it. The man was half shaven, his suit rumpled, his
linen dirty, his hair unkempt. His face had once been lean
and tough, like a hawk, but now there was puffiness of the
eyelids and a burst of spider-web veins across the bridge of
the nose. Yes, no doubt this was Dr. Mordikay.

The group broke up in a hurry, in gratified relief, as soon
as the visiting dignitary released them. Crest was tired. He
wanted to get home to bed. But he was also a little dry and a
little nervous, and he thought he might sleep better if he had
a bottle of beer. He headed in the direction of the cocktail
lounge. None of the others turned in that direction except
one: Dr. Mordikay. Mordikay shambled over and touched
Crest on the elbow.

"Buy you a drink," he said.

Crest hesitated. He wanted a quiet bottle of beer alone. And
he was not sure that he should be seen drinking with Dr.
Mordikay in a public place on this, his first night in town.

"What's the matter, Doc?" said Mordikay, with a sardonic
twist at the corners of his mouth. "Afraid of your reputation,
to be seen in the company of the well-known notorious town
drunkard?"

Crest made a sudden decision. "Sure," he said. "I'll let you
buy me a drink if you'll let me buy us the second round. After
that, however, I'll have to be going home."

Mordikay smiled at him. It was a curiously warm and almost youthful smile which came quickly and fled quickly, as
if controlled by a switch. Suddenly Crest knew that he could
like this man.

They entered the cocktail lounge and sat down in a far dark
corner at a table for two. Mordikay held up a pair of fingers.

The waitress served them instantly, bringing two whiskies. Crest had wanted beer, but he accepted the drink. Crest had noticed, earlier in the evening, that service in this place was slow; at the moment, several other customers were hollering for service and were being ignored. It was obvious that Mordikay was a favorite and well-known customer here. The waitress treated him with a prompt and cheerful courtesy which combined affectionate warmth with maternal solicitude.

"I'm Mordikay, in case you hadn't guessed."

"John Crest."

"Yes, I know. The new dummy on the knee of the master ventriloquist." Dr. Mordikay grimaced, took a healthy slug of his whisky, sighed, set down his glass, and lit a cigarette. "I didn't mean to offend you," he said.

"No offense," said Crest.

"Look, I'll tell you a secret, just between you and me. I'm not really a drunkard. I drink only in public and only at such times when I'm tapering off from the other stuff. Morphine is my weakness, actually. The yearly strife between myself and the narcotics division of the Treasury Department, when it comes time for me to renew my narcotics license, is a thing to behold. Most men do battle with the income tax. I prefer to keep a second drawer on narcotics. The Treasury boys find it difficult to understand how I manage to dispense and prescribe more morphine than Dr. Parkindale. I have spent several pleasant visits down in Lexington, Kentucky."

Crest knew that Lexington, Kentucky, was the location of the U. S. Public Health Service Hospital, reserved for treatment of the narcotic addict.

"I don't know why I'm telling you this," said Mordikay. "The Treasury knows, but my professional colleagues in Sentryville don't. They prefer to peg me as a drunk. I prefer it that way. Drunkenness is more socially acceptable."

Mordikay polished off the remainder of his glass and beckoned the waitress for another. Crest held the palm of his hand

over his own glass to indicate that he wasn't ready. Mordikay
took a slug of his fresh drink.

"This stuff does nothing for me, absolutely. I wouldn't touch
it except for my reputation, which is very valuable to me,"
said Mordikay. "I'll take a needle every time. How do you
enjoy working for Dr. Parkindale?"

"This is my first day."

"A long day?"

"Yes," said Crest.

"You can always quit, you know."

"Probably I couldn't," said Crest. "I seem to be stubborn,
and I imagine that I'll stick it out. I remember my first day
in medical school. There was a balcony overlooking a high
stone wall, and the legend said that a student had to flick a
cigarette butt over that wall if he hoped to pass the course.
I wouldn't wait for more experience. I had to clear the wall
the very first morning."

"Medicine does take stubbornness," said Mordikay. "Your
employer, for example: he's as stubborn as an ox."

"So are you," said Crest. "Dr. Mordikay, if you dislike
medicine so much, why don't you find another line of work?"

"I don't need the work. I inherited a lot of money."

"Doesn't your reputation bother you?"

"As a drunkard? No, I foster that. It covers so many little
sins."

"I meant your reputation as a physician."

"You probably won't believe this," said Mordikay. "My reputation as a physician in this town has always been rather
good. It is generally recognized that if you can get Dr. Mordikay, he's the sharpest doc in town. Of course, you can't get
him very much. If I stayed sober and available, I'd put on
quite a competitive battle with old Parky, nip and tuck, which
is more than can be said for Hamilton and Rhodes, sober and
available though they be. Even so, unavailable and tipsy
though I be, there are several hundred people in this town
who wouldn't go to anyone but me. You ask me why I stick

in the profession? That's it. I don't like my patients very well, but I couldn't bear the thought of having the poor souls subjected to the mercies of Dr. Parkindale."

"What's wrong with Parky?" asked Crest.

"You've been with him one full day? And you don't know what's wrong with Dr. Parkindale? What's the matter, boy, are you blind? Don't you notice little things?"

"As a matter of fact," said Crest, "I noticed a number of little things today."

"Well, let's not discuss it in a public place," said Mordikay. "This is an ethical profession. And, besides, this man is your boss and your daddy-in-law. It wouldn't be quite nice."

"All right. What's good with Parky, then?" said Crest. "There must be something good about the man. The people come to him in droves. Why? How does he get away with it? What does he give these people that you and I can't give?"

"Ah," said Mordikay, and he polished off his glass. "You have a problem there. This has bothered me for years. This man Parkindale must be a wonderful physician, but I'll be damned if I can tell you why. And I'm not so stupid as you might suppose. I graduated first in my class in medical school. Parky didn't, by the way."

"His son was in class with me," said Crest, "and Sam says that Parky would have flunked out of medical school if he didn't belong to the dynasty."

Mordikay waved for another drink, and Crest joined him this time, paying for both drinks.

"In case you want to worry about me," said Mordikay, "don't, because I like it this way."

"Are you married?"

"Twice. One dead and one divorced. My only daughter is grown up and married, and I'm a grandfather, yet. I am all alone in this cruel world. I like it this way," he said, drinking thirstily. "You have a beautiful wife, Dr. Crest."

"Thank you."

"You have a beautiful problem. I prefer my own."

"And I'll take mine, thanks," said Crest.

"In me, you see a nightingale with broken wings," said Mordikay. "I'm not sure that men should apply wings to their backs with wax when they have to fly too close to the sun. My trouble is this: if I could think of the patient as a problem in diagnosis or an object on which to perform some surgical technique, there's no better doctor in the town of Sentryville than Mordikay. But their humanity keeps cropping up at me, damn it! They keep telling me they're people, not patients at all. Why can't they keep their humanity out of my sight?"

"In school, we were dissecting the eye, I remember," said Crest. "Suddenly the man inside seemed to take a look at me. I stepped back and dropped my scalpel on the floor."

Mordikay laughed. "In Sentryville, you pick up the scalpel, spit on it, and start dissecting again. Another drink, my boy? For a physician, you seem remarkably like a human being to me."

"No," said Crest. "I've got to get home. Tomorrow I must get up early and start doing it all over again."

"So do I," said Mordikay. "So do we all. That's why I need another drink before I go to bed."

Crest got up. Mordikay walked to the door with him.

"Thank you, I enjoyed it," said Mordikay. "I hope I haven't ruined your reputation."

"I'm not as proud of my reputation as you are of yours," said Crest. "We'll do it again some night."

"But not regularly?"

"No, not regularly," said Crest.

"If I ever get around to writing my autobiography," said Mordikay, "I'm going to call it *Dr. Death*. Good night."

Mordikay walked back to the table, and the last Crest could see, he was calling for another drink.

Crest slept later the following morning. He awakened slowly to discover Emerald sitting and smoking by the window, looking out over the valley. She was wearing a light negligee over her nightgown, although it was going to be another hot day.

"Stranger, howdy do," she said.

"Good morning, wife," said Crest.

"Where you been hiding, kid?" she said. "Didn't see you yesterday. Woke up in an empty bed. Didn't see you for breakfast, lunch, or dinner, and I went back into an empty bed again last night. Have you left me for some other dame already, chum?"

"Blame your father for that," said Crest.

"So you love Daddy more than you love me."

"I wouldn't quite say that. Your father leads a rather hectic pace, in case you didn't know. There's none of this every other night and every other weekend stuff in Sentryville. Medicine is a full-time job. Toss me one of your cigarettes, kiddo."

She threw the pack at him, without much accuracy; he had to lean far out of bed to grab it.

"Do you want to leave?" she said.

"I beg your pardon?"

"You're not yet committed to Sentryville," she said. "We could leave today. Tomorrow might be too late."

"Why leave? I just arrived," said Crest.

"John Crest: is this what you really want to do?"

"Sure. Why not?"

"Well, if you're staying, I am staying too," she said. "And I better seize you now, while I have you in my power, before my daddy gets hold of you again!"

She walked over to the bed, snubbed out her cigarette, removed her negligee and then her nightgown, and climbed into bed beside him.

"Did I ever tell you that you're beautiful?" said Crest.

"Not recently. I haven't even seen you recently. When do you have to go to work?"

"I choose my own working hours, and your father handles the overload," he said. "Say, that's a pretty good arrangement for the junior partner of the team, now, isn't it?"

She took his head in her hands and cradled it against her breast. "Don't choose to go to work quite yet," she said. "Brrr."

"I know. I need a shave."

"I wasn't thinking of that," she said. "I was thinking of the future. I shivered because somebody was walking over the grave of our marriage."

"Did I ever tell you—"

"Yes. The line of the breast from clavicle to nipple is Nature's most beautiful curve. You said that several days ago. You also said something about the interplay of gluteal muscles that I didn't quite understand. Probably you meant it as a compliment, although it sounds dirty to me. I'm not exactly sure where the gluteal muscle is."

"Right there," said Crest.

"I thought so," she replied.

"Emerald," he said, "I love you."

"Right between the clavicle and the gluteus," she said.

"No, all of you," said Crest, "but most especially the real Emerald who's hiding somewhere underneath."

"You mean it, John Crest?" she said. "Because if you don't, I'm going to scratch out your eyes."

"I would even love you blind."

"That's good," she said. "I'm never going to let you get away. Not to your profession! Not even to that greedy father of mine! Let's get out of town, before it's too late, my love!"

"Let's stay here and make the best of it," said Crest. "We're on to a pretty good thing."

"You like my father, I presume."

"Sure."

"You like my father better than you ever liked me."

"Emerald, it's too late to be coy," he said. "The deed is did. You can't get away, and neither can I. We're signed, sealed, legal, and delivered. Hey, where are you going?"

She had gotten out of bed and slipped on her negligee.

"I'm getting cold," she said.

"Cold? This is July, and the temperature is eighty degrees already. It'll be a hundred in the shade by noon."

"I can feel cold if I want to."

"No doubt of that," said Crest.

"Let's talk," she said. "At a distance. I talk better when I'm cold."

"Shoot, but don't be too verbose. I feel better when I'm warm," he said. "And we haven't much time. Soon I'll have to go to work."

"Do you really like my father, Dr. Crest?"

"Well . . ." said Crest.

"Ah," she said. "So you really don't like my father, Dr. Crest?"

"Well, I think that—"

"Speak up, be a man," she said. "What do you really think of Foster Merritt Parkindale, M.D., resident genius and right-hand man of God?"

"Serious-type conversation?"

"Could be damn serious later on," she said. "Forget the family connections and tell me the truth, John Crest. I love my daddy, in some curious fashion, but I never did like him very well. Sam hates him, always has. If you want to hate him, that's perfectly legitimate by me."

"I only hated one person in my life," said Crest. "I learned to love him, in my curious fashion, when it was too late. I wouldn't make that same mistake again."

"You're straying, friend."

"I'd rather stray," said Crest. "I want to do a dirty little Anglo-Saxon word with you, and then I have to go to work."

"With him?"

"I'm on my own today."

"Will you ever be on your own in Sentryville?"

"Okay. You asked for it, and don't blame me if it doesn't sound quite right," said Crest. "Your father has a hell of a practice, the busiest one I've ever seen, and the patients are crazy about him. He holds Sentryville in the palm of his hand. The size of his practice speaks for itself."

"Even if he's not a very good physician?"

"In many ways he's an excellent physician," said Crest. "None better."

"But in other ways he's not?"

"According to the way I was taught," said Crest, "and according to the standards of the other members of your family, Parky may be a bad doctor, perhaps dangerously bad. I think he aligns himself on the side of the disease."

"Get out of town," she sang. "Before it's too late, my love!"

"Exactly what I am *not* going to do," said Crest. "I thought of that last night when I was drinking with Dr. Mordikay. Did you know I was drinking with Mordikay?"

"Don't stray," she said.

"Funny, but I could be convinced that Mordikay is a better doctor than your father. And yet, obviously, Dr. Mordikay is a dangerously bad physician."

"Will you reform the town of Sentryville?"

"Emerald, your father has something to teach me. They don't teach bedside manner at the university. There's a lot I can learn from him about the art of medicine. As a matter of fact, he could learn from me about the science of medicine."

"Ha!" she said.

"I concede that this may take a little time."

"How much time have you got? My father is pig-headed. We come from a stubborn and pig-headed clan."

"I agree with you," said Crest. "Now, since this discussion has reached an agreement, I hereby declare the discussion closed. Come, my love, and permit me to perform my vulgar little Anglo-Saxon word."

"Okay," she said. "So maybe you can learn to be a Parkindale. But then, I couldn't love you any more. Incest isn't legal any more."

"I know something legal. Come."

"All right," she said. "Men have no sense of intuition. You

must discover the facts of life all by your very little self."

"Speaking of the facts of life . . ."

"I'm coming, damn it. I'm ready for your vile indecencies. But I wish you had a little common sense."

"So does your father," said Crest. "Come on. It's getting late."

It was already too late. Emerald was removing her negligee when the telephone on the bedside table rang.

"Damn," said Crest.

The phone rang again.

"God damn it," said Crest.

"Your master's voice," said Emerald. "Pick it up. Answer it. Or would you prefer to get out of town, my friend?"

Crest answered it. Parky was calling from the hospital. There'd been a bad accident, and the operating room was ready, and they would begin as soon as Crest arrived. Crest hung up.

"My error," he said. "Time to go to work."

"I know," said Emerald. "Don't just lay there gawking at me, chum! Get up! Get dressed! What do you think this is, a honeymoon?"

"Give me a kiss to get me going."

"We really don't have time for that," said Emerald.

Part 4

"She's going to die," thought the mother.

In the still of the night, the shack wasn't creaking. The kids were quiet. There wasn't any noise from the hounds. Even the baby wasn't coughing any more, but she wasn't breathing right. There would be a lot of short fluttery breaths for a minute or so, and then for another minute, no breathing at all.

"I gave her Parky's medicine," thought the mother. "Just like he said, five and five, but it isn't doing any good."

The child was eating poorly. All the vomiting from Parky's medicine for croup was taking the flesh away from her. She was nothing but a skeleton covered with skin, and nothing alive except two big eyes, staring out the sockets of her skull, and even the eyes weren't lively any more.

The father, beside the mother in the bed, was asleep, stupid and heavy from liquor, like he always was. She prodded him.

"Get up," she said. "Get up and call Parky right away."

Stupid and heavy as he was, he got right up, without a complaint or protest. Even he could feel the hand of death in the house. With fifteen children, he wouldn't mind one less mouth to feed, but no man can rest in the shadow of death. There was no telephone. He had to wander half a mile down the road to the next house, taking three or four of his best hound dogs with him. It was twenty minutes before he got back.

"Parky ain't coming," he said.

"Oh, Lord! You should have paid him cash money. I've told you that a hundred million times."

"Dr. Crest is coming instead."

"Who?"

"The young feller. You know, he was out here with Parky the other day."

"Oh, Lord!" said the mother again.

Parky was the only doctor who could save the life of her child. No young doc would understand the case. If Parky wasn't coming, the child was going to die.

At this moment, the mother abandoned hope. She did not grieve, because she had seen death in the house before, and life is for the living, and there were other problems in this house, God knows. God knows best!

Crest didn't come for nearly an hour. He had been dead asleep when the telephone rang, and it took him some time to get going. His eyes were fuzzy and he had trouble seeing the road. He drove around the village square three or four times before he could remember where he was trying to go, and after that he managed to get lost in the hills.

There was only one flickering kerosene lantern in the shack. Crest could scarcely see the patient, but he could see and hear her well enough to know that she was dying. She was unconscious and breathing in the so-called Cheyne-Stokes pattern, which is often a terminal event.

"Hospital," said Crest. "At once."

He expected an objection from the father and the mother, but there was none. Country people of this type still considered the hospital to be a pest house, where patients are taken to die. The child was as good as dead in their opinion, and they were thinking of the funeral. The mother was thinking how pretty the funeral would be. The father was thinking how much it would cost.

"I won't take time to call the ambulance," said Crest, thinking out loud. "I'll take her to the hospital in my own car. Who's coming with us?"

"Nope, Doc, not me," said the father.

"I have to stay with the kids," said the mother.

Neither the father nor the mother would set foot inside a pest house until their own final time had come. Crest bundled the child in her blankets and laid her on the front seat beside him. Now he drove dangerously fast on poorly lit and unfamiliar country roads. He often took his eyes from the road to glance at the child. As far as he could tell, she was still breathing in the Cheyne-Stokes rhythm.

He stopped in front of the hospital. He was taking her into his arms to carry her in when he realized that she was dead. Crest would have broken the hospital rules and exposed others to the risk of infection if she had been alive. Now there was nothing to do but take the body to the funeral home. Afterward he would have to drive back out to the hills again in order to inform the relatives. There was no telephone.

"Don't take it so hard, my boy," said Parky to Crest the following day. "I told you that kid would never live to reach a sanitarium. We did everything we could."

In the white house on the village square, the plump and sassy girl with the appendectomy scar was in bed under the pink silk sheets. She was complaining of belly pain again.

"Where's Parky?" asked the mother.

"He's tied up in the delivery room," said Crest. "If you care to wait, he could probably call at the end of the afternoon."

"Well!" said the mother. "Imagine! I didn't expect this sort of treatment from Dr. Parkindale."

"I'll tell him to stop by," said Crest, preparing to depart.

"You might as well have a look at her, young man, as long as you are here."

Crest went into the bedroom and spent three quarters of an hour alone with the child.

"I hope you won't operate without consulting Dr. Parkindale," said the mother when Crest left the room.

"There's nothing to remove," said Crest.

"And Parky will stop by this afternoon?"

"If you wish," said Crest.

At this point, the child appeared in the hall. She was smiling. She slid adroitly down the banisters.

"Tummy ache's all gone away," she said. "I'm feeling fine. I want to go out and play."

"Go back to bed, dear," said the mother.

"She can be up," said Crest.

"We'll wait for Parky," said the mother.

"I don't want to see Parky," said the child. "I hate that horrid old Parky. I love Dr. Crest."

With which sentiment she jumped up and threw her arms around Crest's neck and gave him a big wet kiss.

"Well!" said the mother.

Crest, not knowing what else to do, blushed.

The father, the mousy little man, spoke up for the first time. "We won't bother Dr. Parkindale," he said. "May we call on you again, next time?"

"If you wish," said Crest.

Later in the day, Parky said to Crest, "I understand you made a small friend today. What was it?"

"Belly pain again," said Crest.

"Did you spank the little brat?"

"Only verbally, sir."

"You found no indication for surgery?"

"It will not be necessary to remove her spleen," said Crest.

The patient was a young adult with loss of appetite, vomiting, and belly pain. The right lower quadrant of the abdomen was tender and rigid. White blood count was elevated. Crest had seen the patient first and made a diagnosis of acute appendicitis. The case seemed typical.

Now Crest was standing, in surgical gown and gloves, prepared to assist Dr. Parkindale at appendectomy. Parky was just painting the belly with red antiseptic solution when Crest suddenly noticed something.

"Hold on, sir, just a minute," he said.

Crest reached for a stethoscope. In so doing, he was breaking sterile technique. It would now be necessary for Crest to scrub and gown all over again, and the patient would have to be redraped.

"What the hell are you doing, son?" said Parky. "This is an operating room!"

Crest had noticed that the right side of the patient's chest wasn't moving properly with respirations. Now, listening over the area with the stethoscope, he could hear diminished breath sounds and crackling fine rales.

"We must X-ray the chest, sir," said Crest.

"Ridiculous," said Parky. "The pathology is in the belly."

"I think it's in the chest," said Crest.

"If we take a picture, we'll have to postpone surgery until this afternoon, by which time the appendix will rupture, and we'll have a critical patient on our hands."

"In my opinion, sir," said Crest, "we'll have a critical patient on our hands if we operate at all."

"What do you have in mind?"

"I think he has a wedge of pneumonia over the right diaphragm," said Crest.

Parky snorted. "Pneumonia? With belly pain? I never heard of that."

"I've seen it at the university."

"Who am I to argue with the university? You're the boss," said Parky. "We'll cancel surgery. We'll take a picture of the chest. If this patient dies, my boy, you can explain to the relatives."

The only necessary explanation was that the patient had pneumonia at the base of the right lung, which was causing pain referred to the right side of the belly.

"That's a new one on me," said Parky. "Nice piece of work, my boy."

"Thank you," said Crest.

"This is why I hired you," said Parky. "We tend to get behind the times, working out here in the sticks. We need a bright young man from the university to keep us on our toes."

Parky and Crest were walking together down Main Street one morning. A shiny new Oldsmobile pulled up at the curb, and a man stepped out.

"That miserable son-of-a-bitch," said Parky. "He's owed me fifteen dollars for more than a year. If he can afford a car like that, he can surely afford to pay me. Watch this!"

Parky stepped over to the man and said, "Good morning, George!"

"Good morning, Parky."

"Nice little car you have there. New?"

"Yeah," said the man. "Just got her last week."

"I wish I could afford a car like that," said Parky.

"Oh, come now!" said the man. "That Caddy of yours is as long as a city block."

"I'll have to be trading her in one of these days. By the way, George, how's your rheumatiz?"

"Not so good, as a matter of fact," said George. "I've been intending to stop by your office for another bottle of medicine. That bottle you gave me last year did me a world of good."

"Any time, George. I charge a dollar a bottle."

"Why don't I pay you now?" said George. "Then I can pick up the medicine this afternoon."

"If you can afford it, George!"

George examined the contents of his wallet. "Put it on the cuff, Parky," he said. "I haven't anything smaller than a twenty-dollar bill."

"I can change a twenty for you, George."

Somewhat reluctantly, George handed Parky the twenty-dollar bill. Smiling blandly, Parky gave him back four dollars' change.

"Hey, what the devil . . ."

"Any time, George, any time," said Dr. Parkindale.

The patient awoke in the middle of the night. Gas pains were oppressing him, crowding heavily down over his belly and his chest, smothering his breath. He knew that he had eaten too much pork and cabbage for his dinner. He got out of bed, went to the bathroom, and passed water. He tried to pass gas, but nothing came.

"What's the matter, dear?" asked his wife from her bed.

"God damn gas," said the patient. "I can't digest cabbage any more. I'll get me some bicarb."

He went downstairs to the kitchen and found the box of bicarbonate of soda. He put a tablespoonful into a tumbler, added hot water, stirred the mixture around, and gulped it down. A wave of nausea passed over him. He shivered. Beads of cold perspiration gathered on his forehead. He belched loudly several times, but the gas pressure was not relieved. He went over to the liquor cabinet, found a bottle of brandy, poured out three fingers, and gulped it neat. Then he sat down at the kitchen table with his head in his hands. He was still sitting there when his wife came down fifteen minutes later.

"Any better, dear?"

"I don't feel so hot," he said.

He didn't look so hot. His complexion was an odd ashen shade.

"Let me call a doctor, dear," she said.

"At this time of night?"

"Harry, I think we better."

"Okay. Go ahead."

This worried her. Her husband never consented to see a

doctor without putting on a tantrum like a child. If he agreed so easily, he must be feeling pretty bad.

"I'll call Parky," she said.

"No, not Parky."

"But he's the best doctor in town."

"No, he's a quack," said Harry. "Parky would come in here with a grin and a big hello and tell me I'm a damn fool to be eating pork and cabbage with this gall bladder of mine. This I already know. He'd tell me a story which I've heard already, and give me a bottle of medicine, which is nothing but bicarb, which I've already taken. He'll tell me to drop into the office next week for a check-up and bring a urine sample. That's the way he'll get his God-damned bottle back!"

"There's a nice young man working with Parky now."

"No," said Harry. "This nice young man would put me into the hospital. Young doctors can't do a God-damned thing outside the hospital. I'll wind up paying a thousand dollars for a little gas. Call Mordikay."

"But—"

"Call Dr. Mordikay," he said.

Against her better judgment, she called Dr. Mordikay. Mordikay wasn't answering his phone.

"Skip it," said Harry. "I'm feeling a little better now. I'll just sit here for a few more minutes and then I'll come to bed. Go upstairs, honey. I'll be right along."

Having lived with this stubborn man for more than twenty years, she knew there was no point arguing with him. All right, let him sit in the kitchen with his gas! He'd want cabbage and pork again next week, and get mad if she didn't serve it to him!

She went back to bed. She lay there in the dark. Things were very quiet in the kitchen. Things were much too quiet in the kitchen. She went back downstairs again.

Harry was still sitting at the table, but he was dead. Now she was free to call Dr. Parkindale.

"If only he'd let me call you, Parky!" she wailed. "If only you could have come!"

"I'm sorry, my dear," said Parky. "You did the best you could."

"I signed him out as acute indigestion," Parky said to Crest the following day.

"I'll bet it was a coronary, sir," said Crest.

"What difference does it make, my boy?"

"People don't die of acute indigestion," said Crest.

"He's just as dead, isn't he?" said Dr. Parkindale.

Parky had seen the child earlier in the week. He called it acute strep throat and prescribed sulfa drug. He said that the child would recover in three or four days, but she hadn't recovered; as a matter of fact, she was getting worse.

Crest took one look at the child's throat and jumped. The entire pharynx was covered with an ugly, gray, sticky, foul-smelling membrane. Crest had never seen the condition, but he recognized it from his reading and the pictures in the texts. He hospitalized the child immediately, putting her into isolation. He took a throat culture. The throat culture came back positive for diphtheria.

"I haven't seen a case in years," said Parky.

"I never saw one," said Crest, "but that membrane was typical."

"Nice piece of work, my boy."

Crest wanted to ask, "How in the hell could you miss it? Have you ever seen a membrane like that in simple strep throat? How many cases of diphtheria have you missed in the last few years?"

Instead, Crest said, "This time the diagnosis is extremely important. The sulfa drugs won't touch diphtheria. On that treatment, the child would die. We may be able to save her with massive doses of antitoxin, if it isn't too late."

"Get to work, my boy," said Parky.

Crest got to work. The patient ran a very stormy course for weeks, but she made a full recovery.

Parky kept poor records in the office. Financial data were filed in complete detail, but the clinical record was kept on a small card that listed only the date of the visit and the treatment rendered. There was nothing to indicate symptoms, signs, physical findings, laboratory studies, diagnosis, or progress. Having come from a teaching center where clinical records must be encyclopedic, Crest was shocked by the paucity of the information on Parky's record cards.

"How do you remember what you're doing, sir?" asked Crest.

"I know my patients, son," said Parky.

"You remember each detail? You see a hundred people every day."

"I have a good memory," said Parky.

Crest had to concede the point. Parky had an excellent memory. He seemed to carry a complete mental dossier on each of the 7,000 citizens of Sentryville. But it was Crest's belief that good medicine means good records. Without records, the doctor is always taking a chance with malpractice, maltreatment, and human fallibility. Crest was filling up the record cards on the patients he saw.

"It's not necessary to write a book about each patient, son," said Parky.

"I can do a better job this way," said Crest.

The patient in the office with Crest that afternoon was a sprightly little old grandmotherly type. Crest hadn't seen her before. The record card stated that she had been coming in for monthly liver shots for several years. The record card did not state why.

"Another shot today?" asked Crest.

"Yes, young man."

"Why?"

"I beg your pardon?"

"Why is the doctor giving you liver shots each month?"

"That's a silly question," she said. "I need them, of course."

"Why do you need them?"

She looked at him in amazement. "Do you have a medical degree, young man?"

"Certainly," said Crest.

"Well, then, don't bother me with such foolishness. Parky's been giving me these shots for years. They've been keeping me alive."

"That's nice," said Crest.

"Don't be impertinent!"

"I didn't mean to be," said Crest. "Your diagnosis isn't entered on your record card, and I haven't consulted with Dr. Parkindale about your case."

"I'm anemic," she said.

"Pernicious anemia?" asked Crest.

"I don't know," she said. "My ill health is certainly pernicious, if that's what you mean."

"When did he last do a blood count?"

"He never did a blood count. Hurry up and give me my injection, young man. I have a dentist appointment this afternoon, and I'm late already."

"I'd like to do a blood count first," said Crest.

"Then do one," she snapped. "I haven't got all afternoon."

Crest grinned at her and did one. It was normal. There was no sign of anemia, pernicious or otherwise.

"You don't need a shot today," said Crest.

"I don't?"

"Why don't we check your blood again in another month?"

"Well, this is delightful news, young man. Those shots were getting to be a pesky nuisance. I can't sit down for two days afterward. Can you really tell that I don't need a shot just by looking at a drop of my blood?"

"That's the only way to tell," said Crest.

"Well, I never! Why didn't Parky think of that?"

"I wonder," said Crest.

At the end of the office schedule, Crest asked Parky about the case. "Why were you giving the old lady liver shots?"

"Because she needs them," said Parky. "Obviously."

"Why does she need them?"

"Why the inquisition, Dr. Crest?"

"I checked her blood this afternoon," said Crest. "Her hemoglobin is in the normal range. There is no evidence of pernicious anemia. That was your diagnosis, I presume."

"My diagnosis was that she needed liver."

"That's all?"

"Isn't that enough?"

"Never mind," said Crest. "Let it go. At least you weren't doing her any particular harm."

The patient was a male. He too had been getting monthly liver shots. His complexion was so pale that it was almost green, and he seemed to be short of breath. Crest did a blood count.

"Sir?" said Crest to Parky later on. "Why were you giving him liver shots?"

"Here we go again!" said Parky. "What have you got against liver shots, my boy? I often use them as a tonic. Liver seems to help the chronically fatigued."

"You give it without a blood count?"

"Surely," said Parky. "Blood counts are not needed in every case of chronic fatigue. You remember that old lady last week. Her blood was normal. You said so yourself."

"This man doesn't have normal blood."

"All right. What does he have? What's the latest poop from the group at the university?"

"He has acute lymphatic leukemia."

"And so?"

"Did you expect to cure leukemia with liver shots?"

"Ah," said Parky. "And what are they using at the university to cure leukemia?"

Crest had no answer for this. There was no cure for
leukemia. The patient was dead within a month.

"Don't criticize me," said Parky. "I didn't expect to cure
him. I did keep him more comfortable for a while."

"I was taught that diagnosis comes first, treatment second,"
said Crest.

"You can be a pretty fine physician and never make a diagnosis in your life," said Parky. "They don't know everything at
the university."

"My boy," said Parky. "Did you see the Miller child last
week?"

"Miller?" said Crest.

Crest lacked Parky's excellent memory for names. Crest
could remember textbook facts. He remembered faces, and
usually the diagnosis attached to the face, but the name was
another matter.

"Your diagnosis was measles," said Parky. "You gave her
sulfa drug."

"Oh, yes," said Crest.

"The mother asked me to see the child today," said Parky.
"She specifically did not want you. She had the feeling you
didn't know her child was going blind."

"Blind?"

"Yes," said Parky. "What's the matter, son? Didn't you look
at the patient's eyes?"

Eyes? Ye Gods! The eye was the organ with which Crest
had never felt at home. When an eye is injured or diseased,
holler for help! Crest thumbed rapidly through his mental
files. He remembered the case very well. The child had a good
exposure to measles and this was the end of the incubation
period for the disease. She did not have a rash when he first
examined her. She had a brassy cough, congestion of the nose
and throat, and a conjunctivitis. The conjunctiva is the membrane lining the eye, and this had been inflamed—yes, surely
he had looked at her eyes. He had also carefully looked at the

mucous membranes on the inner side of the cheek. He was looking for the so-called Koplik spots, which may often be seen in this location as the first manifestations of measles before a skin rash appears. He had found no Koplik spots. But the rest of the picture seemed typical for measles in the pre-rash stage, and Crest had made this diagnosis without reservation. He had prescribed sulfa drug. The drug does not touch the virus causing measles, but it does prevent the complications of secondary infection, which can be serious in this condition. Crest had seen the patient two days later. Now she did have a rash. He had thought his diagnosis completely confirmed.

"No, this was not measles, my boy," said Parky. "The child had a simple cold. The rash was due to drug sensitivity—caused by the sulfa drug which you gave, my boy. So is the present trouble with the eyes."

"She had conjunctivitis when I saw her, sir," said Crest. "This is part of the picture of measles."

"At the moment, her cornea is involved. I believe they'd call it keratitis at the university, my boy."

"Holy smokes!" said Crest.

"You doubt that the rash and the keratitis are due to a drug sensitivity?"

No, Crest didn't doubt it. He had a strong intuition that Parky was correct.

"If we kept on with the drug, my boy, I think the child would have gone blind," said Parky. "Don't worry. I stopped it. I believe she will recover."

Crest was flabbergasted.

"Why were you giving sulfa drug?" asked Parky. "Will it cure the measles?"

"No, sir," said Crest defensively. "I give it prophylactically, to prevent secondary pneumonia and otitis and nephritis and so forth."

"Diagnosis is your forte, my boy," said Parky. "Did you see any Koplik spots? What in the hell ever made you think that child had the measles in the first place?"

"I don't know, sir," said Crest miserably. "I guess I wasn't thinking very well. I surely messed that case up, for fair!"

"You did indeed," said Parky. "But don't let it worry you, my boy. You can't win 'em all. However, I hope you will remember this case the next time you feel inclined to criticize me."

The patient was insane. There was a long history of schizophrenia and now she was turning paranoid and violent. She had to be committed to a public institution. Parky had examined her at home and had signed the commitment papers. Now it was necessary for Crest to sign. The signatures of two physicians were required, according to the provisions of the law. Parky discussed the case with Crest, giving her long history in detail

"You agree with my diagnosis?" asked Parky.

"Yes, sir," said Crest. "There seems no doubt that she should be committed."

"Fine," said Parky. "Run on down to the town offices and sign the papers."

"I'll examine the patient first."

"Not necessary," said Parky. "I've given you the history. You just agreed with my diagnosis."

"I can't sign papers on a patient I haven't examined."

"Have it your own way," said Parky. "Examine her. You better bring along a cop for your own protection. This girl is a witch, and she can give you trouble."

"Did you take a policeman?"

"I know the girl," said Parky. "But you're strange to the ways of this town, my boy."

Crest did not bother to request a policeman. If Parky didn't need one, neither did he. There was nobody at home with the patient; her family had departed to a safer place. Crest rang the bell and walked in. The patient took one look at him and screamed. Then she quickly removed all her clothing. And then, stark naked, at high noon, she ran out the door and down the street. Crest felt obligated to run after her. He finally brought her down with a flying tackle halfway down the block. It was then that a policeman appeared and, it seemed, almost everybody else in Sentryville.

Parky was highly amused by the incident. So was Emerald. So was everybody else in Sentryville with one exception: Dr. Crest.

The patient was a delicate and modest spinster. Parky had been giving her shots of female sex hormone every week.

"Why is he giving you these shots?" asked Crest.

The patient blushed. "Female complaint," she said.

"What sort of female complaint?"

"I'm bleeding, Doctor."

"How long have you been bleeding?"

"Ever since he started giving me the shots."

"For a matter of eight or ten weeks?"

"Yes. I've had trouble before, but never as bad as this."

"You are bleeding steadily?"

"Yes, and it's getting heavier all the time. I'm worried."

"What did Dr. Parkindale find on pelvic examination?"

"He never examined me," she said. "Nobody has examined me in my entire life."

Crest was shocked. To treat vaginal bleeding without a pelvic examination was a crime for which they would have demanded capital punishment at the university.

"I insist that we examine you now," said Crest.

"I wish you would, Doctor," she said.

Crest examined her. On the cervix, there was a large, dark, oozing, cauliflower-shaped mass. Crest knew it was malignant at a glance.

"Carcinoma of the cervix, sir," Crest said to Parky later on. "You never even examined the woman. You just gave her shots."

"Can you cure carcinoma of the cervix better than you cure leukemia?" asked Parky.

"There's radium," said Crest. "You get a lot of five-year cures of cancer of the cervix if you catch it in time. In this case, I'm afraid, we may be too late. Your hormones were making that cancer grow a little faster, I believe."

"Crest," said Parky, "this woman is a spinster, a virgin, a prude. She wouldn't let God almighty touch her private parts."

"She let me," said Crest.

"So, maybe you're God almighty!"

"Sir," said Crest. "I was taught that a pelvic should be done on every female patient."

"In theory, perhaps," said Parky. "In practice, you can't. Women don't submit to pelvic examination willingly. If I examined them all, a lot of them wouldn't come back. This is no problem at the university, but I have to earn a living. Sure, maybe I miss a cancer once or twice a decade. You can't win 'em all. But at least my female patients do return to me. This is private practice, my boy, not the university. You can't forget that the customer is always right."

"We're not running a shop," said Crest. "Aren't we in business to cure the sick?"

"We're in business to serve the sick," said Parky. "You don't serve a female patient by making her ashamed to enter a doctor's office."

"You don't serve the patient by killing her, either," said Crest.

"I don't believe I've missed more than three carcinomas of the cervix in the past five years."

"That's three too many," said Crest.

"Try your radium, my boy," said Parky. "Maybe we're not too late."

Crest referred the patient to the city, where radium was tried. She died in great pain within a few weeks.

Crest had now been working for Parky for several months, and he decided to take an evening off. He asked for, and received, Parky's permission.

"That's wonderful, darling, you need a break," said Emerald. "Your skin looks like a cup of bad coffee with cream. You smoke too much and you're losing weight, and your hands shake. You don't get to bed on time. And when you get to bed—"

"I know," said Crest.

He thought she might accuse him of being an inadequate husband, and this was true enough.

"Let's go out to dinner, dear," she said.

"Emerald . . ."

"Yes, dear?"

"I'd like to go out to dinner by myself," said Crest. "I have some thinking to do. I need a couple of hours alone. Would you mind?"

He could tell that she would mind. Like any wife, she had a legitimate complaint: her husband never took her anywhere. She hated to admit that her husband needed to be alone. She could have forced him to take her. However, she was smart enough to know that this would only spoil the evening for them both.

"Run along, dear," she said. "Have fun."

"I'll be home early," said Crest.

He kissed her good-by and got into his car. It was four o'clock on an afternoon in late autumn. The leaves, having already turned crimson and scarlet and yellow, had fallen, leaving only a few sere stragglers on the boughs. The sun was low on the horizon. Crest took the highway out of town, across the valley to the hills, and he drove to a lookout point on top. There he parked and watched the dusk creeping over the valley. He could see the sweep of the river, the automobile headlights creeping along the highways, the early twinkling lights of Sentryville. He thought of the 7,000 citizens below, for whom he was now partly responsible. Some of them might have babies tonight, and some of them might try to create babies for delivery next summer. There might be an accident on the highway. A man might wake up with pain in the chest or the belly. A woman might begin to bleed. A child might awake with a fever. Some husbands would yell at their wives, and some wives would retire early to bed with a headache or cramps. Some of them, men and women, might address themselves to a bottle or a book. Some would meditate and some would pray. A number of the men would go bowling. A number of the women would attend the monthly meeting of the literary club.

Philosophical generalities are cheap, Crest was thinking, especially when you are alone on a mountain top at dusk, but it seems fair enough to state that all those people below were seeking the same few fundamental things: excitement, satisfaction, consolation, security, and hope for tomorrow. It was their constitutional right as American citizens to engage in the pursuit of happiness. There was, however, no constitutional guarantee that they would ever catch it. Each, in his own fashion, was fighting the battle against the twin enemies of anxiety and fear. Each, at some time or other, must lose. Whenever they were losing, they would cry for help. Often they would pick up the telephone and call for a doctor. Most of the time the doctor would come.

Up here, the problems seemed comfortably remote and impersonal. Down in the valley, the fighting was hand to hand. You can't think well when you're covered with the blood and dust. On the other hand, comfortable generalities don't really do much good.

Crest turned the ignition key and started his car. He drove back to town. It was quite dark when he reached Ye Olde Sentryville Tavern. A crisp frosty hint in the air suggested that there would be snow in two or three more weeks.

Crest entered the cocktail lounge and ordered a Martini. It was tame and warm. He downed it rapidly. Then he ordered another to be sipped. He finished the drink and went into the dining room, where he had reserved a table for one. The room was full of people, chattering to each other, a low merry buzz. Flames crackled from the charcoal grille. There was a delicious smell of sizzling steak and lobster. Crest ate slowly, heartily, and with vast enjoyment. As he finished his dinner, he was feeling physically better and more relaxed than he had felt for weeks. He thought he might enjoy one bottle of beer before he returned to his wife, and he went into the cocktail lounge for this purpose. The minute he entered the room, he changed his mind and started to leave, but he was too late. Dr. Mordikay had spotted him and was waving at a table from the far corner of the room. Crest walked over and sat down with him. Mordikay held up a pair of fingers. The waitress instantly produced two whiskies.

"Trying my patented method of relaxation, Dr. Crest?" said Mordikay.

Crest grinned at him. "Not regularly," he said. "This is my first evening off since I came to Sentryville."

"Then I should think you needed that drink."

"Maybe I do," said Crest, taking a pull at the whisky and water.

"We were discussing a problem the last time we drank together in this joint," said Mordikay. "Have you solved it yet?"

"I've been studying it," said Crest.

"Any conclusions?"

"Two things seem obvious," said Crest. "In some ways, Parky is the best doctor I have ever met. Using the yardstick of his practice, he is certainly a great success. The patients return to him by droves and they love him. On the other hand, using the yardsticks of the medical standards I have been taught, he's a bad doctor, dangerously bad, perhaps a menace to this community. His rate of error is alarmingly high. Some of his mistakes are bad ones."

"Two sides to the coin," said Mordikay. "You have heads. Tails for me."

"He has a gift with the neurotic patient in particular. They love him. But they love him because he tells them what they want to hear. He doesn't bother them with unpleasant truth.

I believe he keeps them sick. He doesn't cure them, and they keep on coming back."

"Have you ever cured a neurotic patient, Crest?"

"I like to try," said Crest.

"Sometimes the patient cures himself while he's seeing the doctor, and of course the doctor must take credit for the miracle, but I believe this cure is a coincidence. You have a great desire to cure the sick?"

"Isn't that the object of our profession?"

"Does it say so in the Oath of Hippocrates?"

"It was hot in the auditorium, and I wasn't listening," said Crest. "If it doesn't say something like that, I must be in the wrong profession."

"I believe that the patient is the means of his own cure, just as the patient selects his own disease."

"You think the patient makes himself sick?"

"I know he does," said Mordikay. "Disease represents a break in the patient's line of defense. Every patient has a certain number of troops to man the line, and he can shift them around to a certain extent. Strengthening the line at one point causes weakness at another. A man's life pattern determines his disease."

"Even when he breaks his leg?"

"Sure," said Mordikay. "A true accident is rare. Most accidents are accidentally on purpose."

"Even if you're struck by lightning?"

"Would you or I be caught underneath a tree during a thunderstorm?" said Mordikay. "Of course not. We're not the lightning-struck type. You and I would be out in the middle of the field where it is wet but safe. I strike myself with a needle. You decided to marry into an impossible situation."

"What do you mean?"

"I suspect you have always resented authority, Crest. Perhaps you resented the authority of your father when you were a child. You chose medicine, where the aristocrats of the dynasty exert a powerful authority. You chose to work for the

most authoritative physician you could find. It wasn't enough
to put yourself in jail. You had to marry into the family. You
locked the door on yourself and threw away the key."

"All right," said Crest. "Now you tell me why you destroy
yourself with the needle and the glass."

"Because I am a disillusioned idealist. I tried to fly too close
to the sun, but my wax wasn't strong enough, so my wings
fell off. Like most patients, you and I have chosen our disease.
Like any sick patient, we could cure ourselves if we ever decided it was worth our while."

"Cure is just a matter of desire? As simple as that?"

"Change of a life pattern is never simple," said Mordikay.
"The recovered patient has changed himself by subjecting
himself to radical surgery of the personality. To stay alive,
you must keep changing all the time. When a man gets tired
of moving his internal furniture, his disease has set and he
will not recover. Do you know any old people, Crest? Have
you followed any geriatric case throughout the years? Old
people are full of dangerous organic disease. Each of them
has a dozen conditions which should have finished them off
years ago. People don't survive because they're strong and
tough. They survive because they're pliant and shifty. The oak
tree goes down in the first heavy wind. The river reed
survives."

"You don't leave much room for the doctor in your theory of
disease," said Crest. "We have been known to cure people
with our medicines and surgery."

"If the patient wants to be cured," said Mordikay. "Otherwise not."

"You're cynical."

"The doctor must be something of a hypocrite," said Mordikay. "He must think of himself as a demigod, capable of
working miracles. If he lacks faith in himself, the patient will
have no faith in him."

"On such a basis, Parky is an excellent physician."

"I give you a toast," said Mordikay. "To your daddy-in-law,

the best damn doctor in this state whenever the patient is curing himself."

"To Parky," said Crest, raising his glass. "The worst doctor in this state when the patient doesn't want to be cured."

"Keep your voice down," said Mordikay. "This is a public place."

"I'm not afraid of unpleasant truth," said Crest.

"That's whisky talking. Of course you are! We're all afraid of the truth."

"Well," said Crest, "if I didn't think a doctor should fight disease and death by facing unpleasant truth, I would change my profession."

"It might be better to change your location."

"And run away?"

"He who writes and runs away, will live to write another day."

"But he won't be writing the truth," said Crest.

"Facing the unpleasant truth is part of the process of maturity," said Mordikay. "The process is painful, too painful for me. Are you strong enough to grow up?"

"Yes," said Crest. "I believe I am. I'm going to try."

"Blessings on you, little man, with barefoot toes and cheeks of tan," said Mordikay. "Let's have another little drink."

It was rather late when Crest got home that night.

"I was drinking with Mordikay," Crest told his wife with a touch of belligerence.

"And so?" said Emerald. "Did anybody tell you that you couldn't?"

Not getting the argument for which he had been prepared, Crest felt suddenly tired. He sat down in a chair.

"Mordikay's a funny guy," he said. "Twisted and cynical. He sees everything upside down. I wonder what defeated him?"

"My daddy, of course," said Emerald. "Who defeats every doctor in the town of Sentryville?"

"Including me?"

"Yes, including you, my love."

She came over to him and kissed him on the tip of the nose with tender affection. Affectionate tenderness was not a usual component of Emerald's personality.

"Mordikay said some funny things," said Crest. "For instance, that I resent authority because I resented my father as a child. I became a doctor in order to combat authority, and it is my nature to fight with the other members of my profession. I chose the strongest enemy I could find, and that's why I came to Sentryville. It wasn't enough for me to work with Parky. I had to marry into the family. Do you agree with that?"

"I always thought you married me because my name was Parkindale, and not because my name was Emerald," she said.

"How could you accept me under those conditions?"

"For the same reason all women marry," she said. "In order to reform their men."

"Will you succeed?"

"Partly," she said. "We always do. Also, we partly fail."

"Well, that sounds like a rather lousy compromise," said Crest.

"John Crest: have you had enough of Sentryville? Are you ready to leave?"

"No," said Crest. "I can't leave a job half done. Will you stay in Sentryville with me?"

"Under one condition, dear."

"What's that?"

"That we live in a home of our own," she said.

"But living in your father's house was your own idea," said Crest. "There's plenty of room."

"I thought it might be temporary," she said.

"You thought I'd be beaten in the first few weeks and run?"

"Yes," she said. "Frankly, I did."

"You don't know me very well."

"I'm getting to know you better, dear. If you insist on doing battle with my father, I don't want to live with him."

"I'll still be working for the man."

"I know," she said. "But under a roof of my own, I won't be tempted to choose up sides."

"Whose side are you on?"

"Silly," she said. "Yours, of course."

"Against your own father?"

"Against the world," she said.

"Okay," said Crest. "You can start looking for a house tomorrow. Let's go to bed."

They went to bed. Within thirty seconds, John Crest was dead asleep. Emerald knew she couldn't wake him. She didn't even try.

Winter swept down the valley from the north, bringing leaden skies and snow and penetrating cold. There was a bitter spell when the thermometer plunged to zero and stuck there for more than a week. The small cottage which John and Emerald Crest had rented on the other side of town was cozy and warm. Emerald enjoyed puttering around playing house. Crest gallantly stretched the point and told her she was a great cook.

"Beware of gallstones and peptic ulcer, friend," she said. "Your digestive tract must pay the price for my freedom from my saintly mother."

"I see enough of your father during the working day," said Crest. "I'm pleased not to have his company at meals."

In weather like this, it was a temptation to keep a house too cozy, too warm. Next door was a ramshackle two-story structure of wood, a converted garage, where an old widower lived alone. On one of the most bitter nights, Crest awoke to see an ominous orange pattern flickering on his bedroom wall. The place next door was afire. The town fire horn was bellowing. There were bells and sirens down the street as the fire engines arrived. Immediately thereafter, Parky arrived in his big black Cadillac. Looking down from the window, Crest could see Parky putting on the yellow slicker, the hip-length rubber boots, and the fireman's hat which he always kept in the back of his car.

"My daddy's never been late to a fire in his life," said Emerald. "He often beats the engines to the scene. Are we in any danger, dear?"

"With your daddy down there taking charge?" said Crest.

"We're pretty close," she said. "I've always been afraid of fire in the night."

"You stand by with buckets," said Crest. "I'll go down and see what's going on."

Crest put on heavy clothes and went outdoors. A sharp wind was screaming out of the north, but it was blowing away from them, driving the flames and smoke toward a couple of vacant lots. There would be no danger to Crest's new home unless the wind should change. The widower's place was going to go, however. Licking tongues of flame were already bursting out of the roof. Firemen were hampered by the chilling cold. Water froze as it left the hoses, garlanding the near side of the blazing structure with sheets and streamers of ice. Crest joined the fire lines. The fire had apparently started at the junction of the chimney and the roof, and the second story was in full blaze already. It was the opinion of the fire chief that nobody was at home. He had inspected the ground floor and discovered an empty bed; he had not deemed it safe to go upstairs. A reliable rumor had been circulated that the widower had been seen in a beer joint a few minutes before.

"I doubt that he's upstairs," said the chief. "If so, we can't get him. He's a gone goose already."

"Chief, we better have a look," said Parky.

"We can't," said the chief. "It's too damned hot up there."

"Maybe it's too hot for you," said Parky, and he walked into the blazing building.

"Where is he going?" asked Crest.

"He's a damn fool. He'll probably try to make his way upstairs," said the chief.

"I thought you said it wasn't safe."

"Parky knows his way around a fire, Doc."

"Shouldn't you stop him?"

The chief laughed. "Did you ever try to stop Parky?"

"Then, shouldn't you be with him?"

"There he is, Doc," said the chief. "See him poking his head out that window on the second floor?"

There he was indeed, in the middle of inferno, surrounded by billowing smoke and flame. Parky was calling out the window, but Crest couldn't hear his voice above the roaring of the fire. Firemen were running over, carrying a ladder, while others played their hoses in the vicinity. By the time they got the ladder up, Parky was gone from the window. Crest was afraid that he might have been overcome by smoke. Then Parky reappeared and there was something in his arms: the limp unconscious form of the widower. They managed to get the widower down the ladder, Parky scrambling afterward. He had no sooner stepped off than everything went: the roof and second story fell in with a tremendous crash, and the walls bent inward in a burst of spiraling flame.

"Warm enough in there, Parky?" asked the chief.

"Damn it, if I'm going to do your work, I ought to draw your salary," said Parky. "Call the ambulance. That old fellow is still alive."

The patient was taken to the hospital by ambulance, Parky following in his Cadillac. Crest went back into his own house. A few minutes later the telephone rang. It was Parky, calling from the hospital.

"Could you take care of the old guy, Crest?"

"What's his condition, sir?" said Crest.

"He's in pretty fair shape," said Parky. "He has some second-degree burns of the hands and face, but mostly he's swallowed a lot of smoke. He'll pull through if his heart stands up."

"I thought I better stay with Emerald," said Crest. "She's afraid of fire in the night."

"You have the whole fire department standing by," said Parky. "I can't be in two places at the same time."

"Neither can I," said Crest.

"There's been a bad accident in the hills, and they need a doctor at once. Shall I call Hamilton and Rhodes while you hold hands with your wife?"

"No. I'll come to the hospital," said Crest. "You go on up to the hills."

At an icy curve in the hills, a car had gone out of control. As if seized by a mighty hand, it had revolved in lazy graceful circles until it smashed the guard rail, broke through, and plunged off a sheer forty-foot drop. The car came to rest about halfway down, supported by a ledge and the tops of a couple of trees. The frame of the automobile was folded like the pleats of an accordion, and the driver's leg was caught by jaws of twisted steel. The police had difficulty reaching him. They had managed to hook up a bosun's chair and lower a man over the side of the cliff; he was trying to free the driver by cutting through the steel with an acetylene torch. Parky arrived and took in the situation at a glance.

"He'll be dead before you get him out that way," said Parky. "Let me go down in the chair. In the meantime, put some ropes on a stretcher so you can haul him up when I get him loose."

"What are you going to do, Parky?"

"Cut off his leg, of course."

Parky worked in mid-air, swaying on the end of a rope. The night was black, the wind was howling, the thermometer stood at ten below. Illumination was provided from flickering torches above. The patient was deep in shock, and Parky did not have to be concerned with pain relief. He threw a tight tourniquet around the thigh and performed a guillotine amputation just above the knee. The surgery was quick and brutal. The patient was then taken to the hospital, where Parky did a proper repair of the amputation stump in the operating room.

The sun was coming up as they left the operating room, but the police were calling for Parky again. This time it was a shooting match, down by the railroad tracks. Two sports had been playing cribbage. The competition of the game was strong, and so was the liquor. One of them had grabbed a shotgun, taken vague aim, and let his companion have it with both barrels. One barrel had missed altogether; the other had scattered a close pattern of birdshot in the soft tissues of the hip and buttock. Having done the deed, the victorious sport decided that he did not care to go to jail. The victim, not badly hurt and feeling no pain, did not care to go to the hospital. By the time the neighbors had complained and the police arrived, the sports were good friends again, united against the world. There were a couple of guns in the house and plenty of ammunition. The police were met with a shower of shot and shell when they tried to approach the place. The police took cover and held a consultation. A call was sent out for tear gas. Parky arrived before the tear gas.

"Hey, Parky, where are you going?" asked the officer in charge from his position of safety behind a rain barrel.

It was obvious where Parky was going: right up to the door, despite the shot and shell. A charge of birdshot whistled uncomfortably close to his hat.

"All right, boys, cut that out!" called Parky. "Who in the devil are you shooting at?"

Nobody in his right mind would shoot at Dr. Parkindale. The gunplay ceased as Parky walked in the door. A moment later he walked out, followed by two unarmed, sheepish, and subdued belligerents. The police hauled one of them to jail. Parky drove the other to the hospital and spent most of the morning digging birdshot out of the gluteus muscle.

"A busy night," said Emerald to Crest. "What do you think of my daddy now?"

"He's a damn fool," said Crest. "A doctor shouldn't make a target of himself and should not go where it's too damned hot for the fire chief."

"I suppose he shouldn't have been swinging from a bosun's chair?"

"He has foolhardy courage," said Crest. "He saved at least two lives tonight."

"What would you have done under the circumstances, dear?"

"I would have been standing by until the police and fire departments had done their duty," said Crest.

"And your duty would have been to sign the death certificates?"

"He's a good man to have around in an emergency," said Crest. "Maybe I'm not."

"This is the stuff from which heros are made."

"I admit it," said Crest. "And I haven't got it myself."

"You might remember this when you are tempted to criticize the man."

"I'll try," said Crest.

One of the patients in the office reminded Crest: this was Valentine's Day. He had overlooked the occasion and had neglected to buy his wife a Valentine.

On his way home after office hours, Crest decided to rectify his error and he stopped at a stationary store. The day was already over from the commercial point of view, and the assortment of cards was unsatisfactory. There were examples of the wise-guy variety which managed to hide any suggestion of love under a veneer of cruelty; and some of the soapy sentimental type; the remainder were suitable only for children. Crest selected the most appropriate of the lot, but felt unhappy over his choice. He gave Emerald the card as soon as he got home, and she had a Valentine for him.

During supper, Emerald was abstracted and remote. Crest felt separated from her by great distances, shrouded by mist. He knew that her feelings had been hurt. He was sure that she had bought her Valentine well in advance and had held it back that morning when she saw that he had forgotten the day.

Did Parky buy his wife a Valentine, Crest wondered? Undoubtedly so. Did a Valentine card truly express his sentiment of love? Did his money and success compensate poor, plump Mrs. Parkindale for Parky's lack of attention during the working hours, which meant all hours of the day and night?

Crest thought he might express his own sentiment in some more tangible way. After supper, he followed Emerald into the kitchen, where she was washing the dishes. He put his arm around her waist and kissed her just behind the ear.

"I love you as much as the day I first laid eyes on you," he said.

"Yeah," she said. "Just about that much."

"You mean everything to me."

"After medicine, I'm in the top spot, no doubt!"

"I never have time for important things," said Crest. "I hope to God it doesn't ring tonight."

"I beg your pardon?"

"I was thinking of the telephone."

"John Crest! What are you doing? Can't you see that I'm trying to finish the dishes?"

"Leave the dishes in the sink," he said.

They went upstairs together. The dishes were still in the sink the following morning. Miraculously, the telephone had not rung. None of the 7,000 citizens of Sentryville had decided to call for help that night.

"It was so sweet and sudden last night that I forgot," said Emerald. "I hope we get away with it this once!"

"Meaning the dishes?"

"Of course not. For a doctor, you certainly can be naïve. Didn't you notice?"

Crest knew what she was talking about. He didn't mind. This was a subject he had meant to broach with her before. She brought the subject up again six weeks later.

"Remember Valentine's Day?"

"Sure," said Crest.

"We didn't get away with it," she said.

Crest grinned at her. "Are you slightly pregnant, dear?"

"Ugh!" She grimaced. "How pregnant can I get?"

"In my experience, a great deal more than you are today."

"Damn it," said Emerald. "I know."

"You don't sound particularly pleased."

"You don't have to lug it around for the next eight months," she said. "Who's going to deliver me?"

"I hadn't considered it."

"It's not your problem."

"Who did the pregnancy test?"

"Daddy, of course," she said. "Who else?"

"Well . . ."

"Should I consult Dr. Mordikay?"

"No," said Crest.

"Hamilton or Rhodes? Old Dr. Klamp? Or perhaps you're interested in delivering this brat yourself?"

"God forbid!" said Crest.

"What else can I do? Were you planning to ship me to the city when the time arrives?"

Crest would have preferred to consult a city obstetrician, but this simply wasn't practical. If they remained in Sentryville, Parky would have to deliver his own grandchild in the fall. There wasn't anybody else.

"Well, he's delivered most of Sentryville," she said. "Obstetrics is easy. You've told me so yourself. You have said that Daddy is very handy with his forceps and that sort of stuff."

"As a matter of fact, he has the makings of a damn good obstetrician," said Crest. "I'm sure he'll do a fine job."

"As usual?" said Emerald, raising one eyebrow into a question mark.

Crest didn't try to answer that.

Spring came to the valley, bringing the springtime floods. Foliage fleshed the trees, and cows were turned out to pasture. Emerald's tummy expanded. She passed through a phase of distressing morning sickness, developed unnatural appetites in the middle of the night, and became quite placid and content. Her disposition reminded Crest of a cow, and her figure was beginning to suggest the shape of a pear.

Summer approached. The citizens began to complain of the heat, and Crest had been working with Dr. Parkindale for one full year. Crest was accustomed to the pace and volume of the work, and he had begun to know his way around town. His relationship with Parky seemed smoother than it had been in the beginning. Crest knew that Emerald's pregnancy had something to do with it. The life of Crest's family was held in Parky's big strong hands, and it was necessary for Crest to place some faith in Parky's judgment and ability. He studied Parky's obstetrical techniques and decided that the older man was thoroughly competent in this department. Crest also began to feel that Parky was treating him as a son, not just as another employee. There had been no major argument between the two men for many months. Crest no longer seemed to notice alarming errors on Parky's part like those that had distressed him in the early months.

"Hasn't Daddy killed anybody recently?" asked Emerald.

"We're learning to work together as a team," said Crest.

Crest no longer debated theory or philosophy with Parky. He made allowances for the difference in Parky's age, temperament, and background. He no longer judged the man by the standards of the university. In fact, Crest knew that university standards do not necessarily apply to practical problems in the field. In the past year, Parky was obviously modernizing and improving his techniques; he ordered more laboratory studies now, blood tests, X-rays, and so forth. This was more costly to the patient, but Parky was beginning to understand that most patients approve of thoroughness. The ratio of diagnostic error was definitely lower, and therapy was being applied more scientifically. In a puzzling case, Parky often asked for Crest's opinion and accepted his advice.

"It took a little time, but I knew I could do it," said Crest. "Parky is learning things from me. Maybe I'll make a doctor of him yet!"

"Or," suggested Emerald, "maybe he'll make a Parkindale of you."

There was something in what she said both good and bad. On the positive side, Crest was learning things from Parky: tricks of bedside manner, little ways to please the patient, arts of economics and of sociology that were never mentioned in the teaching hospital. Crest would never have a magnetic bedside manner, but he was becoming more at ease in the presence of the patients; he was learning to control both his temper and his tendency to blush.

"Yes, I've also learned a lot from him," said Crest.

"And perhaps your own professional standards are beginning to slip?" said Emerald wickedly.

Perhaps. Crest was vaguely aware that he was less sharp than he had been a year ago. Medical progress had been made since he left the university, but he was too busy to keep up with the literature. He would have liked to take post-graduate refresher work. As a matter of fact, he would have liked to take a vacation, but Parky had never taken a vacation, and Crest didn't dare to ask. Crest was not sure that a vacation would be possible: he was busy up to the total limits of his physical and emotional strength, and Parky was a great deal busier, being the stronger man. If either of them took time off from Sentryville, who would take care of the patients? Should sick people be entrusted to Hamilton or Rhodes, Klamp or Mordikay?

The patient was pregnant and she was close to term. Dr. Mordikay was her physician; she had gone to him for years. She knew that he was sometimes unavailable, but he had always come whenever she had called. She had heard many rumors that Dr. Mordikay was a drunkard, but she found them difficult to believe. Mordikay was completely sober every time she saw him. He seemed to understand her case better than any other doctor would.

On a warm July afternoon, this patient had begun to bleed. The bleeding was only moderate, and she was not alarmed, but she thought Dr. Mordikay should see her. She phoned him. He answered the telephone. She described her complaint. He promised to come to her home within a half-hour. Right on the button he arrived, and he was sharp and sober. He did a careful examination.

"You may have a partial placenta praevia, my dear," he said.

"What's that?" she inquired.

"In this condition, the placenta is implanted abnormally low in the uterus," Dr. Mordikay explained. "Towards the end of pregnancy, the baby drops lower in the womb, and the internal opening of the cervix begins to expand. This may tear off a portion of the placenta, and bleeding results."

She did not completely understand what he was talking about, but she was glad that he had attempted to explain. This was one reason why she liked Dr. Mordikay. If you asked him a question, he sat right down and gave you a careful and complete explanation. When he had finished, you had the impression that he had told you frankly everything he knew. In this way, disease became a matter of common sense and logic. Without mystery, there would be no fear. Other doctors she had seen would give you an evasive answer or no answer at all, as if you were a child and had no right to know what was going on within your body. Parky, for example, never seemed to give a direct answer to a question. He would grunt or grin and change the subject.

"Is this dangerous?" she inquired.

"It can be," said Mordikay calmly and frankly. "This depends on how low the position of the placenta may be. If too much of the placental attachment is torn off prematurely, this can endanger both the mother and the child."

She wasn't frightened. She found this interesting. She had

enjoyed biology in high school. There was a time when she had considered becoming a doctor or a nurse.

"What do you do?" she said.

"As long as possible, we wait," said Dr. Mordikay. "Sometimes the mother will go all the way to term with this condition. The longer you can wait, the more developed is the baby, so you want to wait as long as it is safe."

"How long is that?"

"Until there is a frank hemorrhage," said Mordikay.

"What then?"

"Then you have to do Caesarian section as soon as possible," said Mordikay.

"Do you want me to go to the hospital?"

"Not yet," said Mordikay. "We'll give you sedation and put you to bed at home. There's a fair chance we can make this bleeding stop."

"And if it doesn't stop?"

"Call me right away," said Mordikay. "It may be very important for your life and the life of your child."

He gave her sedation and put her to bed. That night the bleeding became quite brisk. The patient's husband telephoned Dr. Mordikay, but Mordikay wasn't answering his phone. The husband wanted to call Parky. The patient wanted to wait. The husband called Mordikay several more times, but still there was no reply. The woman was almost dead from hemorrhage before she permitted her husband to call Dr. Parkindale. Parky hospitalized her and did an immediate Caesarian section. Multiple transfusions were necessary, but the mother survived, and so did the baby.

"That son-of-a-bitch, Mordikay," said Parky.

"Well," said Crest, "he was on the right track. He did suspect placenta praevia, but she wasn't bleeding much this afternoon. I think it was good judgment to sedate her at home. Would you have hospitalized her?"

"I would have watched her like a hawk," said Parky. "When I'm sitting on a case like this, I'm surely going to keep myself available. He abandoned this patient, my boy, and left himself wide open for a malpractice suit. I'm going to talk with the husband in the case."

"You're not going to suggest malpractice?"

"A few frank words may prevent a malpractice suit," said Parky. "I'm doing Mordikay a favor, though I'm damned if I know why."

The husband was concerned with the welfare of his wife and newborn son, and the possibility of a malpractice suit had not occurred to him until Parky mentioned it. The husband decided not to sue; he did, however, file charges of complaint with the county medical society against Dr. Mordikay.

"Do you think that was right, sir?" asked Crest.

"What do you mean?" said Parky.

"You talked the husband into this."

"The complaint was his own idea."

"Why not let sleeping dogs lie? The whole thing would have blown over," said Crest. "No damage has been done, after all. The mother and the baby will survive."

"Are you defending Mordikay?" said Parky.

"We all make mistakes from time to time," said Crest, "but we must present a united front to the public. This is an ethical profession. I once heard you say there was too much criticism in our profession. The faith of a patient in her doctor must never be taken lightly. If she loses faith in one of us, she will lose her faith in the profession as a whole."

"We can't use ethics to cover up error," said Parky.

"We shouldn't attack each other's credentials to the patient," said Crest.

"At times we must clean our own house," said Parky. "We have the obligation to protect the welfare of the community. Mordikay represents a dangerous situation, and I think we have been ignoring it too long."

"I'm not sure that this is the proper way to handle it," said Crest.

"You are not the county medical examiner," said Parky.

"You are not the chief of the hospital staff. You are not the president of the medical society. I am. You will have the opportunity to present your views at the proper time."

A special meeting of the medical society was called to deal with the problem of Dr. Mordikay. No social hour was held before the meeting. No wives were in attendance. Dr. Mordikay had not been invited to attend.

"Gentlemen," said Parky, "this is a distressing problem, one which has been with us for a great many years. As everybody knows, this man is a drunkard. The personal habits and private life of any member of this group do not concern us, but we must be concerned with maintaining high ethical and professional standards in this community. One night last week this man refused to answer his telephone. As we know, he often refuses to answer his telephone, and we know the reason why. He abandoned a bleeding woman, and her husband has filed formal charges of complaint before this society. We can ignore the problem no longer. We must deal with it. The question is this, gentlemen: what are we going to do?"

"Kick him out of the society," said Dr. Hamilton.

"Perhaps the man is sick," said Dr. Rhodes.

"Have we the right to deprive him of his means of earning a living?" asked Dr. Jones.

"He doesn't need to earn a living: he inherited a lot of money," said Hamilton.

"Sick people should be treated," said Rhodes.

"And who's going to treat him?" said Hamilton. "You?"

"This is only a county medical society," said Parky. "We are not the state board of registration. We didn't give him the license to practice medicine, and we can't take it away. We can't remove him from the community. We can't commit him to an institution."

"As a matter of fact," said Dr. Jones, "we can't do anything at all."

"We have only two choices," said Parky. "Pass a motion of censure against him, or expel him from the group."

"Neither one of which will do any good," said Hamilton.

"What do you suggest?" said Parky. "Shall we ignore him, as we have been doing for so many years? Last week he almost killed a mother and her child. Next week he may succeed. Do I hear a motion from the floor?"

There was a long and painful silence. Each man present had an opinion. Each man would have felt free to express an opinion and to vote on any motion presented. None of them was eager to make the motion. Nobody wanted to cast the first stone.

Crest got up his courage and said, "Sir?"

Everybody glared at him. As the junior member of the group, Crest's opinion had not been solicited.

"Are we discussing Dr. Mordikay?" Crest asked.

"Who in the hell did you think we were talking about?" said Parky.

"The name has not been spoken," said Crest. "I believe we should have the courage to call the man by name. Is this an official meeting of the society?"

"Did you think we were having a bull session for our own entertainment, son?" said Parky.

"I note that the secretary is not keeping minutes," said Crest.

"This is a closed executive session," said Parky.

"Dr. Mordikay isn't here," said Crest.

"He wasn't invited," said Parky. "For obvious reasons."

"Does he belong to this society?" asked Crest.

"Where the devil have you been for the past ten minutes, son?" asked Parky.

A small and malicious titter spread through the room. Dr. Mordikay was not loved by this group, but there was no surplus of love for Dr. Parkindale, despite the fact that he was perpetual president of the society. His election was based on power, not popularity. Being Parky's associate and son-in-law, Crest could expect to share any animosity against Dr. Parkindale. Any sharpness between Parky and Crest, any hint of difference of opinion, would give pleasure to the other members of the group.

Crest fought down discomfiture and spoke his piece. "In my opinion, this meeting is not official, since minutes have not been recorded and since one of the members has not been notified. We should not judge this man in whispers behind his back. He has the right to inspect the written minutes. He has the right to be notified as long as he is a member of the society. He should have the opportunity to hear the testimony against him and to speak in his own defense.

Parky was about to snort, but there was a murmur of approval from the other members, small but definite. This was, after all, an ethical profession. Since the day of Hippocrates, the medical profession had bound itself to a voluntary code of behavior. Direct competition between physicians is prohibited. Physicians may not advertise. Physicians may not bear false witness for commercial purposes. Doctors are free to criticize each other privately, and they always do, but they are bound to present a common front and to stick together in the public eye. This code is archaic, and unrealistic, and unenforceable, but without it, the medical profession would collapse. Lawyers may correctly accuse physicians of a conspiracy of silence. The public may complain that doctors always stick together. The ethical code may prevent the profession from cleaning its own house. But every doctor in that room was acutely aware of his own shortcomings, errors, and human fallibility. Each man knew that if the code of ethics ever did break down, his own habits and morals, his own personality and competence, his own standards and his ancestry would be fair game to every other doctor in the room and would swiftly become available to every dirty tongue and guttersnipe in Sentryville.

People who live in glass houses should not take baths in the daytime.

"All right," said Parky. "My bright young associate has made his point. This meeting is not official. If action is to be taken, we shall take it at our next regular meeting, when minutes will be recorded and Dr. Mordikay will have the opportunity to attend. In the meantime, what are we going to do? Have you any suggestions, Dr. Crest?"

Crest was not anxious to suggest, but he was on the spot. His own opinion was that of Dr. Rhodes, the weakest ally in the room.

"I agree with Dr. Rhodes and take the position that Mordikay is sick," said Crest.

"No doubt," said Parky. "He's been sick for years."

"Sick men should receive treatment."

"Since we are all doctors here tonight," said Parky, "I doubt if there is any great objection to this generality."

"If a group of doctors can do no better for a sick man in our own group than to slap his wrist or kick him out," said Crest, "I doubt if we are strong enough to do anything at all."

Crest had not intended to steer himself into this position. It placed him on the side of ignoring Dr. Mordikay, and yet Crest did not think that Mordikay was necessarily right. It allied him with Dr. Jones, who seemed to maintain that the society was too weak to take action, and Crest hoped that this was not the case.

"For myself," said old Dr. Klamp, speaking up for the first time, "I agree with Dr. Crest."

This was strong support from an unexpected quarter. Although Dr. Klamp only played at medicine as a hobby now, he retained the mantle of authority from a previous generation. Dr. Klamp had been president of this society when Parky was in medical school. There was a murmur of approval in the room.

"I am willing to accept that position," said Parky. "We agree that Mordikay is sick. As doctors, we agree that sick people should be treated. How shall we achieve this end? We cannot compel a patient to accept treatment against his will. No one of us has authority to treat him unless he should present himself to us for treatment. We are unable to commit him to a public institution, unless one of us wishes to file papers at the town offices to the effect that Mordikay is legally insane. He may be a drunkard, but none of us believes he is a lunatic."

"I think we should speak with him privately," said Dr. Klamp.

"Would you speak with him?" asked Parky.

"I don't really know the man," said Dr. Klamp.

"None of us knows him," said Dr. Jones.

"Perhaps," said Parky, "Dr. Crest knows him best of all. The rest of us don't drink with him in the cocktail lounge."

"I've had exactly two conversations with the man," said Crest.

"That's two more than any of the rest of us have had," said Parky. "I hereby appoint Dr. Crest as a committee of one to speak to Dr. Mordikay and make a report to the next regular meeting of the society. Are there any objections?"

There was an objection, from Crest, but he did not know how to express it.

"If there is no other business before the society, I hereby declare this meeting adjourned," said Parky.

The members streamed out of the room in relief. Nobody stopped to talk with Crest. They acted as if they had thrust an armful of dirty linen upon him and did not desire any of the dirt to be rubbed off on them.

"Well," thought Crest, "I don't like it. I should have kept my big mouth shut! However, I'm stuck, and the job won't seem any less dirty tomorrow. I might as well take a crack at it tonight, if I can find him. Probably Mordikay won't be answering his telephone."

Before trying the telephone, Crest glanced into the cocktail lounge, and there was Mordikay in his usual dark corner. Mordikay waved. Crest went and sat down. The waitress produced a pair of whiskies.

"Did you have a good meeting?" asked Mordikay.

"You weren't supposed to know about the meeting," said Crest hastily, without thinking.

Mordikay laughed. "There's a grapevine in this town, my friend. A man can't take a crap without the neighbors knowing the minute he steps into the john. Is that what you boys were doing here tonight? Taking a little crap on me?"

"I won't pretend that you were not the subject of discussion," said Crest. "I got the dirty job. I was appointed to speak with you."

"How did you get stuck?" asked Mordikay. "Were you talking out of turn? Were you such a fool as to speak up in my defense?"

"I said we had no right to judge a man behind his back," said Crest. "I gave my opinion that you are sick and that all sick people deserve proper treatment."

"How ethical!" said Mordikay. "How noble!"

"Look," said Crest, "I don't relish this assignment, and you're not making it any easier."

"Do your dirty job. I'm listening."

"I suppose you recall your placenta praevia case last week."

"I do."

"She had a hemorrhage and you were unavailable."

"I try to carry these women as near as possible to term. Hemorrhage is a calculated risk."

"It seems to me that you were cutting a close corner."

"Don't be self-righteous," said Mordikay. "We all cut close corners."

"When this woman was bleeding to death, you wouldn't answer your telephone."

"Maybe I was out on another case. Maybe I had been called away from town on a family matter. Maybe I was asleep."

"And maybe you were drunk," said Crest.

"You'd have a damn hard job proving that in court," said Mordikay.

"I think this woman could establish a malpractice claim in court," said Crest.

"That's why I carry malpractice insurance," said Mordikay. "Every doctor does."

"In other words," said Crest, "you deny that you made a serious error in this case?"

"I deny nothing," said Mordikay. "This was a sin of omission, not commission. I regard it as less serious than if I had tried to treat this poor woman while I was under the influence of drugs. Nevertheless, I know it was a sin. I don't expect absolution of my sins from my professional associates."

"A complaint has been made to the medical society. We believe that the complaint is justified. What can we do?"

"Unfortunately, there's only one thing you can do," said Mordikay. "You could expel me from the society. You can't prevent me from practicing medicine in this community. There are many practicing physicians who do not belong to their county medical society or to the A.M.A. Some doctors don't like organized medicine, and the general public happens to agree with them."

"Then why don't you resign?" said Crest. "You can take the pressure off the rest of us."

"I am not the worst doctor in the group," said Mordikay. "And I am not the only one who makes mistakes. If you start quoting cases at me, I have a few interesting case histories of my own."

"Are you attempting to threaten us?"

"Not unless you threaten me. I can fight fire with fire, if necessary."

"It is the opinion of the society that you are sick," said Crest. "You deny it?"

"Of course I'm sick," said Mordikay.

"We would like you to consent to treatment."

"How very kind of you!"

"Will you accept our advice?"

"Not necessarily," said Mordikay.

"You refuse treatment?"

"Every patient has the right to select the treatment of his

own choice, and this also includes the right not to submit to treatment if he so desires. I'd like to see any of you self-right-eous bastards try to deprive any patient of that right! You are not the representatives of God, you know! You are in business to serve the sick but not to bully or badger them!"

"Good night," said Crest.

"Don't go away mad."

"I used to think you were a reasonable man, but now I agree that you are dangerous to this community."

"And you sound more like Parky every day."

"I think you made a bad mistake," said Crest. "One of these days you'll make such a bad mistake that even you can't face it any more."

"An occupational hazard," said Mordikay. "How can doctors shave? How can we face ourselves in the mirror every day? In the last century, every doctor wore a beard."

"I can't dismiss this matter with a joke."

"Nor I," said Mordikay. "I am a sick man. I have received treatment of my disease at a specialized center, but I am not cured. Knowing my own disability, I refuse to be on call at such times as I am unfit to practice medicine on account of my disease. This is wrong?"

"Of course not," said Crest. "But whenever you accept a case, you make an unspoken contract with the patient to be available whenever the need should arise."

"A doctor should accept every call under any circumstance?"

"Obviously he can't," said Crest. "But he should provide coverage for such times when he cannot be on call. And I do not think he is doing the job when he can never be reached at night."

"As Parky would say, a doctor cannot keep banker's hours."

"In this case, Parky happens to be right," said Crest.

"What a pity he's not right more often!" said Mordikay.

"I believe we can keep Parky out of this discussion."

"Parky makes more mistakes of judgment in any given year

than I have made in all the years since I first came to Sentryville."

"He sees more patients than you do."

"Ah," said Mordikay. "And now you're defending the man!"

"I'm talking about you, not Dr. Parkindale."

"Dangerous corners. Knotty and devious problems," said
Mordikay. "How does a doctor live with his mistakes? Parky,
for example. Or doesn't he even know when he makes a mistake? Does he keep himself so God-damned busy that he never
has the time to think?"

"You don't need the money," said Crest. "You don't like the
work. You have lost all sense of dedication. Why don't you
quit?"

"Why don't you?" said Mordikay.

"I don't suffer from your disease."

"We all have diseases of our own," said Mordikay. "You
make no mistakes?"

"We all make mistakes. We're human."

"I saw one of your patients this afternoon," said Mordikay.
"This was a child whom you treated last fall for the measles.
You treated her with sulfa drug. The virus of measles is not
cured by sulfa drug. The child did not have the measles in the
first place. She happened to be sensitive to sulfa. Now she
happens to be blind."

"I haven't seen her since," said Crest. "I heard that her
visual loss was temporary."

"You heard wrong," said Mordikay. "She has corneal scars.
It's permanent."

"I'm not proud of that case," said Crest. "I know I made
a bad mistake."

"But you still treat children with the measles?"

"I try to learn from my mistakes," said Crest.

"As a matter of fact, so do I," said Mordikay. "There was
another patient of yours. She died of carcinoma of the cervix
several months ago. Although she was bleeding, she had never
had a pelvic examination, and I find this incredibly bad

medicine! You were giving her hormone shots to make her little cancer grow."

"That was Parky's error, not mine."

"And yet, I believe, you work with Parky every day. I know another case of yours, a funny one. Don't tell me it was Parky who was seen chasing a naked woman down the middle of Main Street at high noon?"

"That was embarrassing, but not serious," said Crest. "I managed to survive."

"Unfortunately, your patient didn't," said Mordikay.

"What do you mean?" said Crest.

"You hadn't heard? I forgot. You and Parky are too busy to follow up your mistakes."

"What do you mean? We committed that patient to the state mental hospital. It was proper."

"About three weeks later, this patient escaped from restraint. She made her way to the laundry of the institution in the middle of the night. She threw a knotted sheet over one of the steam pipes and hanged herself."

"I'm sorry. I hadn't heard."

"In other words, you frequently don't even know when you have made an error?"

"Why is that my error?" said Crest. "I don't work at the state mental hospital. I did not permit that woman to escape."

"Which frees you from responsibility, I suppose?"

"Just how could you hold me responsible for that?"

"You know why that woman hanged herself?"

"Because she was insane."

"Because she was afraid," said Mordikay. "She had hallucinations: she was always running from the form of a ghost and goblin in the night. The ghost that was chasing her had the shape of a male and the genital organs of a male. Until she met you, Dr. Crest, this woman's favorite ghost had no face. But you walked in on her one day without warning, and you frightened her. She thought you were the ghost. You gave her ghost a face, my friend: your face. For the last few weeks of

her miserable life, this poor woman was running away from
you. In the hospital laundry, she finally managed to escape
from you."

"What point are you trying to establish?" asked Crest.

"That we can't win 'em all. I quote your esteemed daddy-
in-law."

"Granted," said Crest. "Does this get you off the hook? What
error will you make tonight? Who will you abandon next
week?"

"I don't know," said Mordikay. "I'll have to wait till next
week to find out."

"Well, I've done my duty," said Crest. "I'll report to the
society accordingly."

"You're a nice guy, Crest. You have the makings of a decent
ethical physician. For this reason, I must respect your advice.
Do you think I should no longer practice medicine?"

"Not until you're better."

"Should I take down the shingle and lock the office door?"

"Until you're fit to work, yes. That would be my advice."

"I'll accept your advice."

"Thanks," said Crest.

"I won't stay in Sentryville. I believe I'll go away."

"Back to Lexington, Kentucky?"

"I may go farther than Lexington," said Mordikay with his
sudden smile.

"Come back when you're cured," said Crest.

"If possible," said Mordikay.

"You're a fine physician when you're in good health. We
need you in Sentryville. I never had the slightest doubt of
that."

"I appreciate the sentiment."

"You must understand that I personally and the society as
a whole are thinking of your welfare."

"Including Parky?"

"Yes," said Crest. "He's the president."

"And who's the greatest menace to the community, I wonder: Parky or me?"

"We don't need to debate that point any more."

"I'm sure we won't," said Mordikay.

"Good night," said Crest.

Crest went home and fell asleep and was awakened by the telephone at 2:00 A.M.

"This is the police, Dr. Crest."

"Yes?"

"There's been a shooting here."

"I'll be there at once," said Crest. "What's the address?"

"Twenty-seven Pine."

As he was getting dressed, Crest thought that 27 Pine Street must be near Dr. Mordikay's house. Arriving at the address, Crest discovered that it was Dr. Mordikay's house. Police cars were standing out in front, and all the lights were on.

"This way, Doctor," said a burly policeman, taking Crest by the arm.

"Gunshot wound?" asked Crest.

"Yeah. Suicide attempt."

"The doctor?"

"Yes. He's in pretty bad shape, but still alive, or, at least, he was a moment ago."

But when Crest reached the body, Mordikay was dead. He was lying on the living-room rug in an enormous pool of blood, and there was blood all over the room. A short distance from the body lay a miniature revolver, an antique: the type women used to carry in their pocketbooks, harmless-looking, like a toy. There were powder burns on Mordikay's right hand.

"Was there a note?" asked Crest.

"No, sir."

"Perhaps there was a prowler," said Crest. "Perhaps Mordikay shot at him, and the prowler shot back."

"The bullet's in his head, Doc. We can match it up easy enough."

Examining the head, Crest saw that there was an entrance wound in the right temple and no wound of exit. The policeman was correct; the bullet was still in Mordikay's head. There was no real question in Crest's mind, however; he was sure that this was suicide.

"This is a medical-examiner case," said Crest. "We must call Dr. Parkindale."

"Parky's coming, Doc."

Indeed, at that moment Parky was coming in through the door, brisk, confident. He nodded at Crest and studied the scene.

"I guess we'll have to dig that bullet out," said Parky.

"Yes, sir," said Crest. "But, considering what's been going on tonight, I'm sure this must be suicide."

"I guess this solves the problem for the medical society," said Parky.

"I'm sorry about it," said Crest.

"So am I," said Parky, "but perhaps this is the easiest solution to the problem. Now you won't have to talk with him."

"I talked with him," said Crest. "Not over two hours ago."

"He informed you of his plans?"

"Not directly, sir," said Crest. "He said he was going to shut the office. He said he was going away."

"He went," said Parky.

"I hope I didn't talk him into this."

"Well," said Parky, "you certainly didn't talk him out of it."

"I can't escape a feeling that we should have prevented this, some way or other."

"Neither can I," said Parky. "I should have entrusted that assignment to a man of more maturity."

"It was a dirty job, and I did my best."

"Your best wasn't very good," said Parky.

"Now, wait a minute," said Crest. "You started the trouble. You forced that patient's husband to file the complaint with the medical society. You were hoping to expel Mordikay from the group."

"We should have expelled him," said Parky. "We would have hurt his feelings and saved his life."

"Are you holding me responsible?"

"Don't you accept responsibility for the things you do?"

The tensions of the evening, his own sensations of disgust, anxiety, and guilt were boiling up in Crest.

"God damn it, sir—" he said.

"Don't swear at me, young man," said Parky.

"I'll swear at whomever I like," said Crest. "Mordikay was a pretty fine physician and a brilliant man and I liked him."

"Mordikay was a drunken bum," said Parky.

The police were listening to the discussion eagerly. Even Mordikay's dead face seemed to bear sardonic interest. He would have enjoyed the argument if he had been alive.

"We were discussing mistakes tonight: errors in medical judgment," said Crest.

"Mordikay made plenty of mistakes."

"Mordikay said that he made fewer errors in all his years in Sentryville than you make in any given year."

"Is that so?" said Parky, icy, ominous.

"Yes, I think it is," said Crest, on the verge of losing his professional control.

"I suppose you can prove that."

"Easily," said Crest. "The man with leukemia, the woman with carcinoma of the cervix—all your unnecessary surgery; the child who died of tuberculosis."

"Since we're speaking frankly, Crest, you are not the greatest doctor in the world. You're a smart young man, brainy, well informed, but you are nervous and unstable and immature. The patients don't trust you, and neither do I. You have no common sense, no self-control, and you panic in an emergency. You might have been good in research, but you are not cut out for clinical practice. You should have stayed at the university. You might have made a name for yourself cutting up dogs and frogs."

"Sir, I—"

"Just a minute," said Parky. "I'm not finished. You're not much help to me here in Sentryville. You don't carry your weight. You can't cover for me, and I do most of the work."

"At least I'm not a butcher," said Crest. "I don't specialize in keeping people happy while they die. I don't specialize in keeping people sick. I don't perpetuate disease, and I don't fill up the cemetery, and I don't—"

"As a matter of fact," said Parky, "you don't do much of anything at all."

"Would you like my resignation, sir?"

"I'd rather fire you."

"It won't be necessary, sir. I'm through."

Pale with rage and tension, Crest turned on his heel and went home. Emerald was awake.

"For Pete's sake," said Emerald. "What's the matter, chum?"

"Mordikay shot himself."

"Oh, dear," said Emerald.

"That isn't all," said Crest. "Your father and I had a hell of an argument, right over the body, with all those policemen looking on."

"I thought you were getting along so much better now."

"I can't work with him, Emerald," said Crest. "He makes too many mistakes. If I stay on with him, I'll be making the same sort of mistakes, as I did tonight."

"What do you mean?"

"Mordikay needed my sympathy and understanding. I gave him criticism. Emerald, I shot that man just as surely as if I had pulled the trigger with my own hands. I made a little child go blind. I made a poor crazy woman hang herself. I made my father hang himself. He looked like a dead giraffe."

Crest went into the bathroom and vomited. When he returned, he was ashen, drenched with cold sweat.

"Can I get you a drink?" said Emerald. "A cup of nice hot tea? A sleeping pill or anything?"

"I've spit it out of me. I'll be all right," said Crest.

"Why don't you resign your job with Daddy? Why don't you quit?"

"I already have," said Crest.

"Wonderful," she said. "Now we can get out of town. It isn't too late."

"I'm not going to get out of town," said Crest. "I intend to open an office of my own in Sentryville, if I can get your father's permission."

"Why?"

"I need to prove something to myself."

"Do you think you could make a living here alone?"

"That's what I want to prove," said Crest. "You'll stay with me?"

She didn't answer.

"I need you, Emerald."

"And I need this town like a hole in the head," she said. "But I'll stay. I should have my head examined. When are you going to quit trying to act like a Parkindale?"

"Immediately," said Crest. "I am not a Parkindale. I shall do battle with the dynasty for the rest of my life."

"Sure," said Emerald, "and I'm a ring-tailed baboon!"

In the morning, Crest phoned Parky and requested his permission to practice in Sentryville.

"My boy," said Parky, "you can practice in hell as far as I'm concerned!"

Part 5

The shingle hung from an arm attached to a post that was planted in the grass outside the office, and it said JOHN CREST, M.D. Crest felt a glow of pride every time it caught his eye. However, he was glad he didn't have a longer name, like Parkindale, for example. That sign had cost him nearly five dollars a letter.

On the outer door, a gadget hung from a nail. One side of the gadget had a clock face with movable hands and an inscription in the center: THE DOCTOR IS OUT. HE WILL RETURN AT . . . On the other side of the gadget, the inscription read: THE DOCTOR IS IN. PLEASE RING BELL AND ENTER. Crest would turn the gadget around according to which inscription was applicable.

Just inside the door was the waiting room, which had been converted from a hall. It was small and dark and often empty. At the far end of the hall was the office, converted from a dining room, big enough and properly equipped, but it still looked like a dining room. There was an examining table,

scales, an instrument cabinet, filing cabinets, a set of stain-
less-steel instruments, gauze, adhesive, bandages, and
quantities of drugs. The equipment was the best that bank-
loan money could buy.

Crest announced the opening of his offices in an ad in the
weekly Sentryville *NEWS*, the biggest possible ad consistent
with professional ethics and good taste. In addition, he mailed
several thousand announcement cards to the citizens of Sentryville. He opened the office on a Monday morning, but nobody came.

"Were you expecting a line of waiting patients all the way
down the block?" asked Emerald.

"It's always slow," said Crest.

There was nobody on Tuesday. The doorbell did not ring
and neither did the telephone.

"But I didn't think it would be quite this slow," said Crest.

After all, he had been in Sentryville for a year. He knew at
least 1,000 of the citizens by name, and 2,000 of the citizens
must have known him. When he had been working for
Parky, many of the patients preferred him to Parky and requested him. Perhaps none of these people happened to be
sick that week.

Wednesday came, but the patients didn't. An epidemic of
good health must have swept down the valley. However, if
Crest drove past Parky's offices, he could see dozens of cars
parked out front. At the hospital, all the sixty beds were full:
fifty-four for Parky's patients, two each for Hamilton and
Rhodes, one for Dr. Klamp, and one for Dr. Jones, and none at
all for Crest.

"String a wire across the sidewalk at ankle level," suggested
Emerald. "Somebody might trip and break a leg."

"It's nice to have ten hours of sleep each night and to get
my meals on time," said Crest.

"You could take your car and run down a pedestrian," said
Emerald.

"Now I have time to catch up on the professional literature," said Crest.

"Or," she said, "you could brew up a batch of pathogenic bacteria and dump them in the municipal water supply. If everybody came down together in an epidemic, surely some of them would call for you."

"I'll wait," said Crest grimly.

"Yes, dear," said Emerald. "You may be waiting quite some length of time."

Crest did not consider her remark exactly cricket. When the husband is in trouble, isn't the wife supposed to be standing by to give him sympathy? Of course, this trouble was of his own creation. Emerald had wanted him to move to another town. She was phrasing that remark so satisfying to the speaker and so galling to the listener, "I told you so!" Crest remembered his pride, his stubborn nature, his determination to flick a cigarette butt over the wall on the very first day. He dug in and waited for the patients to arrive.

The office bell first rang on Thursday. Crest, reading a magazine in his office behind closed doors, had to keep himself from leaping out to greet the visitor. He made himself wait inside the office long enough to indicate that he was busy, but not so long that the visitor would give up hope and go away. Finally he entered the waiting room with his most professional smile.

It was a detail man, one of those suave and personable representatives of a drug manufacturer who visit doctors door to door. The man was detailing a vitamin B preparation that day. Crest knew that the drug in question was identical with the brand of twenty other companies, the only difference being that of price. This one was considerably more expensive. Crest listened patiently to the spiel, which was very persuasive and only partially untrue. Parky, Crest remembered, used to welcome detail men; like many physicians who are too busy to study and to read, Parky got most of his information on new drugs from detail men, a biased and untrustworthy source of

post-graduate education. Crest accepted an armful of beautiful printed material and a pocketful of samples in cute and
cunning containers. He went back into his office, promptly
dumped the literature and samples into the wastebasket, and
picked up his magazine again.

On Friday there was another detail man, and an insurance
salesman, and a nice old lady soliciting for the Community
Chest. Crest gave her a couple of dollars; he didn't have the
heart to turn her down. There was no business over the weekend. On Monday there were two detail men; two insurance
salesmen; a middle-aged boy working his way through college
selling subscriptions; a Girl Scout selling cookies; and a passing tourist who inquired directions to the office of Dr.
Parkindale.

"I'm getting busier all the time," thought Crest. "Soon I may
even get a patient."

The first patient happened to be a dog. The day was hot; the
asphalt on the pavement was melting; and the animal's pads
were full of sticky tar. Her worried mistress brought her into
the office.

"But, madam," said Crest. "I'm a doctor, not a vet."

"Well, if you refuse to take care of my poor little Fidele, I'll
find somebody else."

"Please come in," said Crest hastily.

Asphalt is soluble in acetone, and Crest had a bottle of acetone. He removed the tar without too much trouble, and accepted a three-dollar fee.

"My first dollars," said Crest. "I'll frame them and hang
them on the office wall."

"No you won't!" said Emerald. "Gimme! We need groceries."

"Don't they have a vet in Sentryville?" asked Crest, remembering that he had seen Parky treat a cow.

"Sure," said Emerald.

Just out of curiosity, Crest looked up the vet in the phone
book, gave him a ring, and asked for a quotation on removing

tar from the pads of a poodle. The fee was quoted at fifteen dollars.

"I understand why she wanted a physician instead of a vet," said Crest.

"That reminds me of one of Daddy's stories," said Emerald. "There's a man living down the valley who calls Daddy every time he wants a ride to town. The charge for a house call is six dollars. It costs fifteen dollars to call a taxi cab."

The next person to enter the waiting room was human, but not a paying patient. She was a woman in her early thirties, smart, chic, with a certain sharpness to her features which seemed familiar to Crest. He couldn't place her, however.

"I'm Dr. Mordikay's daughter," she said.

"Oh," said Crest. "Please come in."

She sat down in the patient's chair and studied Crest quite carefully. He felt uncomfortable.

"I came to thank you for what you did for my father," she said.

"Thank me?" said Crest.

"Yes."

"I tried to help him. I failed," said Crest.

"I never understood what was wrong with my father," she said, "but I realize that he was beyond any sort of help. I wasn't surprised at what happened. As a matter of fact, I had been expecting it for years. He was making threats long ago, even when my mother was alive. He was a brilliant man, but I don't think he was cut out to be a physician. On the surface he was hard, but I think he reacted too deeply to the suffering of his patients. I never knew him very well, I'm afraid. He was a lonely man."

"My own father committed suicide," said Crest.

She smiled at him, the Mordikay smile, youthful and quick, as if it were controlled by a switch. "Then you must understand," she said.

"I understand very little in certain complex problems of this nature," said Crest.

"My father had no friends," she said. "A number of his patients loved him, a surprising number considering the circumstances, but he had no social acquaintances. He shut himself off from the world. I think you were the closest to a friend that my father had in Sentryville."

"Me?" said Crest. "I barely knew him. I talked with him exactly three times."

"He often wrote of you in his letters. He seemed to think you understood his point of view."

"Only a very small part of it," said Crest.

"I won't take up any more of your time: I know you're a very busy man."

"I have plenty of time," said Crest.

"I wanted to thank you for everything and to pay your bill."

"Bill?"

"For your professional services to my father."

"I rendered no services," said Crest.

"I'd like to pay," she said. "I know doctors treat each other without charge, but my father hated this custom. He wasn't much of a man for professional courtesies."

"Honestly," said Crest. "There was no treatment and no fee."

"I wish there was something I could do to express my gratitude."

There was only one thing Crest could think of. Those patients who were faithful to Dr. Mordikay, those people whom Mordikay did not wish entrusted to the tender mercies of Dr. Parkindale—was there any way these patients could be persuaded to consult Dr. Crest? Of course, Crest couldn't ask her that!

The first real patient was an elderly man who lived alone in the hills, not far from the home of the child who had died of tuberculosis. It was a small and filthy tumbledown shack just big enough for a bed, a stove, a chamber pot, and the patient himself. The sheets, once white, were now a rich brownish shade from lack of exposure to soap and water, as was the patient himself; the stove was red hot, even though this was summertime.

"What can I do for you, sir?" said Crest.

"Well," said the patient, "it's rather personal."

The patient looked like an ancient bawdy Caribbean buccaneer, but underneath a layer of sunburn and accumulated grime he seemed to be trying to blush.

"You can take me into your confidence, sir," said Crest.

"Well," said the patient, "I thought I might get married again. There's a nice young widow living down the road a piece."

"Do you want a blood test?"

"First you better look me over, Doc. Tell me if it's worth my while."

Crest examined the patient. He was not in very good condition, to say the least. In fact, he had enough pathology to fill the museum at the university. The heart was failing; the liver was large; there was emphysema, bronchitis, and bronchiectasis in the lungs and possibly carcinoma too; blood pressure was incredibly high; there were residuals of a little stroke, and hemorrhoids, and double hernia the size of baseballs and . . . Crest gave up. It seemed unlikely that the patient could survive for the remainder of the day.

"Sir, you're not in very good shape," said Crest. "I'd like to put you into the hospital."

"No," said the patient.

"You wouldn't consider it?"

"Absolutely not. I can't get married in a hospital."

Crest considered the problem. There was so much pathology here he didn't know where to begin. On the other hand, he knew that some old people may be laden with disease and survive at home, in their own environment, for incredible lengths of time. Sometimes when you put these people in a hospital, they fall apart like the one-horse shay and die within the week. As for marriage, well, it is nice for a lonely invalid to have a woman to take care of him. Surely at his age and his condition, he couldn't have anything else in mind.

"Doc," said the patient, "I get along pretty good during the day, but it's the nights I'm worried about."

"Short of breath?" said Crest.

"That ain't what I'm short of," said the patient. "Can't you give me something to restore my powers?"

Crest absorbed this request with astonishment. The old fellow was probably dying of combined disease of the heart, blood pressure, and lungs, but this didn't bother him. He wasn't looking for immortality. He preferred the fountain of youth. At his age and in his condition, it was an aphrodisiac he required! This request filled Crest with a feeling of helplessness.

"Sir," he said, "at your age and in your condition, I can't promise very much."

"Doc, let's give her a try. We got nothing to lose what ain't already been lost."

Crest reached blindly into his bag, picked up the first pill vial that came to hand, poured out a few of the pills into an envelope, and gave it to the patient. It happened to be pink aspirin. He expected to hear nothing further from this patient.

However, a few days later he received a request to send out a supply of "them little red dynamite pills" to the old man in the hills. Crest doubted that they worked; but if the old fellow thought they did, he supposed that was all that was required of him. Intermittently for the next few months, and on and off for some years to come, strange dirty people came wandering out of the hills into Crest's office, wanting little red dynamite pills.

"I'm in business," thought Crest, "thanks to the miraculous power of the aspirin tablet, pink, of course!"

During the first two weeks, the patients were so few that Crest was still counting them. The doorbell rang, and Crest knew that the thirty-second person was about to enter his waiting room. He remained in the office for the customary minute and walked into the waiting room with his professional smile. Then he stopped with the shock of recognition.

"Sam!"

"John Crest, M.D., the best and busiest practitioner in Sentryville," said Sam Parkindale.

"Best, but not busiest," said Crest. "Come into the office, Sam. It's been a long, long time."

"I don't want to keep you from your patients."

"Patients? Are you kidding?" said Crest.

"It seems lonely as hell in here."

"It is," said Crest. "Have a seat."

Sam sat down in the patient's chair and studied the office furnishings while Crest studied Sam. He had last seen Sam at the wedding, a year before in June, when Sam had been best man. On that occasion, Sam was flying high on champagne and Crest had been in the bridegroom's customary state of agitated befuddlement; there had been no opportunity to discuss old times. Prior to the wedding, Crest hadn't seen Sam since the day of their graduation from medical school.

This was the same old Sam: apple cheeks, devil-may-care manner, still wearing jauntiness like a pork-pie hat. And yet there was something new, an elusive darker side that Crest could not properly define. Although this was early on a weekday afternoon, there was a faint aroma of expensive Scotch exuding from his friend. It was to be hoped that Sam was not beginning to explore the devious avenues of a Dr. Mordikay.

"This place reminds me of an empty tomb," said Sam. "Let's go out and get drunk."

"I can't afford to leave: a patient might come," said Crest.

"Lock the door and fetch that extremely pregnant sister of mine, and let's all go out to Joseph's place."

"Where's that?"

"I thought you lived in this vicinity," said Sam. "My uncle

has a summer cottage on Crystal Lake, about ten miles up-river. Come on! This is too nice a day to be indoors."

"I'm trying to earn a living."

"It doesn't look that way," said Sam. "This is summertime, and the living should be easy. Crystal Lake is dappled with shadows and the water is cool. Joseph's liquor cabinet is inexhaustible. We can have a drink and a swim and, when the evening shadows begin to gather over the barbecue pit, we can roast a fatted calf. Then we can fill the night with beer and bull."

"That sounds wonderful," said Crest, "but my conscience says no."

"That damn conscience will be the death of you yet."

"I'm still in business," said Crest.

"I expect to earn eighteen thousand dollars this year. How about you?"

"Not that much," admitted Crest.

"Well, if you're facing bankruptcy, you might as well enjoy it."

"There's something in what you say. I'll get Emerald. Shall we drive you out to Crystal Lake?"

"What are you driving these days?" asked Sam.

"A second-hand Ford coupe. I suppose you have a Cadillac?"

"Duesenberg," said Sam. "Fire-engine red. You better come with me and give the citizens a thrill."

Joseph's cottage on Crystal Lake was small but luxurious. There was a gravel drive; a lush green patch of shaded lawn; a pier with canoes and a Cris-Craft; a float with diving boards anchored fifty feet off shore in the shimmering water.

Sam pulled into the drive and screeched to a halt in a shower of pebbles. Joseph, dressed in a sports jacket and white flannel pants with a razor crease, walked across the lawn to greet them, a highball in his hand. There was a woman with him, a willowy, regal ash blonde, and Crest remembered her: the one with the new aristocratic nose who was as silent as a clam. Wasn't her name Diana?

Emerald kissed her uncle on the cheek. Joseph extended a friendly greeting to Crest. Diana had nothing to say. The five of them walked into the cottage.

The living room was long and low, furnished in quiet but expensive taste. A picture window fronted on the lake. There was a great stone fireplace and a well-stocked bar. Sam disappeared into the rear of the house and soon returned in bathing trunks. He was tanned and muscular, but Crest noticed that he was putting on a layer of flab around the waist. Sam took a large quick drink at the bar, ran out onto the pier, and dived, knifing cleanly into the water. Diana had been wearing a robe of many colors in terry cloth. She shed it now to reveal a bathing suit underneath: azure blue, of some satin-like material, skin tight. It would have been possible for Crest not to stare at her if he hadn't been male. She paraded along the pier as if it were a runway and swam out in a crisp Australian crawl, joining Sam on the diving float. Emerald's figure was no longer to be displayed in a bathing suit; she wandered out onto the lawn and sat underneath a tree, placidly smoking a cigarette. Crest found himself alone in the living room with Joseph.

"One of the milder forms of sexual exhibitionism, wouldn't you say?" said Joseph.

"Sir?" said Crest.

"Swimming."

"I hadn't thought of it," said Crest. "Yes, maybe so."

"The water is fine. We have an extra pair of trunks that ought to fit you."

"I think not," said Crest. "I swim in a desperate dog paddle. I could save myself from drowning if the distance wasn't too great, but I don't enjoy myself in the water."

"Can I get you a drink?"

"Scotch," said Crest. "Make it fairly weak, if you please." Joseph rattled some ice cubes at the bar. "What are you breeding with Emerald? Triplets? She's shaped like a flatulent hippopotamus!"

"She does protrude," said Crest. "Of course, she is a small-boned girl."

Joseph sat down beside Crest on the sofa in front of the picture window. He put his long legs on a coffee table, carefully adjusting his slacks to preserve the crease. He looked at the lake. Sam and Diana were having a rather intimate puppy scuffle on the float.

"If I were a younger man, I should be jealous of that," said Joseph, motioning toward the lake.

"Sam and your wife?" said Crest.

Joseph laughed. "What gave you the impression that Diana was my wife?"

Crest fought back an inclination to blush.

"It's a natural error on your part," said Joseph. "I used to change my women with the seasons, but Diana has been with me now for a number of years. It requires energy to change one's mistresses. I suppose I'll marry her some day out of sheer inertia. How does Sam look to you after a couple of years?"

"Sam doesn't change," said Crest, "except . . ."

"Yes?"

"Does he drink a lot?"

"No," said Joseph, "but he drinks too much."

"He's not married or engaged, I suppose."

"There's no suggestion of latent homosexuality in Sam, if that's what you mean. He enjoys girls. But he enjoys them in quantity, as I used to do when I was a younger man. Perhaps he considers marriage as a trap. Or perhaps, in attempting to be considerate toward women, he doesn't wish to inflict himself upon one of them in any sort of permanent relationship. Sam is superficial. He avoids any personal relationships in depth."

"I would have thought some smart young woman would have hooked him long ago."

"Damn it," said Joseph, "I wish that young puppy would

stop imitating me. Have you any remaining influence with Sam?"

"I never had much."

"It was you who dragged him through medical school by the lobe of the ear."

"I don't think Sam would have flunked out of any medical school."

"How about dentistry?"

"Emerald says that tartar and cavities didn't fascinate him very much."

"No," said Joseph. "It must be obvious to you that Sam never wanted to become a doctor, let alone a dentist. He is a father-driven man. I'm sure you know what I mean by that."

"You're not satisfied with his work in plastic surgery?"

"The patients like him. That is no surprise," said Joseph. "He is clever with his fingers, which is likewise no surprise. But his work is mechanical: he shows no flair."

"What would Sam have liked to be?" asked Crest.

"An artisan, I suppose: a worker with his hands. Sam hates cutting into bleeding human flesh. He would prefer to express himself by carving some more durable material: wood, for example, or stone."

"But you do sculpture as a hobby, sir."

"As a hobby, Sam goes out and raises a little hell," said Joseph.

"Sam always liked to play."

"Like a puppy," said Joseph. "Sam is gifted with superficial charm, and everybody likes him, but he can't involve himself with people on any deeper plane. In a way, he's afraid of people."

"He certainly doesn't act that way."

"He acts," said Joseph. "All Parkindales are actors. I am worried about Sam. He lacks any sense of dedication to his work, and I'm afraid that he won't amount to a hill of beans."

"He's a late starter, but he'll find himself one day," said Crest. "I have great faith in Sam."

"How do you get along with Emerald?"

"Very well."

"Is she happy?"

"I don't think she cares for pregnancy," said Crest.

"I also worry about your wife," said Joseph. "I worry about the entire family. Despite our arrogance and pride, we are an unhappy lot. I think we're missing a screw somewhere. With the exception of my brother, of course, who has one screw too many. Screw Parky! I'm glad you were able to break away from him, Crest, although I am not sure it was a mature decision for you to settle here in Sentryville."

"I'm also a father-driven man," said Crest. "In my case, I fight authority. I find it necessary to battle with my fathers."

"If you can recognize that fact, you are not entirely lacking in maturity."

"The fact was pointed out to me," said Crest. "Did you know Dr. Mordikay? He was one of our local men in Sentryville."

"Surely. Mordikay was the most brilliant young brain surgeon in the city when I was in medical school."

"He did brain surgery?"

"Yes."

"How did he end up as a general man in Sentryville?"

"There was a rumor," said Joseph. "I don't know if it was true. They said that his wife developed a brain tumor and wouldn't let anybody touch her but Mordikay. She died on the table. They say it broke his nerve. It takes a peculiar courage, or lack of sentiment, to be a brain surgeon, I suppose. They have a thirty per cent operative mortality, and many of their surviving patients become human vegetables."

"He never told me anything of that."

"Medicine can twist a man in curious ways. Another drink?"

"Not now," said Crest.

"Your wife looks thirsty sitting underneath that tree."

"I believe she would accept a cold, dry Martini, sir," said Crest.

"Fine. I'll mix it and you can carry it out. We must take

care of the future generation. They will be taking care of us in our old age."

Joseph blended a Martini and Crest carried it out, walking carefully in order not to slurp the drink over the edges of the glass. He smiled at Emerald, handed her the drink, and sat down beside her on the grass. She took a sip.

"Uum, good," she said, but then she set the glass aside and did not touch it again.

"You're strangely antisocial this afternoon," said Crest.

"Ruminating," she said. "Vegetating. Breeding like some fat old animal. Isn't she beautiful?"

"Who?"

"See Diana on the float with Sam?"

"You're the one who's beautiful," said Crest, and he kissed her on the cheek. Her skin was damp in the heat.

"You're drunk," she said. "There ought to be a law: pregnant females should be hid. Their husbands should be permitted to act like bachelors between the fourth and ninth months. Doesn't it sort of drive you nuts?"

"What do you mean?"

"Don't men go wild and insane when they haven't had a woman for a period of time?"

"I have you," said Crest.

"Bulls' tails," she said. "How could a night with a cow in my condition compare with a beautiful bitch like that?"

Crest decided to be daring. "You were a beautiful bitch," he said, "and will be one again."

The remark fell flat. "If you wanted to make a pass at her tonight, I'd understand," said Emerald.

"Nothing could be further from my mind," said Crest.

"It isn't fair," she said, patting her tummy. "It isn't fair to you."

"A woman in your condition is far more important than anything in a bathing suit," said Crest.

"You're a sissy," she said. "You'd be afraid to make a pass at Diana."

"She doesn't interest me," said Crest. "She's cold."

"Afraid you couldn't warm her up?"

"A vacuum, a void, no personality, nothing but a body. Joseph cut out her tongue when he fixed her nose."

"The perfect female," said Emerald. "Perfect body and no tongue."

"Nonsense," said Crest.

"A woman to be had and never heard."

"And therefore an utter bore."

"Chum," said Emerald, "next you'll be telling me that women are human beings too."

"Now, Emerald, stop that!"

"Neither you nor Sam nor Joseph have taken your eyes off her since she stripped off her robe."

"But, dear, neither have you!"

"Oh, John," she wailed. "How could anyone desire a fat old cow in my condition?"

"I desire you more than any woman who ever lived."

"Even now?"

"Especially now."

"Then you're a perverted idiot," she said.

"Do you want to go home?"

"No," she said. "I want to sit under a tree. Go away. Go make a pass at Diana, I don't care."

"I'd prefer to get drunk with your brother if I can't sit under a tree with you."

"Do that!" she said.

Pregnant women can be moody. Crest understood. He patted her fondly on the shoulder and carried his empty glass back into the cottage. Diana and Sam were leaving the water. Diana dripped her way toward a back room and Joseph followed her. Sam toweled himself briskly and put on a robe over his still damp bathing trunks and then mixed himself a generous drink at the bar.

"One for me. Scotch and water," said Crest. "Your sister's in a sulky mood, jealous of Diana's figure."

"Dames are funny," said Sam. "Diana was just telling me that she was jealous of Emerald's pregnancy. I told her I'd be willing to be of assistance at any time, but that didn't go over well."

"Diana can talk?"

"Only when jealous," said Sam. He brought Crest's drink and sat down beside him on the sofa. "Man to man and buddy to buddy," he said, "what happened between you and that pompous son-of-a-bitch that Emerald and I call Dad?"

"It's a long story," said Crest.

"I have long ears."

"There was a fundamental difference in opinion," said Crest. "We couldn't see eye to eye."

"That I understand," said Sam. "I didn't think you'd get along. How could you stay with him for an entire year?"

"It was a valuable year," said Crest. "I learned plenty."

"How to keep the patients happy while you're killing them?"

"He makes mistakes," said Crest. "Sometimes serious mistakes. But in the art of handling people, he's a magician."

"You've changed, my friend," said Sam. "I think some of Parky has rubbed off on you."

"Others have said the same."

"Don't you punch them in the nose?"

"If I could acquire some of the Parkindale magic, it would be very much worth while," said Crest.

"What made you break up with him at last?"

"There was a man we were trying to help," said Crest. "The fellow died. I blamed Parky and your father blamed me. We were both upset by the way that it happened. I think we both handled it wrong. In the heat of the moment, we suddenly couldn't stand the sight of each other, and divorce was inevitable."

"You sound as if you'd go back with him if you had the chance."

"I was busier last year," Crest admitted.

"Why did you decide to open an office in Sentryville?"

"They need another doctor here."

"Like flit they do!" said Sam. "Not while my old man is still in business! The patients will never leave him."

"Why wouldn't they?"

"They'd be afraid that Parky wouldn't take them back. He won't give you a single crumb off his table, boy, even though he's got indigestion from having too much to eat. One more question, the tricky one: is he still going to deliver Emerald? . . . What's the matter? I distinctly saw you wince."

"There's nobody else in town," said Crest.

"Does Emerald like that?"

"As much as she likes anything else concerned with pregnancy."

"Do you trust my father's judgment, handling her case?"

"Have I a choice?" said Crest.

"Boy, you're a nut," said Sam. "I never could have a reasonable discussion with a lunatic. I move that this meeting be adjourned. Let's go out and start a fire and scorch a little meat."

"Fine," said Crest. "I'm hungry."

The red sun was low over the lake, and there was a dank delicious smell in the air. Joseph had already lit a fire in the outdoor fireplace and wood smoke blended with the fragrance of the lake. Joseph was wearing a big chef hat, askew on the side of his head, and an apron embroidered with cute and clever aphorisms. Diana had put on a hostess gown, deep cut down the back and almost as deep to the breasts. The gown concealed more of her figure than a bathing suit and yet it seemed to reveal the figure more. This was not the costume for an evening picnic, Crest decided; it was the sort of thing to be worn indoors, for an intimate gathering of only two or three, when there was a male to be seduced.

"I hope the mosquitos bite the holy hell out of her," said Emerald to Crest spitefully.

"Biting mosquitos are the female ones," said Crest. "Males

are inoffensive little midges who get their nourishment from the sap of plants."

"I'd like to bite her all the same," said Emerald.

"As a matter of fact, so would I," said Sam, who had managed to tune in on the conversation.

"What's the subject of discussion, boys?" Joseph said from the smoky region over the fire.

"The rape of a goddess of the moon," said Sam.

"The huntress of the chase?" said Joseph.

If Diana understood the conversation, she did not react. Joseph put raw steaks on the grillework, and the smell of roasting meat percolated through the air. There were bottles of beer in a bucket of ice; Crest opened a bottle for himself; it tasted cold and delicious. Sam rummaged through a bag of potato chips. Emerald was munching on a pickle. Diana rattled a silver cocktail shaker and poured something pink out of it into a glass.

"Does Diana ever get drunk?" Crest asked Sam.

Sam was eating a steak with his fingers, getting grease all over himself. "Sure," he said. "She drinks and drinks and drinks, and nothing seems to happen, and then one last sip and she suddenly falls apart."

"Sounds interesting," said Crest.

"Believe me," said Sam, "it is."

Joseph approached, bearing a long-handled fork, which he flourished like a weapon.

"Can't you two young stallions discuss some other mare?" said Joseph.

Crest thought this was a fine idea. He got a steak for himself and another bottle of beer and joined his wife. Emerald was still eating pickles.

"You can't make a meal of those things," he said.

"Fancies are strange in my condition, chum," she said.

"You don't seem to be having much fun."

"Oodles," she said. "I'm watching the situation develop. I'm laying odds on you."

"What do you mean?"

"Odds on which one of you lays her first."

"Stop that, Emerald," said Crest. "You don't want me to make a pass at her."

"I don't?"

Emerald walked, or rather waddled, over to Diana.

"Darling, you'll freeze," Emerald purred. "All that lovely bare skin is showing, dear, and the mosquitos are ravenous tonight. They will bite you. Particularly there!"

She put her hand on Diana, reaching down and touching the cleft between the breasts. Diana jumped. Probably Emerald's hand was cold. Crest found the behavior of his wife embarrassing, and yet he was perversely pleased by Diana's reaction. It was the first time he had seen her react to anything.

"You are cold, dear," said Emerald, "and with all these men around, too! Can't John get you a wrap? John, dear, get the lady a wrap."

"John, dear, go wrap yourself around the lady," said Sam.

"Wrap, wrap, who's there?" said Joseph, apparently enjoying the strange moment that had developed.

Crest, uncomfortable, wanted to escape, so he walked toward the cottage.

"Oh, look, isn't that sweet!" came Emerald's voice behind him, loud and clear. "They're going into the house together."

Crest discovered it was true. Diana was going into the cottage with him. They passed through the living room and into a dark bedroom, obviously hers. She brushed against him in the darkness, and he was conscious of warmth and womanhood. Crest pulled himself together as she turned on the light.

"I'm sorry," he said. "I don't know what was going on out there, but I think we owe you an apology. We are a rude family."

Miracle of miracles, she spoke. "They don't bother me," she said.

This was not the cool, husky, intimate voice Crest had been

expecting. Diana's voice was shrill, high-pitched. Crest knew why she never spoke if she could avoid it.

"Are you jealous of my wife?" asked Crest. "She seems to be jealous of you."

"Sometimes I could almost kill that man," she said.

She took Crest's hand and placed it at the spot Emerald had touched, at the cleft between the breasts.

"See? I'm not really cold," she said.

Temptation was facing him. Why not? Emerald had been asking for this. But Crest's own nature rescued him; he snatched his hand away, as if it had been resting on a hot stove. Diana smiled at him. The smile spread slowly across her face as if she were afraid that she might crack open the network of fine scars around her nose and make them bleed. Crest wondered what her face had looked like before the plastic surgery.

"Your wife is luckier than me," she said.

She found her coat and Crest helped her on with it. Then she took him by the arm and they went outdoors together, more or less triumphantly.

The sun had set and it was now quite dark. The fire was burning low. Joseph was staring into the dying flame, nursing the residue in his highball glass. Sam sprawled on the grass nearby. Emerald stood apart in the darkness; she was smoking a cigarette and Crest could see the coal glowing on and off. The silence out here was of the kind that had been lying around for a period of time. Diana released Crest's arm and went over to Joseph, touching him with her body. Joseph whispered something low, which Crest could not catch; then Joseph and Diana went into the cottage together. The cottage remained quite dark. Sam, on the ground, let out a soft, sibilant sigh. Crest went to Emerald's side. She tugged him deeper into the darkness, away from the fire, toward the lapping edges of the lake.

"I thought you were never coming out of there," she said.

She took his hands and placed them on her breasts. The

breasts were fuller than they used to be, preparing for milk. Crest could feel the nipples stiffen through the material of her maternity dress and loose brassiere.

"Hold me very hard," she said.

"Emerald," said Crest, "what were you trying to do?"

"In my condition, a woman shouldn't have feelings, but I can't help it," she said.

She tried to kiss him, but there was a mechanical difficulty. His hands on her chest and the swelling of her abdomen made it impossible for her to reach his lips.

"It's hard to get at a woman in your condition," said Crest.

"Pretty funny joke. It's easy to get at Diana."

Crest put his arms around her. "Those who play with desire for pleasure are cheating themselves," he said. "Man is entitled to some pleasure and is required to endure some pain, but pleasure for its own sake destroys and degrades. As a sport, sex is silly; the positions are undignified. As a lust, sex is either shabby or revolting, depending on the amount of violence. Sex is worth while only as a means of expression and communication between two lovers, for the sole purpose of creating children to be loved. Anything else is an itch. The more you scratch an itch, the more it itches."

"You're quite a remarkable guy," she said. "You deserve something better than a Parkindale. We are not a marrying family."

Suddenly Sam materialized out of the darkness. "I hope I'm not interrupting anything, friends."

"Between us," said Crest, "it's already happened."

"The eternally fascinating subject of conversation," said Sam.

"It shouldn't be," said Crest.

"It isn't," said Sam. "Except to those who are unsatisfied. Which is all of us."

"Sam," said Crest, "when are you going to marry?"

"To get a glass of beer, I have to buy a brewery?" said Sam.

"Is there any other way to be satisfied?" said Crest.

"Female propaganda," said Sam. "Don't believe everything you read."

"What do you believe?" said Crest.

"That I don't come from a marrying family," said Sam.

"I just said the same thing," said Emerald.

"You should have heard the silence when you and Diana were in the cottage together," said Sam. "Brother, it was profound!"

The lights in the cottage suddenly flashed on.

"About time," said Sam. "I was thinking I should go in and offer Joseph a little help."

A string of lights along the pier also went on. The reflection shimmered in the water of the lake like jewels. Joseph and Diana walked out onto the pier. She had changed her clothes again: a skin-tight black leotard this time.

"An extensive wardrobe," said Crest.

"She's always getting into things and out of things," said Sam.

"I suppose she likes to change in the dark," said Crest.

"Why should she?" said Emerald.

"Why do we always discuss Diana in her presence? She can hear us. They're only thirty feet away from us," said Crest.

"We're taking a spin in the Cris-Craft, chums," called Joseph. "Care to come along?"

Crest looked at Emerald.

"I guess not," she said.

"We must be getting home," said Crest.

"Johnnie and Em will need a ride, so I'll have to be chauffeur," said Sam.

"You'll pardon us, then?" said Joseph.

"Sure. Go on. We had a fine time tonight," said Crest.

"See you again," said Joseph.

Diana didn't say a word. Joseph stepped lightly down into the Cris-Craft, helped Diana aboard, and started the engine with a roar. The trim boat spun neatly on her heel and roared sharply out into the darkness.

"They like to go zooming all over the lake at any time of night," said Sam. "Perhaps it has some sexual significance. The neighbors frequently complain."

"Now you might take us home," said Crest.

Sam drove fast. The ten-mile trip to Sentryville took no more than twelve minutes. Crest and Emerald said good night to Sam at the door and went upstairs. They hadn't finished undressing for bed when the telephone rang. Crest answered the infernal instrument.

"Dr. Crest speaking."

"You better get out here quick."

"Who is this speaking?" said Crest.

"Me, of course. Sam."

Somehow it didn't sound like Sam.

"What's the matter?" asked Crest.

"There's been an accident. We need a doctor out here."

"You have two doctors," said Crest. "Joseph and yourself."

"Some other time for the small talk, buddy," said Sam. "Why don't you make it snappy, if you don't mind?"

The usual banter was there, but there was an undercurrent of alarm in Sam's voice.

"Hold the fort: I'll be right along," said Crest, hanging up.

"House call, dear?" said Emerald.

"There's been some sort of an accident out on Crystal Lake," said Crest.

He tried to sound matter-of-fact, but she could catch the alarm in his voice.

"Oh, dear!" she said.

"It's probably something trivial," said Crest.

"Want to bet?" said Emerald.

Crest didn't want to bet. He covered the ground to Crystal Lake almost as quickly as Sam had done. The lights in the cottage were on and so were the string of lights along the pier. Crest parked in the drive and went into the living room.

"Sam?"

"Out here," called Sam from the lake-front side of the cottage. Crest went out.

"What's the trouble?" he asked.

No reply was required. Crest could see what the trouble was. The most striking thing was the boat, the Cris-Craft; it was halfway out of water, bow high in the air, mid-section resting on the float, stern buried in lake water. The float had been split as if by a blow of an ax. The hull looked enormous out of water, gleaming in the lights. The steel-edged keel was as sharp as a knife.

"They must have rammed into the float head on, going full speed," said Sam. "Look at that float. These things generate a lot of speed."

Thirty feet away, at the rock on which Emerald had been sitting half an hour ago, was Diana. She was partly sitting, partly leaning, against the rock in a jerky and unnatural position. Crest went over and shined his pocket flashlight in her eyes. Always cold, she was colder than ever; always white, her face was whiter than ever, except for the network of scars which now stood out with lividity. Her tongue lolled, as if she had been sticking it out in defiance at the world; there was pink froth at the lips; she was unmarked as far as Crest could tell.

"She's dead, buddy," said Sam. "Nothing can be done for her."

"I see no evidence of injury," said Crest.

"Put your hand in back of her head," said Sam.

At the back of the head, the scalp had been almost entirely avulsed. She had struck her head a glancing blow against the rock. There was almost no blood, evidence of instant death. At Crest's touch, her head moved too freely on her neck, and Crest could feel the crepitus of broken bone in the region of the mid-cervical vertebrae.

"On impact, they must have flown out of the front seat of the boat like birds, both of them," said Sam. "Diana turned around in mid-air and struck that rock. Clunk! Curtains!"

"Is Joseph dead?" asked Crest.

"Not quite."

Crest shined his light on Joseph. He was also unmarked. Joseph was unconscious, ashen, drenched in sweat, breathing with slow, shallow, labored respirations.

"Shock?" said Crest. "Internal bleeding, perhaps?"

"He also must have turned backwards in mid-air," said Sam, "and he caught the trunk of that tree directly across the middle of his back."

Crest noticed that a tree six inches in diameter had been snapped off near the base.

"He was conscious when I got here," said Sam.

"What did he say?"

"He didn't have any pain. He was worried over that. He was also worried because he couldn't move below the waist. He thought he must have broken his back."

"Paralyzed?"

"He mentioned the word 'paraplegia,'" said Sam. "Perhaps it might be better if he died. If he survives, he'll probably be permanently crippled."

"Paraplegia can be temporary."

"Yeah," said Sam. "Also not. Joseph said one more thing before he passed out in shock. He asked me to call you."

"Professionally?"

"Yes. He was very clear on that. He doesn't want treatment from a Parkindale. Me or especially Parky. He doesn't want Parky to touch him with a ten-foot pole."

"I'm not sure," said Crest. "Your father has more experience with traumatic surgery than anyone in this area."

"Joseph was sure."

"I don't know," said Crest. "I have no experience."

"You're in charge," said Sam. "What next, Doc?"

"We'll have to get him to the hospital."

"All right," said Sam. "If you dare to move him."

"There's nothing we can do out here. I'll call the ambulance. I'll also have to notify your father."

"Why?"

"On account of Diana, if nothing else," said Crest. "He's the medical examiner."

Crest went into the cottage, phoned for an ambulance, and alerted the hospital. He also phoned Dr. Parkindale. To Parky, Crest said very little; he identified himself and said that there had been a fatal accident at Joseph's summer cottage on Crystal Lake. Parky conducted no interrogation; he merely grunted and hung up. Crest went outside again.

"How do you suppose it happened?" said Crest.

"Search me!" said Sam. "Those lights on our pier are visible all over the lake."

"Perhaps the steering gear jammed."

"I suppose a mechanic can tell us in the morning."

"I wonder if we had anything to do with it?" said Crest.

"We?" said Sam. "What the hell! This must have happened while we were on the road. What do you mean?"

Crest wasn't sure what he meant. He filed away the thought for future reference. In the distance, he could already hear the wail of the ambulance siren. The noise came closer and soon the ambulance screamed into the drive, its red eye blinking. Two white-clad attendants stepped out and brought a stretcher. Another car pulled into the drive. It was Parky's Cadillac.

"Good evening, boys," said Parky blandly.

"Hello, Dad," said Sam.

"Good evening, sir," said Crest.

"A little trouble here?" said Parky.

"She's dead," said Sam, nodding toward Diana, "as you can see for yourself."

"What happened?" said Parky.

"No witnesses," said Sam. "You'll have to figure it out."

"Joseph is alive," said Crest. "We think he has a fractured spine with probable cord injury. He is deeply in shock and his condition is poor."

"Don't move that man!" thundered Parky in the voice of authority.

The ambulance attendants, about to place Joseph on the stretcher, suddenly stopped, awaiting further instructions.

"John wants him in the hospital," said Sam.

"I'm not interested in what John wants," said Parky. "I'm in charge."

"You're in charge of that," said Sam, again nodding toward Diana, "but Crest is in charge where Joseph is concerned."

"On whose authority?" said Parky coldly.

"At the request of the patient," said Sam. "He told me very clearly before he lost consciousness. Also by my authority. I am the closest relative."

"The man is my brother," said Parky.

"I am still the closest relative," said Sam.

"Crest can't handle a case like this," said Parky.

"He's going to handle it," said Sam.

"Crest knows nothing whatever about traumatic surgery."

"That's Joseph's business," said Sam, "and mine and Crest's. Diana is your business. You can leave the rest of us alone."

"Crest?" said Parky.

"Sir?" said Crest.

"Would you be such a fool as to take a case like this?"

Crest hesitated. He did not want to take the case. Equally, he did not want to refuse it.

"You see?" said Parky to his son, "Crest is useless in an emergency. He goes into panic. He doesn't know what to do."

"Come on, John," said Sam. "Don't let me down, buddy boy!"

"Crest," said Parky, "if you accept this case and my brother dies, or in any way fails to recover on account of your management, I shall hold you personally responsible."

"Don't let him bully you," said Sam.

"Why don't you stay out of this?" said Parky to Sam.

"Why don't you?" said Sam.

Sam and Parky stared at Crest. The decision was up to him.

They couldn't stand here arguing a family matter over a critically injured man. Crest took a deep breath.

"It's my case," said Crest.

"Good," said Sam.

"I credited you with more intelligence," said Parky. "If anything goes wrong, I shall hold you fully responsible."

"I am responsible for every patient I treat," said Crest.

"If anything goes wrong, you may face a malpractice suit," said Parky.

"Are you attempting to threaten me, sir?" said Crest.

"I am attempting to clarify your position so that there may be no misunderstanding later on," said Parky.

"Thanks," said Crest. "Now we must get this man into the hospital. Since we suspect a fractured spine, we must move him very carefully. All five of us should lift him onto the stretcher together: very gently, very carefully. Your assistance would be appreciated, Dr. Parkindale."

There was no further argument. Parky helped, and they all lifted Joseph carefully onto the stretcher. Crest then followed the ambulance to the hospital; he supervised the transfer of the patient onto the bed. An oxygen tent was ordered. Crest started an intravenous and made arrangements for a blood transfusion to follow in order to overcome the element of shock. Then he had decisions to make. Should X-rays be taken? Motion of the back must be prevented in order to prevent any further damage to the spinal cord; rolling the patient on a hard X-ray table could be dangerous. A portable X-ray could be taken with the patient still in bed, but this would also involve some motion of the back, and a portable X-ray may be of poor technical quality. Crest decided to omit X-rays, even though this meant he did not know what bones were fractured and to what extent. There was also the question of surgery. If a fragment of loose bone were sticking into the spinal cord, it ought to be removed. On the other hand, it was just as dangerous to roll the patient on an operating table as on an X-ray table.

This type of decision was frequently encountered in an emergency: whether to be conservative or radical. Crest had always felt that when there was any question, the conservative approach was safer and gave the best results over all. Above all, thou shalt do no harm! Nevertheless, if he did nothing, and there were poor results, he would be open to criticism. Parky's attitude had left no doubt of that. In this particular case, it seemed that a poor result was inevitable: death or permanent disability.

In order to cover himself, Crest put in a long-distance call to the city, contacting the best neurosurgical specialist he knew. The specialist was very pleasant, very reassuring. Crest suspected that at the university the radical approach would have been chosen, but the specialist agreed that in Sentryville, conservatism was best. Joseph's condition was such, of course, that he could not be transferred to the city.

Crest returned to Joseph's room and made sure that the patient was in the position of hyperextension of the spine, which position would force bone fragments outward and minimize the pressure on the spinal cord. There was nothing else to do but watch and hope and, possibly, pray.

Crest left the room, preparing to go home; as he passed through the hospital lobby, he saw Parky sitting there. Parky did not look like the figure of authority, chief of the hospital staff, responsible for the patients in almost every hospital bed. He looked like an anxious waiting relative. Crest averted his eyes and attempted to pass by, but Parky stopped him.

"Crest!"

Crest was immediately on the defensive. "He's deep in shock, sir. I can get no blood pressure. I've got him in oxygen and we're starting a blood transfusion. If he doesn't pull out of shock, of course, he'll die, and we're doing everything we can. I decided not to take X-rays. I'm afraid of further damage to the spinal cord. There is a paraplegia: no muscle movement, no reflexes of any kind below the waist. If he survives, the paraplegia could be permanent. I've phoned Dr. Black at the university. He was our teacher in neurosurgery, the best man I know in the field. He agrees with my approach. He is willing to come up here in consultation, but he doesn't think there's anything to do that we're not already doing, and neither do I."

Parky seemed scarcely interested in the details; he wasn't even listening. "I regret our conversation out at the lake," he said.

"So do I," said Crest.

"My son and I don't seem to get along. I suppose it's my fault, although Sam doesn't leave much of an opening. I hope you forget my remarks about a malpractice suit. I didn't mean it. The words were spoken in the heat of the moment."

"I understand," said Crest.

"If there's anything I can do, please don't hesitate to call on me. I know you're doing the best any man could do, and have this situation under your full control."

"Yes, sir," said Crest.

"Exactly what happened on the lake tonight?"

"I don't know," said Crest.

"God damn it, how could they hit that float? The lights were visible all over the lake."

"Perhaps the steering gear failed," said Crest.

"It didn't," said Parky. "I've examined the boat. Were they drinking?"

"Emerald and I had been out there on a picnic," said Crest. "The accident happened while Sam was taking us home. Yes, we had all been drinking except Emerald, but not very much. Nobody was drunk."

"I never understood that boy." Crest realized that Parky was referring to his younger brother. "All that talent gone to waste. My brother was a man of great ability, and could have been the finest doctor in the family, but he chose to waste himself on play. Busy work on the nose and breasts of various society women; living with these women afterwards; decadence and shame. He had no sense of dedication, no sense of service to the patient. He never seemed to care."

Parky got up and fatigue drenched every line of his massive body.

"At least you do have dedication, boy," said Parky. "Keep in touch with me."

"Yes, sir," said Crest.

Crest drove home, feeling as tired as Parky looked. Emerald was waiting up for him. Sam had telephoned and she knew the details of the situation.

"You look ninety-three per cent dead yourself," she said.

"I am."

Crest sat down on the edge of the bed and took off a shoe. "Maybe I'll quit practicing medicine," he said. "I should go back to the university. Maybe I should do research."

"What brings this up?" she said.

Crest took off his other shoe. "I have such a feeling of vast futility. I'm not cut out for the work."

"You didn't cause that accident to happen."

"Didn't I?" he said.

"For Pete's sake," she said. "Don't bring up your father and Mordikay and that poor old woman who hanged herself."

"I'm jinxed," said Crest. "I cause accidents to happen. Most accidents aren't accidents, according to Mordikay."

"You weren't driving that motorboat."

"If a man is jinxed, does he have any right to meddle in human affairs?"

"If he was a god, he should be ashamed of himself," she said.

"Of course I'm not a god."

"Then stop talking cosmic," she said. "I don't buy your theories, chum. You weren't responsible for Mordikay or your father. You weren't responsible for anything that happened on the lake tonight."

"I'm not responsible for the things I do?"

"Kiss me," she said.

"If I were more mature, I could learn to prevent accidents," he said.

"Kiss me at once," she commanded.

He kissed her. Then he put on his shoes again. "I'm going back to the hospital," he said.

"Why?"

"The doctor belongs at the bedside of the patient."

"If you're needed, the telephone will ring."

"I'm going back," he said.

"Okay. Far be it from me to keep you from your duty," she said. "You know what I would have done if I had you in a dark cottage alone with a figure like Diana's, with or without a hostess robe?"

Crest grinned. "Tell me," he said.

"Well, you wouldn't have caught me messing around in motorboats," she said.

"You have far more important things to do."

He patted her on the tummy. He could feel the little man inside give a sudden lurch.

"I'm not going to be pregnant forever," she said. "I'm warning you."

"I'll be around," said Crest.

He kissed her again and returned to the hospital.

Joseph was awake. Through the transparent hood of the oxygen tent, Crest could see his lips moving and knew he was trying to speak. Crest shut off the motor of the oxygen pump and raised the edge of the hood.

"Get this damn thing off me," said Joseph, weak of voice but strong of spirit.

"Take it easy. Save your strength," said Crest. "How are you feeling?"

"Suspended."

"I beg your pardon?" said Crest.

"Halfway between life and death and undecided which way to turn. Are you the doctor in my case?"

"Yes."

"Good," said Joseph. "I managed to avoid a Parkindale. How is Diana?"

"Joseph, I . . ."

"She's dead, isn't she?"

"Yes," said Crest. "She was killed instantly. Have you any pain?"

"No, nothing. There's an absence south of the umbilicus. I have no pain or sensation of any kind. I guess I broke my back on that ratty little tree."

"We're not sure," said Crest. "We haven't dared take an X-ray yet."

"I broke it," said Joseph. "I heard bone cracking when I hit the tree. Eleventh and twelfth thoracic vertebrae and perhaps first lumbar, I should say. I'm paraplegic, aren't I?"

"You are paralyzed below the waist, but it may be temporary," said Crest. "Function may return. We won't know for sure for many weeks or months."

"I'll think it over," said Joseph.

"I beg your pardon?" said Crest.

"Whether, under these conditions, I prefer to live or die," said Joseph.

He closed his eyes and lapsed back again into partial coma.

For the next day and night, for many days and nights, for a good portion of the next two weeks, Crest spent much of the time in Joseph's room. There was little for him to do. Most of the time he was sitting and watching and waiting.

In Joseph's case, Crest realized, he was doing something that very few doctors are ever privileged to do: continuous bedside observation of the patient. The doctor is busy; he cannot afford to spend more than a few minutes a day with any given patient; if he is a doctor, he never has the time to be a nurse. In this instance, Crest's practice was so small that he could afford the time, and his connections with the Parkindale family were so close that he preferred to spend his time in Joseph's room.

Crest realized that it is just as well a doctor cannot also be a nurse. The doctor should retain perspective and impartiality and must wear the mantle of authority. Constant contact with the patient would reduce the doctor's usefulness in these respects. On the other hand, the doctor loses something by being unable to sit and watch with the patient through the long hours of the day and even longer hours of the night. Nothing in medicine is static; disease and health have an ebb and flow. Crest could observe Joseph's courage come and go, his vitality and life force wax and wane. At times the black mist of depression would settle over Joseph and he would turn his face to the wall; at such times the touch of the hand of death was close to him. Crest was very well aware that the survival of the patient often depends on the will of the patient to survive. At any time, if Joseph had decided to die, he would have died, but his vital spark, though often very faint, did not go out. It was not a good sign when Joseph was too passive or docile; when he submitted to an enema or needle without protest, the state of his morale was low; on the other hand, if he kicked like a balky mule and acted with cantankerous irascibility, the vitality spark was burning brighter.

"God damn hospitals!" said Joseph in one of his better moods. "A strong man couldn't take it, and you subject this torture on the sick. They wake you up to give you a sleeping pill. They wake you up at five in the morning to give you a bath. They conceal you in a robe which conceals everything except the private parts. They starch the sheets to give you bed sores. The food they feed a dying man would make a strong man sick. More people have been killed by bedpans than bullets, and more people have been killed by beds than bombs."

"And yet," said Crest, "we meet a lot of patients who like to be in the hospital."

"We meet a lot of people who were never weaned from the nipple of their mothers," Joseph growled.

After waxing and waning for many days, the vital spark

turned into a steady flame, and Joseph decided that he would not die; from that moment, nothing could kill him any more. Joseph was a doctor and a realist and he knew what lay ahead of him. Although Crest had nourished hope that the paralysis might be temporary, Joseph had known from the beginning that his paraplegia would be permanent. He would never walk again. He would be a prisoner to the wheelchair and the bed. His bowels and his bladder would never function normally; his sexual capacity was lost. Bed sores, urinary-tract infection, kidney and bladder stones would be continuing hazards.

"There are compensations," Joseph said. "I'll never have to walk into trouble; ambition and status will never need to bother me; I won't make a fool of myself over a woman again. I can't move below the waist, but I can feel no pain sensations either. Give me a hot-foot or kick me in the balls. I won't ever feel a thing. Since I now have no reason whatever to be afraid of death, I can enjoy being alive. This puts me one up on the rest of you ambitious, healthy, and unhappy slobs."

"I admire your courage," said Crest.

"Balderdash," said Joseph. "Courage requires fear, and I have none. I am only a paralyzed animal. I enjoy the animal sensation of being alive too much to give it up quite yet."

On another occasion, Crest asked him, "Do you have faith?"

"Religious faith?" asked Joseph.

"Yes, or the equivalent."

"No," said Joseph. "I wonder what happened to the religious faith of physicians? In another day, we were the pillars of the church. Now the only doctors seen in church are looking for social advantages."

"I have the feeling that most of the community has lost any real feeling of religious faith."

"Times change," said Joseph. "The modern physician considers himself a man of science and, as such, he is somewhat embarrassed by discussions of the soul. You knew my father, the dean. He was a man of faith. My grandfather, who was the dean before him, was even more so. He lived and practiced in the era of faith; in medicine, it was the era of pathology. In that day, the study of disease was the primary concern of the physician. His most important skill was diagnosis and after that prognosis. He could tell the patient what was wrong with him and inform him what to expect for the future. For treatment, he depended entirely on faith, and this was good enough for the patient, too. The era of pathology and the era of faith has passed. It was replaced by the age of reason and the age of surgery. Anxiety could be dispelled by inductive reasoning and logic; disease fixed by mechanical manipulations of the surgeon's hands. This era too will pass. In fact, I think it is beginning to pass already. The great age of reason, the great age of surgery, becomes replaced by a different era, of course."

"What next?"

"The age of drugs and of insecurity, I think. We'll have to wait and see. This is one thing which is keeping me alive. I am curious about what is going to happen next."

Crest asked, "Have you any plans for the future? Regarding your career?"

"I suppose I could do plastic surgery from a wheelchair," said Joseph, "but I won't. I'll turn over my practice to Sam. He is greedy for it anyway."

"You plan to retire from medicine?"

"No," said Joseph. "I am thinking of trying something else. Please don't laugh. I am tempted to become a psychiatrist."

"A very important field," said Crest.

"A miserable field, the last lost continent," said Joseph. "Full of darkness and shadows, tom-tom drums, the thick-skinned elephant and the long-legged giraffe, the impala, the hyena, the vulture, and the tse-tse fly. I would have to be starting out from scratch. At that, I'd be even with most of the psychiatrists I know."

"That would be an interest and a challenge," said Crest. "An entirely new field, starting all over again, from scratch."

Joseph looked down at his useless legs, already beginning to wither and atrophy. "Have I another choice?" he asked.

Plans were made at last to transfer Joseph to the city. Here he would begin the long road to rehabilitation. And also, incidentally, he would begin to study the field of psychiatry. It was only toward the end of Joseph's stay in Sentryville that Crest got up courage to ask the question which had bothered him.

"What really happened on Crystal Lake that night?"

"You never accepted it as an accident," said Joseph.

"It seemed hard to explain," said Crest.

"I was seated at the wheel. The engine was finely tuned. We were going like a bat out of hell."

"The lights of the pier were visible all over the lake."

"Like a target," said Joseph. "Diana was in a lousy mood. She was obviously jealous of your wife's pregnancy."

"And Emerald was jealous of her."

"There we were, zooming around the lake, Diana feeling bitchy and I feeling rather good. I always took pleasure in her bitchiness. I remember thinking—and you'll pardon this, Crest!—how glad I was that Diana hadn't become domesticated and gross and housebroken like your wife. I was considering what I might do with this gorgeous, bitchy, unhousebroken creation when I got her home. Then Diana grabbed the wheel out of my hands. Next thing I knew, we had hit that float like a bolt of lightning. I remember being afraid of the windshield. I wasn't worried about myself, but I was thinking about Diana; if she cut her face on the windshield glass, I'd have to do plastic surgery on her again, and I was thinking I could never again get such a perfect result. I remember being astonished to find myself flying completely over the windshield. Then I wrapped my back around that tree."

"Joseph, could you tell me this: why didn't you marry Diana?"

"I'll answer that question when I'm old enough: I'm only

forty-eight," he said. "After I've learned some psychiatry, perhaps."

"Were you in love with her?"

"I was in love with her nose," said Joseph. "Which I had made, with my own hands. Strangely enough, she used to think there was something more to her than her nose. Now I'll never have the opportunity to find out."

A month after the accident, Joseph was transferred to the city by ambulance.

"Thanks for saving my life, Johnnie."

"Thanks for giving me a lesson in courage and fortitude," said Crest.

"It takes one fool to know another," said Joseph. "I can never pay your fee."

"There's no fee, of course."

"I wouldn't dream of trying to pay you in coin. And I managed to hoard up a supply of that. My average fee was five thousand dollars a case."

"How else would you pay me?"

"In kind," said Joseph.

"I don't follow you," said Crest.

"If you ever need help, you know that you can depend on me."

"That's true."

"Which, Johnnie, can be a thing of very great treasure and value."

Crest was aware that this was also true.

Part 6

In the middle of the night, Emerald said, "Oh, dear!
I seem to have made a mess."

Crest, beside her in the double bed, was sound asleep; he
gave a grunt as a response but didn't really hear her.

"Wake up, John," she said, shaking him. "I think I've developed an internal waterfall."

He became aware then that the bed was wet, quite
drenched, in fact. He came fully awake.

"What's the matter, do you suppose?" she said.

He turned on the light and examined the bedding. At first
all he could think of was that one or the other of them had
committed a childish nuisance, which would have been embarrassing. Then he knew what was going on and he laughed.

"Big joke?" she said.

He patted her shoulder affectionately. "Not a joke," he said,
"but a normal and promising development. Your bag of waters
broke."

"This is good?"

"Labor is coming soon. Are you having any pain?"

"No. What should we do?"

"Nothing," said Crest. "Put on fresh sheets and go back to sleep."

"This isn't dangerous?"

"Usually it will start labor within a few hours," said Crest. "Sometimes there's a delay."

"That's bad?"

"The so-called dry labor," said Crest. "They used to be afraid of it before the sulfa drugs. Dry labor was associated with a definite increase of infections. Now, with the drugs, we can cope with it, and we don't worry at all."

"I'm going to have a complication. I know I am," she said.

"Nonsense."

"The wives and relatives of doctors always do," she said, and then she said quite loudly, "Ouch!"

"What's the matter?"

"Ow! It hurts."

"Where?"

"Ooooooo! OUch!" she said.

Crest went over to her, slightly alarmed.

"Now it's going away, thank goodness," she said.

Crest laughed again.

"This whole business is pretty funny to you, bud?" she said.

"That was a labor pain," said Crest. "The first. Not the last."

"Oh," she said.

The expression on her face seemed to state that she had just realized this affair was going to hurt. Quite a lot. Why the devil did she get herself into this situation, she was beginning to wonder, and how the devil could she get out of it? Without the pain?

"It's a common experience you're going through," said Crest.

"Sure, and you've been through it many times yourself."

"No, but half of the population is female, and most women

have this experience. Only the unhappy and the lonely ones do not."

"Sure, and we all die, and that must also be a lot of fun," she said.

"Emerald," said Crest, "the tough things in life come for all of us. We endure, we survive, and then we rest. The tough things are the matters of great value; the pleasures and the candy and the cream don't mean very much, no matter what you read or hear over the radio. Surely you're mature enough to know all that."

"I'm immature enough to be scared," she said. "I wish you were going through all this, not me."

"As a matter of fact," said Crest, "so do I."

"Shouldn't we call my father now?"

"Bother a doctor at the first labor pain? Hell no!" said Crest.

"When?"

"When those pains of yours become regular and frequent and hard."

"That pain wasn't hard?"

"Probably not."

"Jeepers," she said.

"There's plenty of time," said Crest. "You won't drop that baby on the floor. This is your first and you're a small-boned girl, and the child is obviously big."

"I'm going to have a long, tough time?"

Although Crest thought this might be possible, he said, "No, dear. We'll go through it together. It won't be long and it won't be bad, and think of the wonderful child that God is giving us."

"You think of it," she said.

"Sit down in the chair. I'll get fresh sheets and make up the bed and then we can go back to sleep."

"Ha!" she said.

The next pain didn't come for nearly an hour; it was weak and unsustained, as Crest could tell by putting his hand on her belly, but she made a lot of fuss. This wasn't going to be an easy experience for her. Some women can seem to ignore labor pains, at least in the beginning; Emerald was the other kind.

Sleep would be out of the question, so Crest tried to read aloud to her, something light and humorous, but neither of them could concentrate.

"Turn off the light," she said.

So Crest lay awake with her in the dark, waiting for the next pain. She didn't want to talk.

He did some thinking on the general subject of physical pain. Mankind fears pain more than anything, yet pain is necessary: nature's burglar alarm. When pain perception is lost, the body is in danger. A drunk man can't roll out of a burning bed. When nerve supply to an extremity is lost, the extremity soon develops pressure sores, ulceration, gangrene. To somebody like Joseph, with complete loss of pain below the waist, this anaesthesia is a constant life-threatening risk.

If pain is useful to an individual, it can be close to pleasure. The virgin on the wedding night; the star athlete with a broken nose; the stoic on his bed of nails. Physical pain associated with guilt, anxiety, or shame is enormously magnified.

There is no such thing as physical pain beyond endurance. At a certain point, shock ensues, and the patient in shock does not feel pain. Anyone can take severe pain of brief intensity; the low-grade but steady pain can be far worse: the toothache, the earache, or deep bone pain from infection or malignancy. Colicky pain follows rules of its own; the patient is afraid of it at first until he learns that maximum pain is followed by maximum relief. In kidney colic, or intestinal cramps, or labor pains, the patient is more at ease when he learns the pattern of the spasm. For this reason, many women mind the early pains of labor more than the later ones, when pain is more severe.

Worse than any pain of the moment is fear that the pain of the next moment may be worse. All men discover this in the dental chair. One can always endure the pain of the moment if one can be sure that it won't get worse. Victims of torture discover this fact. Pain without fear can be ignored. Torturers and doctors know this. One cannot remember pain. Mothers know.

"I wish I could tell her these things," thought Crest.

"Don't mind if I holler," said Emerald. "It really doesn't hurt this much, but I seem to feel better when I yell."

"Bellow your head off," said Crest. "It's in a good cause."

By morning, her pains were regular enough and hard enough, and Crest phoned Dr. Parkindale.

"True labor, Crest?" asked Parky.

"True enough for her and also for me," said Crest. "It's been a long night."

"Send her in," said Parky. "I'll notify the hospital."

Emerald was already packed. "Will Daddy see me when I arrive?" she asked.

"Not necessarily," said Crest. "The nurses will look you over and get you ready. They don't bother the doctor until the time arrives. The doctor hasn't got time to sit around for hours."

"They'll give me something for the pain?"

"Oh, sure. You don't have to worry."

"And you don't have to feel it," she said. "Let's go, chum. I want to get this damn business over with."

He took her to the hospital and kissed her at the door of the maternity wing.

"You'll drop in on me from time to time?" she asked.

"I certainly will not," said Crest. "Fathers are not wanted here. You're on your own, and I'll be sweating it out alone. When I see you next you'll have the baby in your arms."

The rest of the day was difficult for Crest. When he was not reassuring his wife, he lost his own assurance. He could do nothing but act like the expectant father of the cartoons: pacing in circles, smoking cigarettes.

"Relax, chum," he told himself. "We never lost a father yet."

But the anxiety of expectant fatherhood, much mocked, is real enough, he decided. It would be easier if the father could share the pain. It would be much easier if he had something to do. The utter uselessness of the male at such a time is part of the anxiety, and the rest of it is a disturbing sense of guilt. He could not forget that she was paying the price, in pain, for his small pleasure in the night nine months ago. No wonder we put women on a pedestal, where they belong. What could be more expendable than the drone?

His impulse was to call Parky or the hospital every ten minutes, but he restrained himself. He finally called the hospital at six that night. Everything was under control, they said: labor progressing satisfactorily, but birth not imminent. Of course, they really couldn't tell him anything. At ten o'clock he decided to call Parky.

"Good pains, but progress mighty slow," said Parky.

"No complications?" Crest inquired anxiously.

"Big head and small pelvis. We've always been aware of that."

"A disproportion?"

"There may be a tight squeeze, my boy."

"Have you taken X-rays, sir?"

"We'll give her a little more time," said Parky.

Crest didn't think he could sleep without a drink or a sleeping pill, and he didn't want to be groggy in case of emergency in the night. He was prepared for another sleepless night, but when he awoke, the sun was up again. He phoned the hospital at once. The report was the same. Then he went over to the hospital. He encountered Parky in the corridor. Parky was calm and confident as usual.

"Had your breakfast, Crest?"

"No, sir."

"You better eat," said Parky. "Nothing's going to happen for a while."

"How is she?" asked Crest.

"Asleep," said Parky. "She was getting tired, so I gave her

a sedative and knocked her out. She can go to work again this
afternoon."

"How about X-rays?"

"She's young and strong. She deserves a good test of labor."

"Thirty-six hours," said Crest. "Isn't that a pretty good
test?"

"Everything is under control, my boy," said Dr. Parkindale.

By afternoon, Crest was beginning to get concerned. He
phoned Parky during office hours.

"She's back to work again, banging away, hammer and
tongs," said Parky. "We'll have something to show for it soon."

However, at eleven o'clock that night, Parky phoned Crest.
"I think she's had it," said Parky. "She's worn out and her
fever is beginning to rise. I think we should do a Caesarian."

"Yes, sir, so do I," said Crest.

"Would you care to assist me in the operating room?"

"No."

"I'll get Hamilton or Rhodes. We'll get right to work. I'll
call you in an hour or two."

"I'll wait at the hospital," said Crest.

Around one in the morning, Parky entered the waiting room
at the hospital. He was still wearing his cap and surgical gown,
which was blotched with blood. He was tired. There were
beads of perspiration on his forehead.

"Sit down, Crest," said Parky. "I have two kinds of news for
you: good and bad."

Crest remained standing. "Let me have the bad news first,"
he said. "How's Emerald?"

"She's fine," said Parky. "She sailed through it like a healthy
cow."

A vast sensation of relief surged over Crest. Somehow, he
had thought that Emerald was dead.

"But the baby . . ." said Parky.

Crest had momentarily forgotten that there were two parts
to this deal.

"Your baby is hydrocephalic, I'm afraid," said Parky.

Crest heard him, but the news did not register.

"It may die," said Parky. "Cyanotic. Mighty poor condition. They're putting it into oxygen."

"Boy or girl?" asked Crest.

"I'm afraid I didn't notice. Sorry, son. One of those things. There was nothing I could do."

"Thank you, sir," said Crest.

Parky grunted, nodded, and went off in the direction of the locker room. Then Dr. Rhodes came into the waiting room. He was also wearing a surgical gown, splotched with Emerald's blood. Always insecure, Rhodes now looked painfully shy and embarrassed.

"Have a cigarette," said Crest. "Sorry I can't offer you a cigar. I'll buy a box tomorrow."

Rhodes shook his head. Crest had forgotten that Rhodes didn't smoke.

"Parky told you?" said Rhodes.

"Yes. The baby is hydrocephalic, but Emerald is fine."

"Oh, sure! She's fine!"

It was funny the way Rhodes said it. Irony sounded unnatural from him. Crest gave him a sharp look. Not ordinarily a perceptive man, Rhodes caught the look and understood it.

"Then Parky didn't tell you?" said Rhodes.

"About the baby?"

"About your wife."

"What do you mean?"

"Parky did a hysterectomy," said Rhodes.

This didn't register on Crest.

"He took out her uterus," said Rhodes. "Sorry. I couldn't stop him."

Now the fact hit home: her uterus had been removed; Emerald would have no more children.

"Why?" said Crest.

"That's a good question," said Rhodes. "Ask him. And if you find the answer, let me know. I'm curious."

Rhodes went away toward the locker room. Things had

been too rapid for Crest to assimilate. The baby hydrocephalic, dying; Emerald without a uterus. But Emerald was
alive. Wasn't that the important thing? Suddenly Crest knew
that he must see his child, and he went to the nursery. The
nurse in charge was a big girl, obese, unmarried but by nature motherly. Crest didn't know her name.

"I'd like to see my baby, nurse," he said.

"Of course, Dr. Crest," she said. "Poor little thing."

"I know," said Crest. "I've been told."

"I'm afraid he's going to die."

"It's a boy?"

"Yes, Doctor, a beautiful little boy."

"Beautiful?" said Crest. "I thought he was hydrocephalic."

"All new babies are beautiful," she said. "Especially the
poor little ones who are different. He's in the isolation room."

She made him put on cap, gown, and mask before entering
the isolation room. Then she left him alone. His was the only
baby in the room. The bassinet was covered by an oxygen
hood. Crest could not see through the hood. He turned off the
oxygen and then pulled back the hood.

Yes, it was monstrously hydrocephalic; the little creature
seemed to be all head: a distended and distorted head with
bulging scalp veins and swinish eyes. The color of the child
was poor. Crest thought it could not live very long without
the oxygen. It gave a cry. The textbooks describe the "cracked
pot" cry of the hydrocephalic child, not a true crying noise,
but a sound like that of a broken saucepan beaten with a
pewter spoon. The poor little thing: was it in pain? Or was it
somehow conscious of its own horrible deformity? It seemed
important for Crest to stop the crying; he picked up the baby
and held it in his arms.

Crest knew that a certain small per cent of hydrocephalic
children can grow up with normal intelligence, despite the
bulging head, but most of them are idiots if they survive at
all. There was hope that the condition could be corrected by
surgery, but Crest knew that few of the surgical procedures

were effective at that time. In a case like this, where the condition was present to an advanced degree at birth, the outlook was very poor.

Whenever he tried to put the baby back into the bassinet, it began to cry again, so he continued to hold it in his arms. He knew that it could not long survive this way, but he could not bear to abandon it. A few minutes later, Crest became aware that the child had died in his arms.

He returned the body to the basinette, replaced the hood, turned on the oxygen, and fled. He wanted to explain to the nurse, but he found himself escaping from the hospital, like a hit-and-run driver, leaving the scene. Crest drove home. As he entered his dark and lonely house, he heard the telephone ringing, and picked it up. Parky was calling from the hospital.

"Crest, your child just died."

"Yes, sir," said Crest.

"I'm sorry, my boy," said Parky. "But probably this is for the best."

"Yes, sir," said Crest, and he hung up.

Emerald was sitting up in bed and she looked fine. She had put on fresh lipstick; it seemed to Crest that the shade was different from that she usually wore, more on the orange side, which heightened her color and natural vivacity. Her black hair had a gloss; it had become a little drab during her pregnancy. Her figure seemed to be returning to its former willowy condition, except for the breasts, still full; but Emerald's breasts had always been, perhaps, a little small.

"Glamour girl," said Crest. "You look wonderful."

"I feel fine," she said, and there was no doubt that she did.

"Dear, about the child . . ." said Crest.

"They told me," she said.

"It was probably for the best."

"Yes," she said.

With finality, she was putting the subject aside. She wasn't going to mention it; she wasn't going to think of it; in fact,

Crest thought, the death of the baby did not bother her. Perhaps she was even glad.

"And, Emerald . . ."

"Why the hang-dog look? What's the matter, dear?"

"Your father had to do a hysterectomy," he said.

"I know it."

"I'm sorry," said Crest. "I'm not sure why Parky did the hysterectomy. I haven't asked him yet. I am not convinced the operation was necessary. I can't think of a good indication."

"I asked him to," she said.

"You?"

"Yes," she said. "I always knew that baby was too big. Just before he took me into the operating room, I asked Daddy if anything was wrong with the child. He said he thought there was. I said that if the baby was dead, or deformed, or anything, I didn't want to go through this again. I asked Daddy to fix it."

"He fixed it wrong," said Crest. "Hydrocephalus is not an indication for hysterectomy. The next child might have been normal. Now you can have no more."

"Yes. Does it bother you, John Crest?"

Crest didn't want to say so, but it bothered him a great deal. This was the end of the dynasty, the end of the line. Emerald's request did not justify her father's act. A doctor should not make a mistake even when his daughter asks him to.

"I didn't want to be a mother anyway," she said. "I'm not the motherly type."

"All right," said Crest.

But it wasn't all right. Crest wanted children.

This lay between them from that moment on. Emerald was pretty and vivacious, glittering, tough-minded, and desirable. Crest could have fallen in love with her all over again, but this was a stranger. He didn't think he knew her very well. To fall in love with her, he would have to begin again, from scratch. And now if he had permitted himself that luxury,

he would have desired, not a wife, but a mistress, a woman
for the night. There was something virginal about her. This
was ridiculous, of course, but Crest was almost afraid to touch
her. No man exactly wants to touch a virgin. She prattled
away, chattering about inconsequential things, but her manner brooked no intimacy. She was acting toward him as she
had acted in the early days, when he was a student in medical
school. She might kiss him suddenly, then run. Once she had
said that no man was going to stand in the way of her plans.
Once she had implied that, by marrying him, she would make
a failure of her life. She was talking about the theater and the
stage quite often now.

"Have you ever thought that you might take another crack
at your career again?" he asked.

"Yes, I have," she said.

"That would mean leaving me, of course."

"I'd have to go back to the city," she said.

"I can't go back," he said. "My work is in Sentryville."

She shrugged her pretty little shoulders. "That would be
for you to decide, of course," she said.

"Emerald . . ."

Something in him wanted to cry out to her. He wanted to
snatch up the past, turn back the clock, go back to the beginning again when everything meant a great deal. But Emerald was a stranger. She only looked like a woman with
whom John Crest had been in love, with whom Crest would
always be in love. This stranger was playing a role. It didn't
seem fair. The real woman was dead.

They kept Emerald at the hospital for a matter of two
weeks. She was still on the maternity wing. This was one of
those unnecessary cruelties which impersonal hospital ad-
ministrations often work on human beings. Surrounded by
women with pretty new babies, Emerald had no baby. Proud
fathers came in to see their wives and children, but Crest was
not a father, only the husband of a beautiful stranger. If Emerald had wanted her baby, life in the maternity wing could

have been unendurable. The new babies were kept in a line of bassinet behind a large glass window, and there were always mothers and fathers on the other side looking in, admiring. Crest walked rapidly past the nursery window whenever he went to visit Emerald.

By the time they discharged her, Emerald was almost back to full strength.

"I heal quick," she said.

"I don't," said Crest.

For an instant, a trace of the love she once must have had for him came peeping through.

"Poor John Crest," she said, "who deserved better things."

She kissed him tenderly on the tip of the nose. Before he could take her in his arms to kiss her back, she was gone. She spoke of gossip in the community. She wanted to be taken out to dinner. She wanted to be taken to a dance. She bought new clothes. She threw away her maternity dresses, and Crest suspected that she had burned them. On the bathroom shelf there was no longer the little container for a certain personal device. Emerald would never need it again.

It was a gray December day, shortly before Christmas. There was a hint of snow. Crest came back from the hospital in mid-morning and went into the kitchen for a cup of coffee. Emerald wasn't there. She had now been home two weeks and it had been a month since the night of her delivery.

"Hey, honey!" called Crest.

"I'm upstairs," she said.

Her voice was very casual and happy. Crest went upstairs and found her in the bedroom. She was packing.

"A trip?" asked Crest.

"My train leaves at noon. Can you drive me to the station, dear? If you're busy with your patients, I can call a taxi."

This was a small and unnecessary irony. Crest was not busy with patients; there were no more than two or three a day. She knew this damn well.

"I suppose it's useless to inquire where you're going?" said Crest.

"You know I'm going to the city," she said.

"Permanently, more or less?"

"I need this town like a hole in the head," she said.

"Am I invited? May I go to the city too?"

"Surely," she said. "Hand me that dress, will you, John? I'd be glad to have you come with me if you want, but I didn't buy you a ticket."

"Where will you live?" he inquired.

"By great good luck, I was able to get my old apartment back," she said.

This conversation was all wrong, Crest thought. You don't break up a marriage this way. Even in her pregnancy, she had been in love with him. Only a few weeks later she was leaving him, for no reason in particular. "We ought to be yelling at each other," he thought; "at the very least, we ought to be discussing things; we shouldn't be so damned impersonal and casual, as if we'd only met last week."

"This is a separation, I presume," he said.

"One could call it that."

"Do you want a divorce?"

"Not to my present knowledge," she said. "I doubt if I'll be marrying again. I'll be glad to give you a divorce, John, if you want one."

"No," he said. "Why don't we let it alone for the moment?"

"I thought so," she said.

"May I come and visit you now and then?"

"I'd be pleased if you did," she said.

"I can't give you much money for support."

"John, don't be ridiculous. I'd never ask money from you."

"I suppose you've discussed the situation with your parents?"

"Yes," she said.

"They agree with you?"

"Daddy does. Mother thinks I ought to stay and try to make

a go of things. I told her that things have already went, as far as I'm concerned."

"You plan to try the stage again?"

"Yes," she said. "Remember Jack? He's a director."

"The other husband? I remember him."

"He's casting something, and he has a part for me. It's nothing, only a walk-on, but maybe I can develop it, if I haven't forgotten how to act."

"I'm sure you haven't," said Crest. "I wish you luck."

"Thanks, darling."

"When you're a star and have your name in lights, you'll find me in the front row on opening night. I'll send roses to your dressing room, as many as I can afford."

"That's one of your best qualities, John," she said. "You're loyal."

"You're not."

"I know it," she said. "I'm a mess. But since I'm unlikely to change, we might as well make the best of it, shouldn't we?"

"Were you ever in love with me?" he asked.

"I was," she said. "Strangely enough, never more so than I am right now."

"Then stay," he said.

"I can't."

"All right. I'll go with you."

"I may be moving around."

"I'll move around too."

"Doing what?" she said.

"Leading the applause for you."

"Giving up your career for mine?"

"Why not?" said Crest. "I'm a lousy doctor. I failed."

"No. I won't let you do it."

"You won't let me live with you?"

"Look, chum," she said, "it's me who failed. Can't you let me run away with my tail between my legs? I'm not very proud of myself. You deserve something better, John Crest, much better. I am not the marrying kind."

"It seems to me you're running away with a good deal of pleasure and confidence. Be honest! You'd rather enjoy your own life than try to have a share in mine."

"Well?" she said. "I'll only be living once."

"This isn't right," he said.

"I tried to give you the child," she said. "It wasn't my fault."

"Of course not. I'm not concerned with children. I am in love with you. At least I used to be."

"Put your weight on this suitcase, will you, John? I can't get the damn thing shut."

He put his weight on the suitcase and closed it. "Discussion isn't going to change your mind?" he said. "You're not amenable to reason?"

"This is not impulsive," she said. "This is not on the spur of the moment. I've given it a lot of thought."

"I can tell. When did you start thinking of it? The moment you married me?"

"Don't turn nasty. That won't help."

"I want to talk it over."

"John, it's too late for that. Will you take me to the station?"

He took her to the station. They stood wordlessly on the platform. The train pulled in, and Crest helped her aboard. She stood on the iron vestibule of the car and waved. A stray snowflake glistened in her hair. Then she walked into the car. Crest could see her through the window. She sat down beside a woman and immediately she was launching into conversation, vivacious, full of charm. The train moved away. Crest went home. He felt very much alone.

Emerald left him in December of 1938. She didn't come back. Now and then he thought he might visit her in the city, but he didn't get around to it. Sometimes he wrote her a letter. She did not reply. She remembered him with presents: at Christmas, on his birthday, and, strangely enough, on the anniversary of the death of their child. Except for the presents, Crest would have known she was alive only from what he read of her from time to time. Her name appeared in print. From what must have been only a little theater group in the city, she was apparently moving toward better things. For a few weeks in 1940 she had a role on Broadway. Sooner or later, perhaps, she might go to Hollywood. Once Crest was thumbing through a man's magazine while waiting in a barbershop in Sentryville and he came upon her picture. It was a full spread, in color; she was in the nude. He shut the magazine at once. He was jolted, shocked. Yet after his haircut, he found himself going to the stationery store to buy a copy of the magazine. He kept it in his files. He never looked at the picture, but he liked knowing he could look at it any time he chose.

The three years between 1938 and 1941 were gray years for Crest. Looking back at them later, Crest could never remember how he spent the time. There was a great deal of it, and he seemed to do almost nothing. There were the concerns of his practice, growing slowly although still small. The patients being few, Crest was able to give a lot of time to each of them. In the evenings he read a great deal. He went out seldom. There was a housekeeper to clean the house and cook the meals, and sometimes she doubled in the office as receptionist: a big, efficient, taciturn widow of Scandinavian descent. He liked her but never felt very close to her. Occasionally on the weekends, he played a little golf. He went to church. He belonged to the Lion's Club. He knew a few men, with whom he played poker at long-scattered intervals. Occasionally he was invited to a cocktail party or a dinner when an odd male was needed. But, as he was frank to admit to himself, he had no friends; at that time he felt no need for them. There were women in Sentryville, more women than men on a statistical basis, and an unattached doctor is not an undesirable catch. There were a number of women who would have gone out with him, but he never asked. Crest was playing a small role in the community and medical affairs of Sentryville; his patients, the few of them, were quite fond of him, and would have missed him if he went away, but otherwise nobody would have noticed if he died.

Dr. Parkindale was busy. Drs. Hamilton and Rhodes and Crest were not. These were the medical facts of life in Sentryville. Crest could accept them, or Crest could move.

He often wondered why he did not move. There were communities, thousands of communities, where a doctor of his caliber would have been welcomed; where he would have been busy night and day; where he could have been a success. Sentryville had nothing for him but a memory, a bitter memory. Why did he stay?

Partly, he decided, he was struck down with the inertia and depression of despair. The months and the years went by. Sooner or later he would shake off the influence of Emerald and the Parkindales. But the influence remained and with it the inertia of defeat.

But there was more than the influence of the Parkindales. These were uneasy years, weighted down with the inevitability of approaching war. Many young men and women forgot to plan and dream in those years. Although nobody would admit it, everybody seemed to feel that war was coming, that this war would disrupt everybody's dreams and plans, that there wasn't any point in doing much until that time arrived.

Crest was listening to the Philharmonic concert on the radio that Sunday afternoon in December 1941 when the program was interrupted. The announcer said that bombs were falling on Pearl Harbor. Like many young men and women, Crest was shocked and deeply disturbed by the news. But, by the following morning, the shock had worn off and was replaced by a sense of exhilaration and adventure, almost a savage pleasure. Crest was not by nature a deeply patriotic individual. And yet it was all that he could do to keep himself from running down to the recruiting office. Many people did, and the lines were long. Some of his generation, in fact, hadn't been able to wait for the declaration of war but had already gone. Sam Parkindale, for example. Crest had heard that Sam had abandoned a flourishing practice in plastic surgery several months before, had enlisted in a Canadian medical group, and was now in London, practicing his trade on the victims of the fire bombs.

Crest waited a few months, but then he could wait no more. He volunteered for a commission in the Medical Corps. He paraded around a cold armory floor, naked, with a bottle of his urine in his hand, together with 200 other naked young men in assorted sizes and shapes. Crest thought that his physical exam was a little like studying physiological chemistry in a nudist colony. They tested his eyes and his reflexes, examined his teeth and his rectum, X-rayed his chest, inquired if he was interested in girls, and decided that he was physically fit to be killed. His commission as a first lieutenant came through. He shut his office, sold his car, gave up the lease on his house, put his office equipment into storage, and said good-by to Sentryville with no particular regret. He went away to war in a train. There was nobody to see him go.

Crest didn't like the Army. Hardly anybody does. Physicians in particular are not adaptable to military discipline. The few doctors who, in times of peace, make military medicine their career are apt to be passive, dependent individuals, afraid of assuming responsibility, who would have failed in civilian life. Physicians are taught to be independent, individualistic, and adaptable. The Army, therefore, is contrary to the medical mind, and doctors are contrary soldiers. Crest didn't complain over the futilities, stupidities, and frustrations of military life any more than all soldiers normally complain, but he didn't like it.

He was sent first to a training camp for the Medical Corps. All Army installations look alike: rows of ugly yellow shacks on desolate ground which is dusty in the summer and muddy the rest of the time. There, he and the others learned soldiering. They learned to keep their mouths shut and their bowels open. They learned to eat rations in the field. They learned military courtesy. Crest shot a rifle for the first time in his life, and he threw a hand grenade, and he crawled under barbed wire as live machine-gun fire whistled a foot over his head. He stayed up all night several nights doing KP. Every weekend, he and the others descended on the village nearby, getting roaring drunk and looking for trouble. On one of those nights, Crest spent fifteen minutes in the bed of a whore: the first time he had ever done so and, as he decided for the next six weeks while constantly inspecting himself for the development of a chancre, the last.

His training period complete, Crest's military career changed from the useless to the ridiculous. His first assignment was of the chair-borne variety, a desk job in the same city where Crest had gone to medical school, the city where Emerald presumably still lived between dramatic roles, one of the last places Crest would have liked to be assigned.

It was a curious job, one of the smallest and most obscure positions in a large befuddled army. His official position was, as nearly as he could discover, assistant public-relations and medical-liaison officer from the Army to the Port Authority of the city. He spent quite a while finding out what an assistant public-relations and medical-liaison officer is supposed to do.

"Don't ask me, Lieutenant," said a fat, balding lieutenant colonel in the Transportation Corps, apparently Crest's commanding officer, the only other Army officer in the Customs House Building on the water front. "In fact, Lieutenant, I'd appreciate it if you didn't bother me at all. Ask one of the girls. I'm busy."

After a quick glance at the "girls," Crest decided not to bother them. They were a pack of scarcely literate secretaries, apparently shanghaied from the hills of Tennessee to meet the manpower shortage: more brawny than brainy and not outstandingly beautiful. When Crest reported for duty, some of them eyed him with a sexual gleam, but when he showed no burning interest, they ignored him, devoting the working hours to crossword puzzles, coffee breaks, fainting spells, gossip, and an occasional letter, typed in quadruplicate.

There was a young medical officer from the Navy, approximately Crest's age and grade, who held the equivalent position from the naval point of view. He made an appearance every day at noon and disappeared promptly ten minutes later. Crest cornered him one day before he could escape.

"What in the hell am I supposed to be doing here?" asked Crest.

"Who knows?" said the naval officer. "Who cares?"

"I care," said Crest. "I like the feeling of knowing what I'm doing from time to time. I'm not treating patients, that's for sure."

"Tell it to the chaplain, if you can find one."

"What do you do?"

"I'm living with a riveter."

"Huh?" said Crest.

"She works the swing shift. Her husband is in the Philippines—at least he used to be; I guess the Japs have him now. She's a very energetic girl, and requires most of my time and energy. While I'm resting, she's riveting. I make it a point to report for duty here every working day."

"Doesn't the Navy object?"

"The Navy hasn't found me long enough to object. Goodby, Doctor. I'm late. I should be riveting."

Not having found himself a riveter with a husband in the Philippines, Crest sat at his desk eight hours a day, five days a week, doing nothing. He soon was dreaming lovingly of foxholes.

During off-duty hours, Crest wandered around the city now and then. It was for him a city of ghosts, haunted by memories of Parkindales: the dean, and Joseph, and Sam, and Emerald.

One day, when Crest was seated at his desk doing nothing, Sam Parkindale walked in, dressed in an unfamiliar blue uniform.

"Sam!" said Crest. "What are you doing in this vicinity?

What type of uniform is that? Do I salute you or do you salute me?"

Sam grinned. "Let's both salute each other simultaneously, and then let's go out and get drunk. Can the military establishment spare you for the afternoon?"

"Hell yes," said Crest. "The military establishment doesn't even know that I'm alive."

Sam and Crest left the Customs Building and found a neighboring bar. Each ordered double Scotch. Sam put away his drink very fast, Crest almost as fast, and they ordered another round.

"Like old times, buddy boy," said Sam.

"Yes," said Crest. "But also no."

"I know what you mean," said Sam. "A certain something seems to be lacking, a juvenile sense of fun, a youthful dedication, an anticipation of the future. So you and Emerald called it a day?"

"She called," said Crest. "I listened."

"She's living in the city. Don't you see her now and then?"

"No," said Crest.

"I believe she's going overseas with the U.S.O. next month. Are the two of you divorced?"

"No."

"I gather you don't want to discuss the subject of my sister, Johnnie?"

"No," said Crest.

"Another drink?"

"I'm not quite ready yet."

"I'm always ready," said Sam.

"I can see that you still enjoy your alcohol."

"My friends tell me that I'm beginning to look like an alcoholic," said Sam. "Are you one of my friends?"

Sam did not look well. His eyes were bloodshot; his complexion was muddy with patches of unhealthy distended venules on the cheeks. His apple-cheeked sunny expression had gone. His forehead and cheeks were lined, as if trouble had been slashing at him with a saber.

"How's your war?" asked Crest.

"Lousy," said Sam. "I'm doing plastic work in London, you know. I hitched a ride with one of our fly-boys, and I've got to be going back tonight."

"What's it like over there?"

"Why don't you come over and find out for yourself?" said Sam.

"I wish I could," said Crest.

"Don't," said Sam, "if you can possibly avoid it. We caught a fire bomb on the woman's wing of our hospital last week. Fried all the girls alive. Great fun."

"I can bet."

"God damn it," said Sam. "Do you know what I'm going to do when this bloody war is finished, if I haven't finished myself with liquor in the meantime? I'm going to find a nice, lonely, uninhabited desert island, and I'm going to sit. I'm going to sit on my big fat ass, and brush away the flies, and watch the sun go down. I won't see a patient for the rest of my life."

"You never wanted to be a doctor, did you, Sam?"

"Oh, I don't mind doctoring," said Sam. "But I don't care for the attitudes of war. I guess it's all right to kill an armed man who's trying to kill you, but I think they could leave the women and kids alone. Frying women, children on a charcoal grille: you'd think there'd be a better way to inhabit a planet."

"My trouble is," said Crest, "I've got nothing to do."

"Trade places with you, son."

"I'd love to," said Crest. "I sat in Sentryville for years doing nothing, and I've been sitting in the Army ever since. It would seem a waste of a long and rather expensive medical education. I am a doctor after all, even though I'm not a very good one."

"Why don't you insult your commanding officer? Maybe he'll transfer you."

"It's a thought," said Crest.

Crest was somewhat drunk when he returned to the office that afternoon. In this mood, he approached his commanding officer and requested a transfer.

"Why, Lieutenant?" said the officer.

"I'm a doctor," said Crest. "This job is a complete waste of my experience and training."

"You don't know when you're well off, Lieutenant. People are getting killed on the other side."

"That's where I'm needed, sir," said Crest.

"This is a good assignment. You can sit out the rest of the war right here if you keep your bowels open and your mouth shut. There are lots of men who would give their right arm to trade places with you."

"I want a transfer nevertheless," said Crest.

"I'll do my best, but don't blame me if it's hot over there."

A few weeks later, orders were cut and Crest was ordered to report to a Port of Embarkation on the West Coast.

Crest knew that Emerald maintained an apartment in the city. Up to that time, he had carefully avoided that particular section of the city, but now, twenty-four hours prior to his departure for an unknown destination in the Orient, he felt a sudden desire to see Emerald again. It had occurred to him that he might not be coming back. He didn't know if she was in the city. She might have been in New York or elsewhere; he remembered that Sam had said she was going overseas with the U.S.O. Nevertheless, he went to her apartment building. In the lobby, he pushed the appropriate button. There was an answering buzz as the main door opened for him. He climbed the flights of stairs and knocked on her door. For a long time there was no reply. He knocked again. Just as he was about to go away, the door opened a crack. Crest could just see the tip of her nose.

"Who is it?"

"Me. Crest."

"Jeepers," she said. "Just a minute, dear."

She closed the door in his face and left him in the corridor for another long moment.

"Come in, John," she said, opening the door at last.

She looked pretty. Also, older than Crest had remembered her. There was something hard on the surface, as if she had been sprayed with transparent varnish. She seemed more tense than the situation seemed to indicate, but when Crest went in, he understood the reason why. A man was sitting in the overstuffed chair.

"John, dear, you remember Jack," she said.

"How do you do," said Crest, extending his hand. "We never met. I've heard a lot about you."

"Likewise, I'm sure," said Jack.

Jack didn't get up. He languidly extended a hand, and Crest shook it. Crest had expected Jack to be a sharp little man, lean, perhaps, bitter or cruel. But Jack was a large man, entirely masculine and virile, dressed in civilian clothes.

"Jack has a heart murmur," Emerald explained.

"And damned tired of telling every jerk in uniform," said Jack.

"I can understand," said Crest. "I'm not exactly an infantry dog-face myself. However, I am going overseas. I leave tomorrow."

"Overseas?" said Emerald.

"At my own request," said Crest.

"Jack, out!" said Emerald. "You must have something to do. Go and do it, dear, without delay."

Jack arose from the chair languidly, yawned, and scratched himself on the belly. "I'll be seeing you tomorrow, dear lady?" he said.

"Out!" said Emerald.

"I'm going already," said Jack. "Nice to have met you, Lieutenant. Kill a few Japs for me."

Jack wandered out, and Crest took the chair he had vacated. Emerald came over to him and kissed him. It was a sudden kiss and a cold one.

"Care for a bottle of beer, John?"

"All right."

She went into the microscopic nook of the kitchenette and brought out two bottles of beer. She handed one to him, and then she reclined on the bed.

"John, I . . ."

"Emerald . . ."

They had both started to speak together. They both stopped. To cover the awkwardness of mutual interruption, they laughed.

"You first, dear," she said.

"No, go ahead," said Crest.

"I forgot what I was going to say."

"Me too."

Crest suddenly recalled another time, long ago, when he had been drinking beer in this apartment. That time they had ended up engaged before morning.

"I was thinking of it too," she said.

"Nice if we could go back and start again," said Crest.

"How do I proceed?"

"For what?"

"How does one seduce a husband?" she said. "One has not seen him for three years. One knows he is going overseas in time of war; some of those don't come back."

"I didn't come for that."

"It is the obligation of the civilian female to maintain the morale of the troops."

"Stop that, Emerald."

"Have you had a woman since I left home?"

"Once," said Crest.

"That's all?"

"And I paid for it," said Crest.

"Funny," she said. "I'd never think a guy like you would have to pay for it."

"I was drunk at the time."

"Would you like another bottle of beer?"

"All right."

This time when she went for beer, she shut the door behind her. The kitchenette also served as dining room and dressing room. She was gone for a time and when she returned she was wearing a black negligee.

"Finish your beer and I'm ready," she said.

She handed him the bottle of beer and Crest thought she had an impulse to sit in his lap, but she returned to the bed.

"Small talk while you're finishing the beer?" she said.

"Stop that."

"I'm ready for you. See?"

Suddenly she stood up and opened the front of the robe for an instant. She wore nothing underneath. Crest could see a flash of skin and female anatomy, but what he noticed chiefly was the white stripe down the middle of her lower belly: the hysterectomy scar. She closed the robe as quickly as she had opened it.

"Oh, damn," she said.

Her bottle of beer had been resting casually beside her on the bed. She had overturned it when she got up. Beer was gurgling onto the counterpane. She swiped at it ineffectually with her hand and, in the process, knocked a package of cigarettes off the night table into the puddle of beer.

"Damnation," she said. "Cigarettes are rare as gold these days."

"They're plentiful at the PX, tax free," said Crest.

"Well, buy me several thousand cartons, chum. I'll have to get the bedspread dry-cleaned. I loathe the smell of spilled beer on cloth."

"Sorry," said Crest.

She turned to him and grinned. "Now I know it's you," she

said. "The uniform had me fooled, but you're the only one I know who apologizes for things he doesn't do."

"I have a theory on accidents," said Crest.

"Yeah," she said. "Accidents are on purpose. This one happened to break the mood, and now I don't have to remove my robe. That doesn't matter. You've seen me before. The contour doesn't change."

"I saw you quite publicly recently," said Crest.

"Beg pardon?"

"A frank picture in a magazine."

"Oh," she said. "That. It's funny the things an actress has to do to earn a buck."

"Such as making love to a photographer?"

"That picture was taken by a woman," she said. "I understand that it is quite popular among the armed forces. I'm a pin-up girl. My friend, I consider that the height of irony. You know how I act with men. Those poor soldiers should ask for their money back. Maybe they can look at me and dream, but if they came up to my apartment now, I wouldn't know what to do."

"Do you see a lot of Jack?"

"This bothers you?"

"It shouldn't," said Crest, "but it does."

"I see too much of Jack. I don't like him. You know that."

"Why?"

"God knows. I can't seem to kick a habit," she said. "You don't know how many times I've nearly taken the train back to Sentryville."

"I wish you had."

"Have we been fencing around long enough, John Crest? Shall we make love?"

"Isn't it too late, Emerald?" he said.

"You're singing our song. Too little and too late," she said.

"Thanks for the beer."

"You're going?"

"I wonder why I came."

"So do I," she said. "Why did you come, John Crest?"

"I suppose it was to say that I love you, Emerald, and I always will."

"As I may have remarked in the past, John Crest, you're an idiot," she said.

"Emerald," he said. "When I come back from the war—if I come back—couldn't we start over, from the beginning?"

"They say it's going to be a long war."

"I need something to look forward to."

"Well," she said, "I'm sure I won't be marrying anybody else."

"That's good enough," he said. "Good-by."

He expected she might try to kiss him suddenly, but instead she shook his hand. And then he left.

As he was walking away from the building, he suddenly decided he had told her a lie. He was not in love with her. In fact, he was sorry for her. Emerald was searching, still searching, for identity in sex. She hadn't found it. She was uneasy in her sex.

"I know what's wrong with her now," Crest told himself with the shock of sudden discovery. "She should have been a man."

Sure. And if Emerald had been a man, she would have been a doctor: perhaps a very fashionable and busy doctor, and a bad doctor, too. Like her father.

He also knew, suddenly, what he had had in common with her. For Emerald was father-driven too.

Crest was following in the footsteps of Kilroy: across the continent by rail, a brief stop in a Port of Embarkation, and then across the Pacific by troop transport. He was leaning on the rail one day, staring over an unwinking azure sea. On the horizon was a faint purple smudge like a wisp of smoke: an island, the first land they had seen for weeks. Their destination, Crest presumed. The transport, crammed with soldiers like a tin of sardines, was not the most comfortable environment Crest had ever known, but he felt a surge of affection for the old tub. To put it another way, there was an inkling of fear for what might lie ahead on that wispy purple smudge. Others were crowding to the rail, and Crest surrendered his place. Others were also afraid. He could smell it. There was a lump in his belly; his mouth was dry; his fingers shook as he lit a cigarette.

Within an hour, the ship was gliding to a halt; the anchor rattled down; there could be no doubt that they had arrived. Now the island was less than a mile away, a little jewel in green and white, its center rising to a lofty mountain peak garlanded with cloud, its edges reaching out in sheltering arms of coral to form a lagoon. Without the throbbing of the engines of the ship, the silence seemed enormous. There were no explosions, no detonation of bombs or rattle of small-arms fire or whine of aircraft. If war was taking place on that pretty little island, it was a silent war. The silence seemed more threatening to Crest than the concussions he had been expecting.

"Now hear this! Now hear this!" said the blatant voice of the public-address system.

An Army general was aboard, and his voice came next over the amplifier, distorted and coarsened by electronic imperfections. This particular island was the end of the line for some aboard, it appeared, but not for all. Some fifty enlisted men and five officers were due to disembark; the others were headed for a destination farther on. The names were read and Crest's was among them.

Crest scrambled below to get his gear and returned to the deck in time to see an LST putting out from shore. The ungainly craft crawled toward them from the lagoon, straddling the ocean like a waterbug. Landing nets were overside the transport, and Crest scrambled down the cliff side of the transport with the others, fighting back his nauseating vertigo. The LST shoved away from the looming transport and puttered toward the maw of the lagoon. The sun was hot and the air was still.

"Where in the hell is the shooting?" asked one of the enlisted men.

The gob at the tiller of the LST merely laughed. The question wasn't worth answering.

The water of the lagoon shelved, turning from a deep blue to a turquoise, then to a sapphire, then robin's-egg green; finally, there was wavering white sand underneath. The LST plowed into the shore; the gangplank slapped down; the men rapidly ran off, jumping into tepid water up to the waist. Just like the movies, thought Crest. His reflexes were prepared to throw him belly down on the sand at the first shot, but the beach was empty. He saw a few broken boxes and crates and the shell of a burned-out half-track, but otherwise the beach was a long, hot, dazzling white virginal crescent of sand. An MP was waiting, hat, belt, and gaiters snowy white. Crest came to the conclusion that there was no immediate danger of sudden death.

"Where is the war?" asked one of the men.

The MP smiled with superior condescension and led the way over a path through scrubby tropical vegetation. Ahead lay the typical Army installation, the same row of ugly yellow barracks in the dust.

"Which one of you men is the doc?" asked the MP.

"I am," said Crest.

"That way, sir. Report to the hospital, the long building behind the officer's mess. The rest of you men follow me."

Crest went to what he assumed was the hospital. Sitting on the front stoop was what might have been a soldier, wearing a tattered fatigue uniform without insignia, smoking a cigarette, drawing figures in the dust with the tip of his forefinger.

"I'm looking for the hospital," said Crest.

"You've found it."

"I'm reporting for duty. Where can I find the commanding officer?"

"You've found him. I'm Colonel Smith. Are you the new man?"

"Yes, sir. Lieutenant John Crest."

"Howdy, Crest." The colonel scarcely bothered to look up. "Welcome to Messy Island."

"I beg your pardon, sir?"

"Officially, the name of the joint is Okramechi Island, or something like that, but we call it Messy Island, for reasons which will be apparent to you very shortly, if they aren't already. I hope you'll be very happy here, but I know you won't. Have a seat."

Crest sat down. "What are my duties?"

Colonel Smith looked blank. "Huh?"

"My work," said Crest. "I hope I didn't come five thousand miles for nothing."

"Do you drink?"

"Sir?"

"Do you indulge in alcoholic beverages?"

"Occasionally, sir."

"Fine," said Colonel Smith. "Your duty is bartender at the officer's club."

Crest thought he was joking.

"You don't have to, Lieutenant, if you don't want to, but it might give you something to do."

"I'm a doctor, sir," said Crest.

"So am I," said Colonel Smith. "I left a busy practice in gynecology in Cleveland to command this installation on Messy Island, and I haven't laid eyes on a woman for months. Let me explain the local situation to you, Crest. Last year, Messy Island was a small Jap refueling station. We landed Marines, who occupied the island after a few bloody hours and turned it over to the Army and went away. The Army spent a few weeks mopping up, then most of them went away.

Now we have a small permanent cadre, some Seabees, and this hospital."

"What's the point?" asked Crest.

"A good question, Doctor, but we don't inquire. I suppose we intended to use Messy Island as a weather station. They have some meteorological equipment, but the weather doesn't change; it's always hot and dry. There's an emergency air strip, but it's never been used. They must have been expecting a lot of casualties, but the war has moved a thousand miles away. We have a fifty-bed station hospital, staffed with fifty doctors and two hundred enlisted men. At the moment, I believe, we have three bed patients and that is a heavier load than usual. Usually there are only one or two."

"Good Lord! Fifty doctors and two patients?" said Crest. "Are there any nurses?"

"No," said Colonel Smith. "This is a combat area."

"I thought you said that the war was a thousand miles away."

"See the mountain over there? There are Japs on it, a few of them, twenty-five or thirty, I suppose. The Marines couldn't find them, and neither could the Army. They live in caves. No white man can negotiate the cliffs."

"Do they give you any trouble, sir?"

The colonel laughed. "Those Japs are as dangerous as a flea on a buffalo. They set off a few explosives every evening at dusk, just to show us that they're still alive up there. I find it amusing, myself. Our general gets mad at them for spoiling Retreat, and he sends a patrol up after them now and again. Invariably, somebody in the patrol falls off a cliff and breaks a leg. That's how we fill three of our hospital beds."

"Colonel," said Crest, "you're beginning to depress me."

"Depression is a common syndrome on Messy Island."

"Sir," said Crest, "I wish to request a transfer."

"You do?" said the colonel. "So do I. Who doesn't? Make yourself at home, Lieutenant Crest. I understand this is going to be a long war."

Crest had thought the colonel was exaggerating, but the appraisal was a good one. Messy Island was two miles broad, one mile high, and a thousand miles from anywhere. It was populated by 52 depressed physicians, 248 enlisted medics, 93 Seabees, 180 soldiers in the permanent cadre, a dozen civilian technicians, a couple of hundred natives, and 31 belligerent Japanese in the caves on top of the mountain, as nearly as Crest could count.

The only ones that Crest found of any interest were the natives and the Japanese. The natives were a placid, moon-faced lot, with a number of fascinating tropical conditions, but they refused to be treated at the hospital. Two of their most common diseases were communicable: yaws, a spirochete disease which is non-venereal, and chancroid, a non-spirochete disease which is venereal. Some of the more venturesome enlisted men, who had managed to cohabit with the females in the native population, appeared quite regularly at the dispensary with these conditions. The first few times Crest saw these diseases he was fascinated, since he had only read of them in books. However, both conditions melted away under penicillin treatment, and the interest was transitory. There were other tropical conditions occasionally encountered from time to time. Those who forgot their atabrine had malaria. There was Dengue fever. There was an interesting variety of deadly snake on the island, and a variety of deadly spider, and man-eating funguses that grew luxuriously in everybody's axilla and groin. However, with one doctor for every ten people, there wasn't enough medical interest to go around. A few of the medical officers did what little medical work there was, Crest among them. The rest drank and played poker and slept in the sun and generally went to seed.

As for the Japanese, Crest kept hoping to encounter one. All he could see was a few distant red flares and an occasional explosion in the distance from the top of the mountain at dusk.

Why, Crest wondered, does the Army invariably waste its

medical personnel? He realized that, perhaps, it was more a
matter of misassignment than actual waste. In all the true
combat areas and, in fact, most rear areas supplying the combat zone, the medical installations were extremely busy. In
such areas, the hospitals were apt to be understaffed and
doctors were working day and night, while in other areas,
doctors sat around in empty hospitals with nothing to do. The
contingencies of war were such, Crest knew, that an area of
combat cannot be predicted in advance. Any potential area
of casualties must have a medical staff; the humanities of
democracy require it, even though other areas are understaffed and doctors may be in desperate need at home. If war
avoids one spot, doctors will sit and hospital beds will lie
vacant.

The military mind is stiff and bristly, like a military brush.
For many, war is hell. But for many more, war is rot and
waste and boredom and nothingness.

Surely, Crest decided, man could devise more constructive
ways to pass the days of his life. It was a long war. Crest sat
out the rest of it on Messy Island.

The Officer's Club at Fort Sam Houston, Texas, is a sump-
tuous establishment; kings and Roman emperors never had it
better; nothing is too good for the battle-stained and weary
returning troops. The food is marvelous and cheap; the liquor
flows, although you have to bring your own bottle into the
place, but you can always find somebody else's bottle if you
forget; women are available. Crest was enjoying himself that
night.

The war, having started with a lot of little bombs, had con-
cluded with a couple of very large ones. Messy Island was
returned to the natives and, presumably, a few remaining
belligerent Japanese. Now he was on temporary duty at Fort
Sam, awaiting discharge, for a couple of weeks at most. Then,
glory be, Crest would become a civilian again. He had no
intention of joining the reserves for any longer period than he

could avoid. Now he was a captain. He would be discharged as a major. He had nothing to do at Fort Sam, but this was not unusual; it had been a long time since Crest had anything to do. There is a large general hospital at Fort Sam, a good one, a busy one. By day, Crest was welcome to spend his time on the wards, getting the feel of clinical medicine. Medically speaking, he had become as rusty as a burned-out half-track on the beach of Messy Island. By night, he could and did enjoy himself in the Officer's Club.

He was dancing with a nurse. She was a grade junior to him, a few years younger than he, and for her it had also been a long, dull war. She was also awaiting discharge. She was not in uniform but wore a pretty and frilly evening gown in white. The evening was warm and she was beginning to perspire; dampness touched down the ringlets at her temples. She danced well. She was a tall girl, sinuous and willowy, not pretty in the face, but, rather, handsome. She was a little shy and retiring. He found it difficult to open a conversation with her. He enjoyed her silent company and the physical sensation of a woman in his arms.

"I swear," he said, "you smell better than anything I encountered on Messy Island."

She gave him a grave smile. "I would be inclined to regard that as a mixed compliment, Captain."

"Please call me doctor: I'm in a civilian frame of mind."

"Yes, Dr. Crest."

Crest stepped back from her. "How did you know my name?"

She smiled. "You never remembered mine."

Her face seemed vaguely familiar. "You took your training at the hospital where I was an intern," he said.

"That's right."

"I know you," said Crest. "I had a date with you ten years ago. We wrestled with a patient in the Accident Room one morning. I wrenched my shoulder. You had a hairline fracture of the external malleolus of your right ankle."

"You're a doctor," she said. "You remember the diagnosis but not the name."

"Nancy Conover. How's that?"

"Brilliant," she said.

"Nancy," said Crest, "don't you find it warm in here? There's a beautiful moon tonight. How about a walk?"

"Are you to be trusted in the moonlight?"

"No," said Crest. "You're the first woman I've had in my arms for three years."

"I'll take a chance," she said. "But I should warn you, Doctor, that I didn't stay an old maid all these years by succumbing to males in the moonlight."

It was a mellow evening. The silver moon rode through wisps of high cloud. Red beacon lights in various locations were blinking, to remind them that this was a military installation, not a country club. Several miles away, over one of the adjacent air bases, they must have been conducting a night problem. The silver speck of an airplane, very high, was transfixed in the fingers of several searchlight beams.

"What became of your other girl?" asked Nancy.

"I married her."

"Oh."

"And she left me just before the war."

Nancy sat down on the grass.

"Be careful," said Crest. "You'll get grass green all over your pretty white dress."

"Small loss. I don't have much use for an evening dress," she said. "Do you have a cigarette?"

Crest sat down beside her on the grass, placed a cigarette between her lips, and lit it.

"I was always giving Emerald a cigarette," he said. "She smoked like a furnace but she never carried any of her own. She borrowed things with no intention of returning them."

"Did you have children?"

"One. He died."

"I'm sorry."

"Born hydrocephalic, lived less than an hour, and expired in my arms. I always thought I killed him, in a sense, since the poor little creature needed oxygen and I couldn't bear to put him back into the tent. Of course, he would have died in a short time anyway. I never told Emerald about the oxygen tent. I never told anyone. Emerald had a hysterectomy, so she can't have any more children, but she didn't want them. I got the impression that she was almost relieved when the baby died."

Nancy blew a cloud of smoke which was faintly luminous in the moonlight. "You don't often discuss your problems, do you?"

"No."

"Why am I favored?"

"Blame it on the moonlight and three long years on Messy Island," said Crest.

"Did you love her?"

"I don't know."

"That's a funny answer. Most people seem very positive on that subject."

"Every man his own expert," said Crest. "Yes, I've wondered about that. If love is a complicated matter—and I think it is —how can people be so sure with no experience? Particularly since most people have no training in dealing with psychology and physiology."

"There's a kid in our barracks," said Nancy. "She has leukemia. Not the acute kind but a chronic case in remission; she feels well enough, and you can't tell she's sick to look at her, but of course she knows it will flare up sooner or later and kill her. I don't know how she managed to get into the Army. They always seem to miss it on the physicals."

"In the Army, this can happen," said Crest.

"Do you know the rather vulgar barracks expression about minks?"

"The fur coat?"

"The animal."

"I know what you mean," said Crest.

"That's her: any time, any place, with anything in pants."

"Perhaps this is part of her disease," said Crest.

"Maybe so," said Nancy. "Knowing that she won't live very long, I suppose she feels she must grab every opportunity for experience. But just in the past few weeks, she's had a greater variety of experience than most of us will have in a lifetime. Curiously, Doctor, I think this makes her more unhappy than the fatal illness she has."

"Perhaps."

"I mean, what is she trying to prove? That she is a woman, I suppose. But why can't she accept that fact without compiling a battalion of expert witnesses?"

"She may be searching for her own identity."

"Yes," said Nancy. "I think that she's trying to prove to herself that she is real. That's a funny way to prove it. I know I'm real."

"Well," said Crest, "have you ever been in love?"

"No."

"You're an attractive woman. Why not?"

"Every time it seems to be getting close," she said, "I get cold feet."

"Why?"

She smiled. "I'm chicken, I guess."

"Any particular reason for you to be afraid of men?"

"I'm not afraid of them," she said.

"Don't like men?"

"I prefer their company."

"Still waiting for the right one to come along, I suppose."

"That's an old-fashioned notion, isn't it?" she said.

"It's a romantic notion," said Crest. "And, like all romance, it's very nice, and false. It is unsound, on the basis of psychology and physiology, to assume that there is only one man for a given woman, and vice versa."

"Will you dissect your next romance on the basis of physiology and psychology?"

"I've had it," said Crest. "More than enough. I'm too old."

"Me too," she said, "even though I haven't had it and never will."

It suddenly occurred to Crest that he could like this woman very much. "Sorry," he said.

"For what?" she said. "What did you do?"

"I didn't do it," said Crest. "I almost did."

"Doctor, I'm afraid I don't know what you're talking about."

"I almost asked you an impulsive question, but I bit my tongue in time."

"I hope you're not bleeding," she said.

"I was going to ask you to marry me."

"Just like that?" she said.

"Sure." Crest grinned. "Is there a better way?"

"Impulsively, on the spur of the moment, to a woman you just met, whom you don't even know?"

"I have the feeling that I know you rather well."

"Why do you see a wife in me?"

"If you'll pardon my frankness," said Crest, "I think that you're a quiet, solid, conservative, old-fashioned girl. This makes the best kind of wife."

"I have liabilities," she said.

"So do I."

"You might not find me fascinating, like that other one," she said.

"As for me, I'm too intense and serious. I have an odd streak, and a stubborn streak. In one sense I am a sensualist, and yet on the other hand, I have a rigid Puritanical conscience, and these two parts of me are constantly at war. I'm not a very good doctor. I have no bedside manner. People frighten me, and I sometimes think I frighten them. I am not a very sympathetic guy. Actually, I'm not sympathetic to myself."

"Do you have in mind a marriage based on mutual liability?" she said.

"Furthermore, I have a family affair," said Crest. "They're

Parkindales. It isn't so much Emerald. It's all of them. I fight
with them, I love them, I'm all mixed up in them."

"You can't fix a marriage like a business deal."

"Nancy, I like you," he said.

"Okay, but is that enough?"

"I'm quite lonely," said Crest.

"Well, so am I," she said.

"You're right. People don't marry like this. I withdraw the
proposition."

"I might remember it," she said.

They looked at each other across a patch of moonlight.

"There isn't much time any more," said Crest. "We are both
still in the Army. They might not discharge us. There might
be another war. Tomorrow they could pick one or the other
of us up and move us half a continent apart."

"I presume we could find each other."

"Then what's the matter?"

"You know me," she said. "Chicken. Cold feet."

"I'm not free. I have no right to ask you."

"Wouldn't she let you go?"

"I don't see why not. We've had nothing to do with each
other for years."

"Sometimes an off-stage husband is useful to a woman like
that."

"I'll ask her," he said, "before I ask you again."

"I hope you won't feel like a small bone over which two
large dogs are conducting an argument."

"I'm not the greatest matrimonial catch. You better think it
over."

"We both better sleep on it," she said.

Crest grinned. "Together?"

"That isn't exactly what I had in mind," she said.

Immediately after his separation from the service, Crest
went to New York. Emerald was in a Broadway play. The
play had been running for nearly two years, and tickets were

not hard to obtain. It was a brittle, brilliant comedy with three characters. Emerald had the only female role, the gamin, a tough little wise-cracking ingénue, whose façade of sophistication concealed an underlying naïve virginity. Her virginity was pursued by a nice but puzzled young man and an unpuzzled gamy old reprobate. Crest scarcely recognized Emerald on her entrance. Although from time to time he caught a stabbingly familiar flash of the Emerald he had known, he was largely absorbed by the character she played. She was good. Although Crest knew that she was not naïve, she certainly carried it off.

After the show, he went backstage to her dressing room. The room was full, people buzzing in and out like flies. Emerald was a dragonfly, poised on invisible wings, sometimes behind the screen and sometimes not, in various stages of undress, without a trace of self-consciousness. On the stage, her hair had appeared as lustrously black as ever, but on closer inspection Crest could tell that there were strands of silver here and there. She acknowledged Crest's presence. After she was dressed, she dismissed her followers, and permitted Crest to take her out to supper. She chose an expensive and fashionable restaurant, although Crest would have preferred some dark and intimate place where they could talk. She ate lightly, drank a good deal of champagne, and chattered at him rapidly. She was talking at him, not to him, a flow of superficial dancing words which didn't say anything at all. In earlier days, the amount of the check would have staggered him, and Emerald offered to pay it, but Crest had accumulated a considerable amount of back pay when he was overseas, and money was not an immediate consideration.

After supper, Crest said, "Let's go somewhere where we can really talk."

"My apartment?" she suggested.

"All right."

The apartment was a long cry from the one of earlier times. It was big, too big for a single woman alone, swank, cold, and, for all the tasteful modern furnishings, empty-feeling. Emerald parked Crest in the high-ceilinged living room and disappeared out back. In ten minutes she returned. She was wearing a negligee, black velvet. She carried a silver tray with two frosty glasses full of beer. Emerald sat down on the floor beside Crest's chair and laid her dark head upon his knee. The white strands of her hair stood out in contrast to the black.

"Well, chum," she said, "the war is over, I understand."

"Until the next one, I guess."

"And where do we begin?"

"Emerald," he said, "that's just the point. We don't."

"All right," she said indifferently. "It's up to you."

"I came to ask you for a divorce."

"Easy enough," she said. "I leave the show in a couple of weeks and go to the West Coast. I have time for a Reno vacation on the way."

"Thanks," said Crest. "I didn't think you'd make a problem at this time."

"Who is she, chum?"

"You don't know her," said Crest.

"Make you a little bet," said Emerald. "Bet you ten to one you don't know her either."

"I know her well enough," said Crest. "I know that she'll be good for me, Emerald, and you weren't. She'll bring out the best in me. You didn't."

"It's a pity you don't love her, too."

"We don't need to discuss it," said Crest.

"How is she in bed?"

"I couldn't say."

"Ah. Honorable. Conservative. Old-fashioned. Virgins till the wedding night. How nice!"

"Emerald," said Crest, "are you still searching for identity in sex?"

"I change my identity with the seasons. I get well paid for it, and people clap their hands."

"That's what you wanted, isn't it?"

"It gratifies the vanity," she said. "I'm not very versatile."

"I thought you were very good."

"I have only one role to play, and I'm getting too old for it. What is your lady's name?"

"Nancy."

Emerald got off the floor, sat down in Crest's lap, and put her arms around his neck.

"I don't suppose Nancy would approve of this," she said.

"I don't require Nancy's permission for the things I do. She knows I've been married before."

"As a matter of fact, I am still your wife, so this is not against the law, is it, chum?"

She unbuttoned his shirt and ran her fingers across his bare chest. He was very conscious of her warmth and presence, and of the fact, which he knew from experience, that she wore nothing underneath her robe.

"Emerald, what are you trying to prove?"

"I've always thought I could get you back at one flicker of a petticoat," she said.

"Well," said Crest, "you can't."

"Oh, come," she said. "You are not reacting as if you had lost all interest in me."

"For reasons that I can't explain, I can't get you out of my blood," he said. "But there's more to this business than that."

"Is there?" she said. "Don't all men have this same itchy and incurable disease? Can any one of you resist the flicker of another petticoat?"

"Emerald, what do you want? I know you don't want me. And you have little interest in physical experience. Physical sensation never meant very much to you unless there was pain connected with it."

She got off his lap. "Since I am losing you to a dame I never met, might not this mean pain?"

"You've gotten along without me now for years."

"That's no problem. I can get along without a man," she said.

"You puzzle me," said Crest. "Who are you? I never knew. What is the real Emerald who is hiding underneath?"

"I'd just as soon not joke about it, chum."

"I'm not joking," he said.

"Emerald is a cat," she said. "She likes dead fish, fat cream. She licks her paws and roams at night. If she had kittens, she would abandon them in a rain barrel, hoping they would drown. She is not a domesticated animal. She will live in a house when necessary in order to get her cream and fish, but she would prefer to snatch a goldfish from a bowl, or go out on the lawn and grab a bird on the wing."

"That's a cruel self-analysis, it seems to me," said Crest.

"Consciously, I'm not cruel," she said, "any more than I could be consciously gentle. I lack moral values. I don't care whether I'm cruel or gentle, and sometimes I don't know the difference. For this reason, it is best for me to live alone."

"Are you lonely?"

"No," she said. "I don't care enough for people to miss them very much. You better marry this Nancy character, chum. I hope she fills your house with sons. Maybe she'll bear you a daughter. Then you can learn from your daughter that women happen to be human beings too."

"Stop that, Emerald!"

"This is my house, chum, and in it I say exactly what I like."

"Mental cruelty."

"We will presume the Reno judge will agree to that. I could scarcely divorce you on the grounds of infidelity. Go on back to Nancy. Treat her like a human being. It wouldn't hurt the cause if you could manage to fall in love with her, too."

"Good-by, Emerald."

"Good-by," she said. "Chum, we really had a ball together, didn't we?"

"We had something," said Crest. "I couldn't define it."

"Let's leave it go at that," she said.

Before returning to Texas to pick up Nancy, Crest stopped off to pay a visit to Joseph Parkindale. Joseph's face was vigorous; he had a dynamic air about him, an attitude of zest. His arms and shoulders seemed more heavily muscled, and Crest presumed that he had been taking special exercises to strengthen the upper half of his torso in compensation for his useless lower half. He managed his wheelchair skillfully, darting around the room quicker than Crest could have walked. Crest noticed his hands: no longer those of a Sybarite but blunter and stronger, like those of a working man.

"You enjoy psychiatry?"

"A fascinating science," said Joseph. "You make up your own rules as you go along."

"You work full time?"

"Twenty patient hours a week is enough," said Joseph. "The rest of the time I occupy my hands. Come with me. I'll show you."

Joseph now lived in a house which had no stairs; different levels were connected by ramps with a gradual slope, to accommodate his wheelchair. Joseph pushed himself briskly up a ramp into a large bare room with a north window. The room was full of statuary, athletic figures, for the most part: running, jumping, diving, leaping.

"Do I detect a Grecian influence in your work?" said Crest. "You used to concentrate on the face, but these feature body motion."

"He who cannot walk must cherish those who do," said Joseph. "There's one I wanted to show you in particular. How's this?"

It was a small statuette, two feet high, in some unusual stone of dark green, veined with streaks of a lighter green. It was a female figure, nude. She stood erect, arms outthrust, legs apart. It was a position of triumphant reception, of victory, except for one feature: the head was bent sharply backward, angulated to the point of fracture.

"Emerald," said Crest.

"I thought you might say it was Diana," said Joseph. "On account of the fractured neck."

"By the way," said Crest, "Emerald is divorcing me. I hope to marry again."

"Congratulations."

"Yes. I think it's a wise move."

"What kind of woman is she, John?"

"A nurse, several years younger than myself. A tall girl, slender, willowy, attractive, quiet, and a little shy."

"Not small-boned, vivacious, moody, glittering, unsure of herself?"

"Hey," said Crest, "aren't you describing Emerald? Did you think I'd marry the same woman twice?"

"I've noticed," said Joseph, "that people have a curious tendency to keep repeating the same mistake."

"Not me. Not where marriage is concerned," said Crest. "Nancy is altogether different. She is not beautiful, by the way. You might call her plain."

"I hope you don't," said Joseph.

"I'm tactful on the subject."

"Tell her she has beautiful eyes. You can't go wrong. Everybody has beautiful eyes," said Joseph. "Are you in love with her?"

"Everybody seems to wonder about that."

"Including yourself?"

"What is love? Define your terms."

"Don't ask me! I'm only a psychiatrist."

"Well, then, was I in love with Emerald?"

"Why don't you tell me?"

"I think not," said Crest. "She fascinated me, sure, and in some way she always will, but that isn't enough. In ways I didn't even like her. She couldn't love me. I don't think she could love any man at all."

"Implying that Emerald could only love a woman?"

"I don't know that," said Crest.

"Don't look at me! Neither do I," said Joseph.

"Regarding Nancy," said Crest, "she doesn't fascinate me. She doesn't overwhelm me. I'm not nervous in her presence; in fact, she relaxes me. I genuinely like the girl. She has the ingredients to be a good wife and mother. She will build a home, and that's what I need. I don't need more fascination. A little goes a long way, at least for me."

"You make sense," said Joseph. "This will be a good marriage. Of course, like all good marriages, it will be dull."

"Go to hell!" said Crest.

Joseph laughed.

"What I really came to talk about is my career," said Crest. "I have no training or inclination to be anything but a doctor. And yet, I have this deep, dark suspicion that I am a lousy doctor. Am I?"

Joseph didn't reply.

"Four years without patients in Sentryville did not help my morale. Three years on Messy Island didn't help me, either. I am seven years away from clinical contact with the patient. I am now taking a post-graduate refresher course, and I'm not far behind technically. I remember the facts. I never did know how to handle the people."

"So what are you going to do?"

"That's the problem. Nancy suggests a salary job. I'm not interested in teaching or research. They always need physicians with the pharmaceutical manufacturers."

"Drug-house doctors are nothing but door-to-door salesmen, my boy."

"There are positions with insurance companies."

"Barracks lawyers."

"Student health. Public health. Ship doctors. Medical missionaries. I could even go back into the Army. The worst doctor can find a good paying job."

"There's group practice. The clinics."

"Yes," said Crest. "But I'm an individualist. I have a feeling that group practice boils down to a matter of politics."

"Get to the point," said Joseph.

"That's the point. What am I going to do?"

"I was waiting for the critical question," said Joseph. "This is poor psychiatry, but I'll save a few hours and phrase it myself. You want me to give you ten good reasons why you shouldn't go back to Sentryville."

"I probably shouldn't."

"I haven't got ten good reasons," said Joseph. "I haven't got one."

"You think I should go back."

"You have already decided to return to Sentryville," said Joseph. "Shall we explore the reasons why?"

"That's what I don't understand," said Crest. "For me, Sentryville represents bitterness and defeat. I couldn't make a living there. It might be different now, but Parky's still alive."

"You're young. You'll outlive Parky in due course of time."

"By which time," said Crest, "some younger, smarter man will come along. Then I'll be an old derelict instead of a young incompetent."

"Your arguments ring of the truth. Do you want me to say they are a lie?"

"What's the matter with me?" said Crest. "Am I a masochist? Do I enjoy despair? Am I accident-prone? Am I driven to place myself in a position where I can't succeed?"

"It will interest me," said Joseph, "to see what happens when Nancy gives you a son."

"Ye Gods!" said Crest. "I've always fought with fathers. Now I'll have sons who will fight with me?"

"Compromise with a father is possible."

"So I've heard," said Crest.

"I'm not giving up on you," said Joseph. "You're a late bloomer, like Sam."

"What happened to Sam?" said Crest. "I've lost track of him. Did he drink himself into an institution?"

"Not exactly," said Joseph. "Sam's unit left London and went to Africa. The rest of the unit marched across the desert, but Sam got left behind."

"Beg pardon?"

"If you should follow a certain African river through the jungles, you will come upon a small native settlement. It's not easy getting there. The climate is lousy; the jungle is thick; the river is full of snags and crocodiles. You might also have trouble with the natives. They ate white men not long ago, and maybe they still do. They're a fascinating tribe, from the medical point of view, full of tropical disease: frambesia, leprosy, elephantiasis, trachoma. They also have white man's disease: tuberculosis, syphilis. The most deadly epidemic, surprisingly, is measles. In the middle of this settlement, fighting witch doctors with one hand and missionaries with the other, you will find Sam Parkindale. He's black as a nigger, working like a nigger. He's alone, and angry, and every night he's drunk. But all day long he's working with his hands. The natives are lazy, and he has to build his own hospital. He's trying to do plastic surgery and abdominal surgery and traumatic surgery and eye surgery with a can of ether, a rusty jackknife, and a dirty spoon. He's trying to cure frambesia and syphilis without penicillin. He has everything to work on and nothing to work with, except his hands, his head, and possibly his heart."

"I'll be damned," said Crest. "Sam found himself."

"He found dedication in the jungles, so maybe there's hope for you."

"But Sentryville isn't a jungle."

"It isn't?" said Joseph Parkindale.

Crest said, "I'm free."

"So am I," said Nancy.

"Then I'll ask you again: will you marry me?"

"I think you'd make a very good husband, John, but . . ."

"I'm not articulate," said Crest. "Personal declarations always seem to embarrass me. I haven't got a very good line. I have no magnetic bedside manner. Furthermore, I'm never quite sure of myself, and never quite understand my own motivations. I don't know what love is, for example. I know about fascination, and know that you could never fascinate me as Emerald did, but I also know my fascination wasn't healthy and I've had enough of it. I know you'll make me a good wife, and build us a home, and that's what I need, but this isn't why I'm asking you. I'm saying, as well as I know how, that I love you, as well as I can. On this basis, I am asking: will you marry me?"

"Of course," she said.

"And live with me in Sentryville?"

"If you feel you must."

"You've never even seen the town."

"No," she said, "but there's trouble there for you."

"A man can't find himself by turning his back on trouble."

"Something to do with Emerald?"

"Not Emerald exactly. Her father," said Crest.

"The man you call Parky?"

"Yes."

"What is he? A monster, or something of the kind?"

"No," said Crest. "Just a doctor. Not a very good doctor, according to the way that I was taught."

"And what are you attempting to prove?"

"That I'm better," said Crest. "That Sentryville needs me too."

"All right," said Nancy. "But one thing must be clearly understood."

"What's that?"

"Parkindales are your problem, not mine," she said. "There will be no room for them in our house."

"All right."

"The past is behind us. I have no argument with that," she said. "But the future belongs to us. I've no intention of sharing you with this woman's family."

"Fair enough," said Crest.

"I think I'm going to like it in the town of Sentryville," she said.

Part 7

Sentryville, a pleasant New England town, population 10,000, had grown during the war. The textile factory had been converted to the manufacture of small-arms ammunition and there was talk of further conversion to electronic parts. The new inhabitants lived in the housing developments, clots of square identical buildings which mushroomed up along the arterial highway to the north and south.

Elms still bordered the village square, but there were fewer of them now. The statue of the sentry still looked for the British in the wrong direction. Except when the square was covered with snow, there were little boys on it playing ball. There were many little boys and, on the green benches, many mothers with baby carriages.

On the north of the square, the rambling old houses were badly in need of paint. Some of them had been subdivided into apartments; some were torn down for parking lots.

During the war, there had been only three doctors in Sentryville. Dr. Jones had been compelled to do a little of everything. Dr. Klamp was forced out of semi-retirement. Dr. Parkindale was busier than ever. By the end of the war, Dr. Jones, a wealthy man and partially disabled by his gout, was more than happy to confine his practice to diseases of the eye. Dr. Klamp, senile, the victim of several little strokes, retired permanently into a nursing home. Only Dr. Parkindale remained active, very active. New men came to town, all specialists. The hospital needed a full-time radiologist and shared a pathologist with another community hospital down the river. Two bright, aggressive young surgeons came to Sentryville as partners; within a year, they had parted in some heat; in future they did not speak to each other and neither spoke to Dr. Parkindale. There was a new pediatrician, a passive and dependent chap, whom anxious mothers seemed to regard as another of their children. There was an obstetrician, a smooth blond man with a wax mustache; he was married, but his extracurricular activities extended in a complicated interlocking network through all the strata of the town.

Three men formerly in Sentryville came back from the war. Dr. Hamilton, white-headed and wearing poorly fitted dentures, had spent his war in the Pentagon. Dr. Rhodes, now nearly bald, had been in the Navy; three ships had been shot out from under him; he had spent thirty-eight days on a raft in the South Pacific and passed the last seventeen months of the war in a Japanese prison camp. And then there was Dr. Crest, who had a new wife.

"Such a pleasant little town," said Nancy Crest. "I know we're going to be happy here."

"I have my fingers crossed," said Crest.

"Won't it be different with me in the house?"

Crest studied her. "Yes," he said, "I think it will."

The epidemiology of Sentryville was in many ways unchanged. Influenza swept down the valley every winter and gastroenteritis in the summer. Almost every child had measles, mumps, and chickenpox in the first ten years of life. Diabetes, hypertension, and arteriosclerosis were common in the older population. Most of the married women got pregnant and some of the unmarried ones. Two per cent of the population was alcoholic. Manslaughter was alarmingly frequent on the highways. Half the people who entered a doctor's office had emotional or functional disease.

In other ways, the epidemiology was different. Appendicitis and tuberculosis were slowly vanishing diseases. Syphilis was rare. Crest had been taught in school that gonorrhea was the most common infectious disease, second only to the common cold, but gonorrhea was no longer seen after the war. Women did not die in childbirth; the death of children was unusual. Life expectancy in Sentryville had increased ten full years. This was, in part, a product of the war. World War II had produced not only the most lethal weapon in history but also the most miraculous drug. On the one hand, the atom bomb; on the other, penicillin. More by fortune than by conscious plan, penicillin saved a hundred thousand times more lives than the atom bomb was able to destroy.

The age of miracle drugs had begun with sulfanilamide, but the sulfa drugs were tarnished miracles at best: unreliable, toxic, and limited in scope. Penicillin promptly took its place with aspirin, insulin, morphine, and digitalis, as the five great drugs of pharmacology.

The age of penicillin produced the needle doctor. Since the early penicillins could be given only by injection, the buttocks of the nation became well punctured. Some men not only gave penicillin for everything the drug could cure, but also for everything the drug could not cure, and in addition gave all other drugs by needle too. The needle is a powerful psychological tool. To some patients, it has a sexual significance. Many neurotic symptoms responded to the needle. Some patients came to believe that a drug wasn't any good unless given by injection, and doctors could always be found to encourage this belief. An office visit without a shot was three dollars in Sentryville; with a shot, ten dollars. It was said that Dr. Parkindale gave more penicillin than all the other doctors in the valley put together, but, of course, he was busier.

For every use there is abuse. Doctors may be smart, but so are bacteria. Resistant strains of bacteria arose which thrived on penicillin. In the laboratory, scientists labored to produce more and better antibiotic drugs. In the bodies of the patient, bacteria labored to adjust to more and better antibiotic drugs. It was like a munitions race. Research is expensive, and drug costs rose. The drug industry is fiercely competitive, and physicians were deluged with mountains of free literature, free samples, free magazines and newspapers and gadgets and gifts from the advertising departments of the drug houses. Some companies spent more money on advertising than on research. Drug costs rose so high as to be out of the range of many of the patients who needed them.

Illness once fatal became curable at great expense. Illness became a financial catastrophe. Insurance plans arose to protect people against such catastrophe, and insurance claims require a lot of paper. Some doctors spent more time filing forms than seeing patients. The pen became mightier than the needle, which, in turn, was mightier than the scalpel or the stethoscope. Doctors began to long for the day when they could spend their time with the sick. Patients began to long for the day when they could see a doctor without bankruptcy. The doctor-patient relationship showed further deterioration for reasons neither doctor nor patient could fully appreciate.

Crest awoke early on a warm morning in July. Later in the day, it would be hot. He glanced across at Nancy, peacefully sleeping in the other bed. She had decided upon twin beds from the beginning.

Her head was turned toward him on the pillow. Even under the relaxing influence of sleep, Nancy had a strong face—not a pretty face. She wore an old-fashioned nightie, severely cut, buttoned to the neck. The thought occurred to Crest that he had never seen her naked. Shortly after the wedding, Nancy had a birthday, her twenty-eighth; Crest gave her a frilly negligee, which he had selected in some embarrassment and with great care. This was the type of garment Emerald had loved and collected in quantity. Nancy had not worn it yet.

She wasn't lacking in femininity, Crest thought; her responses, though slow to build, were more sustained and intense than Emerald's had ever been. Her thermostat was set; neither too hot nor too cold, she tended to run a level temperature.

"She's good for me," thought Crest.

He was inclined to kiss her and to wake her up, but he had discovered that Nancy was unapproachable until after the first cup of coffee in the morning. In the evening, on the other hand, she was likely to begin an involved and serious conversation just as Crest was about to fall asleep.

He went downstairs and fixed breakfast for himself. His days were quite busy. He had gotten into the habit of eating a hearty breakfast. He had gained ten pounds since he returned to Sentryville.

The telephone rang three times during his breakfast. It was ringing quite frequently these days. Sentryville had been doctor-starved during the war. Although most patients doubtless would have preferred Dr. Parkindale, Parky was too busy, and there was plenty of business left over. Crest was getting his share and more. His practice was far more firmly extablished than it had ever been before.

There are four basic practice builders, Crest decided: the emergency; kids; old folks; and the neurotic woman.

In an emergency, nobody cares which doctor comes, so long as one comes in a hurry. Many of the patients will return to their own physician after the emergency, but many of them will stick. The smart young doctor keeps himself available. Although every emergency is a true emergency to the person

calling for help, many are not true emergencies from the doctor's point of view. The timid soul; the hysteric; the hypochondriac; the drunkard; the psychopath: these are some of
the crosses the doctor has to bear in the name of emergency.
Crest especially disliked the patient with a cold that started
on Monday who doesn't phone the doctor until Saturday
night. The experienced physician can learn to tell the true
emergency from the false with a high degree of accuracy, but
the young man is advised to take them all.

Kids are a fine practice-builder for the doctor who isn't
afraid of them. Children are responsive and honest and quick
to heal. There is no more grateful patient than the difficult
child who has not been able to frighten his physician, unless
it is the difficult mother of that difficult child.

Old folks have a variety of organic disease and they do not
recover. They are stubborn and suspicious and resentful; they
do poorly in hospitals, and they don't respond to medication.
However, they are surprisingly grateful and steady patients
to the doctor who listens, who is wise enough not to over-
treat, and who has a sense of humor. Old people are apt to
survive a surprisingly long time under proper management.

And finally, the neurotic woman. Every practice has many.
She refuses to be cured. The doctor could cure her easily if he
could change her husband or lack of a husband or her psychosexual prejudices, but he can't. However, if the doctor
sympathizes without smiling, gives enough harmless medicine, and permits the patient to fall in love with him while
not permitting himself to show the slightest sign of a response,
she will return. She may return so often that he dreads the
sight of her name in the appointment book, but, without her,
he couldn't make a living.

Of these four types of practice-builders, Crest decided that
he liked the old folks best and, after that, the kids. Emergencies are the fascination and the challenge of the trade, but
after a few years the doctor no longer seeks challenge which
doesn't seek him. As for the neurotic woman, well . . . it isn't

the doctor's fault that there happened to be a snake and an apple in that garden with the first of them.

Crest washed his breakfast dishes and went to the hospital. Hospitals had changed as a result of the war. Once the doctor's workshop, supervised by doctors, the hospital was now in charge of that curious breed of cat, the administrator. Doctors had been too busy during the war, and they had lost control. By its nature, a hospital is an inefficient business, running at a loss; the administrator, therefore, is an expert in inefficiency. He seems to regard the institution itself as more important than the patients in it, and to him, by-laws and paperwork are more important than pain. Doctor and patient seemed to exist in order to support the hospital and not the other way around.

Crest encountered Parky in the hospital corridor. Parky had not changed: still dynamic and vital, still brisk and confident, fully in control.

"Congratulations, Crest," said Parky.

"Thank you, sir."

It was a very surprising thing. At the meeting of the medical society the night before, Parky had not been re-elected president, after eighteen consecutive terms. Crest was president. Crest had not been aware of it, but there was a considerable undercurrent of resentment against Parky on the part of other members of the group, led by the two young surgeons with probable backing from Hamilton and Rhodes. Since the rebels were divided into two hostile camps, none of them could provide the leadership. Crest realized that he was a candidate on compromise, not on power or popularity.

One of the new young surgeons, Dr. Ardz, was alone in the doctors' locker room when Crest stopped in for coffee.

"Do you know what your chief duty is to be as leader of our group?" said Ardz.

"Sure," said Crest. "To keep down signs of professional jealousy and to run a quiet group."

"I did a gall bladder on one of Parky's cases this morning," said Ardz. "In theory, he had already taken her gall bladder out. He just scalped it, however, and left half of it behind, and the patient developed more gallstones in the pocket, as you might expect. This is surgery?"

"I would never take the position that Parky is a man of the highest competence," said Crest.

"The man is a menace to this community. In my opinion, the medical society should run him out of town. That's your job for the year."

"I decline," said Crest.

"What the hell, Crest, the patient can't evaluate the skill and judgment of his doctor. Only other doctors know these things. The rest of us know about Parky's fabulous mistakes. Can't we do something about it?"

"All of us are judged by the jury of our patients," said Crest. "The fashionable physician can therefore do no wrong."

"It's no wonder we lose the respect of the public," said Ardz. "We're afraid to clean our own house."

This was a problem. Crest thought about it. According to medical ethics, doctors do not criticize each other, and ethics are necessary to the profession. Would it be fair to say, however, that ethical standards are justifiable only in a truly ethical profession? If all doctors were dedicated to the service of the patient, no criticism would be warranted. To the extent that doctors are dedicated to power or prestige or money, however, they lose the privilege of the public confidence.

Crest had heard much conversation about socialized medicine after the war. It was apparent to him, no matter what the talk, that a tendency in this direction was historically inevitable. The A.M.A. had a powerful lobby and spewed out propaganda like Madison Avenue, but the profession had a blind side to the problem, in Crest's opinion. The public didn't want socialized medicine. Would any patient want to be treated by a doctor in the manner in which he is treated by the Department of Internal Revenue, for example? Would he wish to present his pain, his fear, and his anxiety to a bureaucrat in quadruplicate? But the public was losing confidence in the medical profession. There was suspicion in many quarters that doctors were fattening and feasting on pain, anxiety, and fear. About the time medicine becomes big business, the public will require inspection and regulation and control, for the public good.

We could stop it, Crest decided, if only we could discover a way to clean our own house. We would have to set up, not only standards of ethics, but of professional competence. We would have to lose our fear of the power of the Parkindales. If we were dedicated to service, why would we fear power? Since we do fear power, is it not possible that we have lost our dedication somewhere along the way?

"I couldn't try to stop Parky," thought Crest. "I'm afraid of him. My only hope is to out-live the old son-of-a-bitch!"

Nancy had a message for him when he got back from the hospital. "You have an appointment, dear, at two o'clock."

"Don't tell me," said Crest. "Put it down in the book."

"Downtown," she said. "At the office of the County Attorney."

"Hell, I can't," said Crest. "That's right in the middle of my own office hours."

"I tried to tell them. No good."

"Why do I have to go to the office of the County Attorney?" said Crest. "Why can't he come to mine?"

"I gather that this relates to his business, not yours," said Nancy.

"What's on his mind?"

"They wouldn't say."

"I'm not going," said Crest. "I'm busy."

"I suppose they could subpoena you."

The same thought had occurred to Crest.

"I've canceled your own appointments between two and three," said Nancy. "That will give you plenty of time."

Crest growled and swore he wasn't going, but he knew he would. When the law summons, the law-abiding citizen goes, no matter what the inconvenience. Was he in any personal trouble with the law? Crest couldn't think of anything in particular, although all doctors skirt legal trouble frequently in the course of their daily work. All Crest could think of was the income tax, but tax trouble would have drawn Federal authorities, not the local County Attorney.

Promptly at two, Crest presented himself at the office of Ralph Timothy, the County Attorney. It was located on the second floor of one of the banks in the business block. Right next to his dentist, Crest realized. At the moment, he almost wished he had a dental appointment, although an hour in the dental chair was not his favorite pastime.

The legend on the frosted panel of the door advised him to walk in, and he did so. The receptionist, a quiet, white-headed old lady in a dress of faded brown, smiled at him. Mr. Timothy would be with him shortly. Crest took a seat. It was a leather couch, old, sway-backed, and the leather was cracked. Sets of ancient brown leather-covered books lined the room; they looked as if they might have belonged to Abraham Lincoln and never been opened since. Crest could not help contrasting the atmosphere with that in waiting rooms of his own profession. Medical offices are crisp, white, and efficient, bustling with tension. The atmosphere of this room, and of this profession, was dusty and musty and brown. There was a loud ticking of an old-fashioned clock on the wall, and it was ten minutes slow.

Soon Timothy came out of his office. Crest rose and greeted him.

"Come in," said Timothy. "Nice of you to drop by."

"I didn't feel I had a choice," said Crest, without graciousness.

Timothy chose to ignore the remark. He was a tall, personable individual of about Crest's age with sandy pinkish hair in a crew cut. Medically, he was the type who might be prone to anemia in the winter and eczema in the summer and who would sunburn painfully. Crest knew him only by sight and reputation. Timothy was new to the job, having been elected the previous fall. During the war he had been a combat company commander.

"You're president of the local medical society?"

"Yes," said Crest.

"I have a problem, Doctor, and I need medical advice."

"In your official capacity, I presume?"

"Yes."

"Why don't you ask the medical examiner?" said Crest. "He is the official who works with your office, I understand."

"True," said Timothy. "But in this instance, the complaint concerns our medical examiner, and I could hardly ask Dr. Parkindale to testify against himself."

Crest's heart gave a jump. Parky was in trouble with the law! Crest had a moment of vindictive satisfaction, but he was ashamed of it. In trouble, physicians stick together.

"Would you care to give me the details of the case?" said Crest.

"Not especially." Timothy gave a grin which was almost boyish. "It's a rather messy business. I would prefer to ignore it altogether, but I can't. It's my job to investigate any complaint officially brought to my attention."

"What's the matter? Was Parky speeding?"

"Not exactly," said Timothy. "Do you know a woman named Lulabelle Smith?"

"Lulabelle?"

"A comic-opera name, but this business isn't comedy." Timothy ruffled through the papers on top of his desk and brought out a sheet of long yellow foolscap covered with notes. "She's age thirty-six; white; three children by a divorced husband; presently married to Master Sergeant Clarence Smith, who is stationed in Germany. Lulabelle lives in the Galen's Corners district."

"I don't know her," said Crest.

"She has been under treatment by Dr. Parkindale for a matter of weeks. She has some sort of female disorder. I suspect it may be venereal."

"That sort of woman?"

"Her children run the streets without supervision. Lulabelle spends a lot of her time in Galen's Bar and Grille. She has two convictions for drunk and disorderly conduct. She was once picked up on charges of solicitation, but we couldn't make it stick. That's the sort of woman she is, Dr. Crest."

"If she is making charges against Parky, I'm on Parky's side from the beginning," said Crest.

Timothy studied his notes again. "This woman has consulted Dr. Parkindale six times in the last four weeks. She always sees him at his office. On each occasion, according to the allegation, her appointment is at the rather unusual hour of eleven o'clock at night."

"Parky sees patients at any hour of the day or night," said Crest.

"At such an hour, there are no nurses or receptionists. The patient is alone with the doctor. According to the allegation, she enters the examination room. She prepares herself for internal examination. She reclines on the examining table in the so-called lithotomy position. Have I the proper word?"

"That's the proper position for a pelvic examination, yes," said Crest.

"What is alleged to happen next, Doctor, is not proper."

"Just a minute," said Crest. "Are you trying to tell me—"

"That Dr. Parkindale is accused of acting in an improper and unprofessional manner with a female patient in an intimate position, alone, late at night? Exactly!"

"The charges are more specific in detail?"

"Quite specific. You want details?"

"Not necessary," said Crest. "With or without details, I don't believe it."

"Neither do I," said Timothy. "But the complaint has been made to my office, and I am required to investigate."

"This Lulabelle: is she attractive?"

"Not to me," said Timothy. "Although such things are considered to be a matter of taste. To me, she looks like a slut. I think she has lice in her hair."

"Parky is a busy doctor and a married man," said Crest. "He treats two thirds of the female population of this town. Most of the women he sees are in love with him. Why should he have the slightest interest in a woman with venereal disease and lice in her hair?"

"Stranger things have happened, Doctor."

"Ridiculous," said Crest. "How far are you required to pursue an investigation into this complaint?"

"I can use my own discretion to a certain extent," said Timothy. "This office exists to protect the public good. Although primarily we prosecute the guilty, we also have the obligation to protect the innocent. The ultimate decision on whether or not to prosecute does not depend on me. I present facts to the Grand Jury. They decide whether my evidence is sufficient for criminal proceedings."

"You intend to take this matter to the Grand Jury?"

"That's my job," said Timothy. "If I think there's the slightest possibility of validity in the charge."

"You want my advice?"

"Yes."

"Drop it," said Crest. "Drop it like a red-hot stove."

"Should I?"

"Absolutely," said Crest. "On face value, the charges are ridiculous. You know it as well as I do."

Timothy got up from his chair behind the desk, walked to the door, which was slightly ajar, closed the door firmly, reached into his pocket for a pipe, filled the pipe with tobacco from a pouch, lit it, and blew out a cloud of smoke. "Doctor," he said, "what do you think of Parky?"

"My opinions of Dr. Parkindale remain my own," said Crest.

"Do you want to know my opinions?" said Timothy. "I think Parky is a pompous and arrogant windbag. I think he's a quack. If I could use the force of my office in any way to remove that man from the practice of medicine in Sentryville, I'd do so. I believe he is a menace to the welfare of this community."

Crest did not reply.

"Dr. Crest, I have reasons to believe that you might agree with my opinion."

"Is that why you asked me here?"

"Perhaps."

"Dr. Parkindale is generally regarded as a respectable, ethical, and highly successful physician in this community."

"You damn doctors always stick together," said Timothy.

"You expect me to violate the ethics of my profession?" said Crest.

"That's the trouble with your profession," said Timothy. "You are unable to clean your own house."

"What have you against Dr. Parkindale?" said Crest.

"He killed my mother," said Timothy. "She expired on the table. I have every reason to believe the operation was unnecessary. I'm going to get that man some day."

"On a ridiculous charge like this? You couldn't make it stick."

"I wouldn't have to make it stick," said Timothy. "Can you imagine what the papers would do with a juicy bit like this?"

"Dirty," said Crest.

"Doctor, it's a dirty world," said Timothy. "But I'm not going to allow you to say that your ethics are any cleaner than mine. I would not use this office improperly. Like yourself, I am ethical and honest. If I can convince myself that the charges of Lulabelle Smith against Dr. Parkindale are false, I'll drop my investigation. I'll go farther than that. I'll use the weight of influence of this office with the papers to suppress this dirty business. If false, such statements could not possibly contribute to the public good, no matter what my opinion of Parky's competence, or yours. On the other hand, if there is any conceivable possibility that these charges are true in any way, I shall do my duty, proceed with my investigation, and let the Grand Jury decide."

"What do you want out of me?"

"Convince me, Doctor."

"I want no part of this," said Crest.

"If that's your attitude, I am already convinced," said Timothy. "I understand medical ethics. If you refuse to help your fellow physician in trouble, I can only presume that the trouble is real, and I will proceed accordingly."

"Wait just a minute . . ."

"I'm not crowding you, Doctor. There's plenty of time."

Crest put a cigarette into his mouth and lit it. "In that event," he said, "I'll have to talk to Lulabelle. Maybe to Parky, too."

"Would you like to examine Lulabelle? Perhaps you could examine her right after she leaves Parky's office next time. Could you tell anything?"

"No," said Crest. "I'd only interview her."

"I'll arrange an interview at your convenience. One suggestion, Dr. Crest."

"Yes?"

"You might conduct your interview in the presence of witnesses."

"Don't worry!" said Crest.

Crest made arrangements to see Lulabelle in the office. Nancy, being a nurse, frequently helped him in the office suite, and Crest would be sure that she would be present during the interview. Then he had a second thought, concerning wives testifying in their husbands' cases, and he decided to interview Lulabelle Smith at the hospital. Two nurses would be present; no, better make that three!

Lulabelle sat down and Crest studied her. When seeing a patient for the first time, he made it a practice not to look at the face right off the bat. Faces are made to be seen. In women, the face is concealed with cosmetics, and all people, men and women, learn to adjust their faces to fit the role they like to act. It was Crest's habit to take a quick glance at the total person, and then to study the most striking characteristic other than the face; then to listen to the voice; and only after he had already formed a first impression of the personality to look directly at the patient's face. You can pick up a good deal this way.

Lulabelle's most striking characteristic was her hair. It was a sort of wild orange shade and it stuck out wildly in all directions. The hair reminded Crest of Harpo Marx. He doubted there were lice in it. On the other hand, there could have been snakes. Instead of Lulabelle, her name should have been Medusa.

He inquired her name, her age, and her address, all of which facts he knew, in order to hear her speech. She had a whisky voice: low, harsh, coarse, and edged with faint hysteria. Then he looked at her. The face was hard and soft at the same time, an undisciplined face. Her lips were big and slashed with lipstick of an orange shade, just enough off color from the hair to make both colors clash. The eyes were large and nervous. Her make-up was suited for the darkness of a bar and grille and looked theatrical in the brightness of an examination room.

This was a wild one, Crest was sure.

"Mrs. Smith, do you know why you're here?" he asked.

"Why'ncha tell me, Doc?"

"It concerns your dealings with Dr. Parkindale."

"Yeah," she said. "Mind if I smoke in here?"

"Go ahead."

Her fingers trembled as she lit the cigarette and her lips were sufficiently shaky to make the cigarette wiggle up and down. She huffed and puffed her smoke, in such a fashion as to make the coal on the end of the cigarette long and hard. The smoke in her mouth would taste hot and harsh.

"I'll bet she drinks raw gin," Crest thought. "Maybe she brushes her teeth with old razor blades." When she was a child, life treated her harshly; now that she has become a

woman, she intends to give as good as she will take. She has
a certain power over a certain kind of man, and she'd use the
power harshly. She'd be damned if she'd give satisfaction; nobody had ever satisfied her! A dangerous woman, if intelligent;
if stupid—and Crest thought she probably was—dangerous
only to the foolish; if mad—and Crest thought she also probably was—she could be quite dangerous to herself.

"What do you want to know?" she said defiantly when
Crest's long, silent scrutiny had begun to disconcert her.

"Only the truth," said Crest.

"What the hell, Doc, are you calling me a liar?"

"Was everything you told Mr. Timothy the truth?"

"I don't care what anybody thinks; it happened," she de-
clared from a defensive position. "And it wouldn't have
happened if my husband was in town. He's in Germany.
Clarence don't let nobody fool around with me. If Clarence
was here, he'd go punch him in the mouth. I wouldn't have
to go calling for the cops, believe you me!"

"And why did you need to go calling cops?"

"I'm decent and respectable. I don't care what anybody
says. I'm taking lip from nobody, from no man!" she said.

"Who gave you lip?" said Crest. "Dr. Parkindale?"

"That ain't what he done," she said, and she made a facial
grimace which Crest would have described as a leer.

"What did he do, Mrs. Smith?" said Crest gently.

"I done told them already."

"Tell me," said Crest.

She looked plainly and directly at each of the three nurses
in the room. They, in turn, looked away and acted as if they
wanted to move away. Her look stated that she wouldn't mind
telling her story, in solid and frank detail, as descriptively as
a limited vocabulary might permit, but her style was cramped
by the presence of a woman in the room. She would coarsen
herself before a man because it was her opinion that all men
were coarse, but she was not inclined to cheapen herself in
front of another woman.

"This is a confidential interview," said Crest. "You can be frank. Nothing will leave this room."

She pouted, and the motion of her lips knocked ash from her cigarette down onto her blouse. She brushed at the ash. The gesture knocked open a button. The pink edge of a brassiere was visible in the gap. Aware of the button, she let it be. She was not in control of this interview. Perhaps some scenery would give her control, since it was a man in charge.

"I already told," she said. "Why don't you ask them?"

"Because," said Crest, "I wouldn't believe anything they told me about you which you hadn't told me yourself."

She smiled at that. She dropped her cigarette on the floor and tromped it. She had a good ankle. She was wearing spike heels. Then she put both hands in her lap and waited. Crest gave her plenty of time, enough to get nervous again, but she wasn't nervous now. She knew men.

"My dear," said Crest, "this business can hardly remain a secret if you tell it to the County Attorney and the police. If your story is true, it must be presented to the Grand Jury. It will all get into the newspapers. Dr. Parkindale is a very prominent man."

"Will they put my picture in the papers?" she inquired.

Crest realized that this was a dangerous approach. She wanted her picture in the paper.

"You will be required to tell the truth in court," said Crest. "If you tell them a lie, you will go to jail."

"Who's going to prove it's a lie?" She had risen to that one, strident, shrill.

"Prove what?" said Crest.

"I done already told," she said sullenly.

"In court you will also be required to tell the whole truth," said Crest. "You've told me nothing. Unless you can do better than that in court, they'll put you in jail. What would Clarence think when he hears they've put you in jail for telling a lie?"

"It isn't a lie."

"What isn't?"

"He was messing around."

"Who?"

"Parky."

"Where?"

"In his office. In the middle of the night."

"What do you mean, messing?"

"He put his God-damn great hand in me!"

"Where?"

And having asked that question, Crest could have bitten his tongue. He was afraid she was going to show him where. Her actual response surprised him. Underneath the cake of paint and powder on her face, she blushed.

"My dear," said Crest, "the doctor was treating you?"

"That's his story."

"You're sick?"

"Yeah. God knows."

"How are you sick?"

"Pains," she said. "Cramps. I got disease of the ovary."

Again she had surprised him. Where had she heard that word?

"Of the ovary?" said Crest.

"Cystic cysts," she said.

Crest almost laughed at that. Out of the mouths of babes and sucklings hast Thou ordained strength!

"I understand," he said. "Dr. Parkindale was treating you for cystic disease of the ovary."

"Yeah. I ain't right. It happened before I ever met Clarence. I was married one other time before. I got three kids."

"Then," said Crest, in his most professional manner, "if the doctor was treating you for cystic disease of the ovary, it was necessary for him to examine you. The internal examination. You know what I mean."

She wouldn't buy that. "He was messing around," she said firmly.

"But—"

"Look," she said. "Why else the poetry?"

"I beg your pardon?"

"Love poetry."

"Hold on, young woman," said Crest sternly. "Let me have that again. You claim that while Dr. Parkindale was in the act of performing a pelvic examination, he was quoting love poetry?"

"Why else did he lock the door?" she said.

"One thing at a time," said Crest. "You claim the doctor was quoting love poetry . . ."

"Reading," she said.

"What?"

"He was reading poetry from a book," she said: plain, loud, and clear.

Impossible! Crest didn't believe it. He glanced at the nurses out of the corner of his eye and discovered them glancing at him. Incredible though this story sounded, it seemed to have a certain horrible ring of truth about it. He knew that the nurses thought so too. He immediately regretted having required them as witnesses. He had originally intended the nurses as witnesses for the defense: they knew Parky; they worked with Parky every day; they had known paranoid patients before; they would instinctively know, as Crest had known, that a man like Parky could not conceivably have done anything improper with a woman of this kind, and yet . . . ! The interview had gone much too far. In a sincere effort to be of help, Crest had a horrible inkling that he had started something he could never stop.

"That's all, Mrs. Smith," he said curtly.

"But, Doc—"

"You may go," said Crest. "We're finished."

"Don't you want to hear the story, Doc?"

"The interview is over, Mrs. Smith. Will you kindly leave the room?"

"I'm going to tell it all in court," she said triumphantly.

"Nurse," said Crest, his voice like ice, "kindly show this woman out."

"It'll be in the papers. All over the papers, Doc. And I'll have my pictures in the paper, too."

They led her out. At the door, she more or less flipped her rear at Crest: the can-can dancer, coy and victorious, after a successful show. There was no doubt in Lulabelle's mind that she had won. Perhaps she didn't know how, but she knew that out of the jaws of danger she had snatched the pearl of success.

The nurses were trying to escape. Crest summoned them back together, all three, and shut the door.

"Girls . . ." he said.

They looked at him and waited.

"Remember your oath," he said. He tried to remember whether nurses swore the Hippocratic oath or some equivalent; he would have to inquire of Nancy when he got home. "This is a confidential matter. A privileged communication. You have no right to tell anybody a single word of what you overheard today. You may not discuss it. You may not even discuss it with yourselves."

"Doctor," said one of them, "will we have to go to court?"

She wanted to go to court, Crest knew. And Lulabelle wanted her picture in the papers. These nurses were good girls, and honest, and ethical, and they understood the responsibility of their profession toward the privileged communication. But could they ever look at Parky in the same light again? Was there any human force that could keep them from discussing it among themselves? Was there any force, human or divine, that could now keep rumors from sneaking along corridors? Some cats cannot be kept in bags.

"No," said Crest. "I can assure you, there is no possibility whatever that you will appear in court."

"Doctor?" said another of the nurses.

"Yes?"

"Doctor, do you suppose—"

"Absolutely not!" said Crest. "There wasn't a single grain of truth in Mrs. Smith's remarks. The woman is insane. You have my word on that."

They had his word. They had their own opinions. They stood around waiting for Crest to tell them more. There was nothing more to say. Except for him to wonder also. Was it possible that . . . ? As Timothy had so truly remarked, this is a dirty world.

"Thanks, girls, that's all," said Crest.

He walked firmly out of the room. The meeting was adjourned.

Leaving the examination room of the hospital, Crest bumped into Dr. Parkindale in the hospital corridor. It was during afternoon office hours, when Parky would not be expected in the hospital, so it must have been an emergency. Parky was striding briskly along, almost on the run, and he was beginning to take off his coat. Crest suspected that the emergency was obstetrical. Probably the nurse in the obstetrical suite was desperately trying to hold back a rapidly oncoming head until Parky could arrive. But Crest was too full of his own concerns to think of another man's emergency.

"Sir?" said Crest.

Parky gave him a brusque nod and kept on walking.

Crest called after him, "Parky!"

It was a form of address and tone which Crest had never used to the older man, and it stopped Parky in his tracks. Parky could detect a trace of urgency, perhaps emergency, in Crest. Like the busy man accustomed to dealing with several emergency situations at the same time, Parky made a fast decision and decided to give Crest a moment of his time.

"What's on your mind?" said Parky. "Make it snappy. I'm in a rush."

"Do you have a book of poetry in your office?" said Crest.

"Poetry?"

The look on Parky's face was almost worth the price of admission. It was a theatrical look, like that on the face of a comic who has just taken a pratfall on a banana peel.

"Love poetry," said Crest, attempting to explain but compounding the original error.

"Love poetry?"

Parky put back his leonine head and gave a roar, a bellow of laughter. Then he resumed his brisk march up the corridor, laughing to himself. Before he disappeared from sight, his pace slowed up and Crest could see that he was shaking his head. Just as he turned the corner at the far end of the corridor, Parky sneaked a quick glance over his shoulder at Crest.

"He thinks I'm crazy," thought Crest. "He's wondering if he should call for the little men in white."

From the hospital, Crest went directly to the office of Ralph Timothy, the County Attorney. He didn't wait on the swaybacked leather sofa this time, but strode directly into Timothy's inner office. Timothy glanced up at him.

"You've examined the woman?"

"Interviewed her," said Crest.

"What's the conclusion, Doctor?"

"Drop the case," said Crest.

"You told me that before."

"I'm saying it again," said Crest.

"In my experience, Doctor," said Timothy, "where there's smoke, there is also fire."

"Lulabelle Smith is a paranoid," said Crest. "She'd make a lousy witness on the stand. Any decent lawyer could tear her half apart. They'd laugh the two of you out of court."

"By paranoid, you mean insane?" asked Timothy.

"Perhaps not legally committable," said Crest, but surely crazy for practical purposes. Paranoid means unnatural suspicion. The trait is often marked with a psychosexual tinge, certainly in this particular case. What I mean to say is this: like so many of Parky's female patients, Mrs. Smith is more than half in love with her physician. She had an unconscious desire for the man to make a play for her. He didn't and she was angry. Out of spite and paranoid suspicion, she therefore accused him of doing what did not take place. She blamed him for what he didn't do, because he didn't do it, if you can follow that twisted logic."

"Hell hath no fury?"

"Exactly," said Crest.

Timothy extracted his pipe and lit it. "She'd certainly make a lousy witness. I'll buy that. Parky, of course, would make a good one. But how about the poetry? This bothers me."

Crest didn't say that it bothered him, too.

"That's the sort of detail I wouldn't expect a woman of her mentality to invent," said Timothy. "So what do you think really took place in Parky's office on those particular nights?"

"I think it might have been only one night, not several," said Crest.

"Once is enough."

"We presume this woman has cystic disease of the ovary, probably not venereal. She got worried over her condition in the middle of the night and phoned Dr. Parkindale. He told her to come right over to the office. He sees patients at any hour of the day or night. That's one reason Parky's patients are so loyal. He comes whenever they call. Many doctors don't."

"All right," said Timothy. "She goes to the office at eleven o'clock at night. There are no nurses or receptionists at that hour. The doctor is alone with his patient."

"He ushers her into the consultation room. He speaks with her. He determines that her complaint is in the pelvic area. Internal examination will be required. This is good medicine. I can recall a few cases, by the way, where Parky treated women without doing pelvic examinations, and this is poor medicine. So he takes her into the examination room."

"Shouldn't he have waited until morning, until he had a nurse in attendance?"

"When Parky makes a decision, he doesn't wait," said Crest.

"Is it not a risky policy for a male physician to examine a female unattended?"

"Many doctors do it," said Crest. "There is a definite risk. This case illustrates exactly the danger of unattended examinations on a certain type of woman."

"You take the position that Parky conducted a proper examination on this woman, in an ethical and professional fashion? His only mistake was that of judgment, doing this exam without a nurse in the room? You feel that her accusation is entirely false, based on her misinterpretation of his actions, due to the twisted paranoid state of her mind, as you have previously described?"

"I do," said Crest.

"And you'd be willing to testify to that effect in court, under oath?"

"As my opinion only," said Crest. "Of course, I wasn't there."

"And how about the love poetry, Dr. Crest?"

Crest didn't reply.

"Bothers you too, doesn't it?" said Timothy.

Crest couldn't deny it.

"And yet you advise me to drop the case?" said Timothy.

"Are you expecting to run for another term?" asked Crest.

"Parky would be a dangerous enemy," said Timothy. "But I would be willing to risk my political career for the public good. I wouldn't duck a case out of fear. I would welcome the opportunity to deprive Dr. Parkindale of his right to practice medicine in Sentryville."

"Do you think you would win this case?"

"No," said Timothy. "I don't think I could ever get it by the Grand Jury."

"Then what would you accomplish?"

"There would be a small smell," said Timothy.

"Would that stop Dr. Parkindale?"

"It might give his patients second thoughts."

"It wouldn't harm his practice in any way," said Crest. "His patients are loyal. Most of them would automatically take his side against a woman of that social level and type. Some female patients might be intrigued. Parky might have an increase of business in the office at eleven o'clock at night."

"Damn it," said Timothy.

"Then I presume you will drop the case?"

"I'll drop it," said Timothy. "But I'm going to watch him. I'm going to keep my eye on Dr. Parkindale. Sooner or later, he'll make another mistake."

"He makes plenty of mistakes," said Crest.

"And you fellows let him get away with it."

"We have no choice," said Crest.

"Ham-strung by your God-damn medical ethics!"

"Mr. Timothy," said Crest, "give me your opinion. Do you think my profession would be better or worse without our ethics?"

"Dr. Crest," said Timothy, "I think your profession is several centuries out of date. We live in a modern world. You practice in the middle ages. In the name of mercy, you fellows get away with murder. Slowly but progressively, the general public is beginning to understand this fact. The public is pretty mad at you gentlemen. When they get mad enough, they'll put you under rigid public control."

"You may be right," said Crest.

Before dinner, Crest had a Martini, as he occasionally did after a hard day. Then he had a second, unusual for him, and then a third.

"Getting drunk?" said Nancy.

"I'm tired and confused," said Crest. "Tough day."

"I hope you're not seeing patients tonight."

"Not unless there's an emergency."

"Let somebody else take the emergencies," she said. "Alcohol and medicine don't mix."

He knew she was right. He would turn down all calls tonight.

"Do nurses take an oath?" he asked. "Like our oath of Hippocrates?"

"Yes, the pledge of Florence Nightingale. What's troubling you, John? Something to do with a Parkindale, I'll bet. Nothing but Parkindales can get you so upset."

"I promised to keep that problem out of the house," he said.

"Your problems are my problems now," she said.

"It's a messy business. I wouldn't want you involved."

"As your wife, I prefer to be involved in anything that bothers you," she said. "Who can tell? Maybe I can help."

So, Crest told her the story, just the general outline without specific detail.

"What a dirty man!" she said.

"Parky? You think he's guilty?"

"I know he is. No woman could invent that sort of thing."

"I'm not sure," said Crest.

"I never knew any such woman," she said.

"I have," said Crest.

"Suppose it got into the papers. Such a mess. And I suppose everybody in Sentryville would enjoy reading all about it. The most proper people might get the most enjoyment. People are too interested in the filthy side of life."

"What do you mean?"

"Read the daily paper. Read any novel on the best-seller list. Listen to the conversation at any party, in any beauty parlor, any bar. All that sort of thing should be suppressed."

"Why?" said Crest.

"Is that a serious question, John?"

"Certainly. Why should conversation and newsworthy material be suppressed?"

"Just the filthy part."

"Matter of definition," said Crest. "What's filthy?"

"You know what I mean."

"No, I don't," said Crest.

"Well," she said, "I don't think we should publicize the fact that man is a filthy and sinful animal."

"But he is," said Crest.

"He shouldn't be," she said.

"Nancy," said Crest, "I'm a doctor. I must take people as they are, not as they think they are or as they would like to be. You've worked with me in the office. We have problems every day which some people might consider filth or sin. The problems remain, and they won't disappear if we close our minds, our eyes, or our ears."

"Sure. This is your work, John. This is disease."

"All people get disease."

"Yes. Let's keep it in the office, then. Why talk about it on the street? Think of it, read and write about it all the time? Why this morbid and pathological interest in disease? Why can't we speak and think and write of health, the fine clean things in life? There are many of them."

"Health is only a relative absence of disease," said Crest. "And we can remain healthy only by exploring, studying, understanding the sources of our disease."

"That's fine for a doctor, John, but most people aren't trained or equipped to study disease. Their morbid curiosity, I think, can make them sick."

"Moral judgments can make them sick," said Crest. "You can't approach the patient from the moral point of view. You can't help a person if you judge him."

"The doctor doesn't believe in evil, sin, or moral weakness?"

"Sick people need understanding. We all need to understand each other."

"I'm sure you're right," she said. "Perhaps I don't understand disease very well. Perhaps I don't want to."

"I honestly believe," said Crest, "that all people should explore and study and try to understand their own motivations and those of the people whom they meet. This means attempting to face the truth. It means exploring matters bravely which are often considered evil or sin or moral weakness. Disease grows in darkness like the mushroom. We need all the light we can get."

"Yes, but it isn't easy for me," she said. "I'm not much of an explorer. I can't cope with matters of darkness."

"It's very easy to get lost," said Crest. "What would you do in my position about this problem of Parky and Lulabelle?"

"I'm not equipped to handle it."

"You think he must be guilty."

"It's hard for me to think of him as innocent."

"I have a feeling that all of us are innocent," said Crest. "However, I still can't understand about the love poetry."

"The what?"

He hadn't told her about the love poetry. He decided that he wouldn't try to tell her now.

Crest encountered Parky at the hospital the following day.

"I see you're treating Lulabelle," said Parky.

"I examined her," said Crest. "Yesterday."

"There's a witch," said Dr. Parkindale.

"Agreed," said Crest.

"You know, my boy," said Parky, confidential, expansive, "that sort of woman can be dangerous."

"Sure can," said Crest.

"We ought to run her out of town."

"This is a democracy," said Crest.

"She came barging into my offices one night last week . . ."

"At eleven o'clock?" said Crest.

"Yes, as a matter of fact. She told you about it?"

"She told me many things," said Crest.

"She has cystic disease of the ovary," said Dr. Parkindale. "But her trouble doesn't lie down there. Lulabelle's trouble is upstairs."

"I thought so," said Crest.

"You know what I think she has? Disease of the morals."

"Huh?"

"No moral sense, my boy. She's nothing but a little animal."

He doesn't know, thought Crest, he hasn't even the slightest inkling of what's going on!

"You know what that woman needs?" said Parky.

"A good stiff dose of salts?" suggested Crest.

"A good stiff dose of old-fashioned religion," said Parky.

"Huh?"

"And I tried to give it to her."

"How?" said Crest, fascinated.

"I handed her the Bible."

"What?"

"I keep a Bible on my desk," said Dr. Parkindale. "Medicine is something more than surgery and pharmacology, my boy. Sometimes when I meet a confused or agitated woman, I prescribe a little Bible, rather than a little medicine. I hand them the book. I have them open it to whatever page they like. Then I read them a few paragraphs."

"What on earth were you reading to Lulabelle Smith?" said Crest.

"Well, that's funny," said Parky. "And that's why I said the woman has no moral sense. Do you know what book she chose?"

"I just asked."

"The Song of Solomon," said Dr. Parkindale. "What's the matter, boy?"

"Nothing," said Crest.

But, as a matter of fact, Crest was feeling faint.

With patient volume heavy, and getting heavier all the time, Crest began to have confidence in his medical ability. These patients were his; he was free to handle them any way he liked; if they didn't trust his ability, they were free to consult anybody else. There were now enough doctors in Sentryville. By the very fact of walking into Crest's office, a patient implied confidence in Crest. This is the pride and the privilege of private medical practice, and Crest was very happy to accept it.

There was still a side of private practice with which Crest

did not feel at home. Probably he never would. This was economics.

A dedication to service is not exactly compatible with a request for payment of a fee. Crest hated to ask the patient for money. The act of accepting a fee somehow made him feel ashamed of himself.

"I'd practice better medicine if I didn't have to earn a living," he thought.

Many doctors feel that way, and many patients agree. Money considerations should be taken out of the doctor-patient relationship, but the doctor works best in independent private practice, and he must earn a living. In fact, he must earn a good living, or the patients won't have confidence in him: nobody trusts the fringe practitioner, and the laborer is worthy of his hire.

"It's funny," Crest thought, "but the patient and I both agree: my fees are too high. Medicine has a unique privilege which is also a responsibility: it is one of the few trades or professions where a man establishes his own fee without public regulation or control. And what are the criteria? How much do you pay a man who may put himself to inconvenience, sometimes hardship, perhaps even danger to come to your help whenever you call? How much, for example, for a night call in a blizzard? What's the monetary value of a human life? No matter what the fee, it's either too little or too much.

"Both I," thought Crest, "and my patient are victimized to some extent by the few greedy members of my profession. There aren't many fee gougers in the profession, but there are enough to make everybody suffer." Almost all of them, Crest knew, were surgeons. That wasn't quite the same as saying that all surgeons are fee gougers. Crest had always believed that surgical fees were too high, and since they were too high, the few greedy men would gravitate in this direction. The standard fee for an appendectomy in Sentryville was a hundred dollars. There is nothing easier in medicine than the simple appendectomy: any medical student can, and does, do it. The average time for an appendectomy is twenty minutes. But if you spent twenty minutes with a man dying of a coronary or with an aggressive paranoid psychotic, the most you could possibly ask for this service was ten dollars.

"Also," Crest decided, "the patient and I are victimized by the rather numerous greedy patients in the community. There are quite a few people with whom it is a matter of pride not to pay a doctor's bill." Crest didn't mind the true charity case. He gave his time and experience, and was glad to do so, to anybody who couldn't honestly pay the fee. True charity cases amounted to something like ten per cent of his practice. Another ten per cent could afford to pay only part of the bill; these were good people, proud people, and for them Crest took pleasure in reducing his usual fee. But there was another segment, perhaps another twenty per cent, who could pay but wouldn't; treating these people was always, to Crest, a matter of extreme exasperation. These people were not exactly dishonest; they wouldn't steal; but the tricks, the dodges, the lies, and the evasions they went through to duck a doctor's fee would astonish even Diogenes. These were the people who screamed for socialized medicine, when they would be able to freeload to their greedy little hearts' content. These were the people who always claimed that you could never get a doctor in an emergency. These were the people who started malpractice suits.

Only after he had been knocked about in private medicine for a time, only after painful aging and maturation, did Crest begin to realize that the deadbeat's attitude toward money was a part of his disease. People who duck a doctor's fee are doing so for a psychological reason and this psychological reason is part of why they need a doctor in the first place. They are masochists who need to degrade themselves. They feel sick because they are ashamed of themselves. Being ashamed of their own shame, they have a need to strike out and punish. They punish the doctor by not paying him, thereby increasing their own punishment by knowing that the doctor will hold them in contempt. Only after he became aware of this curious psychology was Crest able to deal with the deadbeat in any comfort. And, once he knew it, curiously, some of the deadbeats would pay him. In other words, he was able to cure a few of them.

There was another curious type of patient at the other end of the economic scale: the rich masochist, ashamed of money he has not earned, ashamed because he knows he can buy anybody, and anybody who can be bought is cheap. You can lose this type of patient, Crest discovered the hard way, by not charging enough for your services. Ask your normal fee, and they don't come back; they think if you're cheap, you can't be good. For the rich, you double your fee, gulp and take a deep breath, and double that figure again. The patient pays promptly, buying you, and both he and you are well aware that you have been bought.

"I don't like to treat the rich," thought Crest. "I even prefer the deadbeat, miserable soul. Obviously I wasn't cut out to be a millionaire."

It would seem logical for the medical profession to abandon the time-cherished notion of the sliding scale of fees. One charge for the given service for all, posted, understood, as in a grocery store. Slowly, painfully, the profession began to head in this direction. But, paradoxically, this logical direction began to interfere further with the doctor-patient relationship. There was a fundamental reason for this. Medical services are not groceries. You can't put a price on human pain.

"Parky always charges the patient exactly what the patient wants to pay," thought Crest. "And, damn his greedy soul, he just happens to be right!"

"I'm pregnant," said Nancy.

Crest was delighted by the news and also a little scared.

"There's nothing to worry about," she said.

"Of course not."

"Then why are you worried?"

Crest denied it.

"It won't be like that time with Emerald. I'm perfectly normal," she said.

"I know you are."

It wasn't her he was worried about; it was himself. Hydrocephalus is not inherited. The chances of another hydrocephalic child were no greater than a hundred thousand to one, but, despite his scientific knowledge, Crest had never been able to rid himself of an underlying superstition that the poor little creature with the enormous head had somehow been his fault.

"Did Emerald think it was her fault?" asked Nancy.

"Perhaps. She didn't want the child, and then it turned out to be deformed. Perhaps she felt guilty over that."

This thought had never occurred to Crest before. Perhaps it explained why Emerald had left him as she did.

"Why did the doctor do a hysterectomy on her?" asked Nancy.

"There was no medical indication."

"Perhaps Parky didn't know any better."

"Perhaps he didn't."

"It was his own daughter. All the more reason not to cripple her, you'd think."

"A hysterectomy doesn't cripple," said Crest.

"Not obviously," said Nancy. "But doesn't it amputate the patient's womanhood?"

This was another aspect which Crest had not considered before.

"Well, anyway," said Nancy, "we won't worry about complications. I'm going to have an easy pregnancy. And obviously I won't consult Dr. Parkindale. I like Dr. Sweetster very well."

"So do I," said Crest.

Sweetster was the new obstetrician in Sentryville. He was well trained and smart, and Crest respected his judgment. He had only one reservation about Dr. Sweetster: the rumors of his extracurricular activity. Probably Nancy didn't know about that. Certainly Crest wasn't going to tell her.

She had an easy pregnancy: no morning sickness, no irritability, no unnatural appetites in the middle of the night. Her labor started promptly on the date of term. The pains were hard and regular from the beginning, but Nancy didn't seem to mind them much. She was in no hurry to get to the hospital. In fact, by the time Crest thought she should be in the hospital, she still wasn't in any hurry. Although it was her first child, they barely made it in time.

"Crest," said Dr. Sweetster, "next time, I suggest you act with a little greater speed. She almost had that baby in the corridor."

"She almost had it in the car," said Crest. "Is everything all right?"

"Uneventful delivery. She's fine."

"And the baby?"

"Also fine."

"Are you positive?"

"Don't take my word for it," said Sweetster. "Go up to the nursery and examine him yourself."

Crest put on cap, mask, and gown and entered the nursery.

"This one is mine, nurse?" he asked.

"Yes, doctor," said the nurse. "Isn't he beautiful?"

"In my opinion, newborns are not beautiful," said Crest. "They're red, wrinkled, little old men."

"You should be ashamed of yourself, Doctor," said the nurse. "Pick him up before you give him a feeling of insecurity."

Crest picked him up. The miniature creature yawned, gurgled, rubbed his eyes, and grinned.

"He has a beautiful smile," said Crest.

"Yes, Doctor."

The nurse turned away because she was smiling herself. The new baby's smile is not a smile; it is a grimace; the little

thing had gas. Really, Crest did know this fact. He put the
baby over his shoulder and patted it on the back. This effort
was rewarded with a short, sharp burp.

"You'll make a wonderful mother, Dr. Crest," said the nurse.

"It's curious," said Crest. "At the beginning of our lives,
when we have pain, we smile. It's a pity we lose this facility
so soon."

Part 8

In 1951, Sam Parkindale fell sick. He was persuaded to leave the jungles; they almost had to drag him out by force; he returned to America and entered the university hospital for a check-up. Crest went to the city to visit him.

"Hello, buddy boy," said Sam from his hospital bed.

"Hi, Sam. How's the battle?" said Crest.

"I think I'm losing it," said Sam.

Looking at him, Crest thought so too. Sam had lost twenty-five or thirty pounds. There was no further suggestion of apples in his cheeks, and his smile was ghostly. His skin was a peculiar color: a combination of fading jungle tan plus fading atabrine and probably jaundice, a shade in the spectrum of yellow-green. Crest got a definite feeling: this was a dying man.

"Have they found the trouble yet?" asked Crest.

"Everything is ganging up in the liver," said Sam. "Some cirrhosis and malaria and filaria and a few other things, I

guess. They can hardly wait to do the post. My liver is a cinch
to end up in the pathological museum."

"Don't be fatalistic," said Crest. "You're going to make it."

"I'm going to make it out of here," said Sam. "I'll get back to
Africa. There's something I need to finish up. It won't take
more than a few weeks. After that, who knows? In fact, who
cares?"

"Africa means a lot to you?"

"Miserable," said Sam. "Climate miserable. Natives miserable. But I don't have any fee problems, and nobody's going
to sue me for malpractice, and there's small chance that I'll
be expelled from the medical society."

"I admire you," said Crest. "I couldn't do it, but I almost
envy you."

"Well, hell, I have the family advantages," said Sam. "I had
to do something worth while doing with this life. All over the
world, little military men are starting wars. They're doing it
in Korea now, I understand. There have to be a few of us
working the other side of the street. Otherwise God might get
mad."

"Seems to me," said Crest, "God is mad, and out of His
anger, He has handed us the perfect final weapon for our destruction. I refer to the hydrogen bomb."

"Global Russian roulette."

"Exactly."

"How's the family?"

"Thriving," said Crest.

"You have two kids?"

"Three sons," said Crest, "and another on the way."

"Damn near a basketball team," said Sam.

"Nancy enjoys pregnancy, and I need the deductions on
the income tax."

"Ever hear anything from Em?"

"We saw Emerald on television just last week," said Crest.

"And I suppose you and my father have come to terms,
dividing up the pot of Sentryville between you?"

"He's very busy. I'm busy enough."

"In other words, you get along."

"We work together, side by side, pleasantly. We speak pleasantly in the corridors and at medical meetings. Other than that, we ignore each other."

"And you ignore his mistakes?" said Sam.

"I still notice them," said Crest.

"Silently?"

"I mind my own affairs," said Crest.

"And this is ethical?"

"I can't influence your father," said Crest. "I never could."

Nothing makes a sick man sicker than his visitors at the hospital, Crest knew. He would have liked to chat with Sam for hours, but it was time for him to go. Crest knew he would never see Sam again.

Sam Parkindale managed to return to Africa, against the advice of his physicians, and he died there a few weeks later. His liver did not reach the pathological museum at the university. Sam was buried beside the hospital which he had managed to finish with his own hands.

Crest knew it would be a bad day. It started bad as soon as possible, with the telephone ringing at midnight. This was one of Crest's least favorite alcoholics, a garrulous and sometimes abusive soul, who invariably phoned a doctor after the fifth drink. Crest thought he might be able to get away with a telephone consultation, but he couldn't give a sedative over the phone. After ten minutes of garbled rambling inconsistencies, Crest allowed himself to be talked into a night call, where he was subjected to another three quarters of an hour of the same at the patient's house.

Back home, returning to bed, Crest discovered Mike, his two-year-old son, wandering around the halls. Mike looked flushed. Crest took his hand to lead him back to bed, and discovered that his skin was dry and blazing hot. He took Mike's temperature; it was 105. He examined his chest with a stethoscope and found a small patch of bronchopneumonia at the right lung base. He summoned Nancy and she took charge. Crest got a bottle of antibiotic in syrup form from his office, gave Nancy directions for administering the same, and returned to bed. He knew he wouldn't sleep, however. Sickness in one of his children worried him far more than it should. Rare diagnoses, serious complications, always kept coming to mind.

At three in the morning, Crest had to go to the hospital. Some woman had gashed open her hand while opening an oyster. She wasn't drunk. What in heaven's name she was doing opening an oyster at 3:00 A.M., Crest couldn't imagine. He didn't inquire. He repaired the laceration.

He had just returned from the hospital when he had to turn around and go right back. One of his patients had dropped dead on a bedpan: probably a pulmonary embolism, from the sudden and unexpected nature of the death. The patient's husband went into complete collapse on hearing the news, and Crest had to treat him, too.

Back home, Nancy had her hands full. Now the twins, Sam and Joe, were also sick. In their case, it was a gastroenteritis, with violent vomiting and profuse diarrhea. Bathrooms were totally occupied, and there would be many sheets for the laundry. Poor Nancy! Crest had a feeling it was the first day of her period, too!

"Anything I can do?" asked Crest.

"No thanks," she said.

"How are you?"

"Crampy!" she said. "Damn it! On a day like this!"

"I think I'm catching cold," said Crest. "I've got a tight congestion in my chest, like a bronchitis coming on. How is John, Jr.?"

John, Jr., was the only member of the family unaccounted for.

"I haven't dared to look," said Nancy. "There's a P.T.A. meeting tonight."

"To hell with that," said Crest. "I have a long day today. Patients all morning, and I've got to go to court this afternoon."

"Court?"

"Yes. That damned accident case."

"John?"

"Yes, dear?"

"Remember the moonlight at Fort Sam?" she said. "That little restaurant with the wine and candlelight and gypsy violins? Our honeymoon?"

"Yes?"

"This is the result," she said.

She swept her hand in an arc to include Mike's bedroom, where the poor little tyke was tossing in a restless doze, and Sam, who was trying to vomit into a basin and getting most of it onto the sheet, and Joe, who was parked permanently in the bathroom, and the dog, who was trying to reach and knock over a bottle of paregoric.

Crest gave her a smile of sympathy and left the house. It was raining. On a rainy day, all patients feel worse, and some will try to blame their doctor for the weather.

Crest got into his car and drove a few feet before he realized that his left front tire was flat. Had he been driving back and forth to the hospital all night on a flat tire? It was seven in the morning. At this hour, only one garage in town had a man on call. The owner of this particular garage had owed Crest ten dollars for more than two years. Despite this fact, he always charged Crest double for any garage service rendered. Crest could wait another hour until the other garages opened up, or he could pay double, or he could change the damn tire himself. Crest changed the tire in the rain. When he had finished, he was wet and weary and conscious of an aching congestion in his chest.

"I should start on antibiotics today, or I'll be in bed by tomorrow night," thought Crest.

Then he forgot his chest. The doctor, careful of the health of everybody else, ignores his own.

He drove through town toward the hospital, driving fast because now he was late. A child suddenly darted into the street, popping out from between two parked cars in the middle of the block. Crest didn't see her until she was almost under the wheels. He swore and jammed on the brakes. The car skidded on the wet pavement, missed the child by fractions of an inch, and struck a lamp post with a metallic clang. Crest rocked forward in his seat, but he wasn't hurt. He got out and inspected the damage; nothing much; just a hundred-dollar dent in the right front fender. He breathed a sigh of relief that he had not struck the child. He continued to the hospital, driving very slowly and carefully now.

He suddenly remembered that he had a dentist appointment at ten o'clock. He decided to omit it.

He was taking off his coat at the hospital when the relative of one of his patients grabbed him and harangued him for more than half an hour. The gist of the conversation could have been summed up in a single sentence:

"Please don't discharge my father today."

The relative wanted Crest to keep the patient in the hospital for a few more weeks at least, but she wasn't paying the bills. Crest knew that the patient intended to sign himself out against advice that day if Crest didn't discharge him. Father and daughter hated each other, Crest knew, and this hatred was making both of them sick, but they were trapped in the same house together by the force of circumstance. How could the doctor alter that? Crest promised to try and persuade the patient to enter a nursing home, but he knew the patient would refuse.

Crest signed in at the doctor's desk and looked in his drawer. It was full of incomplete records. There was a peremptory note from the medical-records librarian asking him, please, Doctor, get your charts caught up!

There were a few out-patient reports in the drawer. One

was an A-Z pregnancy test, and it was positive. Crest had been expecting this, but it made him feel a little sick. The patient was thirteen years old. The boy in the case was fourteen, only son of the Episcopal minister. Neither parents knew about this yet. Crest would have to explain.

There was another report that bothered him, a sputum test, positive for tuberculosis. He had also been expecting this; X-rays had been suspicious. The patient was the mother of nine small children; Crest would now have to X-ray each of them; probably every single one of them would have tuberculosis!

Crest's name was being paged. Telephone. He took the call. It was from a little old spinster, and Crest promised to stop by her house later in the morning. Her trouble was vaginitis, pelvic pain, pelvic guilt, and itch. He knew why she had the trouble, and so did she, but the subject was too delicate for discussion. Every time he saw her, they skated around the topic like thin ice. He was afraid that if he talked frankly to her, she might try suicide out of shame. He wanted to tell her that this was not a crime or a moral sin; that she wouldn't go to hell for it; that God would understand. But he sensed that she could no more accept the fact than stop the act. Well, maybe he could find a way to explain later in the morning.

He hung up, and Sweetster, the obstetrician, buttonholed him.

"There's a newborn I'd like to have you see for me in consultation," said Sweetster. "Delivered it by Caesarian last night."

"What's the trouble?" said Crest.

"Hydrocephalus."

Crest winced.

"Anything new on hydrocephalus?" asked Sweetster.

"Not to my knowledge," said Crest. "I don't suppose you did a hysterectomy on the mother?"

"No," said Sweetster. "Why in the hell should I do that?"

Crest didn't pursue the subject. He went into the nursery

and examined the hydrocephalic child. Then he went down
to the lab and checked the morning bloodwork on his hospitalized patients. One of the counts was way out of line:
100,000 white blood cells.

"Do you have the smear on this patient?" Crest inquired.
"Yes, sir."

Crest examined the smear under a microscope. You can't
make a count on the smear, but with experience you can make
a reasonable estimate. Crest was sure that the correct figure
should have been 10,000, not 100,000; an extra zero had been
added by mistake.

"Jeepers," thought Crest, "I'm glad I checked! Ten thousand is normal. A hundred thousand would have implied leukemia. I'll bet Parky would have told that patient she was
going to die without thinking twice!" Many an error is made
by those who make diagnosis by laboratory test instead of by
clinical judgment.

Crest went across the hall to the X-ray room and consulted
with the radiologist. Crest had been right about the patient
in room 7 with anemia; X-ray studies revealed that she did
have a cancer in the bowel as an underlying cause of her
anemia. This patient had just been studied at one of the big
university hospitals, discharged with the diagnosis of anemia,
treated with liver extract. They never did an X-ray. They
never felt the mass in her right lower belly. "By God,"
thought Crest, "they don't know everything at the university!" He went upstairs.

One of his patients had fallen out of bed during the night.
Crest didn't think he had broken his hip but ordered an X-ray
to be sure. Crest checked the chart. He had written an order
for restraints and sideboards; there it was on the chart; the
nurse had forgotten them. Crest wrote the order again and
underlined it twice.

He went into room 7 and told the patient about her cancer
of the bowel. She was scared to death. Crest didn't blame her.

He went into room 10. This patient was in an angry mood,

infuriated at one of the nurses, who had been insulting and personal and fresh, she claimed. Crest found the nurse in question, who was also angry: the patient had been rude and insulting and personal, claimed the nurse. Well, both of them were right! The patient happened to be slowly dying, afraid and angry because nothing could be done, and she took out her fear and rage on everybody she encountered. The nurse was the smartest and most capable girl on the floor, but she had a harsh manner and a hair-trigger temper. It happened that the nurse was sensitive; fear and pain upset her; she covered her sensitivity with a harsh exterior. Crest soothed the patient and the nurse as well as he could. They were no longer angry at each other, but now, he thought, both of them were a little mad at him.

"Sometimes," thought Crest, "the gruff, brusque, irritable nurse or doctor is the one who really cares. The smooth, placid, unruffled ones don't give a good God damn any more."

"I wish I could tell people these things," he thought. "I suppose they wouldn't believe me."

The hospital administrator buttonholed him next. The rule on admissions was going to be more strictly enforced in future: no earlier than two and no later than three in the afternoon. Crest promised to abide by the rule as well as he could. A pity people didn't get sick by the clock: it would be so much easier for the hospital! The administrator reminded Crest that doctors were supposed to write their whole names after every order on the chart. Crest had been putting down only initials. He promised to reform. He did not remind the administrator that his handwriting was distinctive and that no other doctor in the county had the same initials. Another thing: the administrator wondered if Crest had any suggestions on the management of the gift and stationery shop in the lobby. Crest had an opinion on lab technicians who put down extra zeros by mistake, and on nurses who overlook orders for sideboards and restraints, but none on the management of the gift and stationery shop.

Then Crest went down to the doctors' lounge for a cup of coffee. A lot of the boys were there. The room was blue with smoke. There had been much talk, in professional journals and the lay press, concerning cigarettes and cancer of the lung, but most doctors were heavy smokers. Didn't they believe it? Personally, Crest didn't, since the evidence was entirely statistical, without experimental confirmation, and statistics can always be juggled by those with a preconceived opinion. Or didn't doctors care? Surrounded by disease and death, did they consider themselves immune? Crest was conscious of the tightness in his chest which had been with him all day; smoke would make it worse; he lit a cigarette.

The boys were talking about malpractice suits that morning. This was a subject of growing concern to the profession. Suits were so frequent and judgments so heavy that many men were afraid to try anything new. For fear of legal suit, doctors felt they had to order every lab test and X-ray in the book, increasing the patient's costs enormously. The situation was such that, seeing an accident on the highway, a smart doctor was advised to drive right by. Crest himself had never been sued, and had been threatened by the word "malpractice" only once. The person who threatened him had been Dr. Parkindale.

Parky was in the group and leading the conversation, as usual. "The man can't be in any group without dominating it!" Crest thought. "If somebody else is talking, Parky interrupts. If Parky is talking, nobody else is entitled to an opinion."

Parky was speaking of greed: greedy patients, greedy lawyers, and general deterioration of national ethics and morality.

"He's a fine one to talk!" thought Crest. Most of the others thought Parky greedy because of the size of his practice. Crest thought that very few of the men present had ever been faced with malpractice claims, but he was willing to bet that Parky's insurance company settled a judgment out of court for him once or twice a year. "And that's the reason malpractice premiums are so high for the rest of us!" Crest thought. It was his own opinion that the malpractice problem was not due to lawyers or patients or the national morality, but to a deterioration of the doctor-patient relationship. Doctors and patients no longer understood each other. Doctors and patients no longer trusted each other. Why? Because of the power of the Parkindales, that was why! Because of doctors who were too busy to think. Because of patients who believed that the only good doctors were the fashionable busy ones. Because of doctors who told the patients only what the patients wanted to hear. Because of patients afraid to face the realities of age, disability, and death. Because of doctors who had lost their dedication to service. Because of patients who had lost their courage and their faith.

"This is a lousy profession," Crest thought.

Suddenly the hot smoky room seemed overwhelmingly close and confining to him. Crest couldn't seem to breath. A cold hand grabbed him around the throat. A crushing weight lay heavy along his breastbone. His left arm was constricted by a vice.

Crest got up and left the room. He had an urge to rush outdoors for a breath of fresh air, but motion made his throat, chest, and arm feel worse. The mounting intensity of pressure froze him in his tracks. He sat down on the floor. Cold sweat burst out of the pores of his forehead. He had a premonition that he was going to die.

Crest made his own diagnosis without any doubt. He knew he was having a coronary heart attack.

He was fighting for the breath of life, drowning in a sea of pressure and pain, but way up in the distance, the observer was looking on with interest: one small part of Crest's consciousness, somehow uninvolved in the life struggle, able to study the scene with scientific detachment. The observer, with X-ray eyes, seemed to be looking at Crest's heart.

The heart: tough elastic bundle of interconnecting muscle

strands; a big fist, squeezing tight with a rotating motion, once a second, every second, from intra-uterine life to the moment of death, without a moment of rest. Inside, the four valve leaflets, opening, snapping shut: the mitral, shaped like a bishop's miter; and the tricuspid, with three teeth; and the two guarding the great arterial trunks, aortic and pulmonic. The electrical impulses controlling the beat; starting at the nodule between the auricles; traversing through the conducting cable of the bundle of Hiss; splitting into the branch bundles to the right and left. The coronary arteries, small tributary vessels off the main aorta, hooking back to supply the muscle of the heart itself with blood. One of the coronary vessels in Crest's heart—the observer didn't know which one —showed corrosion in the lining, sludgy patches of cholesterol, like rust in a dirty pipe. The sludge in that vessel had caused narrowing; the blood stream slowed; and clotting suddenly occurred to block off the vessel completely. An area of heart muscle supplied by the blocked vessel was deprived of blood, blanching white, critically injured. Pain impulses from dying muscle fled up the nerves, causing the pressure and pain in Crest's chest, throat, and arm. The area of injured tissue, perhaps the size of a quarter or a dime, would die. If the area was big enough so that the heart could no longer perform its thrusting pulsations, the heart would stop and Crest would die. If the mass of uninjured muscle could limp along efficiently, Crest would survive. Then the area of injury would turn dark and rot, like any dead bit of flesh; the processes of repair would begin; collagen fibers would creep into the area of decay; white scar tissue would form. If he was lucky, after a period of six or eight weeks, his heart would be almost as strong as it was before. If he was half lucky, his heart would function under limited activity but would not permit him to lead a normal life. Or he might die. He might die of shock; of heart stoppage; or, if the electrical impulses were badly disturbed by the area of injury, he might die of short circuit, a sort of internal self-electrocution. If the scar that formed was

too weak, it might blow out like a badly patched tire. He might
die suddenly of pulmonary embolism. Or he might die gradually of slowly progressing heart inefficiency.

The observer watched. It would be of interest to see what
was going to happen next. At the same time, down below,
Crest was fighting for his life.

Several of the doctors left the lounge together, and discovered Crest a few feet away, collapsed, slumped to the floor,
leaning against the wall. He was in pain and shock; his color
was gray; his lips were blue; he was laboring for breath; his
skin was drenched with cold perspiration. A brief question on
their part, a brief grunted reply from Crest, and they all knew
the diagnosis at once. Parky, of course, automatically took
charge. He called for an eighth of morphine and gave it intravenously. A litter was procured. Crest was supported and
lifted onto the litter. He was wheeled to one of the private
rooms upstairs. He was bundled off the litter onto the bed.
His clothing was removed. He was clad in a hospital johnnie.
Parky listened to him with a stethoscope, front and back, and
took his blood pressure. The nurse took his temperature, pulse,
and respiration. Another dose of morphine was given subcuta-
neously. Parky had ordered an oxygen tent; an orderly
trundled it into the room; the transparent plastic hood was
placed over the head of the bed and tucked under the sheets.
A few minutes later a technician came along and drew some
blood from his vein. Later in the morning, another technician
came and did a cardiogram: gritty paste and cold electrodes
on arms and legs and chest.

Crest was only vaguely aware of these things. The morphine
took hold and he drifted away on a soft cloud of rose. The
observer noted that he was still conscious; that the pain and
pressure was still present; but although he was still aware of
pressure and pain, the symptoms did not bother him any more.
Great God Morphine! The truly miracle of miracle drugs.

The observer was tired then, and so was Crest, and he went

to sleep. He slept intermittently but naturally through the rest of the day and the night and then part of another day.

Then he woke up. Naturally. Through the oxygen hood, the world looked wavery and misty, as if he was under water. He was nauseous, light-headed, cotton-mouthed, but the pain and pressure had gone. Experimentally, he moved one arm: no pain, no pressure. Boldly, he heaved himself over in bed. This caused just a vague ghost of a gassy feeling under his chest and in his arm. It wasn't enough to bother, but he didn't want any more of it. He decided he would just as soon lie quietly.

It occurred to him that he had forgotten to cancel his dentist appointment. He had never gotten around to seeing the spinster with the vaginitis. There were a hell of a lot of things he hadn't gotten around to doing. His conscience told him to get the hell up and out of bed. His chest and throat and arm told him not to. The exertion of thinking made him tired, and so he went to sleep again.

Waking up on the morning of the third day, some forty-eight hours after his coronary attack, Crest really did feel fine. He could move quite freely in bed without a trace of the pressure or the pain. Breathing was quite natural. He did not need oxygen any more. There was no light-headedness, no cotton mouth, no hangover effect. He felt, as a matter of fact, somewhat better than usual when waking up in the morning. Then he began to question the diagnosis. He wondered if the events of the past two days were only the vague memory of a bad dream. He became rebellious. The jury was all wrong. Let's have an appeal to a higher court and see if we can't reverse the sentence. I'm an innocent man, jailed to my bed on evidence of perjured witnesses.

Parky came into the room, strong, bustling, confident, oozing cheerful health from every pore.

"Well, my boy," said Parky, "it looks like you're going to make it after all."

"Get me out of here," said Crest.

"I guess you don't need the oxygen any more," said Parky.

Parky turned off the motor of the tent, peeled off the hood, and pushed the machine away.

"I'm getting out of bed," said Crest, and he started sitting up.

"No, my dear, you're not," said Parky.

Parky put a massive outstretched hand on the middle of Crest's chest and exerted the slightest pressure and Crest fell weakly back on the pillow. He was weaker than he thought. He felt a surge of resentment against Parky's size and strength and force and vitality and confidence.

"Are you the doctor in my case?" asked Crest.

"It was a small one," said Parky. "We have every right to expect that you will pull through. Of course, you better give up any of your active plans for the next three months."

"Three months?" said Crest, resentful and unbelieving, although he had given similar advice to many coronary patients on many occasions.

"Four weeks in bed. Two weeks bed and chair in the hospital, and then another six weeks of progressive ambulation at home. You'll be back in harness by Thanksgiving."

"Do you think I had a coronary?"

"How old are you now, my boy?" asked Parky.

"Forty-five," said Crest.

"That's young," said Parky.

Crest knew what he meant. The long-range outlook for a young man with a coronary wasn't so very good. The man who has a coronary will some day have another one. The long road might not be so very long: one year, two years, five, ten, at the very outside fifteen.

"Are you sure of the diagnosis in my case, Dr. Parkindale?"

"Aren't you?" said Parky.

"Have you had a report on the cardiograms as yet?"

"It's typical," said Parky. "Would you like to examine the tracings yourself?"

Crest wanted to say yes. He also wanted to say no. The observer was interested in his dilemma.

"No," said Crest at last.

There was no real doubt in his own mind about this diagnosis. To see the abnormality on the tracing in black and white would not make him feel any better, or heal any quicker, and it might deprive him of a nourishing grain of hope. Man needs the nourishment of illusion, at least a little bit of it.

"That's right," said Parky. "You rest. Take it easy. Heal yourself. And leave all the worrying to me."

Crest wanted to fire Parky as his physician. He intended to fire Parky as his physician. But he didn't feel up to it now. Later on he would do it.

"I'll see you again this afternoon," said Parky, and he stormed out of the room.

Nancy came at visiting hours that afternoon. She looked very strained, tense, worried. She looked sick. Crest was sure he looked better than she did.

"Say, you better occupy this bed instead of me," he said.

"How are you, dear?" She was hesitant, almost afraid to inquire.

"Me? I'm fine," said Crest. "That was a damn fool selfish thing for me to do."

"Rest. Get well," she said. "You've got to get well."

"I'll get well," said Crest. "I'm too stubborn to die."

She blanched. He wished he hadn't mentioned death. Dying didn't seem to bother him. To go at once: all right! So what? It was disability that he was afraid of. But of course, Nancy knew that a coronary is a very tricky thing; life can go in a snap of the finger tips, like a candle flame blown out. She was afraid he might expire suddenly before her very eyes. Was she going to handle him for the rest of his life, however long that might be, like a delicate, expensive, and fragile vase, liable to shatter at any time?

"Look," he said, "I intend to live for the rest of my life."

"That was a silly way to phrase it," said the observer: "everybody lives for the rest of his life."

He tried it again. "It is my solemn intention to survive Dr. Parkindale. Have you seen him this morning? Does he look as if he were about to die?"

"I wish there was another doctor in the case," she said, worried.

"He's as good as any," said Crest. "The diagnosis is obvious. The treatment is obvious. There's nothing for him to do. Everything is up to me. And I intend to live."

Asked the internal observer, "How long?"

"How's Mike?" said Crest, to change the subject.

"He's fine," she said, brightening slightly. "Temperature is normal today."

"And Sam and Joe?"

"They're back to school already."

"And John, Jr.?"

"He didn't get sick," she said. "I think he's in trouble with his math at school again, however."

John, Jr., had apparently been born with the conviction that two and two makes five. Nothing much was going to change him.

"And yourself?" said Crest.

"I could use a little sleep," she said.

"Take a Nembutal tonight," said Crest.

And then, quite suddenly, he was tired and wanted to sleep himself. He wished he knew a tactful way to inform her that he had had enough, that visiting hours were over. So very often the visitors, with the best of intentions, can talk the patient to death. Nancy stayed another fifteen minutes, though. When she finally left, he was very happy indeed to see her go.

He did not fire Dr. Parkindale. Parky bustled in to see him—hearty, cheery, optimistic—twice a day. Crest found himself looking forward to the visits, as he looked forward to meals. The hospitalized patient, out of pain and trouble, finds the greatest problem monotony and welcomes anything to break it. This is particularly true of the coronary patient, who often has no symptoms of any kind after the first two or three days but who must remain at rest for weeks if he wishes his heart to heal. Between visits, Crest resented Dr. Parkindale. Before the time and at the time, however, he fell under the spell of Parky's strength and confidence.

"He's making a baby out of me," thought Crest. "He cradles me to sleep in his great strong hands. He hands me sugar teats to suck."

Maybe this was true. But maybe, he was almost willing to admit, this was the way to handle a sick patient: like a strong father with a fractious child.

Crest realized that something else was true. Parky was permitting Crest to dictate his own treatment. Whether or not to continue anticoagulants; when next to test the prothrombin level of the blood; when to do a cardiogram—Parky would invite suggestions; Crest would offer a tentative opinion; and Parky would follow it.

"He's telling me what I want to hear," thought Crest. "I'm treating myself. Is that right? Am I in any position to treat myself? I've never even seen my own cardiogram."

Right or wrong, this was the way it was being done. Crest accepted it. He even suspected that if he needed a physician again, he might consult Dr. Parkindale by choice.

As he approached the end of the necessary hospitalization period, Crest sometimes tried to alter his relationship with Parky. He tried to break away from being Parky's patient or his son. But whenever Crest tried to discuss medical topics, concerned with anything except his own condition, Parky would grunt and change the subject. If Crest mentioned Sam or Joseph Parkindale or Emerald, Parky would ignore him. Parky could not even seem to acknowledge the existence of Nancy or of Crest's four sons, two of whom were actually named for Parkindales.

"One level only," thought Crest. "Parky erect and dominant, while the patient is flat on his back."

Theoretically, Crest thought that this was wrong. Parky's attitude tended to perpetuate Crest's feeling of dependence and passive submission.

"Damn it," thought Crest, "it's taken me years to try to mature and stand on my own two feet; Parky's knocked it out of me in a month. It would be much easier to be a child and leave all responsibility to Parky and his friends. Once Parky's seized the advantage, he won't relinquish it. I suppose that's why his patients always do come back. If I submit and anything happens to me, it's Parky's fault, not mine. If I defy him, anything that happens to me is my own damn fault. So I'll be a good little boy. It was always too hard for me to be a man."

When the time came for Crest to be discharged, he was almost afraid to leave the hospital.

The convalescent period at home was difficult. He loved Nancy and was glad to have her around; he loved his four children more than anything. But he felt like a useless antique chair. Everybody was afraid to sit on him. The doorbell rang, but Crest couldn't answer it. The telephone rang, and Crest must ignore it. When little Mike fell down and skinned his knee, Nancy would bandage it. When John, Jr., argued that two and two made five, Nancy would try to persuade him otherwise. Even the dog didn't quite dare let Crest scratch him on the belly.

He had a good deal of anginal pain at home, minor variants of that crushing gassy pressure in the throat, chest, and arm. He had had none at all in the hospital. Whenever the suspicion of pain and pressure arose, he slipped a nitroglycerine tablet under his tongue and it would go away. But he was constantly aware of his bruised and battered heart.

He fought out two conflicting desires. He knew he didn't want to die. On the other hand, he didn't want to sit around like a useless antique chair, afraid to move. Should he quit trying? Learn to be as happy as a vegetable? Some people could, like Joseph Parkindale, for example. Crest suspected that he did not have the inner resources of a Joseph Parkindale. Or should he say to hell with it? Ignore his heart. Live fully, even though briefly, and drop in his tracks when the time arrived? He swung like a pendulum between these two poles, not content with either. Most of the time he was suspended somewhere between: wanting to get up while wanting to lie down, clutching the bottle of nitroglycerine, waiting for the next attack of gas and pressure.

He took steps at the proper time. He walked at the proper time. He went outdoors. By six weeks, he was almost fully active. By the end of two months, his activity was in a normal pattern. Increased activity didn't seem to make him any better or any worse.

"I'm not gaining an inch," he thought.

The time was coming when he would have to make his decision: get up like a man, or go to bed like a child. Ten weeks after his coronary attack, he still hadn't made it.

"Nancy," he said, "I'm going to the city."

"I think a trip might do you good," she said.

"I want to see a specialist, a good cardiologist," he said.

"Fine. I don't think you should accept the judgment of Dr. Parkindale. We'll make plans. I'll find a baby-sitter for the kids."

"Nancy," he said, "I've got to go alone."

"But, dear . . ."

Nancy didn't like it. Perhaps she was allied with the forces to keep him a child. He wasn't old enough to go to the city by himself.

"I'm well enough physically to take the trip," he said. "As long as I have plenty of nitroglycerine."

"I'm sure you are," she said.

"My decision for the future must be made alone."

"We're a family, dear. It's all of us together."

"We are," said Crest. "But this is not a family heart. It's my own. It carries me or it quits. Nobody but me can make the final decision on how much mileage to get out of the God-damn thing."

She couldn't understand this. She was hurt. Crest had become a stranger to her. He looked like the man she loved, father of four sons, master of the house, but something had changed.

"All right," she said. "I understand."

But she turned away quickly from him, and there were tears in her eyes.

Crest remembered the cardiologist from his student days as a red-faced, brisk, dynamic man. The red face was there, redder than before, but the manner seemed to contain uncertainty. This was an old man and Crest was not sure he could accept his judgment. On the other hand, in his present mood, he might not have been able to accept anybody's judgment.

"You practice in Sentryville, Doctor?"

"Yes," said Crest.

"Lovely little town."

"Ye Gods," Crest thought, "I'm wondering whether I'm going to live or die, and he's discussing Sentryville! Probably we'll discuss the weather next!"

"You fellows are lucky," said the cardiologist. "I envy you. Small-town practice is clinical medicine in its purest form, I think. In the city, we can never really know the patient, his family background or environment, and you fellows can see a lot of things we miss. One of my classmates practices in Sentryville. Probably you know him. Parkindale."

"I know him," said Crest.

"A very able fellow: strong, competent, and dedicated."

"His practice is enormous," said Crest.

"And now, Doctor, shall we consider your problem? A recent coronary, I understand?"

Crest gave a complete history. The cardiologist examined

him, studied the cardiograms and lab findings from Crest's hospital stay in Sentryville, did a new cardiogram and chest fluoroscopy.

"There's no doubt about the diagnosis," said the cardiologist. "Small posterior coronary, now well and firmly healed. Physically speaking, your heart is nearly as strong as it ever was."

"Do you think I should go back to work?"

"Yes."

"Full time?"

"As full a schedule as you can handle in comfort," said the cardiologist. "A certain moderation is advised. For example, you must run your practice and not permit your practice to run you. When you're tired, quit for the day. Don't be afraid to turn down emergencies or get rid of nuisance patients who bother you. In other words, practice as much as you enjoy. But don't try to do everything. Try to lose, if you can, the feeling that you are under obligation to the community. Forget about ambition and prestige and status and all that sort of thing. Don't try to solve insoluble problems. Do your best; then quit; and don't worry about the problems of tomorrow. Under such a program, you have a long, rewarding life ahead."

"That would mean changing my entire personality," said Crest. "I don't believe I was ever a moderate man. I have a tendency to throw myself at things. I batter brick walls with my head."

"That must change," said the cardiologist, "if you wish to postpone your next attack."

"You think I'll have another attack?"

"Most coronary patients do."

"How long?"

The cardiologist smiled. "As you very well know, Dr. Crest, nobody can predict. Statistically, you should have several good years left. With luck, ten or fifteen. Maybe even longer than that."

"On the other hand," said Crest, "I could have another attack tomorrow."

"You might get run over by a truck this afternoon. Who can predict these things? However, we can make certain statements of probability. The chances are very good, nine out of ten, that the eventual cause of your death will be coronary artery disease. It is very unlikely that you will die of cancer, for example. It's also unlikely that you will get run over by a truck. Coronary patients learn to take care of themselves, and they seem to avoid accidents. Furthermore, although I don't know why, it is unlikely that you will ever be confined to a mental institution. I have rarely seen a coronary patient with a nervous breakdown."

"We don't live long enough."

"No. Not true. But you fellows live differently."

"I'd like to live normally," said Crest. "But I feel as if I were carrying a firecracker in my chest. It might explode at any time."

"All of us live under the sword of Damocles. Most of us, however, are not aware of it. You people have an advantage. At least you can appreciate the odds."

"One of my teachers said that the best way to live a rewarding life is to develop a good chronic disease."

"And Osler said that we must learn to live in day-tight compartments. One day at a time. This is sound advice for all of us."

Crest knew that the cardiologist had presented the problem to him honestly and wisely. Crest must learn to accept himself on these terms. He must change his life pattern. It wouldn't be easy for him. He would need help.

"Joseph," said Crest, "I'm sick. I need guidance."

"Come in, John," said Joseph Parkindale.

"I come as a patient. Should I lie down on your couch?"

Joseph smiled. "I don't have a couch. You can take your

choice of a variety of chairs. You may walk around the room. One of my regular patients always sits on the floor."

Crest selected a chair and sat down. He didn't know how to begin the interview. The silence was awkward.

"I was expecting that you might offer me congratulations," said Joseph at last.

"What for?" said Crest. "Are you married?"

"I have been appointed dean of the medical school."

Crest had not heard this news. He was gratified and, frankly, surprised.

"This establishes several firsts," said Joseph. "The first dean who ever was a plastic surgeon. The first dean selected from the department of psychiatry. The first bachelor dean. The first dean confined to a wheelchair. Of course, I am not the first dean named Parkindale; as a matter of fact, I'll be the last; there aren't any more of us."

"It seems a shame to break the continuity of centuries," said Crest.

"We need new blood," said Joseph.

"You're a busy man. I have no right to take your time."

"I have plenty of time."

"I don't know where to begin," said Crest. "You heard I had a coronary?"

"Yes."

"I seem to have made a good recovery. I have been advised to return to active practice, with moderate limitations. I may live well and long, with moderation. But I'm afraid of myself."

"Why?" said Joseph.

"I was hoping you could tell me that," said Crest.

"The psychiatrist does not supply answers. He merely stimulates questions and listens to the discussion."

"It's a matter of tension," said Crest. "I know that. My life is filled with an undercurrent of anxiety, insecurity, and low-grade tension. It's been that way since I first walked into the medical school in 1931."

"Our profession is not a relaxing one," said Joseph.

"It ought to be a rewarding one," said Crest. "But it doesn't seem to me that I have gotten a sufficient dividend of satisfaction on my investment. I watch other doctors. I see people like your brother, for example, working night and day and loving every minute of it, but I can't get rid of my tensions. I know it was tension that caused my heart attack. I know I'll have another if I can't get rid of tension. I think I know why I am tense. I'm a bad doctor, aren't I?"

"I've known several thousand doctors, John. I never knew a bad one yet."

"You don't mean that!"

"I do," said Joseph. "I never met a bad physician."

"Come off the roof!" said Crest. "The selfish doctors, the greedy doctors, the stupid doctors, the weaklings, the self-righteous, the pompous, the arrogant, the drunks, addicts, and psychopaths, the ones concerned with power and prestige and money. Don't you know any of them? You ought to come to Sentryville."

"I know them all," said Joseph. "There isn't a bad doctor in the bunch."

"Explain yourself!"

"All right. Take any one of these men that you describe in Sentryville, or anywhere else. Suppose this man, just once in his life, cured one patient. Suppose, just once, he drove out fear, anxiety, and pain. At such a time, was he a bad physician?"

"Just once, out of thousands of times?"

"Suppose this man has a patient, just one patient, who thinks he's the greatest doctor in the world, the only doctor who could ever understand the case."

"Every doctor must have at least a few of those patients," said Crest. "Even I do."

"*Quod est demonstrandum*," said Joseph Parkindale.

"I don't know," said Crest. "An occasional success; many failures; many serious mistakes. This is good medicine?"

"Who's the judge?" said Joseph. "Where is the table of standards? Who shall set the criteria?"

"Does this excuse the errors that we make?"

"What are we, John? Gods? Demigods? Magicians?"

"Just ordinary men and women with a long, fancy education."

"Extraordinary men and women," said Joseph. "Why? Because we and our continuing lifelong education are dedicated, not to our own welfare, not to personal enrichment in terms of money, power, knowledge, or prestige, but for the benefit of others."

"It should be. That's the point," said Crest. "But the point is that we've lost our dedication. I have, at least. So have the other men in Sentryville."

"I take exception to the statement," said Joseph. "Is there any man in Sentryville who turns down genuine emergencies? Suppose the doctor is sick. Suppose he's tired. Suppose it's snowing a blizzard. Suppose he knows the patient will not pay. Suppose he hates the patient. But the patient has called and the doctor knows the call is genuine. Will he turn it down?"

"Well . . ." said Crest.

"Would Parky turn it down?"

"Never."

"Would Hamilton, Rhodes, Sweetster, Ardz, or any of the rest of them?"

"I don't know," said Crest. "I think we all turn down cases from time to time for no good reason other than selfishness or perversity."

"All right," said Joseph. "We're human, and humans do act selfishly and perversely. But when a doctor turns down a call for help, he worries about it, doesn't he? His conscience keeps giving him fits."

"I suppose."

"Surely. Because even at his most perverse, the doctor is still trying to put the welfare of the patient first. Doctors are disagreeable, rude, selfish, lazy, greedy, ambitious, proud, arrogant, and stupid, but they put the welfare of the patient first. For this reason, I maintain that I never knew a bad doctor in my life."

"And yet, it seems to me that patients don't trust the doctor any more, and that doctors no longer find medicine a satisfactory way of life."

"Modern medicine is technical," said Joseph. "The newer pharmacology, the newer surgery, our new diagnostic methods are complex and highly technical. For this reason, many of the men drawn into medicine these days are good technicians, and technicians, by their nature, often do not get along with people very well. On the other hand, the extrovert who is socially inclined and who does get along with his patients is often not very good at the theory and complex techniques that modern medicine requires. The patient longs for the day of the good old country doctor, when the patient was treated like a human being instead of a code number in an I.B.M. card. On the other hand, the few good country doctors left cannot handle the newer drugs, the newer diagnostic and therapeutic techniques."

"Like your brother, I suppose," said Crest. "Parky is a good old country doctor, but he makes mistakes. He makes too many mistakes, and some of them are bad ones. How can I live silently next door to that?"

"This is not a perfect world," said Joseph. "Progress is painful and slow, and for every gain, we sometimes show a loss. Our technical advances are so rapid that we can't keep up with them, but on certain levels, we haven't advanced since the Middle Ages. We remain unsure of what we are and why we're here. The physician cannot change the world as he finds it. He is an individual, working with individuals. His tools are imperfect, his knowledge limited, and he is bound to make mistakes. Since his mistakes concern human life and suffering, they may be horrible to contemplate. But our very weakness is our strength, John. We are a human profession. Science serves us, but we do not enslave ourselves to science. We fight bureaucracy and mass production and gadgetry. Perhaps alone among the professions, and certainly alone among the sciences, we fight for the integrity of the individual."

"And we lose," said Crest.

"Humans always lose," said Joseph. "We fight, and get knocked down, and rise again. Our strength is our humanity."

"Since all patients get sick and since all men die, the doctor's work must end in failure every time," said Crest. "In other words, a doctor cannot succeed."

"Osler said that medicine is the science of uncertainty and the art of probability."

"Did Osler say everything about this profession?"

"He gave some mighty good advice," said Joseph. "For example, Osler considered that there are two qualities that every physician requires, in times of success and also in the hours of failure. The first of these qualities is imperturbability."

"In other words, hardness of heart?"

"No," said Joseph. "Coolness and presence of mind, exterior calm, clearness of judgment in moments of emergency. The doctor must learn not to panic. This can be acquired by self-discipline. It can, and must, coexist with warmness of heart. The other quality that Osler describes is equanimity."

"That's the same thing, isn't it?" said Crest.

"No. Imperturbability is exterior calmness. Equanimity is inner peace of mind."

"That's what I lack," said Crest. "How do I get it? Did Osler have some fabulous suggestions?"

"Osler was a realist," said Joseph. "He gave no mystical chestnuts, no quasi-religious platitudes for obtaining peace of mind. He suggested merely that the doctor must not expect too much of the people with whom he deals."

"If you expect the worst of people, you seldom are surprised?"

"The doctor is at the mercy of his patients. Sick people are children, hostile, rude, silly, stubborn, frightened, mean, and stupid."

"Then the doctor must not like people very well. He expects to see them at their worst. People are no damn good. The doctor must therefore be a cynic."

"Not necessarily," said Joseph. "The more you study human nature, the more you will discover that the meanness, the weakness, the sickness of the patient is very like your own. The worst of us and the best of us are basically the same; we differ from one another only in degree. We all have the seeds of the same sort of weaknesses; we all have the capabilities of the same sort of strength. Intensive study of this phenomenon leads the true doctor away from cynicism. It leads him in the other direction: towards tolerance, patience, humor, gentleness, understanding. It leads him towards the paths of love."

"I accept that in theory," said Crest. "In practice, the weakness that I see, in myself, in my patients, in the other doctors in town, exasperates me and causes inner tensions. This makes me sick."

"You are a romantic, John, an idealist. A doctor must keep high ideals, so high that he can never attain them, since perfection is the province of the god, not the man. But since you fail to meet your own standards, you can't escape feelings of frustration and futility. You're a man of thought, not a man of action, and for this reason, you can't handle a heavy practice load with any peace of mind. You need time to think. You are by nature shy and reserved and therefore you cannot acquire a magnetic bedside manner. You will never be a fashionable physician. But you're a good doctor, John. You've always been a good doctor. There are hundreds of people in Sentryville who will tell you that. You'll be a better doctor in the years to come. You need more experience. You need the imperturbability and equanimity which comes with maturity. You need more time."

"That's exactly what I haven't got," said Crest. "Time."

"None of us has enough, but everybody has too much," said Joseph. "There's only one question: what to do with the time we have?"

"What do you suggest?" said Crest.

"That's one question the doctor can never answer for the patient," said Joseph. "What the patient is to do with the time the doctor has saved for him. The patient must decide for himself."

"But you suggest that it is better to give time trying to help others than to hoard it on yourself?"

"That would be the physician's point of view," said Joseph. "Many patients can't accept it."

"I have just been advised, by a good cardiologist, to live my life in moderation, to quit when I am feeling tired, to turn down calls when I am feeling sick. Could I practice medicine that way?"

"No," said Joseph. "Unfortunately not."

"Then," said Crest, "unless I retire from practice, I guess my profession will kill me."

"Our profession kills most of us," said Joseph.

"Then it isn't a question of how I'm going to live. I've got to decide how I want to die."

"To dedicate your life to the welfare of others," said Joseph. "Such a policy has been recommended."

"I'm not sure I'm big enough."

"You have to be," said Joseph. "This profession doesn't give you any other choice."

"Long live Florence Nightingale!"

"Poor Florence," said Joseph. "I suspect that she was frigid, and I know that she was paranoid. Many paranoids dedicate their obsessions to constructive causes."

"I'm glad I'm not a psychiatrist," said Crest. "How does it feel to know that everybody, yourself included, just happens to be insane?"

"Feels wonderful," said Joseph. "I find myself in the best of company."

When Crest got home, he said to his wife, "I've made my decision."

"You're going to retire," she said.

"I'm not. Doctors don't retire. I'll open the office next week, business as usual."

"And let your profession kill you, I suppose."

"No," said Crest. "I'm growing up. My heart has plenty of mileage for physical activity, all that I'll ever need. It was tension that was killing me, and my tension was due to the frustration and futility of the whole damn thing. But I've had some pretty good teachers, Nancy, and they showed me how to conquer tension and anxiety. It seems to be a matter of equanimity. People won't bother me as long as I know that they and I are in the same damn boat. Nancy, I didn't build the boat and I didn't steer it on the rocks. All I've got to do is bail it out, and I can keep working with a bailing can until the end of time. I'm not even going to fight with Parky any more."

"They've beaten you," she said.

He kissed her. "No, dear, they haven't," he said. "In due course of time, I'll be stronger than they are. You just wait and see!"

Part 9

The telephone rang. Crest awoke and glanced at his wrist watch: a few minutes after midnight. He answered the phone.

He recognized the voice at once. She was a curious patient, a sort of female Jekyll and Hyde; no doctor would see her, not even Parky. She was a normal and respectable member of the community during the day, but at night her personality seemed to change, and she had irresistible urges to throw herself at men. She might call anybody in the yellow pages of the directory: doctors, lawyers, policemen, firemen. Doctors quickly learned that any politeness to this woman would mean a call late at night, many nights in a row. Crest hung up on her. If this woman ever had a medical emergency, she could never find a doctor who would come.

Crest got up and went to the bathroom. He glanced out the window. Still snowing, and the drifts were piling up. There would be several feet to shovel in the morning. Shoveling snow is not recommended for a man who has had a coronary heart attack. Each winter, Crest engaged a man with a jeep to plow out his drive. He had had no trouble from his heart since his attack, three and a half years ago, and he could shovel snow if he had to in an emergency, but he preferred not to take a chance.

Returning to bed, Crest heard foreign noises in the house. He listened with a parent's ear, and knew that one of the children was stirring, and listened further, and knew which one: Mike. Mike seemed to be the weak physical link in the family, the child most likely to develop sudden fevers in the middle of the night. Crest located Mike stumbling around the hall. He took the child by the hand, expecting to find the skin dry and blazing hot, but it was cool. Mike had no fever.

"What's the matter, sport?" asked Crest.

Mike mumbled. He was two-thirds asleep. Crest guided him back into his own room. Mike obediently snuggled underneath the covers, but then he suddenly spoke up, loud and clear:

"Daddy, why are lobsters red?"

"Huh?" said Crest.

"Lobsters," said Mike. "You know. The things with claws."

Crest knew. A few weeks before, there had been lobsters for sale in the A & P, and Nancy had bought them experimentally. She had not realized that the creatures must be boiled alive, and she called Crest out of the office suite to perform this task. Crest didn't enjoy it. He found himself wondering whether crustaceans suffered pain.

"Daddy, why are they red?"

Mike was stubborn, and he wouldn't go to sleep until Crest supplied some sort of satisfactory reply. Crest fumbled through his mental file, crowded with the names of several thousand patients and several thousand drugs and other problems of one sort and another.

"Mike, they're not red until they're cooked. In the natural state, they're green."

This was the best he could do, but it satisfied the boy. Mike's next remark was a statement, not a question.

"I'm going to be a doctor when I grow up."

"Why?" said Crest.

"Because doctors know everything," said Mike, and he promptly fell asleep.

"No, sport, they don't," thought Crest, "but I regard it as a compliment."

Leaving Mike's room, returning toward his own, Crest became aware of something else out of kilter in the house. A light was on somewhere. Crest placed it: from John, Jr.'s room, on the floor above. He tiptoed up the stairs, carefully avoiding the hazard of a roller skate on the landing. Crest had just poked his head inside the door when the switch snapped off and the room was dark again. Crest had caught just enough of a glimpse to know that John, Jr., was reading something half concealed underneath the covers. What was it? Homework? Unlikely, for John, Jr., was not a notable scholar. Pornography? *Lady Chatterly's Lover* or *Ulysses,* or a girlie magazine with nudes? John, Jr., was approaching puberty with frightening speed. Crest's impulse was to turn on the light, throw back the covers, and reveal the incriminating evidence. But wouldn't he feel silly if it was *Popular Mechanics?* John, Jr., was still convinced that two and two made five, but he could take apart a car and put it back together again. Nancy hoped the boy would go to M.I.T. Crest thought the boy should get a job in a garage after graduation from high school. It is not mandatory for all sons of professional people to enter a profession. There should be no stigma against a mechanic in this mechanical world where born mechanics are so rare.

"Save your reading for the morning, son," said Crest.

"Yes, Dad."

There was something in the boy's voice which told Crest that pornography was more likely than *Popular Mechanics.* "Well, and what about it?" thought Crest. "Let him read and study and look; let him learn as much as he can while he's still young enough for it to do him some good. If I had my way," thought Crest, "art studies and the classics of pornography would be freely available in the public library. Why keep the best examples under lock and key, when the worst examples are available at any corner drugstore to any kid with fifty cents? There seems to be a conspiracy of silence in our culture, the remnants of our Puritan tradition, which would deny the young access to the realities of the body. Formal courses in sex hygiene are not enough. The textbooks are too technical, too statistical, and too dry; they take the fun out of it, and the beauty, and don't dispell any of the darkness; novelists and artists have always been in closer contact with such matters than the scientists. I could not say this at the P.T.A., even though mature parents might secretly agree with me and even though the physician presumably can see the results of poor sex education in his office every day. The net effect of our Victorian cultural heritage seems to make us ashamed of what we are and to block our attempts to understand the reasons why. This is good soil for disease. But a doctor can't say these things, for they lie in the province of the parent, the teacher, and perhaps the minister. It takes courage to break through the barriers. Medicine is not the only profession which requires courage. Who comes off strongest in the last analysis: parent, teacher, minister, or physician? Are doctors the only ones who can be accused of losing dedication?"

Passing by the bedroom of the twins, Crest glanced in. In the double bed, where there should have been two sleeping bodies, there were three: on either side a boy, and in the middle of the sandwich, a dog. In the morning, Nancy would wonder why the twins were covered with little red spots: what sort of measles, German measles, or tropical disease was this? Crest would have to tell her it was flea bites. For completeness, Crest glanced into the baby's room, the little girl, just nine months old. There is no more cozy or reassuring smell than the humid, hothouse, uriniferous aroma of sleeping babyhood. Nancy was awake when Crest got back to bed.

"Anything wrong?" she inquired.

"John is reading what he shouldn't be reading; the dog is in bed with the twins; the baby is sound asleep," said Crest. "Snow is falling; I love you; and all is well with the world."

"I'm a little concerned about John," she said. "Shouldn't you have a talk with the boy?"

"It's normal," said Crest.

"I better give the dog a bath. If I can't keep him out of bed, at least I could reduce the ratio of flea bites."

"Nancy," said Crest, "I'm glad I'm not young any more."

"What brings this up?" she said.

"The dividend has been worth the investment," he said. "If my heart stands up a few more years, do you know what I'll be?"

"An old goat?" she suggested.

"A grandfather."

"Holy smokes!" she said. "Good night, Grandpop."

At three in the morning, the telephone rang again. It was the hospital. Somebody had dropped a sledgehammer on his toes. Crest managed to get the car out of the drive without shoveling, gunning the motor and plowing through the drifts, and he skidded over to the hospital.

"Were you drinking?" he asked the patient.

"No, sir."

"Then, how on earth . . . ?"

The patient gave a sheepish grin. "Stupid thing for me to do," he said.

"I'm inclined to agree," said Crest. "Was there any particular reason for this accident?"

"I couldn't sleep. I went down into the cellar for no particular reason, and saw this sledgehammer. It isn't mine. It must have belonged to the previous owner. At any rate, I picked it up for no particular reason, and . . ."

"Dropped it on your toe," said Crest. "At least you didn't go upstairs and slug your wife over the head with it."

"It seems a pity to get you up at three A.M. in the middle of a blizzard."

"That's my job," said Crest.

"I should think you fellows would sometimes get mad at the whole human race. Doctors need sleep as much as anybody else."

"We have a feeling of kinship with the whole damn human race," said Crest. "Do me a favor in the morning, and throw away that sledgehammer. You only broke one of your toes. You have nine others."

"I don't know how you doctors do it. Three in the morning, and you still have a sense of humor."

"It's better to laugh than to growl your way into a coronary heart attack," said Crest.

Dr. Ardz, the surgeon, intercepted Crest as soon as he reached the hospital in the morning.

"I'm seeing too much of a certain kind of surgery. I call it the Parkindale procedure."

"What do you mean?" said Crest.

"When you do an appendix, you take out the right ovary," said Ardz.

"I didn't think you fellows did appendectomies any more," said Crest.

"I don't," said Ardz. "Parky does it two or three times a week. And once a week, I think, he also takes out the right ovary. Why?"

"Does it do the patient any harm?"

"Does it do the patient any good?"

"No," said Crest.

"Why in the hell the right ovary?" said Ardz. "Why never the left?"

"Because the right ovary is closer," said Crest.

"This is supposed to be good surgery?"

"Ardz, don't worry about it," said Crest. "You'll drive your-self into a coronary."

"I had a three-year residency in surgery," said Ardz. "I'm Board qualified. I don't do anything else but surgery. I think I'm fairly good. I take a post-graduate refresher course at least every other year. Parky never had a residency. I'm not even sure he had an internship."

"He did," said Crest.

"Well, anyway, he's a general man. He taught himself to do surgery. At the expense of his patients. Scarcely a week goes by but what he doesn't make some horrible mistake in the operating room. And yet, you know, his operative load is five times heavier than mine."

Crest grinned. "What do you propose to do about it?"

"You think I don't like Dr. Parkindale because I envy his volume? Professional jealousy?"

"Not entirely," said Crest.

"I've got nothing against him personally. He can be quite charming and persuasive."

"But you think he's a menace and we ought to run him out of Sentryville?"

"I'm a surgeon. He's a hacker and a quack. How can I prac-tice silently next door to that?"

"Don't be silent. Speak up."

"And what would happen if I did?"

"You tell me," said Crest.

"Nothing," said Ardz. "I might hurt myself, that's all. There's nothing I can do to stop Dr. Parkindale. How old is he?"

Crest did some mental arithmetic. "Seventy-two or three, I think."

"He doesn't act it," said Ardz. "He's as strong as a bull. I couldn't keep up with him. He's going twenty-four hours a day."

"He's been slowing up recently," said Crest. "You should have seen him in the good old days."

"Isn't there a hospital rule about retirement? Shouldn't a man stop operating when he's past the age of sixty-eight or something of the kind?"

"Why don't you bring it up at the next meeting of the staff?"

"Yeah. Why don't I stick my head into a lion's mouth? Parky's been president of that staff since before I was born. He'd bring up some counter-motion, barring left-handed surgeons from the operating room, since I'm the only left-handed surgeon in the county."

"When rape is inevitable, relax and enjoy it," said Crest. "Remember your coronaries."

"Why do you always take Parky's side? Do you owe him any debt or obligation? Weren't you married to his daughter once?"

"I owe Parky what Parky owes me: nothing," said Crest.

"We'll never get rid of the son-of-a-bitch unless the rest of us all stick together. I've given up all hope of out-living him. That tough old bastard will still be working at the age of a hundred and three!"

"I have enough problems of my own," said Crest. "I'll let you worry about Dr. Parkindale."

"Crest, I don't understand you. You're a good man, well trained, ethical. You can see Parky's mistakes as well as the rest of us. You know that he's a bad physician."

"Is he?"

"Isn't he?"

"Parky is a good physician and a bad physician," said Crest. "Something of both. He's too busy to read or think; he makes snap judgments and some of the judgments are wrong. He keeps neurotic patients sick, and sometimes he's a butcher at surgery."

"You know what I think is worst of all?" said Ardz. "He's greedy. He has the need to dominate this community. It isn't enough for him to have a bigger practice than he can manage. He tries to destroy the rest of us. He wouldn't be happy unless he had driven the rest of us out of town, even though the town needs all of us. The rest of us stick only because we're stubborn."

"And yet," said Crest, "Sentryville also needs Parky. He's strong, he's loyal, he's dedicated, he's on twenty-four-hour call. His patients worship him."

"Well?" said Ardz. "So patients are stupid. They don't know what's good for them."

"And so," said Crest, "would you deprive patients of their freedom of choice of a physician?"

"You've got me," said Ardz. "But I don't have to like it."

"No," said Crest, "but on the other hand, you do have to live with it, and so do I."

Crest didn't want to see the patient in room 16. This was a good example of what Dr. Ardz had been speaking about. The patient was an elderly male with urinary complaints. He had gone to Parky six or eight months ago. Parky had interviewed him, examined the urine, and dispensed some sulfa drug, but had not done a rectal examination. As any medical student knows, a rectal is mandatory in any male with urinary complaints. If Parky had done it, he would have felt the cancer in the prostate gland, and at that time, possibly, the cancer had not spread. The prostate might have been removed. Castration might have been indicated. Hormones might have helped. Propaganda aside, malignancy is very seldom cured, but means were available to prolong a useful, active life. Now it was too late. The cancer had spread, involving almost every bone in the body. The patient was doomed to a lingering and painful death.

"We all miss cancers now and then," thought Crest. "This is the horror of the disease. By the time a malignancy causes symptoms, it is already too late. A majority of the X-rays and tests we do are performed in the hopes of picking up cancer early enough, usually with negative results. Management of cancer is the doctor's most depressing and discouraging failure, unless it might be management of emotional disease. No wonder all of us—doctors and patients too—are so afraid of cancer and so aware of it all the time!

"But this doesn't excuse Parky from doing a rectal exam," he thought. "I should go down into the doctor's lounge. Parky is there, expansively discussing loopholes in the income tax to a captive audience of younger physicians who don't have enough income to worry about the tax. I should interrupt him and tell him about the patient in room 16. I should make him confess his error to the group. Then I should make him go up to room 16 and tell the patient! 'Parky,' I should say, 'haven't you killed enough of the population of Sentryville in the last half-century? Glance at the cemetery the next time you drive by! Most of those patients are yours. Why don't you quit and grow roses, sir, before somebody catches up with you?'

"But I haven't the courage. I have to watch my coronaries. I must recall that this is not a perfect world, and that no physician is a bad physician if he puts the welfare of the patient first."

Before he could go into room 16, Crest was paged over the loud-speaker system: telephone. He welcomed the interruption.

"Crest speaking."

"Doctor, this is Timothy, County Attorney."

"Oh, yes."

"Can you spare me a few minutes this morning?"

"What's on your mind?" said Crest.

"I need your advice."

"Concerning whom?"

"Who do you think?" said Timothy.

"Dr. Parkindale again?"

"Crest, I've got him," said Timothy, a note of exaltation in his voice. "I've been watching him all these years, and he's finally made a mistake that nobody can explain away. I'm going to nail him to the wall. I thought you might like to help."

Although he was ashamed of it, Crest felt a moment of exaltation himself. "I'll be with you in five minutes, Timothy," said Crest.

Instead of going into room 16, Crest went down to the office of the County Attorney. He was going to help nail Parky to the wall. Finally, after all these years!

"I hope this won't be a waste of time," said Crest.

"Would you consider nailing Dr. Parkindale a waste of time?" said Timothy.

"What have you got on him this time?"

"The number one."

"What?" said Crest.

"Murder."

"I don't believe it," said Crest.

"You never seem to believe anything bad about Dr. Parkindale."

"Not the sort of things that you dig up," said Crest. "Where's the body? It has one of Parky's scalpels sticking out of it, I suppose."

"This is not a joke."

"I didn't imagine that it was. Would you mind giving me a few details?"

"I was poking around the probate-court records a bit," said Timothy. "Several well-to-do widows have died recently. And I discover that they seem to have willed money to Dr. Parkindale. In one or two instances, the sum was rather substantial."

"Grateful patients sometimes mention their doctor in a will," said Crest. "It never happened to me, but I've heard of it. In fact, it would surprise me if it had never happened to Dr. Parkindale."

"There are several cases, but one will do."

"Well?" said Crest.

"A certain Mrs. Lyme, elderly, widow, wealthy, who left some money to Dr. Parkindale."

"And you maintain Parky killed the woman?"

"He did."

"For her money, I presume."

"That's a fairly good motivation, Dr. Crest."

"In this case, I think it's a lousy motivation," said Crest. "Do you have any idea what Parky makes out of his practice?"

"I don't have access to his income-tax returns."

"Well, neither do I, of course," said Crest, "but if he hasn't grossed at least fifty thousand dollars in each of the last fifty years, I'll eat his income-tax return. He's too busy to spend it. Parky makes more money than he knows what to do with."

"All of which is neither here nor there if he killed this Mrs. Lyme."

"I'll grant you," said Crest. "Did he use a poison dart or a death ray or a cavalry sword?"

"He used the weapon all doctors have immediately to hand," said Timothy. "Drugs, of course."

"Ah," said Crest. "The faint aroma of bitter almonds. The scent of new-mown hay. Arsenic in the coffee. Strychnine in the sugar bowl."

"You read too many detective stories, Dr. Crest."

"You're so anxious to nail Dr. Parkindale that you snatch at a straw."

"Is three grains of morphine a pretty good dose?"

"A stiff dose," said Crest.

"Given intravenously?"

"Probably lethal, unless the woman was addicted."

"She had cancer," said Timothy. "She had received morphine fairly frequently, but no dose greater than a quarter-grain, which is normal, I believe."

"A quarter-grain of morphine is a usual dose, yes."

"On the morning of her death, Dr. Parkindale gave her three grains intravenously, and she expired of respiratory failure four hours later."

"I would expect that she might."

"Doctor," said Timothy, "that's murder."

"You can prove that?"

"I haven't exhumed the body. This can be done. I understand that toxicological studies should be able to demonstrate the presence of a lethal dose of morphine even in the embalmed body."

"I'm not a toxicologist," said Crest, "but I imagine so. What gives you the impression that you'd find all this morphine?"

"I have obtained the hospital record on the case."

"And?"

"Dr. Parkindale wrote the order, gave the drug, and signed the chart."

"Maybe it was a mistake."

"Look for yourself, Dr. Crest."

Timothy handed Crest a photostat of the order sheet of a hospital chart. There it was, in Parky's distinctive scrawl over his signature: three grains of morphine, given intravenously.

"Maybe he meant a third of a grain," suggested Crest.

"He didn't," said Timothy. "I interviewed the nurse who made up the morphine solution for the syringe. There is no doubt whatever in her mind. Three grains. There was no doubt of Parky's intentions. Since it was such an unusual dose, the nurse checked with Parky. She had never heard of such a dose. That's what he wanted: three grains."

"Now, wait," said Crest. "Does it sound like murder to put it down in writing and sign it on a chart?"

"I don't care if he wrote it in red paint down the middle of Main Street," said Timothy. "He killed that woman just as surely as if he had asked for a revolver and shot her in the head."

"Maybe he wasn't thinking properly. He sometimes gets too busy to think."

"Are you trying to say that Parky didn't know three grains was a lethal dose?"

"It's possible. He may have forgotten."

"I called Parky on the telephone this morning," said Timothy. "I asked him what three grains of morphine would do to a patient, given intravenously. Parky said he thought such a dosage might be fatal."

"There must be extenuating circumstances."

"In murder, there are no extenuating circumstances."

"You think he killed this woman deliberately?"

"I God-damn well know he did," said Timothy.

Crest thought. There didn't seem to be much doubt. Why would Parky do a thing like this? Surely not for money! "Did Parky know about the will?"

"I don't think that makes much difference," said Timothy.

Neither did Crest. "The woman was in pain?"

"Yes, I believe so. Cancer spread to the bone."

"She was terminal?"

"She was going to die of her disease. When, I don't know. People with cancer in their bones do die, don't they, Dr. Crest?"

"Yes."

"I don't know how long she would have lived. Perhaps you can tell me."

"Perhaps she would have died that same day, or within a day or two, from her disease alone."

"Possible."

"Then, isn't that extenuating circumstance? Parky merely hastened the inevitable. He gave her a painless death instead of a painful lingering one."

"A mercy killing?"

"Well, yes," said Crest.

"There is no provision for this sort of thing in the eyes of the law," said Timothy. "I'm not going to argue the euthanasia question with you, Doctor. There's a lot to be said on both sides. But murder is murder in the eyes of the law."

"Do you hold the brief that useless suffering should be prolonged?"

"I hold no brief. I'm a law officer," said Timothy.

"I suppose I've killed some people," said Crest. "Terminal cases. When I am sure the end is coming, I often do not prolong the suffering. I stop giving IVs and antibiotics and so forth. I merely keep the patient comfortable, and let him slide away naturally. Maybe you better arrest me."

"I'd have no argument and the law has no argument with that."

"I sometimes think you should arrest the doctor who keeps the patient alive to suffer uselessly."

"We're discussing the case of Mrs. Lyme."

"Well . . ."

"You think he's right, Dr. Crest?"

"No," said Crest.

"Even if this poor woman was going to die five minutes later of natural causes, the act of giving a lethal drug, in full knowledge of the effects of that drug, with obvious premeditation, is an act of murder, Dr. Crest."

"Yes," said Crest. "I guess it is, although I am sure he was putting the welfare of the patient first."

"He chose an unfortunate case, wouldn't you say? When Mrs. Lyme was willing him a substantial sum of money?"

"I should say."

"I think I've got him."

"I'm rather afraid that you have," said Crest.

"I thought you might be pleased," said Timothy.

"Are you pleased?" said Crest.

"I am only doing my job."

"Frankly," said Crest, "this makes me sick at heart."

"Nancy," said Crest, "what am I going to do?"

"Why do you have to do anything?" she said.

"There's trouble," said Crest. "A doctor is a trouble-shooter. I have to do something if I can."

"You've grown up, remember? You're not fighting with the dynasty any more. Equanimity. People are no better than they are. Just bail out the boat. You didn't build it, and you didn't drive it on the rocks."

"Yes, but I can't just close my eyes and let a mess develop."

"Remember the tension and the coronary arteries," she said.

"No," said Crest. "I've got to do something. I can't stand by and see him go to jail."

"Why not?" she said. "He made a mistake. Shouldn't he have to pay?"

"I ought to be able to protect him."

"Why? Wouldn't it be better to protect this community?"

"Damn it," said Crest. "I don't think you understand."

"I understand that you're all wrapped up in that family, and you've always been, since the day you first walked into medical school."

"All right," said Crest. "They taught me many things. Is loyalty a crime?"

"John, he made a mistake. A serious mistake. And now he has to pay for it."

"I'm sure he was working for the patient's good."

"He had no right to kill her."

"He had the obligation to relieve her suffering."

"Are you defending him?"

"No, I'm not."

"You know he made a mistake."

"Damn it," said Crest. "He's been making errors of judgment all his life. He's too busy. A million people are waiting for him. He walks in, makes a snap decision, and acts on it, no matter what the consequences. Many of his mistakes are worse than this one. What he did to his own daughter, for example: he amputated her womanhood and destroyed her chances for a normal life. He drove his son to drink. He pushed me into a coronary heart attack."

"And just thinking of him is going to push you into another."

"He ought to bear responsibility for his mistakes," said Crest. "I was hoping he'd trip himself up many years ago. Many times I would have been delighted to see him nailed to the wall. Many times I would have gladly given testimony against him in a court of law, but . . ."

"But what?"

"I can't hate my fathers any more."

"All right. That's to your credit," she said. "Now, if you could only shake off the influence of that entire family . . ."

"I think we need Parky in this town," said Crest. "If only he wasn't . . ."

"If he wasn't what?"

"I was going to say, if he wasn't so greedy; if he didn't have to dominate; if he could keep his practice within reasonable limits; if he didn't need to destroy the other doctors, and his daughter, and his sons; if he wasn't so pompous, arrogant, and self-righteous; if he could ever admit that he was wrong; if he ever gave himself time enough to think!"

"In other words," she said, "if he belonged to any other family, you could see him in a reasonable light."

"Are you jealous of that family?"

"John, I think they've done you a great deal of harm."

"Don't you think they've also taught me everything I know?"

"I wish we could be free of them," she said.

"Will it help to have that old man locked up in jail?"

"No local jury would convict Dr. Parkindale," she said. "You know that."

"He's a doctor," said Crest, "and in the last analysis, doctors stick together. I've got to try to help him, no matter what my feelings toward the Parkindales. Surely he has the right to be warned about the developments in the case of Mrs. Lyme. He should have time to formulate some defense before the sheriff arrives with a warrant for his arrest. I'm going to try to find him first."

Crest went to the hospital. Parky's car was in the parking lot, the unmistakable long black Cadillac. Crest couldn't locate Parky at first. He checked in the operating room, the delivery suite, the locker room, the wards, the private rooms. Then he had Parky paged over the loud-speaker system. When this produced no immediate response, Crest began to prowl the less likely portions of the hospital: lab, X-ray, dining hall. Finally, in the basement, among the steam pipes, not far from the boiler room and the morgue, Crest found Parky standing at the end of a corridor. The light was not very good. Parky seemed to be leaning against the wall, and he didn't look well.

"Dr. Parkindale . . ."

"Yes, my boy?" said Parky. The voice seemed to lack some of its customary vigor.

"Sir, there's been a little trouble . . ." Crest didn't know exactly how to phrase it, and Parky wasn't helping him. "Do you remember the case of Mrs. Lyme?"

Parky didn't answer.

"She died a few months ago, I believe," said Crest. "Cancer with metastasis. I heard she left you money in her will. There was some question of the manner of her death. A dose of morphine intravenously: three grains. Timothy, the County Attorney, seems to think . . ."

Parky wasn't listening. He was leaning weakly against the wall and he seemed to be perspiring.

"I'm not feeling well this morning. Excuse me," Parky said. Then he made a curious noise in his throat and bent over, and Crest could see that he was vomiting.

"Sir," said Crest, "is there anything . . ."

Parky vomited again. Although the light was poor, Crest could see vomitus on the floor of the corridor and it looked red. Parky was vomiting profusely. The material was all over the floor now, and definitely it was blood. Parky was having some kind of a hemorrhage.

"I'm sick," said Parky. "Help me."

Crest didn't exactly know what to do.

"Damn it," said Parky. "Don't freeze in an emergency. Can't you see that I need a little help?"

Crest unfroze himself and ran into the nearest room, where there would be an extension telephone. He phoned the front desk. He identified his location, said that Dr. Parkindale was ill down here, requested a litter and a couple of orderlies, suggested that Dr. Parkindale be admitted into a vacant private room. Then he returned to Parky's side.

"They're coming, sir," he said.

Parky had slumped down toward the floor, half sitting in the pool of vomitus and blood. He was showing signs of air hunger, shallow, labored respirations. Crest felt for the wrist. The skin was clammy, covered with cold perspiration; the pulse was thready and weak. Parky was going into shock.

The litter and orderlies promptly arrived. Crest helped put Parky on the litter and then, as soon as he was free, ran upstairs into the doctors' locker room. The room was full, blue with tobacco smoke; most of the boys were there.

"It's Parky," said Crest. "He's sick. Having some sort of a hemorrhage. They're taking him upstairs."

"From the lungs?" asked Hamilton.

"No. He's vomiting blood, a lot of it," said Crest. "Upper GI tract, I think. Stomach or duodenum. Probably an ulcer. Maybe a cancer."

"Could be esophageal varices," said Ardz. "With cirrhosis of the liver."

"But Parky doesn't drink," said Rhodes.

"I didn't take the time to examine him," said Crest. "Does anybody know his medical history?"

The men looked at each other. None of them knew Parky's medical history. Nobody could remember Parky's having been sick a day in his life.

"Who's his doctor?" asked Crest.

There was no reply. Parky had no doctor here.

"Damn it," said Crest, "he's a sick man. Who's going to take care of him?"

"Don't look at me," said Hamilton.

"It might be a surgical problem," said Rhodes.

"Parky wouldn't let me touch him with a ten-foot pole," said Ardz.

"Fortunately, I limit my practice to obstetrics," said Sweetster.

"Well, somebody's got to take the case," said Crest.

All of them were looking at Crest.

"Not me!" said Crest.

"Do you think we should flip a coin for the privilege?" asked Hamilton.

"You're the obvious man," said Rhodes.

"You're elected by default," said Ardz.

"Why don't you ask the patient?" said Sweetster.

"He's going into shock. He's too sick. This is an emergency," said Crest.

"Why don't you phone his wife?" said Sweetster.

This was the obvious suggestion. Crest had forgotten that Mrs. Parkindale was alive. If Parky was too sick, the choice of physician was obviously up to her until the emergency was over, and then Parky could make up his mind for himself. The room had silently but definitely emptied and Crest was alone. The other men had all suddenly remembered very important things they had to be doing some other place.

"My buddies!" thought Crest bitterly. "Doctors stick together!"

Crest telephoned Mrs. Parkindale. She was very pleasant, as, indeed, she had always been on the few occasions he had ever spoken to her: poor, plump Mrs. Parkindale, always in the background, as nearly anonymous as any person could be. She told him that Parky had never had an ulcer, had never been sick, as far as she knew, and had never had a personal physician.

"Who do you want to be the doctor in the case?" Crest asked her.

"You, John, of course," she said.

"I'm not sure that Parky would want me."

"Of course he would," she said. "Parky always claims that you're the smartest young doctor in the state."

Indeed? This was a surprise to Crest.

"We are all very fond of you, dear," said Mrs. Parkindale. "We always have been, especially the doctor himself."

Under these circumstances, Crest felt he had little choice about the matter. He would accept the case and do the best he could. Crest went up to room 1. Parky was deep in shock and his condition was poor. He had not vomited again, but this was no guarantee that the internal bleeding had stopped.

"Place him on the critical list," said Crest. "I have already notified the family."

"Yes, sir," said the nurse.

"I'll want oxygen."

"Yes, sir."

"And blood in a hurry. Type and cross-match the donors. I'll start some saline intravenously in the meantime."

"How many donors?"

"Four or five at least," said Crest. "And morphine, now. I'll give that intravenously."

"How much morphine, Dr. Crest?"

"Three grains."

"Sir?" said the nurse.

"Sorry," said Crest. "I didn't mean that. One eighth of a grain."

"Morphine grains one eighth?"

"Correct," said Crest.

The nurse left the room. "Why in hell did I say three grains?" Crest wondered. He had entirely forgotten about the episode of Timothy and Mrs. Lyme.

"Please don't let me panic in this emergency," Crest thought. "Don't let me get too busy that I forget to think. Let me consider the differential diagnosis of upper GI bleeding. Please don't let me make some horrible mistake!"

Crest drew back the sheets, pulled up the hospital johnnie, and went over Parky's belly, quickly but carefully. There seemed to be slight tenderness high in the epigastrium. Digging deeper with his fingers, Crest thought he could feel the suspicion of a mass. Moving his fingers up under the right lower border of the rib cage, he could definitely feel the liver edge: hard, irregular, slightly nodular. The nurse came in with the syringe of morphine.

"Grains one eighth?" asked Crest.

"Yes, sir."

"You're positive?"

"Yes, sir."

Crest gave the morphine. Fortunately Parky had big veins. They were bringing in the saline-infusion set. Crest started the infusion. The lab technician was already getting blood from the other arm for cross-match and typing purposes. The orderly trundled the oxygen into the room and stood waiting to catch Crest's eye. Crest nodded: go ahead! There was nothing further Crest could do at the moment in the patient's room. His next job was to think. From room 1, Crest went down to the doctors' locker room. Dr. Ardz was there alone.

"Crest, I didn't mean to abandon you," said Ardz. "I don't want to leave you holding the bag. If there's anything I can do, please don't hesitate to call on me. It's just that I never got along with Parky very well."

"Thanks," said Crest.

"What's he got?"

"It's kind of a tricky differential, as a matter of fact."

"Upper GI hemorrhage? Yes, it often is."

"I have no history," said Crest. "I don't think Parky ever consulted another doctor in his life."

"He wouldn't trust one," said Ardz.

"He's never been sick, to anybody's knowledge. He's bleeding like a stuck pig internally. I saw him vomit. There must have been a quart of bright fresh blood, I'd say."

"He vomited? He didn't cough it up?"

"It's not coming from his lung," said Crest. "Esophageal varices from cirrhosis; or peptic ulcer; or carcinoma of the stomach, I suppose. That's it?"

"Those are the important ones," said Ardz. "Or a blood dyscrasia? Could be leukemia, perhaps."

"We can rule that out with a simple CBC," said Crest. "He

has a spot of tenderness high in the epigastrium, and I think there's a suggestion of a mass. I can feel the liver edge. It's nodular and hard."

"I'll lay my money on cancer of the stomach at his age," said Ardz.

"Or cirrhosis, with that liver edge."

"He doesn't drink. No other signs of portal obstruction?"

"No," said Crest.

"I think you must assume it's ulcer or cancer until you prove otherwise."

"I can prove it by X-ray," said Crest.

"Yes. When he's well enough. But first you've got to make that bleeding stop."

"Should we consider surgery?" said Crest.

"You have to if you can't stop that bleeding otherwise."

"At the moment, he couldn't stand a haircut."

"If he's got to bleed to death, I'd prefer that he do it in bed and not on the operating table in my hands," said Ardz. "If that's all the same with you."

"Blood; oxygen; morphine; rest; keep him quiet; hope the bleeding stops. Is there anything more that I can do?"

"Just keep your fingers crossed and watch him, Crest. That's all until he stabilizes, or until it's obvious that the bleeding isn't going to stop. I'll be around. If you need me, give me a buzz."

"Thanks," said Crest.

"Don't mention it," said Ardz.

"Dr. Crest? Telephone. Please take line one," said the loud-speaker.

Crest picked up the phone and pushed the button to clear line 1.

"Hello? Crest speaking."

"Doctor? Timothy. Office of the County Attorney."

"Oh, yes," said Crest.

"I think we have enough evidence. Is Parky at the hospital?"

"Parky's at the hospital," said Crest.

"I'm going to send out an officer with a warrant and put him under arrest. Do I have your approval?"

"I think you better not," said Crest.

"Are your thumbs still tied by medical ethics, Doctor?"

"There's been a new development," said Crest.

"The evidence better be good, Doctor."

"Parky is a dying man. Is that good enough?"

"No!" said Timothy. "Suicide?"

"No. Massive bleeding from his stomach, we believe."

"Oh," said Timothy. "Then I guess I shouldn't send my officer today."

"I don't think it would be suitable," said Crest.

"Any chance that he might pull through?"

"I hope so," said Crest. "We're fighting for him now."

"Well," said Timothy, "if there's any change in his condition, you'll let me know?"

"I'll let you know," said Crest.

"Thank you, Doctor. I appreciate your interest."

"Don't mention it," said Crest.

Mrs. Parkindale was waiting for him in the lobby: pleasant, not so fat as Crest had remembered, getting old, white-headed, somewhat shaky on her feet. She was faintly worried, but far from hysterical. Perhaps she wasn't even as worried as the serious nature of her husband's condition might indicate. The thought occurred to Crest: perhaps she wouldn't mind if Parky died. It wouldn't change her life a great deal, he imagined. Parky was always busy with the patients, night and day. Crest wondered if she saw him more than once or twice a week.

He explained the situation to her: the present danger, the possible diagnoses, the choices on management and therapy. Since she was a doctor's wife, he felt that he could get technical and sensed that she could understand. She asked a few questions. He answered her honestly and frankly. She never referred to Parky by name, Crest noticed; she always called him "the doctor"; perhaps she thought of him, not as a man, not as her husband and the father of her children, but as "the doctor"; perhaps, from her point of view, there were no other doctors in the world.

The interview apparently over, Crest turned to go, but she called after him in a different voice and stopped him.

"John?"

"Yes, ma'am?"

"One thing," she said. "Please don't make an invalid out of the doctor."

"I beg your pardon?" said Crest.

"If there's anything you can do to make him busy or active again, do it," she said. "But on the other hand, don't try to keep him alive if he's going to be a prisoner to his bed. He couldn't lie around doing nothing. He'd go crazy, and drive the rest of us crazy too. Rather than retire, I am sure my husband would prefer to die."

"Well . . ."

"It may sound cold-hearted, John, but that's God's honest truth. He'd tell you that himself, I'm sure. If he couldn't see his patients, he wouldn't want to live. He has nothing else. He never had anything else."

"I suppose that must be true," said Crest.

"Bless you, dear, I knew you'd understand," said Mrs. Parkindale. "I always think of you as one of the family."

Crest returned to Parky's room at the end of the afternoon. Parky had a special nurse. Crest requested her to leave, and he sat down and examined the chart. Parky had received three pints of blood. Blood pressure was low but stable. Crest didn't want the pressure to climb too high; if a clot had formed over the bleeding vessel, he didn't want that clot blown off. Pulse and respirations had slowed to normal levels. Parky was out of shock. He was awake.

"You don't need this at the moment," said Crest, turning off the oxygen and pushing away the hood.

"Hello, son," said Parky.

"How are you feeling, sir?"

"Fine," said Parky. "I'm going to get up."

He started to raise his massive body on the bed. Crest gently put a hand on Parky's chest and pushed him down. The former vitality and strength was gone. Parky was as weak as an empty potato sack.

"Maybe you're right," said Parky. "I guess I'm not as strong as I thought."

"You lost a lot of blood," said Crest.

"Are you the doctor in my case?"

"Yes," said Crest, immediately on the defensive. "I took charge in the emergency. Your wife wanted it that way. Now that you're better, I'll be glad to step aside. I'll get whatever doctor you want."

"I don't want anybody else," said Parky, brushing the suggestion aside. "Ridiculous. You're in full charge of the case. I had a bleeding peptic ulcer, didn't I?"

"We're not yet sure of the bleeding source," said Crest.

"I'm sure," said Parky. "I've had ulcer symptoms for the past few weeks. I took some Gelusil, but not on a regular basis, and of course my meals have never been regular."

"You'll have to take better care of yourself in the future."

"I suppose," said Parky. "I've been worrying too much recently. I worry too much about my patients. You'd think I'd be old enough to know better than that, wouldn't you, my boy?"

Crest, who was under the impression that Parky had never worried about anything in his life, said only, "Yes, sir."

"That damn case of Mrs. Lyme," said Parky. "That's been worrying me most."

"You knew about it?" said Crest.

"What do you take me for, a fool?"

"You knew what the County Attorney was planning to do?"

"Timothy and his damn-fool warrant on a manslaughter charge? Sure."

"He was planning to serve the warrant on you this morning."

"I know it," said Parky. "Why did you think I had my hemorrhage this morning? Sheer coincidence?"

"I see," said Crest. "Sir, did you really kill that woman?"

"Cancer of the breast killed her, my boy."

"And three grains of morphine . . ."

"Yes, I gave it to her, certainly," said Parky. "The final cause of death was respiratory depression from morphine. You'll find that on the death certificate. You'll find my order on the chart."

"Why?"

"Why did I sign the order on the chart? I'm not ashamed of the things I do. Did you want me to falsify the record?"

"Why did you kill her?"

"She asked me to."

Crest knew he shouldn't bother Parky at a time like this: the man was sick, weak, just out of shock. Excitement could start up the bleeding very easily, but Crest couldn't leave it alone.

"She asked you to kill her, sir?"

"She was a dying woman. She was in great pain. She asked me to stop the pain. She asked me to put her to sleep. Hell, boy, we were the best of friends. I've known Rosie Lyme since I was knee high to a grasshopper. As a matter of fact, I was in love with her once, and I almost married her. That was before I met Mrs. Parkindale. A wonderful woman she was. The very best."

"Yes, sir," said Crest. "You needn't talk any more if you're tired."

"She said to me, 'Parky, get me out of this mess. Put me away.' I said to her, 'My dear, you know I can't, not the way you mean.' She said, 'Can you put me to sleep?' I said, 'Sure, if I give you a lot.' She said, 'And stop the pain for me too?' I said, 'If I give you a lot, but it may be risky.' She said,

'Risk? Good God, Parky, what are you, a monster or a man? What have I got to lose?' This was a brave woman, Crest, and she'd had more than any human should be asked to endure. She wasn't afraid of death. I'd do it again. Wouldn't you?"

"I'm not sure. We can't do everything the patient asks."

"Think about it, Crest."

"Yes, sir."

Crest got up and started to leave the room.

"Doctor?" said Parky.

"Sir?"

"Are you in a hurry tonight?"

"No," said Crest, "but you're tired. I don't think you should talk any more right now. You need rest."

"I'll get enough rest, plenty soon enough," said Parky. "Sit down for a few minutes. Sit with me, please."

Crest sat down again on the chair by the bedside. Parky was looking peacefully out the window. The evening shadows were falling over Sentryville.

"I always loved the evening of the day," said Parky. "This is a pleasant town."

"Yes, sir."

"I wanted to tell you about Emerald," said Parky.

"Emerald?"

"Why I did the hysterectomy."

Crest wasn't sure that he wanted to hear.

"I don't know if you ever noticed, son," said Parky, "but all my family has big heads."

"Yes, sir, the famous leonine Parkindale head."

"I cut into her that night and I pulled out the child. Crest, I forget—was it a boy or a girl?"

"Boy, sir," said Crest.

"My only grandchild. You'd think I'd know that, wouldn't you? Sometimes I'm so busy I don't even know the time of day."

"Yes, sir."

"I pulled him out, and there was nothing but head. 'God damn it,' I said to myself, 'this is the greatest head in the family, and there's always been too much head and no heart! We need no more big-headed Parkindales,' I thought."

"Hydrocephalus is not inherited," said Crest. "There was every reason to expect that other children would be normally developed."

"Yes, I found that out later when I looked it up in the book," said Parky. "But once I took her uterus out, I couldn't put it back."

"If you had to sterilize her, you could have just tied the tubes."

"I also thought of that later on," said Parky. "Rhodes tried to stop me. Poor Rhodes. He's a weakling. He doesn't have the guts to stand up for his own convictions, even when he's right! As I was walking across the lobby to speak to you, I suddenly realized my mistake. I had castrated my own daughter. Crest, it isn't easy to live with a thing like that."

"I should think not."

"I was thinking of the baby's head and the family name, and you were worrying about Emerald. You had even forgotten that there was a baby in the case. I realized at that moment that you did love Emerald. I had always thought you married her just to join the family."

"Well . . ." said Crest.

"I saw Emerald on television last week. She was pretty good."

"She's wonderful," said Crest.

"You have a fine new wife, whatever her name is."

"Nancy."

"Strong girl. Smart girl. You have a fine family. You're a lucky man."

"Yes, sir."

"That wasn't the first mistake I ever made," said Parky, "and it wasn't the last. Why, I must have made hundreds of mistakes throughout the years. Nobody knows how many, not even me."

"Sir," said Crest, "why did you allow yourself to get too busy? Did you intend to dominate the area?"

"You younger men resented this, of course. I don't blame you. You're good men, smart men, well trained and ethical, and you kept wondering why all the patients came to me. Well, consider my point of view. I didn't want all those patients. I had so many patients I couldn't take care of them properly. I wonder who'll take care of them now?"

"You could have turned them down. You could have stopped taking more when you had too many."

"Boy, I'm a doctor, and a doctor does not turn a patient down. When they call to me for help, I come!"

"Surely that is to your credit, sir," said Crest, "but—"

"I may not be the best doctor in this area. In fact, I may be the worst, but who's the judge? Who will decide? I always figured the patients should decide. If you young men are so good, why don't you take the patients away from me, as I took patients from the older men when I first came to Sentry- ville? Why can't you build a busy practice of your own? I always let the patients choose, and I was content to abide by their decision. If they wanted to come to me, I took 'em."

Parky closed his eyes, and Crest thought he had fallen asleep, but Parky was only resting.

"It's been a lonely life, my boy," said Parky, his eyes still closed. "I'm surrounded by a crowd but always alone. Pa- tients never love a doctor. They admire him, respect him, and trust him, but they are also afraid of him, and you can't love a man you fear. The other doctors in the area didn't like me. They would vote me president of the staff but only be- cause of the power of my practice; I could always see the hate and jealousy in their eyes. My wife? She stopped loving me many years ago; I don't even see her more than once or twice a week. My son hated me. Sam was a friend of yours, and he must have told you that. How could Emerald love me after what I did to her? I never wanted to be a doctor, Crest. My father drove me into it."

It was difficult for Crest to accept this statement.

"I come from a family of doctors," Parky went on. "Father, Grandfather, Great-grandfather: back through the generations. I was the ugly duckling of the family: big, strong, clumsy, and dumb. I had an older sister who went to medical school. There weren't many women doctors in those days. She was built like Emerald: a small-boned, vibrant, black-headed little girl, screwy but a genius. She was first in her class. During her internship, she cut her finger at the autopsy table, developed septicemia, and died. You know my younger brother, Joseph; he may be peculiar, but he's smart, and he also led his class. And me? I held down the bottom of the class. They would have flunked me out if my name didn't happen to be Parkindale. As soon as I could, I left the university and came to Sentryville. Here it didn't make any difference whether my name was Parkindale or Smith. In the country, I figured I could do my best, run a quiet practice, and enjoy myself. I planned to go fishing in the spring and hunting in the fall. I did promise myself I would be loyal to the few patients who might be loyal to me, and that I would come whenever they called. Perhaps, I thought, I could make up in loyalty for what I lacked in brains. Well, they called and they called and they called. They kept on calling. I never had a moment to myself. Somebody else can be loyal to them now."

"How is he, dear?" said Nancy when Crest came home for supper.

"Better," said Crest. "You know, I think I understand him now. I know why he did that hysterectomy on Emerald, for example."

"Does that matter any more?"

"It was an unconscious gesture of hostility against the brainy members of the dynasty: his father, grandfather, great-grandfather, and even me, I suppose. He wanted to be sure the line would stop."

"Does this excuse the error that he made?"

"He made errors out of pride, and fell into a very common trap. Because so many people thought him the greatest doctor in the world, he began to believe it himself. What began as loyalty became self-deceit, and then he got all tangled up in the crowd."

"Was Parky a bad doctor or a good one?"

"Nancy," said Crest, "please don't require me to make such a judgment in black and white. Like all human beings, Parky is neither bad nor good. He's both."

"But for the patient, he must be better or worse."

"That depends," said Crest. "If you are trapped in the wreckage of an automobile halfway down a cliff, you better call for Parky. He would amputate your leg while suspended in mid-air and save your life. Not many doctors could. On the other hand, if you are sick because of psychosexual prejudice, stay away from Parky! He will keep you sick."

"How could the town control a man like Dr. Parkindale? Utilize the good in him and minimize the bad?"

"I don't know," said Crest. "I suppose the profession should set up some method of control. We have the state license boards, of course, but once you pass the test, they never examine you again. There are testing boards in all the specialties, but again it's only a question of examinations. The ability of a man to pass an examination has nothing whatever to do with his skill or judgment as a physician. The competence of a doctor can only be assessed by the other doctors in the same town who work beside him every day."

"But the other men in town can never speak. Your hands are tied."

"In the last analysis," said Crest, "I think the patients always decide."

"But patients can't assess the skill of the physician. Patients are like children. If children were permitted to choose their own diets, they'd eat nothing but ice cream, candy, and cake, and keep themselves sick."

"We are a nation of emotional immaturity," said Crest. "If a patient is too immature to acknowledge the fact that he will some day get sick and some day die, he will make an immature choice of his physician. He may wait until the last moment, when it's almost too late, and grab a name at random out of the yellow pages, as if he were selecting a plumber. If he gets a plumber, he has no complaint. We are a nation of fads and fashions. Therefore, I suppose, immature people will always go to the fashionable physician in the community, not knowing that the busiest man in town may not necessarily be the best, and, in fact, for many patients, is the worst."

"And what in the world can you do about that?"

"A doctor can do nothing about it," said Crest. "A doctor cannot teach his patients emotional maturity. By the time they are sick, it is too late. This is the province of the parent, the teacher, and the preacher, and the time is long before."

"You sound fatalistic about the whole damn thing."

"The Parkindales have always been among us. The Parkindales will always be among us until such time as both doctors and patients learn to grow up and think. For this reason, I believe, every community and every patient in the community gets almost exactly the kind of medical care that he deserves."

"Then perhaps we should put the whole system under rigid public inspection and control."

"Probably we will," said Crest. "In which event, things will get a hell of a lot worse before they get better. The federal employee behind that desk is not famous for wisdom, judgment, and emotional maturity!"

Parky spent a comfortable night and the bleeding apparently had stopped. Crest thought it might be safe to do X-ray studies. Parky was opposed.

"What's the point, Crest? We know where that bleeding was coming from."

"No, sir, we don't!" said Crest.

"Maybe you don't," said Parky peevishly.

Crest talked him into it. Then he had a conference with the X-ray man, warning him to handle Parky gingerly, in order not to start up bleeding again. Doctors sometimes think of X-ray as harmless and benign, forgetting that certain X-ray procedures can be as rough on a patient as major surgery. When the study had been done, Crest spoke to the radiologist again.

"There it is: enormous," said the radiologist, pointing to the dripping X-ray film.

These things are sometimes difficult to see for a doctor without special training in radiology, but this one was unmistakable: a huge ulcer crater in the stomach.

"Not duodenum," said Crest.

"Stomach," said the radiologist.

The point was important. The common location for a peptic ulcer is in the duodenum, and almost without exception an ulcer in the duodenum is benign. Ulcers also occur in the stomach, where many of them are also benign but where a significant number of them are malignant.

"Question of cancer?" said Crest.

"Can't tell short of surgery," said the radiologist. "However, the index of suspicion in this case is high. Look at this film. See the liver shadow there?"

"Large; irregular; nodular," said Crest. "So you think we have a stomach cancer with spread to the liver?"

"Those are the odds," said the radiologist.

Next, Crest consulted with Dr. Ardz.

"Whether or not to operate is entirely a question of judgment," said Ardz. "If it is cancer, you'd like to prove it. On the other hand, if it has spread to the liver, we're too late to cure it. Some men feel that you prolong the patient's life by removing the primary site. Here we don't even know whether the stomach is resectable. If it were me, I think that I'd want surgery."

"If it were me, I think I wouldn't," said Crest.

"In this case the patient must decide," said Ardz.

Crest went to room 1 and said to Parky, "Sir, you have a hell of a big ulcer in the stomach, and the liver is large. Now, the question is: should we operate?"

"Cancer?" said Parky immediately.

"Maybe," said Crest.

"I want to go home," said Parky.

"You wouldn't consider surgery?"

"Absolutely not."

Parky tried to get right up out of bed. He moved too quickly; he was weak, anemic from his loss of blood, and he fainted momentarily. With the assistance of nurses and orderlies, Crest got Parky back to bed.

"I guess I'm not ready to open the office yet," said Parky with a weak grin.

"I guess you're not," said Crest. "You better plan to stay with us for a few more days."

"I don't like it," said Parky. "I've always been as strong as a horse."

"Perhaps you must learn to think of yourself in a different light."

"No surgery," said Parky.

"All right. That's up to you."

"And another thing, Crest."

"Sir?"

"No more blood."

"Not even if you bleed again?" said Crest.

"Especially not if I bleed again. Oxygen and morphine to keep me comfortable, but no more blood, you understand?"

"But, sir," said Crest, "I couldn't watch you bleed to death right under my own eyes."

"You'd prefer to wait and watch me die when the cancer spreads into my bones?"

"Well . . ."

"I'm not afraid of death," said Parky. "I've seen too much of it. But long, painful dying doesn't appeal to me."

"But I have to practice according to the principles of good medicine."

"You have to use your heart and not your head."

"Would you like to change doctors, sir?" said Crest.

"Grow up!" said Parky.

"If I'm to be your doctor, I'll have to use my judgment in the case."

"The patient has the right not to be treated if he so desires," said Parky. "If you use blood on me without consent, that's assault and battery. I'll turn you in to the County Attorney."

"I suppose you'd prefer three grains of morphine intravenously."

"Maybe I would," said Parky, "but you wouldn't have the guts to give it to me."

Crest turned on his heel and left the room before he lost his temper.

"Damn that man!" he thought. "Even now, when I'm beginning to understand his point of view, I disagree with him to the point of violence. I never could work with him."

Crest was so angry that he scarcely noticed where he was going and he almost crashed into Emerald, who was standing waiting for him in the corridor.

"That's right, chum, run me down!" said Emerald.

"Oh," said Crest. "Hello. What are you doing here?"

"Where else would I be at a time like this?" she said. "I would have come last night, but the traveling was tough, thanks to the blizzard."

Crest studied her. She retained the figure of the Emerald he had known, but her black hair had turned completely white. She noticed his glance.

"If you see me on television, it's black," she said. "I have too much figure to be playing little old ladies yet. I fool the customers, but I don't try to fool myself. How are you, John Crest?"

"Fine."

"You had a coronary, so I heard."

"I made a good recovery," said Crest.

"We live fast, you and I," said Emerald. "How's Dad?"

"Your father had a nasty hemorrhage," said Crest. "The bleeding has stopped and he's much better today. We've done X-rays. There's a huge ulcer crater in the stomach and his liver is large."

"Malignancy?"

"We think so. Parky won't let us operate."

"Well," she said, "he's the boss."

"And furthermore," said Crest, "he refuses any more blood, in case that bleeding should start up again. What in the hell am I supposed to do? Watch him bleed to death?"

"You're supposed to treat him the way he wants to be treated. Isn't that always the case, John Crest?"

"He's as stubborn as a mule."

"Sure," she said. "And aren't we all? May I visit him now?"

"Yes. Don't stay too long. Don't tire him."

"Chum, I'll see you around," said Emerald.

That night, in the middle of the night, as Crest had feared, Parky began to bleed again. Crest went to the hospital immediately. He found Parky in poor condition, deep in shock again, drenched with perspiration, pulse weak and thready, blood pressure low. He had vomited another pint or two of bright red blood.

"I started the oxygen, Doctor," said the nurse.

"Good," said Crest, "and I'll want morphine intravenously."

"How much, Doctor?"

"One eighth of a grain."

"Shall I call the lab? We need more blood."

"No blood," said Crest.

"But, sir . . ."

"You heard me, nurse," said Crest.

She tried again. "Sir, he's lost nearly a quart of blood and he's in shock."

"I'm in charge of the case."

"Yes, sir."

The nurse knew what ought to be done, but Crest was in charge of the case.

"I don't like it," thought Crest, "but I'm doing it. I let him dominate me again. I let him dictate his own treatment. I should call Timothy and turn myself in. Mr. Timothy, sir, I'm letting this man bleed to death before my eyes. Is this murder, sir? What am I supposed to do?"

Twenty minutes later, Dr. Parkindale expired.

Crest immediately telephoned the Parkindale home. Emerald answered the phone.

"It's me," he said. "Crest. I'm sorry. Bad news, I'm afraid."

"He's dead?" said Emerald.

"About a minute ago. He began to bleed again. He died of shock. There was no suffering. Please tell your mother."

"I know you did your best," she said.

"I know I didn't," said Crest. "I didn't give him any blood."

"Isn't that what he wanted, chum?"

"If you don't mind my saying so, Emerald, I'm not always sure your father's judgment was the best."

"If you don't mind my saying so," she said, "you're going to be a pretty nice guy some day, when you grow up."

"I'm tired, Emerald. Let's not fight."

"No, dear," she said. "Thanks for everything. I'll tell Mother. Go on home to your wife. Probably you're needed. There is nothing more that you can do for us."

Crest went home. "It's going to be mighty quiet around this town," he said to his wife.

"Good medicine in Sentryville for a change," said Nancy.

"I couldn't fill his shoes."

"You won't make his mistakes."

"I couldn't afford it," said Crest, "but could I afford to turn people down when I get too busy?"

"You always worry, John, usually about something you haven't done."

"Is a doctor any good if he doesn't worry about his patients all the time?"

"You're good," she said. "The best in Sentryville."

The telephone rang.

"Damn," said Crest.

The phone rang again.

"God damn it! My master's voice."

"Let it ring," said Nancy. "You've had a long, tough day."

"It might be a genuine emergency," said Crest.

He answered the phone. It was the police. There'd been a bad accident in the hills, and they needed a doctor at once.

"I'll be right there," said Crest. He got out of bed and started to dress.

"John," said Nancy, "do you have much experience in accident cases?"

"They need me," said Crest.

"You're not a surgeon. Dr. Ardz is better qualified."

"They didn't call Ardz," said Crest. "They called me."

Nancy laughed.

"What's the joke?" said Crest.

"For all your fancy talk, you've joined. You've become a member of the dynasty yourself. I suppose it was inevitable."

"Maybe I should call for Dr. Ardz."

"Maybe you should, but you won't. They called for you. The welfare of the patient comes before that of the doctor, but even more important is the call itself."

For better and for worse, Crest knew that she was right.

"I hope I don't get arrogant and proud. I hope I don't get greedy. I hope I don't try to dominate the patient and the younger men in town."

"I hope you don't," she said. "I'm not as tolerant as Mrs. Parkindale."

"You wouldn't leave?"

"Nope," she said. "Somebody's got to stick around and prick you once in a while. You better get dressed. The patient is waiting."

"I ought to call Ardz."

"Run along," she said. "If it's something you can handle, take care of it. If you need help, you wouldn't be too proud to call for Dr. Ardz."

"Of course not. I like Ardz."

"Go on, but be careful. Remember there's snow in the hills."

Crest left the house, got in his car, and set off for the hills, driving fast, but carefully.

The End